PATHS OF THE NA'GEE

REFLECTIONS OF WORLDS VOLUME 1

ERIC RITTER

Kravitz and Sons LLC
204 E Arlington Blvd. Suite B
Greenville, NC 27858

Published by Kravitz and Sons LLC.
ISBN: 979-8-89639-374-0 (sc)
ISBN: 979-8-89639-373-3 (e)

Library of Congress Control Number: 2025920853

Because of the dynamic nature of the Internet, any web addresses or links contained in this book may have changed since publication and may no longer be valid. The views expressed in this work are solely those of the author and do not necessarily reflect the views of the publisher, and the publisher hereby disclaims any responsibility for them.

TABLE OF CONTENTS

Part 1 Top-Siders

Chapter 1: Samuel 1
Chapter 2: Victor 9
Chapter 3: The Visit 20
Chapter 4: Homecoming 39
Chapter 5: Dante 63
Chapter 6: 'The Spot' 73
Chapter 7: Camacho 86
Chapter 8: "Always Go Right" 93
Chapter 9: "Our Prized Knife Fighter" 106
Chapter 10: "I Never Get Kicked In The Face" 114
Chapter 11: "You're Holding Yourself Back" 122
Chapter 12: Plans Unfold 137
Chapter 13: Polo 148
Chapter 14: "We'll Just Take Two." 152
Chapter 15: The Base 159
Chapter 16: Agent 17 180
Chapter 17: Sous Chef 193
Chapter 18: It's Too Big! 202
Chapter 19: "You Forget Your Place Top-Sider" 207
Chapter 20: Halbred 213
Chapter 21: Framed 220
Chapter 22: Special Unit: Gene 6 227
Chapter 23: Primo 233
Chapter 24: Primary Objective 237
Chapter 25: Eva 239
Chapter 26: Hotel 'The Deluxe' 248
Chapter 27: "What Have You Got Us Into?" 258
Chapter 28: Intercepting The Target 270
Chapter 29: The Same Side 275
Chapter 30: Reinforcements 279

Chapter 31: Mila 289
Chapter 32: Steph 295
Chapter 33: The Rooftop 306
Chapter 34: The Parking Deck 315
Chapter 35: The Escape Route 328
Chapter 36: Aftermath 338

Part 2 The "Other Side"

Chapter 37: Arrival 347
Chapter 38: From Child To Warrior 366
Chapter 39: "Anyone Know How To Cook Snake?" 388
Chapter 40: Dishonored 396
Chapter 41: A Different Warrior 408
Chapter 42: High Ground 417
Chapter 43: A Promise 426
Chapter 44: The T'kche 435
Chapter 45: Re-Match 446
Chapter 46: To The Settlement 460
Chapter 47: Rebirth 468
Chapter 48: Preparations 480
Chapter 49: Arrival 490
Chapter 50: The "Back Door" 497
Chapter 51: Family 507
Chapter 52: Showdown 522
Chapter 53: The Jobs Not Done 537

Epilogue 1 541
Epilogue 2 543

For everyone who is filled with creativity
and ambition, find your art form and
share it with the world.

This is mine.

Hope you enjoy the ride!

Part 1
Top-Siders

CHAPTER 1:
SAMUEL

As he slowly pulled to a stop in front of the old house, Samuel was overwhelmed with feelings of déjà vu. He'd seen the old white house, with its tattered blue shutters and black screen door at least a thousand times in head. He'd parked his black four door luxury sedan in front of the mailbox, slowly got out and made his way up the stone walkway at least a thousand times in his head. The only difference this time, was it wasn't in his head… he was here. Finally, here. Months of planning every step and the day had come.

Samuel put the sedan in park and unbuckled his seatbelt, opened the sleek door and stepped out into the cool summer evening. He didn't bother grabbing his 9mm pistol off the passenger seat, there'd be plenty of time for that later. What he did do was check the pocket of his black sports coat to make sure the trash bags were there. Sure enough, they were just where he placed them. As his hand touched the cold plastic of the black trash bag in his pocket, he felt a wave of guilt wash over him. Was he just as bad as the people who put him in this situation? After all, these were innocent elderly people, or at least as innocent as anyone could possibly be. Their only crime was to have this perfectly placed house, tucked away so perfectly that it had to be the one. That and the fact that it was paid off, with solar panels, well water and a septic tank… completely self-sufficient. Yes, this had to be the house, it was just too perfect. The elderly couple that lived here had no family, no friends, and no bills… they had practically disappeared already, he would just speed up the process.

Samuel let rationalization push the guilt away. The ends would justify the means, he thought. They were a small price to pay for what the people owed that pushed him to this. "Not just for me", he thought. "For every family that suffered and is still suffering… no more. This must be done. Someone needs to step and be the Hero. If no one else would do it, that left it up to him".

With that final thought he found his usual confident resolve and began his steady walk up the stone path.

Moments later, Samuel gently opened the black metal screen door. He didn't want that in his way. Positioning himself in front of the screen door, letting it rest against his back, he firmly knocked on the old wooden door.

He didn't worry about them not answering, Samuel had done his homework…they were always home. He also knew that while it was still light out, albeit dusk, they would open the door without a second thought. He'd sent packages in the weeks leading up to this, to be sure of that. Oh yes, old Mr. Greenwell would open the door right up and smile welcomingly to anyone knocking. There would be no awkward dialogue through a wooden door aimed at convincing an unsuspecting lamb to let in the wolf. Not this evening.

"Knock, knock, knock".

It didn't take long for Samuel to hear the slow plodding footsteps of the elderly man inside. "There's someone at the door sweet", he heard Mrs. Greenwell shout.

"I know my love. Don't you get up, I've got it." Mr. Greenwell said lovingly to his elderly wife.

"They're so adorable" thought Samuel. "They must be in their early 80's, at least, and yet still so kind and loving to one another after all these years". "Am I wrong for this" thought Samuel?

"Should I walk away now?" "Can I really do this to these old gentle souls?" "Am I the Villain?"

Samuel didn't have time to second guess himself any further… the door opened.

"Why hello there, Young Man" Mr. Greenwell said with a grandfatherly smile. "What brings you to our humble abode dear boy".

Just like that, it had truly begun. The planning phase was over. The path to justice had now truly begun. Samuel responded to Mr. Greenwell with a cold smile, the kind of smile that is almost more unnerving than a scowl.

Samuels clean shaven face and head, coupled with his cold blue eyes didn't help to soften the smile. Neither did the fact that he was every bit of 6'1 and wore his 265lbs like a professional athlete. No, Samuel was quite intimidating, even when he didn't want to be.

Mr. Greenwell had immediately started to notice just that. As the cold smile hit him like a chill in the air, he began to look Samuel up and down. He noticed the sleek black boots, well-fitting black jeans that looked almost more like suit pants, especially when coupled with Samuels black sports coat. The coat and the black t-shirt under it, did very little to hide his muscular physique.

Samuel knew what had to be done, but paused just long enough for Mr. Greenwell to take it all in. It wasn't a boastful gesture or even an attempt to instill fear into the old man, but more so that Samuel felt the need to let Mr. Greenwell see his adversary clearly. He owed him that much at least.

A split-second later Samuel made his move. It wasn't a hostile or violent move, on the contrary, it was nothing more than a gentle touch of his finger on Mr. Greenwell's hand. That was all it took. That was always all it took.

Mr. Greenwell instantly froze in place. Not frozen like ice or cold, it wasn't like that at all. Just stuck, staring, immobilized, paralyzed or whatever it was. It was just what it was. What it always was.

Samuel gently eased past the "frozen" Mr. Greenwell and entered the house.

He knew where Mrs. Greenwell was. The same place she was every evening at this time. Sitting at the kitchen table knitting. Right in front of the large bay window in the old kitchen, the same large bay window that Samuel had spent so many evenings looking in. Watching, calculating, planning for this very moment.

Unlike his feelings for Mr. Greenwell, Samuel did not wait for Mrs. Greenwell to turn around and see him. That would just be cruel and terrifying to the sweet old lady. No, he wasn't a bad guy, he wasn't here to terrorize, it just had to be done. A small sacrifice for the greater good. No point making it cruel, that's the type of thing "they" did. "They" were the reason these poor old souls had to be sacrificed, "they" were the reason all of this was necessary. No, he wouldn't be like "them".

Her chair at the head of the antique wooden table faced the large bay window and had its back towards the entrance from the main room into the kitchen. Samuel silently approached and heard Mrs. Greenwell's soft humming. So sweet, so soothing.

She had her silver hair up in a bun, held in place by a wooden hair pin. With one light touch to the back of her exposed neck, the humming was instantly swallowed by utter silence. It had been done. Both Greenwells "frozen" in place. Now time to clean up and get some rest.

Samuel leaned Mrs. Greenwell back in her chair and slowly drug her towards the hallway. She didn't flop, her arms didn't fall down or even quit holding the knitting she had been working on. That's not how it worked. She stayed completely still, "frozen", the exact same way she was when he'd touched her.

He didn't know how long it lasted or if it was more tied to his proximity of the frozen individual. As far as he knew there wasn't really a time limit to it, but if he got far enough away it just "turned off" and the individual was "back". As long as he was around, anyone he "froze", stayed "frozen". That is of course unless he "willed it to stop". After all these years, Samuel didn't really know a better way to explain it. Once he touched them and froze them, he never had to touch them again to "Unfreeze" them or release them or whatever… he just kind of willed it. He didn't even have to be in the same room as them or see them, once he froze someone, he just kind of felt them and could release them at will.

Unfortunately for the sweet old Greenwells, that's not something he could do this time. There were grander plans in motion and the Greenwells didn't fit into them.

Samuel opened the double doors to the large hall closet. "yes" he thought. "This will do just fine".

He carefully pushed Mrs. Greenwell into the closet, chair and all. Making sure he had her facing away from the door and pushed far to the right, so there would be room for Mr. Greenwell too.

With that, he headed back down the hall to the front door. Once there, Samuel grabbed Mr. Greenwell under his arms and pulled him down the hall to the opened closet. He gently pushed Mr. Greenwell in the closet facing the wall, next to his seated wife.

He really dreaded this part, everything up to this point could be undone, but the next step couldn't. He quickly reached into his pocket before he had any more time to consider another path and pulled out the garbage bags. Samuel made short work of tying each bag firmly around the head of each Greenwell. "They won't even feel a thing" he told himself.

"I'll bury them tomorrow" he thought.

After Samuel had finished pulling his car around to the back of the house, bringing in his luggage and closing the curtains on all the windows, he headed upstairs to shower and get some rest. The next few days would be busy, he needed rest. He'd worry about eating tomorrow, after the morning burial.

As he lay in bed, Samuel pictured the look on Mr. Greenwell's face. He pictured the instant change in Mr. Greenwells eyes as he touched him. That part always haunted him. That instant change from a lively, eyes full of thoughts and ideas to hollow "frozen" eyes that seemed no more real than a manikin at a department store. Samuel wondered, as he often did, if there was anyone else out there like him. If there was anyone else haunted by the change of eyes like him.

He knew a lot of people had "the gene", it wasn't common, but it wasn't super rare either. Some people just had it. It didn't affect them like him though. Most people with "the gene" could move really fast, or were abnormally strong, there were also those who could move things with their minds and there used to be a lot who could fly, but those ones don't last long. Most of them get shot down by the gangs when they're just learning how to fly. No, there were definitely some unique ones out there, but "the gene" didn't seem to affect anyone like it did Samuel. It's why he had to be the one. Why he had to stop "them". Too many had suffered. Someone had to bring about justice. Someone had to step up and be a hero.

The teapot whistled and Samuel snapped out of his trance. It was only 11am, but it had already been a long day. After very little sleep, the "burial" activities and then showering and getting cleaned up Samuel felt exhausted.

He told himself "You just need to eat; you didn't have breakfast or dinner." but he knew the real exhaustion could be attributed to his heavy conscious. He knew he was doing what must be done, but he hated the sacrifices that had to be made along the way.

Regardless, a quick meal and a hot cup of tea and he'd be on his way. This was just the beginning, there was much to be done and next on the list was a friendly visit to Mr. Wiser. Oh yeah, good old Victor Wiser didn't know it yet, but his adventure was just about to begin too.

CHAPTER 2:
VICTOR

Victor Wiser, was a tall, tall man. He stood just a hair under 7ft, was slender in a muscular sort of way and had pale skin, pale grey eyes and a blonde buzz cut. Give him a black robe and a scythe and you had one hell of a grim reaper, that was for sure. He often thought these things and chuckled to himself while he gave himself one last look in the mirror before heading downstairs.

"Yeah, I'm the damn Grim Reaper" he thought. "Everyone better recognize it too, when they cross my path". The thoughts were definitely encouraged by his all-black attire. Black pants, black boots and an untucked black oxford button up, that hung just low enough to hide the large chrome 45 caliber pistol stuffed into his belt. He grinned that blonde headed, grim reaper grin and headed down the stairs two at time.

As soon as Victor hit the bottom of the stairs and started towards the kitchen he was hit with attempted tackles from both sides, right at his knees. The tacklers, his daughter of 10 and his son of 7 gave wild roars and they attempted to tackle their tall father.

"roooaarrr!" they yelled. "We've got you now sucker! Say your prayers!" They said in unison. "Who you calling a sucker, you little rascals?" Victor roared back, as he grabbed them both, one in each arm and in one swift motion swung them over each of his shoulders.

"Well, well, well looks like I've caught me a couple rascals for breakfast!" Victor playfully shouted. "I guess my pretty wife has some cooking to do".

"Noooo! Nooo! Don't eat us daddy!" The children screamed through uncontrollable giggling. "Oh yeah" Victor said, keeping the fun going as he marched towards the kitchen. "When I catch rascals, I eat rascals!". Both children Mila and Steph laughed wildly at their father's comments.

Victor walked into the kitchen only to be greeted with a huge smile and a gentle scolding from his beautiful wife Eva. "Now, now Vic" she said kindly. "Put them down and let them eat their breakfast. I've made you eggs and bacon dear, there's no need for you to eat dirty rascals." Before Victor could say a word, Mila and Steph both cried out "come on mom" in unison once again.

The entire family laughed together as Victor put the children down in their seats at the table. He kissed Eva and thought the same thought he had every day… "wow, I'm one lucky guy".

Eva, Mila, and Steph were his world. Sure, he worked, was loyal to his job and loved to spend his free time practicing his martial arts (although he needed no practice), but none of it mattered compared to them. They were everything. They were why he did it all. "Wow, I'm one lucky guy" he thought again.

As Eva handed a plate towards him, he smoothly dodged the handoff and reached his long arm right past her to grab the coffee that she'd just poured for herself. "Gotta go, babe. Camacho's coming to the spot early before his big club opening tonight. I've got to open the place up and make sure it's cleaned up before he gets there. You never know how the fellas may have left it."

"Vic!" Eva said sternly. "It's Saturday. I thought we were all going to do something as a family today. The kids were hoping we'd take them to the park."

"Yeah Dad" the children once again said in unison. "The park sounds like a great idea guys! You go have a good time and I'll be back from work before too late. Love ya." With that Vic flashed his sweetest grin to them all, gave Eva a quick kiss and bolted out the kitchen and through the front door before they could contest him any further.

Once out the door and in the driveway, Vic, walked past Eva's white minivan, shaking his head like he did every time he passed the minivan. "We only have 2 kids, why the hell did she insist on a minivan?" he thought for the millionth time, as he opened up the door on his black SUV. It was a two-door black SUV 4x4 with black wheels and big tires. It had a black row bar across the front bumper and the across the back one. The guys always gave him a rough time about the rugged look, when most of his time was spent driving around the city, but he didn't care. He loved his ride and felt ready for anything while in it. He started it up and off he went.

Victor worked for Juan Camacho. Well, the way Vic saw it, everyone worked for Juan Camacho one way or another. He was mostly doorman/security for "The Spot", but he occasionally did other odd jobs like "collections" or serving as a bodyguard. Sometimes Camacho or one of his underbosses sent Vic to "send a message" to someone, those were the times Vic made the real money. He didn't mind it all. With his size and his passion for martial arts, Vic was the perfect messenger, and he was quite alright with that.

"One day, maybe I'll even get a seat at the table" he thought. "Or at least get the quit watching the door and take up collections full time". Until that day, Vic mostly manned the door and served as security for the "The spot".

"The Spot" was Camacho's hangout if you will. It was where all of his underbosses usually gathered, connected, turned in monies owed and in the later hours often drank heavily and gambled. The ground floor had a huge open room with three large tables in the center of the room and a bar towards the back. Two small offices sat on the right side of the large room and a bar ran across the back of the room. To the left there we restrooms and elevators.

The building or "the spot" had 6 floors and at least one underground level, maybe more… no one knew for sure, because no one was allowed to go down. Camacho had a penthouse apartment on the sixth floor (one of his many homes away from home) and a large office that took up most of the fifth floor. Victor wasn't really sure what floors two, three and four held, but he was sure that it wasn't a good idea to ask.

Vic parked his beloved SUV in his usual spot in the alley

behind "The Spot" and walked around to the door of the six-floor building. Vic's usual spot was in the alley behind the building, where he could get in and out much quicker than the large parking lot out front allowed and also, where his vehicle couldn't be seen by prying eyes. Once at the front door, Vic typed in the security access code and entered the grand building.

As soon as Vic entered, he took it all in… he couldn't help it, this was how he was wired. He noticed that the place had been cleaned up, that was usually his job when opening "The Spot". As a matter of fact, the place was too clean, everything was perfectly in its place, every chair was perfectly tucked into the table and the smell of bleach lingered in the air. Vic instantly knew that something had gone down last night, something bad, that was the only time that "the shop" got this clean.

"Of course, it would be the one night that Camacho sends me on another task" Vic thought. "So many dreadfully boring nights, watching the door, standing alert as underbosses and their guys gambled drank and traded boastful stories in efforts to one up each other and shit pops off when I'm on another assignment. Damn." Although Vic was lost in his thoughts of what he may have missed out on, he didn't fail to notice Camacho sitting at the end of the bar, sipping on what had to be his black Columbian coffee. Vic casually made his way towards the boss.

Camacho rarely arrived before Vic. "He must've slept in the penthouse apartment upstairs" Vic thought. Camacho wasn't a big man, rather small actually. No more than 5'9 and probably 185lbs. To Vic he looked kind of like one of those lucha libra Hispanic wrestlers. He was definitely some type of Native American, not Hispanic, but that's still what he reminded Vic of. Bronze skin, dark eyes and dark hair, that was buzz cut very low, with a modest short mohawk. Black dress pants, perfectly ironed, shiny black dress shoes and a long sleeve silk button up shirt was the usual look and the look he wore today. The shirt today was white with red streaks all over it like an abstract painting or blood splattering. Of course, the jewelry always stood out the most. That same heavy golden watch on his left hand and huge gold chain that hung over his shirt with the peculiar old stone looking pendant. The pendant never seemed to go with the gold. It was old, stone looking and circular, about the size of a silver dollar. Nonetheless, Camacho always wore it, on that same gaudy gold chain.

Despite his modest size and gaudy attire, Vic knew Camacho was not be underestimated. It wasn't just that he was the boss. It wasn't just that he ran almost half the city or even the fact that he seemed slightly crazy, like he needed to prove himself through violence over and over. No, it was because he was one of those damn freaks Vic thought. "The gene" is what they called it. Vic called it "bullshit". For a man of Vic's size and martial arts skillset, he felt personally offended that there were people who just randomly developed "the gene" and could do amazing things without even working for it. Without even struggling and training and pushing yourself. "Bullshit" Vic thought again.

As he approached the bar and Camacho who pretended not to notice him, he was greeted with "How did he pay Vic?".

"He didn't pay right boss and he still owes." Vic said. Only then did Camacho set down his coffee mug and turn in his bar stool to face Vic. He raised an eyebrow as if to asking, no expecting Vic to continue. With that Vic reached into his left pocket and pulled out the small black velvet jewelry bag. He untied the delicate string and dumped the contents onto the bar.

Four golden teeth clattered softly onto the bar. Two of the teeth had been designed to look like fangs and the other two were definitely front teeth. Camacho let out a rough chuckle and then instantly turned stern and stoic again. "Good job Vic" he said. "Where did we leave it?"

"He's transferring all his funds into the account number you gave me when the bank opens this morning" Vic said. As he said it, he looked at his all-black rubber watch on his left hand, "Should have seen it come through about ten minutes ago boss."

Camacho, picked his phone up that had laying on the bar by his coffee mug and quickly typed a few things then set it back down. "Damn that was fast" Vic thought. That was what "the gene" had done for Camacho. It made him fast, very fast and abnormally strong too. Not many people had multiple effects like that from "the gene", but Camacho sure did, and he enjoyed showing it off.

No one knew much about Camacho, other than the effects 'the gene" had on him and that his family was slaughtered when he was very young by the cartels. It had been a long, hard road for Camacho and he was dead set on never being a victim again. His approach to this was to make sure everyone else was a victim instead.

"Whatever" Vic thought nonchalantly. "It's a good gig. Pays the bills and lets me take care of Eva and the kids. I'll pull peoples teeth every night for this little freak and do it with a smile, if it keeps my family living comfortably and happy.".

Camacho interrupted Vic's thoughts with the curt question "how do you know that's all he had Vic?"

Despite asking the question, Camacho had no doubt whatsoever that Vic had made sure he got every penny that the degenerate had. Vic was good at collections. Hell, Vic was good at everything and smart too. That's precisely why Camacho kept him spending most of his time as a doorman. He'd learned long ago, guys that are smart and skilled get greedy and insubordinate quick if they're given a little power. If they're used too much. No, guys like Vic need to feel like they haven't made it. They need to always be reaching for that carrot. That's what kept them loyal and it's what drove them to execute orders without question, as they were positioned to constantly feel that they need to prove themselves.

It was this perspective that drove Camacho to question Vic. He knew the answers, but Vic needed to feel pressured to explain himself. To prove his worth. "That's how you train good dogs" Camacho thought.

"I made him pull up all of his accounts and show me the balances" Vic replied. "Then I pulled two more teeth to make sure". He couldn't help but smile after the last comment. He was the grim reaper after all. "I expect you saw just over five thousand dollars transferred to your account boss?"

He was right too. Five thousand, one hundred dollars and

sixty-four cents. "Vic was good." Camacho thought. "He still owes just over five thousand more, you'll get half deposited this Friday and the rest two weeks later" Vic stated. "I had him show me his direct deposit history. Unless the governor's office gets wise and fires him in the next two weeks, you'll get what he owes boss."

While Camacho was once again impressed with Vic's thoroughness, it instantly triggered two thoughts… "Damn, I sure know how to find talent" Camacho thought, but the other thought, the darker thought quickly drowned out his moment of self-adoration. "He's too good. Probably needs a reminder of what happens when I'm crossed, even when people try to make it right" Camacho thought darkly. "Matter of fact there are others at the governor's office that he knew owed me, they need to know it too. Can't let any of them think I'm a victim. Especially Vic. Yeah, he's too good. He needs a reminder. He needs to be tested." As Camacho's dark thoughts kept wondering he began giving the instructions and watching Vic closely to gauge his reaction.

"Fuck the money. He's an example now Vic. Too little, too late." Camacho said sternly. "Wait for his kids and wife to get home this evening and then take out the house."

Vic was hardened. Vic was violent. Vic had grown up like that and he made a living because of that, but he didn't think of himself as a bad guy. No, he just did what he had to do to take care of his family. He figured the people he did it to had it coming… but kids? The guy's wife? Camacho had never asked him to do something like that to innocents before. That was bad guy shit. "I'm not a bad guy" Vic thought. "I just do what I have to do to take care of my beautiful wife and those amazing children".

As images of his family flooded his mind, he also was struck with the other thoughts "he's testing me". "This little freak wants to make sure I follow orders, any orders. If I don't, there's no doubt little Napolean over here will take out my family". With that thought Vic felt a flush of anger. He pictured himself punching Camacho in the throat, kicking the barstool out from under him and putting two 45 bullets in his little head before the man could get up. "Wonder if the little freak is fast enough to stop that?"

"No. It wasn't worth it. If this little man's "gene shit" saved him, that would be it for Eva and the kids" Vic thought. Followed by the justifying thoughts of "hell, maybe this will be the job that gets me a seat at the table. Maybe, he'll realize I'll do whatever it takes, and I can start making real money!" Vic thought. "a couple years of real money and I can get the family out of here and live happily somewhere remote, without a care in the world. It sucks, but it's his family or mine and I choose mine."

With that Vic replied, "No problem boss. Thought I was supposed to be watching "The Spot" tonight though?".

"You are. That shouldn't take all night Vic. Stock the place, then go home get a quick nap and be back to the spot by midnight. Drive by our friend's house on the way in and use the RPG, when you know everyone will be tucked in safe and sound for the night" Camacho said. "I'll be at the club opening, with Tony and Hector. The rest of the guys will be here. I don't need them making a scene up there on opening night. Stump will watch the door with you and help you clean up once the fellas have finished."

With that Camacho stood, looked up at the tall man "damn, he's tall" Camacho thought as he often did and headed towards the elevator. "The place has already been cleaned; we had a little incident last night. Just get the bar and fridges stocked and then go home. Don't forget to take care of business on your way back in Vic!". Camacho said and he stepped onto the elevator and was gone.

Vic chose not to think, he didn't want to think about this. He was a good guy after all. He just worked with bad guys. It's what had to be done though. "Has to be done for Eva and the kids", he thought. So instead of dwelling on it, Vic began making his list of things needed for the bar and the fridges.

CHAPTER 3:
THE VISIT

As soon as the black rugged looking SUV pulled out of the driveway and drove away, Samuel pulled his black sedan out from his discrete parking spot down the street and headed to the house. Some might give it some time before pulling up to make sure the coast was clear, but not Samuel. He figured, it would be much easier to walk right in and leave the unsuspecting family thinking "dad forgot something and came right back" or something like that. Less risk of quick phone calls or texts. The kids were young, but there was no such thing as too young to call or text these days. Besides, if "dad really did forget something and come back home, it wouldn't matter. Sure, it would change plans a little bit, but they would all end up in the same spot at the end.

Samuel pulled his black sedan into the same spot in the driveway where the SUV had been parked. This time he did grab his gun and placed it neatly in the underarm holster that his black sports coat hid nicely. He didn't intend to use it, but it could definitely come in handy. He checked his pocket to make sure the zip ties were there and eased out of the car.

Once out he made his way to the door, no knocking today, no he immediately tried the handle. Bingo. Unsuspecting Victor had left it unlocked.

Since the incident had shattered Samuel's life, he'd spent plenty of time watching "the bad guys" and one thing he was shocked to learn was that when they weren't on the job, they were just as careless as the rest of the normal joes in the world.

Take Victor for instance. Samuel knew what Victor was capable of, he'd done his research. He knew how intelligent and careful Victor was to pay attention to every detail. He knew that Victor was a loyal solider but was smart enough to know he was working for a very bad man. After all, these were the reasons that Samuel had specifically chosen Victor. Yet at the end of the day, Victor still was a loving husband and father smiled to his family and left them home to enjoy a beautiful Saturday… with the door unlocked.

Samuel walked right in took a left and silently stepped into the kitchen. The children were at the kitchen table. The boy, who smaller sat at the head of the table facing his mother's back who was doing something over the stove and the girl who while still young was a little bigger and definitely older sat on the side facing the window and looking back and forth between her brother and her mother.

She'd be the one to see him. She'd be the one to scream, to run, to text, to call. Yes, she'd be the one. He had to move fast.

With that Samuel entered the kitchen as quickly and quietly as possible. In one fluent motion he touched the boy lightly on the back of his neck, freezing him in place, while simultaneously he reached for the girl's arm. Too slow!

The little girl saw him from the corner of her eye, she saw him touch her brother and her brother freeze with a bite almost to his mouth. She saw him reaching for her and she immediately jerked her arm back and yelled "Mommy!!!" in the loudest screeching voice that only a little girl like her could muster.

No time to dally, he didn't want to hurt them. Not yet. Not if he could avoid it. After all, he was the good guy. Not to mention, his plan would be more difficult to execute if they looked visibly beaten. So, he dove, catching the girl with his finger on her leg just as she had slipped out and began to dash out of the kitchen. "Got her!" he thought. Just then the frying pan hit him in the face. Hit him hard in the face.

She had him in a tough position, as he was still sprawled on the floor from his dive. He did all he could do and reached for her leg, just as she was rearing the frying pan back for a second shot to his face. No luck, she saw him reaching and responded with a swift kick to his arm, followed by another frying pan swing that he just barely dodged by rolling backwards. He jumped to his feet as nimble as a cat and the two squared off in the kitchen.

He tried to be convincing in a calm soothing voice, that was little more difficult to orchestrate with his face having just been bashed by a frying pan. A hot frying pan at that. Maybe he was targeting the wrong Wiser in the family, Victor's wife was no joke.

As he spoke, he noticed her surveying the children,

the room and looking him up and down for any potential weakness or opening. He'd have to watch out for her in the future. She could make things much easier or much worse, depending on how he played his cards. "No time for that now Samuel." he thought.

"Hey, hey, hey, calm down." he said. "Who the hell are you?!" she screamed, followed by "and what have you done to my kids?!".

Throughout the exchange, he noticed her eyes continually going back to the bread box on the counter. "Bread box, huh? Who the hell has a bread box?" Samuel thought. "No this must be the cheesy gun stash." He thought.

He eased forward, cutting her off from the bread box and continued talking, calmly, smoothly. "I didn't hurt them; they're just frozen for a moment. I can show you if you calm down."

"Don't you touch them again, you Bastard!" She roared. She sounded less nervous and more ferocious. He needed to end this quickly, one way or the other. "Ok, Dammit!" he said much less calmly as he pulled out the 9mm pistol from its holster under his jacket and aimed it at her.

"This is happening and you're going to listen or you're going to watch them die, before you join them." He said as he pointed the gun at the little girl's head, who was still frozen with her back turned towards him in mid run form.

Eva immediately stopped. All of the fight in her, faded away in an instant. She had to keep her babies safe. She didn't know what to do, so instead of doing anything she just asked again in a much softer, pleading voice "what did you do to them?"

Samuel clearly saw the realization and the emotions all over her face. "Ok this was better" he thought. "This is where we needed to be" he thought.

"Put the pan down and sit down at the table" he said firmly. "I'll show you they're fine, but you'll have to do as I say, or they won't be. I can undo the freeze, but I can't undo a bullet. It's all up to you."

Shuddering, terrified for her children, Eva complied and sat down. Samuel tossed a zip tie onto the table in front of her. "Tie it in a large loop, then put your hands through it palm to palm and use your teeth to pull it tight" he said. Before she could think about it, he followed the instructions with "If you don't, we're done and so are your kids". With that he emphasized the pistol in his hand still pointing at the little girl's head.

That was all the convincing that Eva needed. She complied and once she did, Samuel put the gun back into its holster. He walked to the little boy, pulled his arms together and zip-tied them similar to how he had instructed Eva to do. She gasped as he touched the boy, but did not speak.

Once the boy's hands were tied, Samuel "willed him unfrozen". The boy dropped his bite, looked astonished at his hands, then at his mother and then at the large man in all black standing in over him. Cautiously, the little boy whimpered "Mommy, why are my hands tied and who's that?".

Eva let out a sigh of relief. "It's ok Steph. It's ok."

"Your names Steph, huh?" Samuel asked the boy gently.

The boy, Steph, did not answer, he only nodded. Then turning to his mother, he asked "What did he do to Mila, Mom?"

"Ok. That's enough for now Steph" Samuel said kindly, and gently touched the boy on the arm. Just like that, Steph was frozen again, and Eva's gasp said she noticed it instantly.

"You see Eva?" Said Samuel as he turned his attention to Eva. Although he was watching her closely, he couldn't tell if she was more surprised at what at just happened or at the fact that he knew her name.

"The children are ok… for now. It's up to you if they stay that way." Samuel said. With that he walked over towards the pot of coffee he noticed was half full, he made it a point to open the "bread box" along the way. Sure enough, there was a full size 9mm pistol carefully placed inside. Samuel picked it up, checked the clip and the chamber to verify his suspicions that proved to be accurate. Fully loaded with one in the chamber, ready to go. "Yeah, Victor had prepped his beloved well, just not well enough." Thought Samuel.

He put the gun in his waistband and opened a cabinet, looking for a mug. The second cabinet proved to be a winner. He removed two mugs and poured two cups of coffee. He turned towards Eva and raised an eyebrow in a questioning manner.

"Uh!" she exhaled, as if breathing her frustrations towards him and then muttered "with cream, it's in the fridge door". Samuel opened the fridge casually, while still keeping his eye on Eva. He poured her a little cream in the coffee and set the mug in front of her. He sat down across from her, in the seat her daughter Mila had previously occupied.

"Eva, my name is Samuel." He began. "I'm not a bad guy, on the contrary, I'm the poor guy who lost everything because of bad guys, and now I'm the guy that's got to stop them. It's really as simple as that, although I understand, you'll need to know more."

"Let's start with your husband. Do you know where Victor, sorry, Vic was yesterday afternoon?" Samuel asked.

"He was working, you crazy bastard. Just like he is today and if he gets home and you're here, he'll kill you." She said coldly. She didn't say it mean or loud or boastfully, just very measured and matter of fact. He knew she believed it. If he was a careless fool, then she'd probably be right.

"If I die, while your children are frozen Eva, they will die too." He didn't know if that was true, he actually thought it might be very untrue. Having never died, he didn't know for sure, but his hunch was that if his ticket got punched then frozen victims would just be released. Maybe, maybe not. It didn't matter, he chose to go with the 'if I die, they die' theory on most occasions. "Why not? You never know it may save my life one day." He thought.

"Now, do you know exactly what your husband was doing at work?" he asked patiently. "We don't talk about his work" she said curtly.

"Fair enough." Replied Samuel. "Allow me to bring you up to speed." Samuel continued. "Victor, I mean 'Vic', was with the governor. He grabbed him while he was leaving work, took him to a nearby alley and commenced to…"

"Stop" Eva interrupted. "I don't want to know. I told you we don't talk work. Why are you trying to tell me this? What does this have to do with me and my kids? If you've got beef with Vic, take it up Vic and see how far your little freeze trick gets you!" Eva shouted.

She'd had enough. He needed to move this along. The clock was ticking after all.

Samuel continued "Ok, we'll skip the details. Let's just say, your husband left with the governor's four gold teeth. You know the front ones and the fangs… the egregious damn things that make it such an irony that he ever made it to governor status, but hey that's what the hell this city has come too."

Samuel caught himself before he began a spirited rant and continued. "The governor owes money to Vic's boss, Eva. Probably for getting him into the damn governor job to begin with, but that doesn't matter. The point is the governor couldn't pay. Don't ask how I know, but I know. The same way I know that Vic's boss is going to send him to kill the governor and his wife and children tonight, probably while his boss is at the opening of his new club. The perfect alibi and a way to smile and gloat and let the entire city know it was him."

"I am sure your husband thinks it's about the debt, but it's not. There's more to it." Samuel said. "Regardless, that's where we're at."

"First off, my husband would never kill kids or even an innocent wife. He wouldn't. Secondly, that still has nothing to do with why you're in my house threatening to kill me and my kids, you bastard!" Eva said, obviously done with this exchange.

"It has to do with you because this is your chance. Your only chance to get out of this mess. To get your children out of this mess. To keep Vic from becoming that man." Samuel said passionately. He was done with this too, time to get on with it. "Vic WILL kill that family, because he knows if he doesn't, they'll send someone else to do it and then they'll send someone to kill all of you too. Do you really believe he'd let that happen to you? To your children?"

Eva froze. She knew what she heard was true. She could just tell by the way this strange man said it. By the look in his cold blue eyes. "This guy was definitely crazy" she thought, "but he isn't lying."

"So what? You're here to help us? Your gonna save us from this bad choice he's being pushed to make, by magicking my kids and pointing a gun at us?" Eva challenged, although much less hostilely than her previous responses.

"Yes." Samuel said. "That's exactly what I'm offering." He paused for effect while he looked her in the eyes briefly. Then he continued "I'm not offering some easy way out for your husband. Let's get that straight. He's got to work for it. He'll have to help me, keep this type of thing happening to other families everywhere." Samuel said.

Eva looked him in the eyes, weighing out the terrible options in front of her… hands tied, children "froze" and a mad man in front of her. It didn't seem like she had options. So she responded with the question on her mind "So you think, you, some crazy gene freak that we've never seen before who broke into our house and held our family hostage, is just going to present this offer to Vic and he's going to believe that its safer to side with you and turn against his boss?" she shook her head, almost sympathetically. "Really? That's your plan, what was it, 'Samuel'?"

Well, she had a point, he thought. He had known it would take more. Time to move along.

"Yeah, that could be tough. That's why you're going with me." Samuel said. "Get up and pick up Steph." He told her. She started to say no, she started to contest, but as their eyes locked, she knew it would only encourage him to remind her of the leverage he had. "Until he unfroze her kids, she couldn't risk it. Maybe, she could catch him unaware and force him to unfreeze them, but not here, not now while he's expecting it" Eva thought.

Eva got up and awkwardly picked up her son with her hands zip tied, while Samuel gently zip tied Mila's hands and picked her up. Eva and Samuel headed to his Cadillac each carrying a frozen child.

They gently placed the kids in the back seat and Samuel instructed Eva to get in the front seat. He started the car and then touched her arm, she froze. It was necessary. She couldn't know how to get where they were headed. No one could know how to get there.

Samuel made his drive to the Greenwell's house. It was the perfect location. That's why the sacrifice had been necessary. While he didn't know for sure how far the freeze would extend too, he did know from practice that this house, tucked away on the edge of this city was plenty close enough to Vic's house and "The Spot". He could leave the family frozen and be back to meet Vic, but first…

Samuel finished delicately carrying the children inside the Greenwells house and placing them in the living room, which was to the right of the front door and directly across the hallway from the kitchen, which was to the left of the front door. Then headed back to the car to get Eva.

Samuel opened the passenger door and stepped back to give Eva plenty of room and "willed her" free from the frozen state. Eva instantly looked around, more trying to soak up her surroundings than in alarm. She turned to face Samuel and recognition washed over her. "You froze me as soon as I got in the car, didn't you?" she asked, almost rhetorically. Samuel simply said "yes."

He didn't have too much time, but this part would dictate how he'd need to handle her and the children. If she reacted calmly, she just might prove to be rational despite the situation.

A look of surprise sprung onto her face, as she instantly turned around to check the back seat of the car. Samuel didn't wait for her to ask. "They're inside, still frozen, but safe and sound." He said calmly.

She turned to face him and continued out of the car until she was standing face to face with Samuel. Again, he didn't wait for her to ask, or demand, instead he simply said "I need to show you something and then you can go to them. I'll even unfreeze them, but I need you to see something first."

Eva, whose frustration was noticeably building again said "then show me."

Samuel pulled his phone out of his pocket and selected the appropriate video he'd previously taken, before handing her the phone though, he paused to explain. "This is why you're here Eva. This is why I chose not to let your husband die with the rest of those bastards that took everything from me…" Samuel paused, looking into the distance as if haunted by an old nightmare. It only lasted a moment, but it was long enough to catch Eva's attention. Samuel continued "unless you and your husband choose to die, unless you are not the people that I think you are, then I refuse to let you be another slaughtered family by the Camacho Tribe." With that, Samuel handed her the phone and said, "push play".

Eva took the phone in her hand, looked skeptically at Samuel and then concerningly at the house, then she reluctantly hit play on the video. Immediately surprise and anger appeared on her face "You were watching our house?! Videoing our house?!" She roared.

"I've watched all of Camacho's people's houses for quite some time now Eva. Keep watching." Samuel said.

As Eva watched her own house, being watched from what appeared to be across the street, she noticed the stocky short man and the well-built dark-haired man get out of the car parked on the street just past her house. She instantly knew the men. She'd met them on many occasions, they worked with Vic. It was Stump and Eli. They were almost like family friends, so, what were they doing sneaking around her house? Her questioning thoughts were answered quickly as she watched the men, open the trunk of the sports car they had pulled up in and removed what looked vaguely like explosives of some sort. They then crept up to the house, stared into the kitchen window for a moment and then worked together to secure the explosive-looking bundle under the front porch. They appeared to be very thorough, as they used a drill and some type of metal strips to screw it into position. Once finished, both men ran back to the car bent over as if trying hard not to be seen. Then they drove off in a hurry.

"What was that?" Eva asked Samuel. "Exactly what I wondered." He said in response. "So, I checked, keep watching."

The video kept playing as the person holding it obviously got out of some car and approached the same spot on the porch that they secured the item to. The camera man went under the porch, turned the light on the phone taking the video and zeroed in on the package. It looked like grey clayish blocks, several of them that were at least the size of bricks with wires protruding from them and all connecting into some sort of device that had an antenna and dim lights. The video abruptly ended.

Eva handed the phone back to Samuel and said "What the hell was that? A bomb? Why would Stump and Eli do something like that?"

"Yes" Samuel responded "C4 to be specific. Connected to a transmitter, so that it could be triggered remotely and as far as your other question, because they were told to. People who work for your husband's boss do what they're told. The same reason your husband will kill the governor and his family… or would've if I hadn't intervened."

"Eva" Samuel continued "take a moment and think about this … Camacho is prepared to kill you, your children, and your husband. He's sent your husband to kill the governor and his family. If Vic doesn't do it, what do you think that means for you and your family? If he does do it, do you think Camacho sets off the bomb anyway to get rid of the trail back to him or do you think he waits for the day your husband says something he doesn't like?"

"If I hadn't seen this, your husband would've died with the rest of them for what Camacho did to my family, but I couldn't let another family die, not if I could help it." Samuel paused, obviously emotionally affected by what he'd just said and possibly from what he recalled by saying it.

Eva looked shocked and horrified, but she seemed to be processing this well.

"Let's go inside," said Samuel. "Take a look at the house. It's yours, if you and Vic are on boar… at least until all this is done and then you can go wherever you like."

"I'll unfreeze the children for a bit, whenever you're ready, but soon, I'll need to go meet Vic and show him the same video."

"Good luck." Eva said as they walked towards the house.

As they entered the old house Eva began taking in all the details, every little one. While seeing the video and hearing the explanation, helped her better understand the situation she was in, it did little to settle her nerves. She was on high alert. Her and her children were after all, kidnapped by this genetic freak who had unreal abilities, and oh by the way didn't look like he'd be too easy to handle without them. The only comfort she had in this crazy situation was that their kidnapper had chosen to spare them from his murderous vengeance driven scheme, because what, he saw that her family would be blown to pieces at some point in time by the psycho her husband worked for… oh and he only knew this because he had been watching their house for who knew how long. No, nothing was good about any of this. She was and had definitely better stay on high alert.

As she walked through the house, two thoughts weighed heavily on her mind… one was that this was definitely not Samuel's house. While it looked like he'd done a good enough job cleaning it up, it was still very obvious. There were a lot of spots on the walls where discoloration made it clear that pictures had been there for some time before being removed. The same thing on dressers, where dust patterns showcased something that had been there a very long time, was no longer there.

Sure, this could've been him discarding every memory of his murdered family, but that wasn't just it. Whoever lived here seemed old, you could just tell from the taste of the décor to the way things were arranged. No, this was some older couple's home, was Eva's best guess and they didn't have kids, at least not school aged children, that's something a mother of two could tell at a glance.

So, where were the owners? How had Samuel come by this house?

The second thought weighing on her mind, was that this psychotic kidnapping freak might just be there best bet to stay alive. Sure there was absolutely no trusting him, but if she had to pick between psychos to side with to keep her family alive, she'd definitely pick the one that showed her the bomb and chose to spare her adorable family from his vengeance driven schemes over the one that her husband was loyal too, yet still planted a bomb to kill them all … oh and by the way was sending her husband to murder women and children. Yeah, she was sick to her stomach to think of it this way, but this nut job might just be their best shot.

With that decision made in her mind, a different kind of fear washed over her. The fear that Vic would kill him before he heard all the details, before this freak unfroze or whatever it was, her children. With that she decided it was time to stop learning and start trying to keep her family alive. For her to stop thinking like a victim and start thinking like the soldier she'd been trained to be long before Vic and the kids.

Eva finished wandering the house and approached Samuel who had been staring out the kitchen window. He didn't seem concerned about letting her walk around by herself. Didn't seem to worry that she might find something like the letter opener from the upstairs writing table, that was now tucked under her shirt now. Didn't seem worried that she might approach him from behind and decide to find out if unfreezing her children were as simple as sticking the envelope opener right through his neck.

No, Samuel let her wander without seeming to worry. Maybe it was that he felt the leverage of the frozen children would keep this poor mother in line. Maybe it was the fact that he underestimated just what Eva was capable of. "No, that's not it" Eva thought. "Samuel really believes he's made such perfect sense, that he's done such a good deed by saving us that he doesn't even realize the lines he's crossed" She thought. Her thoughts were reinforced as she approached him, quietly, and heard him muttering something like "I'm a good guy, but it has to be done". No Samuel's strong sense of self justification was downright unnerving, not to mention certifiably crazy and its exactly what would lead Vic to killing him before he had a chance to explain... Unless Eva helped that is.

"Ok, Samuel" Eva said firmly from directly behind him. In truth, she kind of hoped for a sign that she'd startled him, but she should've known better. Samuel slowly turned around, calmly raised and eyebrow and said "Ok what, Eva?". He clearly knew she had been there the entire time. Good thing she had decided against the envelope opener, that might not of went the way she hoped.

"Ok, if you've got any hope of convincing Vic before he kills you, you'll need my help." Eva said. "Your freeze ability is handy, I'll give you that, but it won't matter if Vic thinks you took or killed his family. You'll be dead before you can reach him, and he'll figure out how to find us later... trust me... that's just Vic." As she finished, she stared into Samuel's eyes and waited for him to respond.

His lack of surprise was not what she expected at all. "I agree Eva. I think your help will be essential. There is far too much to be done, to be wasting time with unnecessary bloodshed." Despite Eva's surprise at how quickly he agreed, she did not fail to notice that he did not say 'whose bloodshed' he was referring to. Rather than dwelling on the disturbing thought, she went on "Samuel, I think we need to make a video for Vic. Me and the kids. I plan to leave out the kidnapping at gun point and freezing of the children, but I want you to know that I will tell Vic everything when we're together." She said.

Samuel simply nodded in understanding and replied, "So you're ready for me to release the children now?" "Yes," Eva said.

In mere seconds she could hear her children muttering "mom?" from the other room and moved quickly to meet them. Eva spent a few minutes explaining to her children that this was where they would be staying for a while and that their father would meet them soon. Both children seemed to except what their mother was telling them, but the older girl "Mila" continued to look around suspiciously. When Eva walked them into the kitchen, the girl immediately halted as soon as her eyes landed on Samuel.

Samuel did not speak, he did not move, and he did not smile. He simply stood there, apparently counting on their mother to explain things. Eva did so promptly "Mila, its ok. Samuel is here to help us. He just isn't that smart and didn't know how to tell us before. He didn't mean to scare us."

"What did he do to Steph before mom? Steph just stopped moving when he touched him." Mila asked, still staring at Samuel suspiciously. Eva replied in a motherly tone by saying "He can pause people like a video Mila. He just didn't want to scare us before he could explain, but you were so fast." She let her smile complete the explanation.

"Now kids, your father is in danger and Samuel is going to help him, but if Samuel scares your dad like he did us… well" Eva was interrupted by the little boy Steph saying "then Dad will kick his butt, huh Mom?". Despite the awkward situation the boy still had the nerve to look at Samuel and grin.

"Well," Samuel thought, "if Vic is half as scary as his family seemed to think he is, then I've definitely picked the right one to save."

"That's right" Eva said. "So, let's make a video for your dad so poor Samuel doesn't get his butt kicked."

In truth, Samuel hadn't really known what to expect from the video, but he felt good about the results when they had finished. Eva had told Vic that they were safe. That Samuel had saved them, that they had to get away from Camacho and that he should listen to what Samuel had to say. After that the kids said their "I love you's", as did Eva and she ended the video. Short and sweet and a little more supportive of him than he thought she might have been. Still, she had told him that she would support him, but also that she'd tell Vic everything when she saw him. "I don't guess he'll be too overjoyed to hear how I got them here" Vic thought.

Now that the Video was all done, Samuel looked at Eva and said, "I'll need to freeze them while I'm gone, but there's no need for me to freeze you." They stared at each other in silence for a moment. Samuel expecting a protest and mentally preparing his response, but Eva surprised him once again by saying "I understand, but… IF my husband agrees to help you, the freezing stops. Agreed?"

Samuel simply said "Agreed." However, he had no intention of releasing them, only to walk into who knew what kind of trap later.

Chapter 4: Homecoming

After Vic had finished picking up everything needed to stock the bar and the cabinets, he looked everything over one last time to make sure it was all set up for the evening to come. He knew that because of his damn "assignment" that the guys would all be here before he was back. Usually, he was here to open it all up for them. Sure, Stump would get the place opened and turn the lights on, but the lazy bastard wasn't good for much more than that, well that and getting on Vic's nerves when the watched to door together. "Everything looks good" Vic said to himself. "Good to go."

With that Vic went out the door, pulling it shut behind him and entering the security code. He walked to his black SUV, that the guys loved to make fun of, started it up and began the short ride home. It was late afternoon/early evening, he had time to go home take a power nap and eat some food. He'd head back out at dark to handle his assignment before making his way back to 'The Spot'. "My damn assignment." Vic thought. "Well, it's him and his family or me and mine, and I'll be damned if it's gonna be mine." Vic told himself.

He kept thinking those thoughts again and again, but it didn't stop him from being haunted by what he was going to do. Killing women and children wasn't what he signed up for. Hell, it wasn't even necessary. This was just Camacho throwing his weight around, with the city and with Vic.

"What if I just loaded Eva and the kids up and we took off" he thought "we've got enough saved up to get far away from here. No, he'd find us. He finds people everywhere. He finds them and he makes examples out of them." The thoughts weighed heavily on Vic. Then he had another thought "What if I just take him out instead? Lord knows the little bastard has it coming." Vic mulled this idea over for a few minutes while he drove. "I'd have to take the guys out too, but that wouldn't be too hard" he thought. "The family though. The damned creepy Camacho family" he thought. There would be no getting away from them. Hell, that's how Camacho finds everyone. Those Creepy family members of his just show up out of nowhere and no matter how far someone goes, it doesn't take long for them to find them and bring them back to Camacho, then just as creepily as they showed up, they disappear. It could be months before they were seen again. No, there's no getting out of this.

After all these thoughts, the one the plagued him the most was the constant thought that after he went through with this Camacho had him. Had him in his pocket to do anything and discard him anytime he wanted too. He wasn't even his own man anymore, not after this anyway. It was that thought that tormented Vic the rest of the way home. It was that same thought that had Vic so mesmerized that he didn't even notice when he drove right past the black sedan parked oddly on the street across from his house. Vic finally snapped out of it when he pulled into the driveway and put the SUV into park. He shook his head, adopting the "It's easier not to think at all" motto for the moment and stepped out of his ride. He noticed Eva's car was exactly like it was when he left this morning. "That's odd" he thought. "I thought she was taking the kids to the park. She always takes the kids to the park on Saturdays."

Slightly puzzled he began to head towards the front door, when he noticed the curtains over the kitchen window were pulled shut. "She never closes the curtains" Vic thought. Instantly he knew something was wrong. The tall man's entire demeanor changed, but his pace did not, nor did the expression on his face. No, not Vic, he just kept walking towards the front door, but instead of turning left to take the short steps up the porch and in the door, he walked right past it and kept going across the yard. His pace gradually increased, and he smoothly ducked his head when passing the windows, without missing a step. When he reached the corner of the house, he went left coming around the side of the house towards the backyard. Vic knew exactly where he was headed, he'd planned for just such an occasion. When he got to the fence, he didn't go for the latch to enter the backyard, instead Vic smoothly pulled himself up onto the top of the fence and from there he pulled himself onto the lower roof. Once on the lower roof, Vic made his way to the upper section of roof, being very careful to walk lightly. On the upper roof, there was a small square glass sunroof that sat above the master bathroom. It opened from a knob on the inside and would let a nice breeze into the bathroom when the occasion merited it. However, this fancy window wasn't meant for feeling the breeze or keeping up with the jones' on house décor, no this was how a guy like Vic planned to get into his house if using a door wasn't "ideal".

Vic got to the sunroof, felt around the edge and engaged the hidden latch that released the locking mechanism from the outside. He then pulled open the sunroof, locked it in the open position and silently lowered himself into the bathroom.

As soon as he hit the floor, he pulled the 45 caliber pistol out from under hist shirt and paused to listen. He hoped to hear the kids laughing and running or even the coughing and sneezing of a summer cold, but he knew better. His instincts told him otherwise and the silence just reenforced it. Something was wrong. Vic slowly and silently made his way out of the bathroom and into the master bedroom. He silently searched the rooms upstairs but did so quickly. If someone was here waiting on him, it wouldn't take them long to notice his truck in the driveway and began to search for him, that could endanger his family even more. He couldn't risk that. It took mere seconds for him to feel confident that the upstairs was clear and begin his descent down the stairs.

As Vic approached the bottom of the stairs he slipped around the steps towards the back of the house, where a den connected to the hallway that the stairs fed into and to the back entry into the kitchen. He figured that he had an unwelcome guest. He also figured that this guest would be exactly where he would be, in the kitchen. The kitchen gave the best view of the driveway, the street and was in direct sight of anyone coming in the front door.

So, Vic headed around to come in the back of the kitchen. The fact that it was silent, and his family was nowhere to be seen, was filling him with growing rage. "In my house!" he thought. "Messing with my family!" he thought.

As he approached the back entry into the kitchen, he saw him.

A well-built man with dark skin and a shaved head. The man wore a black a sports coat and black jeans, that almost looked like dress pants from the way that they fit with the jacket. He had black boots on. The man was staring out the window with his back facing Vic. Obviously noticing that the SUV was parked in the driveway. Yeah, this trespasser knew what he was doing, looked like he could handle himself, looked like a professional. "I have to do this fast, or I may not get a second chance" Vic thought. "I also can't kill him, or it'll be hell trying to find my family… well I'll try not to kill him" Vic thought. He knew all too well, that if this guy gave him a reason, he wouldn't think twice and would just deal with the more difficult task of finding his family without the aid of this man's answers after it was all over.

Vic leaped in the Kitchen and the kicked the closest chair over the table hitting the man directly in the back with enough force for his head to crack the window he was staring out of. Before the man could turn around, Vic shoved the entire table forward, pinning the man's legs against the window. The man started to shove back and turn around, but by then he already had Vic's pistol firmly pushing against the back of his head.

"Don't turn around. Don't move. Don't do anything or I pull the trigger and find my family without your help." Vic said coldly. "Please know I mean it" Vic said, or at least tried to say… he didn't quite get the last part out before the table he was leaning across gave way on the far end sending him crashing head towards the floor, at the same time the table gave way from a firm back kick to the right leg by the trespasser, the man moved fast, very fast to the right.

"He was true to his word" Samuel thought has the window shattered from a .45 caliber bullet going through it right where his head was. Vic spun free of the table and then kicked it from the far end so that it sent Vic from flying head towards the floor across the table, to riding the broken table towards the hallway.

Samuel didn't hesitate, he needed to end this quickly. Vic had already caught him off guard. He ran towards Vic, leaping on the leaning, sliding table, which stopped it in its tracks and allowed Samuel to place a firm kick to Vics face.

"Shit, this guy's fast" Vic thought right as he took the boot to the face. What Samuel couldn't see was the smile that appeared on Vic's face immediately upon getting kicked. "He don't know the grim reaper" Vic thought as he quickly grabbed the man's ankle before he could pull his foot back. "He got my face, and now I got him" Vic thought viscously. In a flurry of hand motions and less than a second Vic had twisted Samuel's ankle, punched his knee, his groin and flipped him backwards off the table.

"Shit he's fast" Samuel thought as he rolled back onto his feet after suffering a flurry of punches that hurt like hell, but not as bad as the damn ankle twist. When he jumped up onto his feet, he noticed the other man doing the same thing, it was either go for the pistol or a leap of faith that could put him in precarious position if not landed correctly. He had a millisecond to make his decision and decided that if he pulled a gun on Vic, he'd probably have to use it… and use it quick. Samuel made his move just as Vic was making a quick move towards him. He counted on the reckless dive taking the other man off balance and he was right. He just dove, arms extended. Vic tried to sidestep, but he was already moving forward and had too much momentum built to get fully out of the way. That's all Samuel needed. That's what he was counting on. He touched him with his finger, freezing Vic in place and then crashed heavily into the pile of debris that used to be a kitchen table.

Vic looked around in confusion. "What the hell? How did this happen?" Vic thought. He was sitting on the only kitchen table chair left in one piece, with each foot zip tied to the front leg of the char. His hands were also zip tied, but behind his back over the back of the chair and to each other.

When he realized the back of his belt was zip tied the one of the rungs in the back of the chair, he knew he'd really made an impression on the fella. As entertaining as this thought was, he knew from the throbbing pain in his head and the stinging of his face that felt like there must be a boot print on it, that the man had a definitely made an impression on him as well.

"It doesn't make any sense" Vic thought frustrated. "I had him dead to rights. Sure, he threw me off with that reckless childish leap, no one would've expected that from someone who handled themselves with the skill that this strange man did, but it was reckless and left him exposed… he should be waking up with my gun in his face." Vic's confusion and frustration continued to build up, until he snapped himself out of it. "Wait a minute, where the hell is he now?" was the next thought that washed over Vic. "Did I put my family in more danger? Did he leave to finish them off?" Vic thought. These thoughts replaced all of his confusion and frustration with fear and guilt. 'What have I done? I should've been faster. Should've let him take me and flipped the script on him once I knew where they were. Damn it Vic. Damn it Vic." Vic's self-reprimanding thoughts were interrupted by the sound of liquid pouring into a cup from behind him.

He immediately began taking in the details of his situation. He was sitting in the middle of the hallway, obviously the man was keeping him away from any walls that he might use as leverage. His back was to the kitchen, and he was facing the living room across from the kitchen. The front door was to his right and the rest of the hallway that led to the stairs and the back door was to his left.

He noticed the shattered table and chairs had been cleaned up and moved somewhere, he didn't know where, but it should've been sitting almost directly to his right. "How the hell did he have time to tie me up AND clean up?!" Vic thought. Before he could go back down the perplexing rabbit hole of thoughts around how this man had gotten the upper hand and pulled of this apparent magic trick, Vic's peripheral vision caught the man walking around the left side of him.

The man gave him a wide berth, obviously cautious about getting too close, yet still appeared casual as he sipped his cup of coffee walking around in front of Vic.

"Sorry, I can't offer you a cup as well Vic." Samuel said sincerely. "It's just better for both of us if I leave your hands secured for now."

"You mean better for you. What's the matter a little

concerned you'll get your ass kicked again?" As soon as Vic said it, he regretted it. He knew he shouldn't provoke the man. Not with his family still at this man's mercy somewhere. Sometimes he just couldn't help himself though.

Samuel wasn't fazed by the response. He was actually a little amused. That's odd "I'm never amused anymore, not after what happened" Samuel thought. He wasn't sure if it was because of all the planning and preparation for this moment, or the fact that this man had such a loving family that reminded Samuel of the family he'd lost or if it was no more than respect that Vic had managed to catch him off guard and give him quite a challenge (which never happened), but Samuel admitted to himself that he liked Vic already.

"Well, you definitely didn't disappoint Vic. My damn ankle will probably hurt for a week." Samuel said with a half-smile. "Not to mention the chair that you managed to what throw into my damn back?"

"kicked" Vic said. "I kicked the chair over table into your damn back."

"Impressive." Samuel said. "I'll give you some ice for your face that I imagine still feels like my boot, once we're done."

"What do you mean, once we're done?" Vic replied. "And how the hell did you manage to pull this off? I had you dead to rights?"

"Well Vic, you only had me dead to rights, because I gave myself up just to pull THIS off." Samuel continued. "My name is Samuel. I can do things that other people can't do. That isn't important right now though. I'm comfortable telling you more about that later, but now we should talk about your family." Samuel paused a moment to let Vic process the words and to let Vic get past the expected emotional response he saw wash over him at the mention of his family.

It only took a moment and despite the fury in his eye, which was to be expected, Vic appeared ready to listen. Samuel continued "they are safe Vic. They are actually safer than both of us right now in this damn house." Samuel couldn't help but glance towards the front door when he said that. Towards the place where he knew there was a bomb that could end everything for both of them at any given second.

A bomb that could leave his family unavenged for eternity. "No, I can't let that happen. Won't let that happen." Samuel thought as he felt a degree of anger and fury in himself. He shook his head and focused his attention back on Vic, aware that Vic had noticed the glance towards the front door and the emotional change of his face. "Vic is definitely observant" Samuel thought. "That is good, considering what we must do, but I'll have to be more careful around him."

Samuel picked up right where he left off "Eva and the children actually made you a video Vic. It was her idea, not mine. She insisted that if you didn't see it, then you wouldn't believe a word of what I'm going to tell you and show you. I'll let you watch it now and then I'll explain more."

As Samuel was getting his phone out and pulling up the video, Vic responded. "You could've made them record it. You could've held them at gun point and told them what to say. You could've killed them as soon as it ended. It doesn't mean shit! I need to see them alive!" Vic's voice got louder as he went on. His response was understandable, Samuel thought.

As Samuel held the video in front of Vic, he made one statement before hitting play "I understand, and you are correct. While I admit I failed to research Eva as thoroughly as I researched you Vic, I think we both know that your wife is more savvy and capable than people may give her credit for being. You decide if this is sincere or forced for yourself."

With that, Samuel hit play. He watched the emotions in Vic's eyes as the tall man watched the video. He watched the realization and relief flood over him when the man realized that his family was ok. That this was legit. The video ended and Vic looked up at Samuel, for the first time seeing him as a person and not an adversary that he needed to figure out how to conquer.

"Why? What does it mean?" Vic asked.

"My family was slaughtered by Camacho Vic. I will destroy him for what he did, and I will destroy his family, his people and the empire he's built. You would've just been another justified casualty along the way had I not seen you with your family, had I not seen that Camacho was intent on destroying another family. Watch." Samuel said. With that he hit play on a second video. The video that showed Samuel watching his house, that showed the men he worked with plant something under his front porch. The video showed exactly what that something was.

Unlike Eva, Vic didn't have to ask. He knew exactly what it was as soon as he saw it. Rage and anger washed over him again, but this time it wasn't aimed at the man who had fought him and tied him up in his own house. This time it was aimed at the man he worked for. The man who just hours earlier had instructed him to kill women and children. To kill another man and his family. The man who had threatened to kill Vic's family if he didn't do as he was told, without even saying it.

Vic was livid and instantly decided that Camacho would die. That all of his key enforcers would die.

"You have been given the gift that was never offered to me Vic. You can commit yourself, your life, to destroying Camacho BEFORE your family dies. You can choose a path of justice, whereas my path is clearly one of vengeance. You can join me and keep him from hurting your family or any other families. I have given you this choice, this gift Vic."

"If you have any doubt's left, go look under the porch for yourself." Samuel said. With that Samuel pulled the small black dagger from the sheath on the back of his belt under his coat and approached Vic. He cut his hands free first, then his feet and then handed him his chrome .45 caliber pistol.

Vic was more shocked that this man would cut him loose and give him his gun back then he was at anything he'd heard so far. So shocked that he didn't know what to do or say, which was rare for Vic. He slowly stood up, he looked at the gun in his hand and looked at Samuel, who still stood in front of him, although he'd stepped back just barely out of reach.

Vic paused for a moment and then headed to the front door, putting his gun back under his shirt while he went. Once outside, he quickly checked under the porch only to see exactly what he saw in the video. Without touching the explosives, he carefully inspected them and came to the conclusion that the odds were very high that they were set to go off if tampered with.

"That explains, why this 'Samuel' didn't remove the damn thing when he saw it." Vic thought.

With that Vic headed back inside. Upon reentering the house, he noticed Samuel in the kitchen. He had just finished pouring another cup of coffee and offered it to Vic. Vic, did not want to take anything from this man, however coffee sounded great after what he had just experienced, so he reluctantly accepted.

Standing in the kitchen, both with mugs in hand looking at each other, Samuel began before Vic had a chance to speak. "You saw it?" He asked.

Vic simply replied "Yeah, I saw it."

"I assume you came to the same conclusion that I did… trying to remove it appears that it would trigger it?" Samuel asked. "Yeah, that's what it looks like to me too." Vic said in response.

"Your family is at a house not far from here. It's safe, self-sufficient and off the grid for the most part. It's yours and your families until this is all over with." Samuel said. "All I ask in return for sparing your lives and securing a safe location for you and your family is for your trust and your help in taking out Camacho. What do you say Vic?"

Vic hesitated before answering, feigning contemplation. It was just night an act to appear less eager than he was. In truth he didn't trust this crazy guy at all, but it didn't matter, if this 'Samuel' had kept his family safe, warned them of the treachery of his boss and secured them a safe house… he was in. One hundred percent in. "Well, one hundred percent in until we kill Camacho. After that we'll see." Vic thought.

Then Vic answered with, "Trust takes time Samuel, but I'm in. Now take me to my family and we can talk through what you've got in mind once we get to them, and I see them safe for myself."

"Fair enough." Samuel replied. "We don't have much time though. Camacho expects you to take out the governor and his family right after his new club's grand opening this evening right?"

Vic was shocked at how Samuel could've known that, but being surprised by Samuel was feeling like the theme of this entire afternoon, so he chose not to dwell on it. Instead, he said "Yeah, that's what that son of bitch expects."

"Then we have to make our move, before he learns that you've chosen a different path Vic." Samuel said. "We'll kill Camacho and all of his lieutenants tonight, Vic. At least all of the ones he's posted here. Tomorrow lay low and figure out how we get at the rest of them, I've got tonight all figured out for us."

Samuel paused staring into Vic's eyes, no, staring more through his eyes, then asked "You ok with this Vic? Even though they were going to kill you and your family at some point, I know you still worked with all of them for quite some time. You sure you're ok with slaughtering them all, tonight, Vic?"

Vic didn't need to think about his answer or hesitate on this one for Samuel's sake. "No point in it" he thought.

"Absolutely" he said staring back into Samuel's soul. "They don't call me the grim reaper for nothing. These assholes died when two of them planted that bomb, all of them died, they just don't know they're dead yet." Vic said it sternly, viciously yet honestly too. Then added "and Samuel, I'm in it until they're all dead, not just the local ones. I expect you to be too. I've been with Camacho too long and one thing is for sure, his creepy Indian family or whatever they are, that seems to appear out of know where is far more dangerous then these fools he has as his lieutenants here. I don't plan on my family hiding and running forever only to get ambushed by some creepy Native American Camacho relatives. So let me ask you, are you in it until they all die or are you stupid enough to think it all ends with Camacho and these local fools?"

Samuel respected the question and appreciated the sincere bravado. He was also relieved and reassured that Vic was completely on board. At least for now. "Wonder how his mood changes when Eva tells him about how I took the family?" Samuel thought.

In response Samuel said "I assure you I have no other purpose in life but to dispatch Camacho and all of his people, employees, friends and relatives. I have no intention of stopping until that is done Vic and I am pleased to hear that you feel the same. Now, we've wasted enough time, get whatever things you need for you and your family. Pack light, but be thorough, I don't think we'll ever see this place again."

It didn't take long for Vic to pack a couple bags for the kids, one for his wife and for himself and get them loaded into his SUV. He also packed what seemed like a small arsenal in three separate bags and loaded them up with the help of

Samuel.

"This guy was equipped for a small war." Samuel thought and that was even before he noticed the RPG in the back seat of the SUV. Once again Samuel felt reassured that he'd picked just the right man to help him, although he wondered in the back of his mind, if the two of them would be enough.

Once they had finished loading up the SUV, the two men stopped in the driveway to look at each other once more. They didn't speak for several moments, just stared as if they were both silently assessing how much they could trust the other, despite having already went all in on this risky course of action. After a few moments, there was an odd feeling of mutual respect that seemed to connect the two men. "This is good. This is needed for what's to come." Samuel thought. "We should be able to work well together."

"Well, I know he can handle himself and if he wanted us dead, he damn sure had his chance. I guess were in it together now." Vic thought.

After the long moment of silence, Samuel reached into his pocket, pulled his hand out and then reached out his closed fist, palm down towards Vic as if handing him something. Vic in turn reached out under the closed fist of Samuel and felt him drop a handful, fifteen to be exact, .45 caliber bullets into his hand.

"Your clip is empty." Samuel said. "That could be a problem later, but I had to be sure earlier. Load up and follow me, I'll lead you to your family."

"How the hell did he do that?" Vic thought. Followed quickly by the thought that if he had chosen a different path, if he had chosen to shoot this man instead of aligning with him, then he would likely have been the one with a bullet in his head. "Yeah, we're in it together, but I've got to keep an eye on this guy. He's no joke." Vic thought as he just nodded in response and got into his SUV.

Once the two men had parked in front of the old 'Greenwell house', Vic willed the two children free from their freeze. They started to make their way up the path to the porch and were greeted by Eva opening the front door before they made it past the first step. Eva saw Vic and Samuel walking together and rushed to hug her husband. Despite the relief and love in her eyes and the genuine embrace, Samuel heard her whisper in her husband's ear, "Are we really with him or not? Tell me now." She said it very quietly, most people wouldn't have heard, but Samuel was paying very close attention as he knew this was still a delicate moment.

He was also once again impressed by Eva. She was far more than he had expected. He wondered what sinister trap she had planned for him, with the children free and Vic home. Vic's response made him think that he may not ever know, but he was still very curious.

"We're with him babe." Vic said in a normal voice, not at all trying to hide the fact that she had asked him. "Samuel is on our side. He warned us and got us to safety. Now him and I are going to make sure we don't have to hide out here too long" he said the rest lovingly and reassuringly then he asked "Are you ok? Are the kids, ok?"

As if in response, both children burst past their mother in unison and each hugged one of Vic's long legs. "Daddy!" they yelled. Vic didn't take his off Eva's eyes though, obviously waiting on an answer. "Yes. We're all fine" she said. "He scared the kids a little, because he's a creepy bastard" Eva said looking sideways at Samuel, "but he didn't hurt us Vic. He was polite and explained everything, that's why I made that video."

As Eva responded, she noticed the large almost foot shaped red imprint on her husband's face and frowned. "Are you ok babe? Did this guy hurt you?" she asked with a hint of astonishment in her voice.

Vic just laughed as he leaned down and picked up both kids, one in each arm. Then he said "I think we both hurt each other babe. Hell, what did you expect? It could've been worse… he's pretty damn fast."

Eva looked shocked and stared at Samuel as if seeing him for the first time. She'd seen her husband compete in martial arts, she'd seen him lose his temper, this 'Samuel' was definitely more than just a guy with a weird power if he'd held his own against Vic and got a compliment from him afterwards.

"Come on Eva, show me the house and then Samuel here can fill us in on his plans. We don't have a lot of time." Vic said. With that, they all headed into the house.

In no time at all, Eva had walked Vic through the house with the kids practically nipping at their heels the entire time. It was really as if the children were seeing it all for the first time too, of course they were, but Vic didn't know that. "At least not yet anyway" Samuel thought.

Samuel gave the family their space, but still listened carefully. From downstairs, he'd heard enough from the children's animated explanations to know that Eva had set them up a room to share. He knew it would be the room on the same side of the hall as the master bedroom. He knew she'd keep the children close to her, if not in the same room as her.

After the brief tour, the entire family came downstairs and both parents got the children settled in the living room watching TV. During their time upstairs, Samuel had definitely heard when Eva had told the children to look around their new room and began talking very softly with Vic. Samuel couldn't make out what was being said, but he assumed this was Eva 'keeping her word' and filling Vic in on everything that had transpired.

He braced himself for what he expected could easily turn into another few rounds with Vic, before he managed to freeze the man. He was starting to be concerned about how little time they had to put the plan in motion, but he knew this part was critical. Vic and him could not operate together as a tactical unit if they had to worry about the other man putting a bullet in his back.

Despite that he thought to himself "I doubt Vic will be frozen so easily next time. The guy's fast enough and skilled enough to go to toe to toe with me and keep my hands off him. This could get tough."

By the time Samuel finished mulling over the probabilities and possibilities of what he assumed would be an upcoming confrontation, Eva and Vic walked into the kitchen where he waited.

"Alright" Vic said "Sit down, tell me how you did your

magic trick or whatever the hell it was and then tell me your plan Samuel. My family's safe. Eva said you got them here without hurting or threatening them, though I still don't quite understand how." He paused to look cynically at his wife, then went on. "But we're here now. You've kept your word from what I can tell, so let's talk about how we're going to take care of Camacho."

Samuel was shocked. He'd definitely expected Eva to tell him every detail and for the man to be extremely angry about what had transpired between Samuel and his family. It seemed however that Eva had decided otherwise.

"What I do, I don't truly understand myself Vic." Samuel said. "It's something like freeze tag if you will. I touch people and they well, freeze, but without the cold."

"It's like a pause button babe." Eva chimed in. Vic just glanced at his wife and raised an eyebrow as if to say, 'How do you know'. But said nothing.

Samuel continued "I don't know how it works, just that I can do it and have been able to for a very long time. I have to touch someone to 'freeze' or pause them" he half smiled at Eva when he said it. "Paused is an interesting way to say it he thought". Then he went on "but I can just kind of will them to be free from the freeze from anywhere. I'm not sure how far it will go, but I know it will cover a decent distance. I'm also not sure if there is a time limit, but if there is it's longer than I've been able to test. Make sense?" Samuel asked as he finished his explanation.

"Not a damn bit" Vic replied, "but now I know how you got me at the house, you slick bastard."

Samuel smiled in return, or at least gave as close as he got to a smile, which was kind of a half-smile. Then he continued "Enough about 'my skill', let's talk about tonight." With that statement made, he looked at Eva and then at Vic.

Vic noticed Samuel's look and awkward pause and then realized that Samuel was waiting for Eva to leave or for Vic to tell her to leave. Vic thought about it for a moment. "I don't like her being involved in work stuff" he thought. "But this isn't just work. This is our lives, and she needs to know what's going down, how serious it is and what to prepare for." With this final thought he responded to Samuel's look.

"She can stay and hear it all Samuel." Vic said. "I don't like her to know the nitty gritty of what I do, but this involves her and the kids. She needs to know what we're planning and understand what to do if we fail."

"Fair enough." Samuel said. Then he continued explaining the plans for this evening. The plans that would finally put an end to Camacho. The plan that would be the first major step in eliminating the madman and all of his people from existence. The plans that he had been working towards for so long.

"It was really rather simple" Vic thought as he was busy unloading the family's things from his SUV. "Not much to it. I head to the spot and Samuel takes the RPG and instead of blowing up the governor's house with his family in it, Samuel takes out the new club that Camacho was opening with the little bastard sitting right in it. Meantime I take my spot at the door and when I see old Samuel walking up, I take out Stump, punch in the code to 'The Spot' and we both walk in and take care of the lieutenants." Pretty straightforward Vic thought.

He'd tried proposing they wait until later in the night for the lieutenants to be good and intoxicated, which was about their usual, but Samuel had shut that idea down with sound logic. "If they hear about the club explosion, they'll be on full alert. They may notify the family and who knows who else. No, Samuel's plan seemed like the best approach. From there the two of them would just scour 'The Spot' and see what they could find to lead them to the rest of Camacho's 'Spots' and people.

After Vic finished unloading his family's things. He talked with Eva briefly. Vic assured her everything would go according to plan and told her that she had nothing to worry about. He mostly believed it. Still there were just two of them. Then he went on with what he really needed to tell her.

"Eva, if we're not back by morning. You need to get the kids and get out of here. I know it seem's safe and that Samuel is definitely all about getting Camacho, but if things do go wrong, there's no telling how quickly Camacho could get him to give up this location. Take the kids through the woods out back. I've packed the tent, a pistol and some essential gear and food for you and the kids in the large backpack by the backdoor. Camp for a few days, a few miles away. Make it fun for the kids. I'll come find you. If I'm not there by day three, I'm not coming. Hike out towards the highway, find a store, get an uber and head north. Canada is the only chance of disappearing. Camacho is too connected in the states and everything south of the border." He finished his passionate instructions. He half expected Eva to protest, to argue, but he knew his wife too well. Hell, she was his wife for a reason. She was calm, rational and wasn't afraid of anything as far as he could tell.

"Ok Vic." Eva said. "I don't feel like fucking camping though, so you better just make it back. Alright?" She said with a loving smile. "Damn, I love her." Vic thought, like he often did.

"Ok babe. I'll see you in the morning. I love you." Vic said and then lovingly kissed his wife. He said his goodbyes to Steph and Mila, separately telling them in sincere whispers that they needed to look out for each other and their mother." They each responded with a since of compassion and duty in their eyes. It was cute to this look on his son's face, but he knew little Steph was too young to be much help in any kind of way. Mila was another thing altogether. Despite her young age, when she said "yes sir" to him, it felt cold, it felt real, it made him feel like his little girl might end up being scarier than both of her parents.

With the goodbyes all taken care of, Vic grabbed his pack and headed out the door. Samuel was waiting in the driveway, leaning on his black luxury sedan with his legs crossed.

As Vic approached, Samuel stood up straight and headed to meet him at the back of the SUV. Vic opened it up and pulled out the large RPG. "You know how to use this thing, Samuel?" Vic asked.

Samuel simply nodded and in reply asked, "How many rockets do you have?"

"Three, but you only need one." Vic said.

The two men loaded one rocket into the RPG and placed it in the backseat of the sedan. Vic suggested putting the other two rockets in the trunk, but Samuel insisted that they go into the backseat too. So that's where they went.

With that, the two men synchronized their watches and turned away from each other, got into their vehicles and were off. Both men clearly understood that the time for talk was over, and they both clearly understood that the other knew it too.

CHAPTER 5:
DANTE

ante was so happy. This had to be the best night of his life. He'd worked so hard to get his family to the states. To get them all settled into the small two-bedroom apartment, which was cramped for the seven of them, but still more spacious then the living conditions they had escaped. He had worked so hard to get them all jobs in the club restaurant, despite them having to come on at half pay. He didn't care about that; he knew once they saw how hard his parents and his older siblings worked that they would be thrilled to pay them all full wages. Not to mention, once they tasted the amazing cooking his family produced. He knew his parents could make gourmet meals out of next to nothing, he'd been raised on it his entire life.

At twenty-three, Dante was the youngest of his five siblings. Despite being the youngest of them all, he was the one that got them all to the states. It wasn't that he was better than the rest of his family, no Dante would never say that or even think it, it was just that he had gifts that they didn't have. So, it had to be him, to get them out of the hopeless conditions that they were stuck in.

At 5'9", Dante wasn't that tall and although he was extremely fit and muscular, he wasn't that big either. He was a good-looking young man, with black hair that he kept slicked back and a well-trimmed goatee, but just considered himself average. He did have 'the gene' though. It affected him differently than anyone he'd ever heard of before. He had the ability to teleport himself to any place he'd ever seen before with nothing more than a concentrated thought and some focused internal effort, almost like lifting weights with his mind, is how he often described it to his family. He also was extremely agile and had incredible aim. He couldn't say for sure, but deep down he knew this was attributed to 'the gene' too. He never missed anything he aimed at and could move with such incredible agility that it was far from normal, even for skilled athletes and gymnasts. It was these gifts that allowed Dante to join the circus and other various performing acts when he was younger and first left his family to 'find them a way out'.

He performed everywhere and saved everything. Ultimately, he found he made the most money throwing knives. Well, that was until some shady gentleman offered him huge amounts of money to fight with knives. Dante hated violence, but the amount of money they offered was unbelievable, so he gave it a try. He hated the violence, but he was good. He was very good. He didn't know if all the men he fought survived or not, he told himself they did and chose not to think or ask about it ever.

It was the knife fighting that paved the way for this opportunity. He asked some of the men that bet on him and paid him if they could help him get his family to the states and help them get jobs. After they laughed and made jokes about only if they could fight like him, they finally gave in and said that if he got them here, they could get them on working in the kitchen at the 'bosses new club'.

He regularly teleported back to his family's house south of the border to bring them food and catch up with them. He had such a close relationship with his parents and all of the older siblings. He couldn't stand to be away. No matter where he went or what he did, he always made it a point to visit. With his teleportation 'skill' there was no reason not to.

It was upon one of these visits that he told his family about the job working in the kitchen. He told them about the two-bedroom apartment he'd saved up for and got for them all, although he didn't tell them how he earned the money. He didn't really lie to his family, he couldn't do that, but he didn't tell them the truth either. He just said he did jobs for men that ran gambling circuits. He evaded questions for more details, almost as skillfully as he evaded knives being swung at him in the fights. Despite everything being set up for them, he still had not come up with a way to help them all get to the states. There were too many obstacles and risks. Very few people actually made it to where they wanted to go now days, when trying to illegally cross the border. It had become more treacherous than ever.

After what seemed like hours of brainstorming, when the family was cleaning up after dinner and getting ready to call it a night, his oldest brother Hugo pulled him aside. "Teleport me back with you Dante" Hugo had pleaded. "If it works, you can bring all the family and we can finally be free."

Dante had told Hugo it didn't work like that; he'd argued

with Hugo for what seemed like forever "it could kill you, Hugo!" he finally yelled. The entire family immediately noticed the conversation that had turned into a loud argument. At that point, Hugo explained to them all what he proposed. He ended it by firmly saying "I am the oldest. Let me try to save us. I would rather die trying this way, than risk us all dying or even worse, by trying one of the other ways we've discussed. It might just work."

That statement had impacted everyone in the room, including Dante himself. Dante would never forget those words or the words of his father that followed. "He's right Dante, but the choice is up to you. You're the one blessed with the gifts, it's up to you how you choose to use them son." His father had said.

That night Dante had tried it and to his surprise it worked. He simply grabbed hold of Hugo, just like he did the food that he brought them so often, concentrated and they were simply there. Both of them. Him and his brother Hugo back at his two-bedroom apartment. He didn't wait. He immediately went back and one by one took them all out of there. Thinking the entire time, how easy it was. He could've done this years ago. It didn't matter though; he had finally got them there.

Now one month later, it was opening night of the club and his entire family was working the kitchen with him. The deal was simple, they got half the wages and he had to keep fighting for half as much money as he made before. However, the men assured him that if they did a good job, they could keep their jobs and earn higher wages over time. Dante was thrilled. He still didn't tell them about his fighting, just that he had jobs to do for the men, but he felt like they knew.

This was the best night ever! His family was all working hard, but you couldn't tell from the looks on their faces. It was nothing but smiling from ear to ear for Dante and his family tonight. He snapped out of thoughts and continued peeling potatoes. "What a great night" he kept thinking over and over while he worked.

Less than two hours later, the club had opened. Red carpet, a grand speech from the owner Camacho and then people rolled in, and music played.

Camacho sat in his VIP lounge, which consisted of a large half circle booth on a balcony directly opposite the grand front doors of the club and slightly over the DJ booth and the dance floor. To both of the sides of the dance floor were dozens and dozens of dining tables, some lounge couches scattered about and two magnificently large bars to either side of the front doors.

Camacho sat in the middle of his VIP booth, with his right-hand man who only went by "Primo" to his right and several scantily clad women. "Primo" as they called him, was everywhere that Camacho was. Very few had ever seen them apart for long. The man was older, at least mid-fifties, of average height, very thin and kept his silver hair pulled back in ponytail. Similar to Camacho he was obviously of some type of Native American decent. He was constantly whispering in Camacho's ear no matter where they were.

There were also two muscular men in suits with sub machine guns on each side of the booth. No one knew if there was really danger or if Camacho wanted to show everyone how powerful he was, but it so customary for Camacho to have an entourage like that, that few paid it any mind whatsoever.

A little over two hours into the club opening, Primo leaned over to whisper in Camacho's ear as he often did. "We must leave now. The place will explode in seconds. I have seen it." he said calmly.

That was all Camacho needed to hear. He knew very well to trust what Primo said, everything Primo said. That was why he always kept him so close. Primo had 'the gene', just like Camacho, but he didn't get extraordinary strength and speed like Camacho, instead he had the unique ability to "glimpse" the immediate future. This skill had left the man half crazed and no one knew how much he saw, but Camacho knew that if it was important, if there was danger, Primo always saw it and warned him. He didn't see far ahead only seconds, but seconds made the difference.

No sooner did Primo whisper the words into his ear, than Camacho stood up, Primo standing with him.

Camacho rubbed the stone circular pendant on his large gold chain and a weird line appeared before them. It looked like the blur you see when the hot sun hits the ground in the desert, only it ran vertically into the air about six feet tall. Camacho and Primo stepped into the "blur" and vanished, just as a rocket came blasting through the front door of the club and exploding right where the VIP booth was.

The explosion was immense. The entire building was turned to flames and ashes almost instantly. Dante was across the back of the lot behind the building taking the trash out when the shockwave from the explosion hit him. It sent him flying into the front of the large dumpster with such force that he struggled to maintain consciousness. He felt like his nose had been broken and struggled to get to his feet, dazed and confused, he managed to turn around and saw what was left of the club. What was left of his family inside the club. He could only stare. He couldn't move, he couldn't think. They were all inside. His entire family. His entire life. Everyone he loved. He couldn't believe it. "This was the best day of our lives" he kept muttering to himself without even realizing it.

He was startled from his horrific shock by a weird glimmer across the back lot. It was on the other side of the dumpster so he didn't have a great look, but he could see some weird blur that was like a line running straight up from the ground about six feet. Out of the blur, out of nowhere two men step out with bright sunlight behind them. For just a moment he thought he saw a grand forest around them on the other side of the blur and then it was gone.

It was just the two men. He knew them right away. The man with the short mohawk owned this club, his name was Camacho. He didn't know the name of the other man, the skinny one with the ponytail but he knew he was always with Camacho. The two men, who were in the club just moments ago, stepped out of the blur and stared at what was left of the place.

"Well, I'll make a fortune on the insurance money Primo" Camacho said. "I knew it would either be the governor, or it would happen this way. Either way both places were getting toasted." Camacho said it matter of factly and then he laughed.

"Where to from here?" Primo asked in his soft raspy voice "The spot?".

"No, that place may be compromised. We'll go back to the other side to converse with the family for a while." Camacho said "First, go ahead and light em both up Primo."

With that Primo pulled a large square device out of his suit coat pocket. It looked like a smart phone but was about two or three times as thick. He typed on it swiftly for but a second and then looked up and gave Camacho the most unsettling grin Dante had ever seen.

"It's done." Primo said. With that they both laughed and then Camacho rubbed the stone-looking pendant on his gold chain and the blur appeared again. They stepped back through and were gone.

Dante, stared at the spot where both men had been in disbelief. He didn't know what to make of any of it. All he knew is that this man talked like he knew that Dante's family would get blown to smithereens and he laughed about it.

A deep kind of anger that Dante had never felt before rushed over his body. Sure, he'd been mad before, he'd mad plenty of times during his fights, but nothing like this. This was something different. This was pure hatred. To think that this man and his people had let Dante and his entire family come to work here, despite knowing that it would be blown up infuriated Dante. He had nothing left. This man had taken everything from him. He'd taken all of Dante's family from him. All he had ever loved. Dante knew in his heart that he would kill this man. He would kill them all, but for the moment all he could do was fall to his knees and cry.

After what seemed like forever, Dante slowly pulled himself up off the ground. He slowly dried the tears from his face, and he began to think on what he should do. Slowly it came together in his head. He would go the place the men had stopped at many times when taking him to the fights. He was never allowed inside, but he'd been in the parking lot, sitting in the car on many occasions. He knew it well enough to teleport there. Once there he'd have to figure out how to get inside and then make the men tell him where Camacho was. Where "the other side was" and then he'd kill them. He'd kill them with the same knives that they paid to use on so many others, during the fights.

That meant going home first. That meant getting ready first. They took everything from him. This was all he had left, then he'd join his family. To Dante, it wasn't worth going on without them.

He concentrated on his apartment living room and an instant later, he was there. He went straight to the closet by the front door and pulled away the piece of false wall on the right. He grabbed his knives. He had several of them. All double-edged daggers. All sharp. All tucked into the two leather belts that were covered in built in sheaths. He wore them crisscrossed over his bare chest in the fights. The belts held four daggers in the front on each side and two in the back on each side. Ten total. He strapped the belts over his dirty soot covered black t shirt. He changed into his blue jeans and put on his black boots.

With a snarl to himself, he let the anger overtake him and he concentrated on the parking lot of that place they often stopped at. "The Spot". Yeah, that was what they called it.

An instant later Dante stood in the parking lot of the spot, but it was not what he expected. The door was wide open, a roundish looking man lay in a bloody mess in front of the open door and Dante heard gun shots from inside the building. Still resolute about his mission, he began to approach, however the fact that someone had seemed to beat him here, filled him with wary caution.

CHAPTER 6: 'THE SPOT'

Vic pulled up to his usual parking place in the alley behind "The Spot". He parked the SUV got out and thought to himself "Samuel better just do his part."

Vic grabbed 3 extra clips from his glove box and tucked them into his pockets. He pulled out his chrome .45 pistol, double checked the clip and cocked the gun. Then he tucked it firmly back under his shirt.

"This is going to be the toughest part" he thought to himself. "I gotta figure out to keep a straight face and not kill these bastards until Samuel gets here." Vic steeled himself and began his walk to the door.

As he approached, he noticed Stump standing guard by the door. Stump looked just like his name suggested… he looked like a tree stump. Short bald and stocky. Stump stood there with his submachine gun on a shoulder strap looking straight ahead into the darkness, with his head slightly cocked to the side like he was trying to listen to the fun going on inside that he wasn't invited to.

Vic approached and was amused at Stump's startlement when he saw Vic. "Stumpy bastard got caught eves dropping" thought Vic. Stump went from looking surprised about getting caught trying to listen in on the guys inside, to even more surprised to see Vic.

"What the hell are you doing here Vic?!" Stump said way too loudly. "I thought you weren't coming until later. Thought you had something important to do?" As Stump said it, he unconsciously adjusted the sub machine gun in his hand.

"Oh, I see" Vic thought. "Old Stumpy knew what I was sent to do and was told to be ready for me to show up with the task incomplete." As Vic thought it, his mind instantly went to what Stump might've been told to do in this situation. Then he thought about the video. The thoughts were enough for Vic to decide in that moment that Samuel wouldn't be his sidekick going into "The Spot", he'd be his backup. Vic would handle these bastards or damn well try right here, right now.

"Eva would be pissed" he thought as he walked up towards Stump casually.

"Everything's done Stump" Vic said. "Why the hell would I show up without it being done, I'm just not as slow about my business as you are lil Stumpy" Vic said with a half-smile. The comment generated the desired effect, Stump's face looked angrier, but he ever so slightly loosened his grip on the sub machine gun, finger moving from the trigger to the side of the gun.

"And just like I always do, I brought a little souvenir back from the assignment" Vic said. With that said, Stump's frown went away, and he smiled. It was true, Vic usually did bring back a souvenir from whatever job he got sent on, a couple teeth, an earring, even a finger once or twice. It was kind of his way of letting them all know this was easy for a guy like him.

"Hell yeah. Well let me see it, you tall lurch looking fool." Stump replied back. Obviously eager to see what Vic had brought.

"Sure man" Vic said, and he swiftly pulled out the .45 and shot Stump in the face. Despite how bad an idea it was. He went ahead and shot him two more times on the ground. Vic then put the .45 back in his waist band, picked up the sub machine gun off of Stump's corpse and typed in the code that unlocked the door.

As the door swung open, Vic instantly took in the room. Six lieutenants getting up from the table and pulling out their guns. Six more at the bar turning around and pulling out their guns.

"Shit. I hoped they all be at the table! Eva's definitely gonna be pissed. Samuel better get here quick." Vic thought as he sprayed the six men at the table with gun fire from the sub machine gun. He began running toward the table after a second of gunfire, continuing to shoot the entire time. When he got close, he slid on the floor as if to slide under the table and instead grabbed the edge of the table with his left hand, still holding the machine gun firmly in his right. Mid slide, he smoothly planted his feet and sprang upward. The result was the table turning up on its side in one fluid motion as Vic came to halt behind it, just in time for the table to catch a flurry of gun fire from the six men at the bar.

The men had all taken positions behind the bar and were peppering the large table with plenty of ammunition. Vic did not return fire. Not yet. He knew he had less than half a clip left in the sub machine gun and one pistol against six weren't great odds.

"Why didn't I wait for Samuel again?" Vic thought to himself.

Vic's thoughts and strategy were interrupted by the hole large hole that blasted through the table just to the right of him. "Great. The idiots found the shotgun behind the bar." Vic thought.

"Alright, no sense waiting for them to turn me and the table into Swiss cheese" Vic thought.

With that Vic jumped up and sprayed the bar with bullets from the machine gun. Still firing he made a dash for the next table to the left of the one he'd flipped. It was smaller, but still plenty big enough for him to slide behind like he done with this one, and it got him just a little closer towards getting around the bar. Most importantly to Vic, was that it got him away from the front door. That was the critical part.

Vic knew that sooner or later Samuel would arrive, and he'd be no help at all if he walked in the door to direct gun fire. No Vic needed to get them shooting away from the front door, so Samuel could come in and help return some of the gunfire.

Vic slid again grabbing the edge of table and flipping it up on its edge to form a wall in front of him. He got there just as the sub machine gun ran out of bullets. Apparently, the gentleman behind the bar noticed the clicking of a gun with no bullets and all started firing at the small table Vic hid behind.

Between the gunfire he heard the shotgun cock and thought to himself "why'd I move to a little table again?" But the blast never came. Instead, he heard the men screaming and noticed them start shooting at the door.

For a moment he thought Samuel had arrived, but he hadn't heard a shot from the door. Then at the large table he'd slid from across the room from him, still turned on its edge, a young Hispanic boy simply appeared crouching behind the table.

Vic didn't know what the hell was going on, but he waited no time contemplating it. He jumped to his feet and lit up the bar with his .45. He caught one of the men and noticed another one laid out over the bar with the shotgun in his hand as he ducked back down behind the table.

As he ducked, the young man who had appeared behind the table to the right of him jumped up and paused just standing in the open and threw one knife. "A fucking knife?!" Vic thought.

The young man quickly ducked back down as they heard the faint gurgling of what sounded like a man with a knife in his throat. "Well, knife it is." Vic thought.

He waited for them to return fire, but the next wave of gun shots didn't come from the bar. They came from the front door. Vic and the young man both looked at the door only to see Samuel, not running, not crouching, not even moving fast, just walking straight in the door shooting with what appeared to be a black 9mm pistol in each hand.

He walked calmly right past them, crouching behind their overturned tables and proceeded to the bar. There was never a return shot. Each man that jumped up to shoot was shot by Samuel before he could get a single shot off. Vic and the young man next to him watched from around the tables as the battle ended with Samuel walking up to the bar, jumping on it and shooting whatever or whoever was left crouching behind it.

Without even pausing, Samuel jumped down from the bar and turned around to face them. "What happened to the plan Vic?!" He yelled "and who the hell did you bring with you?"

Vic looked at the young man next to him and as he stood up, he said "Thanks man. I don't know who you are, but these evil sons of bitches had me in a pinch until you arrived."

Dante's first instinct was to teleport out of there as fast as he could. He almost did, but as the tall pale man next to him rose and thanked him for his help, he hesitated. He didn't know either of these guys at all, but it didn't take a lot of intelligence to figure out that they were here to kill the same men that he was here to kill. He also knew that this was the only place he knew to look for Camacho, so he was lost after this. If he intended to kill that monster and then join his family in death, he might need some help finding them.

Dante slowly stood. He nodded at the tall man that had thanked him and then followed that man's lead as he turned to face this dark-skinned man that had casually walked into gunfire and ended it all with relative ease.

Vic gestured for Dante to follow him, with a slight wave of his end and casually made his way towards the bar where Samuel stood shifting his eyes from surveying the room and to watching them approach. As they got close enough to talk without shouting, Vic spoke up "I know Samuel, I know. I should've waited, but as soon as I saw that damn Stump and remembered that he tried to kill my family, it was all over. My bad man." For a tall, pale man that did in fact resemble the grim reaper, he managed to pull off a slightly apologetic and almost even humble look.

Dante spoke next, completely ignoring Samuel, he turned to Vic with excitement and rage all mixed together and said "They tried to kill your family too?! It was Camacho, wasn't it?!" he yelled.

"Yeah man." Vic said in a comforting kind of way. "It was that damn Camacho. He would've killed my family if Samuel here hadn't warned us."

"What about you?" Dante asked, turning to Samuel. "Did he kill your family tonight too? Is that why you came here too?" Dante had a desperate tone to his voice and a desperate look in his eyes. It was almost as if he were longing for someone to be feeling the same agony and torture that he had experienced tonight.

Samuel did not respond immediately. He was measuring Dante with his eyes, calculating everything about the young man before him. After a moment that seemed like forever he responded in cold shallow tone "Yeah, he took my family from me too. If you're here to kill him then you're too late kid. Camacho died earlier in his new club. We're just cleaning up what's left of his crew." As Samuel finished talking, he watched Dante's eyes more closely than before.

"The eyes don't lie" Samuel thought. "Are you really here to kill him?" he wondered to himself.

"He's not dead!" Dante exploded. "He blew up his own club on purpose! I know! I was there! My family was there!" as Dante finished tears began to stream down from his eyes and he continued to stare at the other two men with the same desperate look in his eyes.

Vic and Samuel exchanged confused looks and then Vic chimed in. "Slow down man, what do you mean he's not dead? He was there, wasn't he? There when the place… exploded?" he asked careful not to say too much about how the place actually exploded.

"He was there and then right when it exploded, he appeared out back. He kind of stepped out of a blur, or something like that. Look I don't know what the hell it was, it was different than what I do, but I do know that him and that skinny Indian he's always with, you know the one who wears the suits, stepped out of some kind of blur and laughed about the explosion. They said now they knew; they'd make a fortune off the insurance and all of them were going to blow or something like that. Then they just stepped back into that blur thing and were gone." Dante's eyes went from tear filled to filled with the fire of anger as he continued. "They laughed! Those monsters blew up my entire family in that club and they just laughed!"

Samuel and Vic looked at each other again. Each thinking

the same thing. This was not good. This was not good at all. As they shared similar thoughts, through silent looks they were interrupted by the breaking news report that was showing on the TV hung high above the bar.

"That's right three separate bombings all within minutes of each other in very different parts of town. While it's unconfirmed at this time, a terrorist attack is definitely what authorities are speculating" The news anchor reported. The screen switched to show three different views at the same time, each of an explosion aftermath with an address listed underneath. It showed the club that had exploded, the governor's house that had been blown up and Vic's house, which had absolutely nothing left to it.

They stared in shock. Then Samuel turned to them both and spoke in that cold deep voice of his "Vic it appears our work isn't done, and the job just got harder. If Camacho can disappear or teleport or whatever, that changes things. Let's search the place, get what intel we can and light this place up."

Then Samuel turned to Dante. "My name's Samuel. Camacho slaughtered my family just like he did yours and was going to do the same to his. We're going to kill him. Come with us and you can avenge your family too, but you do what I say so you don't get us all killed. Deal?" With that Samuel reached out offering a handshake to Dante.

As Vic heard Samuel invite the strange guy to join them and then reach out his hand, he had no clue if Samuel was sincere, was going to freeze this guy or would just kill him. It unnerved him that he knew Samuel was quite capable of all three and wouldn't think twice. It also unnerved him, that this kid had lost his entire family because of the rocket that Samuel had shot into that club.

Dante on the other hand, had a look of hope in his eyes. He looked as if he'd been sent a guardian angel to help him avenge his family. Before he said a word, Vic knew this guy was all in.

Dante reached out and shook Samuel's hand. "My name is Dante. I would be honored to join you if it means killing that murderous monster, Samuel."

Samuel shook the young man's hand firmly. Looked him in the eyes and then nodded and said "alright let search this place quick and get out of here."

The three men headed for the elevator and Vic punched in the access codes that he wasn't supposed to know. Paying attention had paid off. They went floor by floor, finding drugs, weapons, and literal tons of cash. Throughout their searching efforts Dante had explained a little about his teleportation skills and had offered to help them get whatever they wanted outside without them having to carry it.

It didn't take much convincing for Samuel and Vic to not only agree, but to wear the young man out by having him transport an enormous amount of cash and weaponry. They had diligently searched several floors and had only one floor left before Camacho's living quarters in the penthouse at the top.

As the elevator opened and they walked out they were all shocked at what they saw. They expected more guns, drugs, or cash, what they got was something that looked more like the NASA room used to navigate rockets into outer space.

There were screens everywhere. They saw different color-coded dots at various locations around the globe. Some of the dots were connected with color coded lines. There were names by the larger dots.

Samuel began snapping photos of everything, as Vic just wandered around the giant room that took up the entire floor with screens on all the walls and rows of computer monitors and chairs down the middle. When Vic got to the far end of the room, he stopped. This was his town on the screen. When he turned around the row of computers closest to the screen each had a different color dot with lines that looked like they indicated travel paths. The one in front of him was red and by the dot he saw the word "Stump". It showed Stump's house, then the line went three blocks down to what Vic knew as Stumps local bar, from there the line went to "The Spot". Vic noticed today's date at the top of the screen.

He stepped back and looked up and down the row. "Shit, he's been tracking all of us." Vic thought. Then a different thought occurred to Vic, and he quickly went down the row until he found his name beside a purple dot. It showed him leave 'the spot', run his errands come back, go home and… "No. No, no, no, no" Vic said growing louder as he went. "He's been tracking us you fool!" he screamed at Samuel still taking photos of everything he could. Samuel paused and looked at Vic questioningly, but Vic's words immediately hit him.

"He's been tracking every movement! He's been tracking all of us! He blew up my house Vic! The club Vic! He knows where Eva and the kids are!" Vic yelled with a panic in his voice that Samuel had not heard before. With that Vic darted for the elevator.

"Vic wait!" Samuel yelled. "If he was tracking you then, he probably still is. He won't go for them, he'll come for you!". It was too late; Vic was boarding the elevator pushing the button over and over while the doors slowly closed like it would make them close faster.

Samuel sighed. "that's it" he thought. "Now it makes sense. This is why a man of Vic's skills wasn't one of the highest paid mercenaries that money could buy. This is why he isn't running everything for Camacho. This is why someone of his talent isn't anything he wants to be… he's irrational. He's a cowboy." Samuel shook his head, somewhat disappointed in his new recruit. "Yeah, it all makes sense now. No one wants a cowboy in an organization, and they don't tend to last long in organized crime." Samuel thought.

"Well, fortunately for me, a cowboy will do just fine with our mission, hell maybe even better than most. Still, it would be nice if he'd listen or stick to a plan. Have to keep working on that." Samuel thought.

His thoughts were interrupted by Dante, who appeared out of nowhere by the elevator. "Ok Samuel." He said huffing and puffing as if he were working much harder than everyone else and in truth he was. "The papers are in the parking lot by the guns and the cash. I'll take these explosives next if you show me how to unplug them."

"Good idea, Dante. Give me just a second." Samuel said as he finished stuffing what looked like two oversized cell phones into his jacket pocket. "We need to finish up here quickly and then go after Vic before he gets himself or his family killed." Samuel took a few more pictures then walked over to where Dante stood staring into what appeared to be an electrical closet, looking very perplexed.

As Dante, noticed Samuel approach he said, "Why did those red blinking lights just come on like that?"

"Oh, shit!" Samuel yelled out.

Then the building called 'the spot' exploded.

Chapter 7: Camacho

Camacho and Primo stepped out of the path. To the uneducated observer it would appear that they were stepping out of some desert mirage or a blur of some sort, but they knew it was just a path. A path to the 'other side'. They knew it well. Despite both men being from the world that many humans knew, the one they were taught to call the 'top side', they were trained and practically raised here on the 'other side'. It wasn't a different world really, even though it was.

It was, well it was the 'other side'. Kind of like the flip side of a sheet. Each side may have different designs, different stains, or other features, but they were both just different sides to the same sheet. If you poked something through one side, it went right through to the other side. This was very similar. Actually, the paths were pretty much exactly that, a hole from one side to the other. Very few could find a path, let alone create one, but when you did take a path, it only took you to the same exact spot on the other side as the spot you were in on your side. Just like poking something through a sheet.

Geographical location is about where the similarities stopped though. The 'other side' had totally different forms of creatures and plants and humans were not at the top of the food chain there. The 'other side' was far less industrial and technologically advanced than the 'top side', but it alternatively had far more mysticism and supernatural properties. Most 'top siders' knew about the 'other side' more than they thought they did. Creatures and people accidentally slipped through paths back and forth from time to time. It's what created most of the stories and supposed sightings of things often not believed to be real. Oh, there was sure to be some bullshit out there, but most 'top siders' wouldn't ever sleep again if they knew how many supposed myths were as real as can be and just mistakenly or maybe intentionally slipped into their world and then out again.

Although he was technically a 'top sider' Camacho considered them all fools. He couldn't understand how so many people in totally different parts of the world could see the same things, have descriptions and stories that matched perfectly in totally different languages and still ignorantly chalk it up to imagination. "fools" Camacho thought as he often did.

He knew he was a fool once, before the Na'gee had recruited him, trained him, raised him to be a real warrior, but his bias memory told him he was never that foolish.

Camacho, like Primo and many others were recruited by the indigenous people of the 'other side'. They seemed to only select 'top siders' of some Native American decent. Something to do with the ancestral lineage tying those peoples together.

They recruited many, but only a select few survived the training. They were brutally savage people. It's probably the only thing that kept them alive on the 'other side' where humans were definitely, not the top of the food chain. The Na'gee thought of all 'top siders' as weak and soft, too dependent on their precious technology. Yet it was the advanced technology of the 'top siders' that they recruited for.

They only selected the most savage of their recruits and then positioned them strategically on the 'other side' of critical Na'gee compounds. Each recruit and each Na'gee warrior had a talisman that they wore around their necks with mystical inscriptions that allowed them to 'cross over' or make a path from one side to another. Once they felt the right recruits had been sufficiently trained, the Na'gee would take them across and support them in taking over key components of the underworld trading and gambling. Their savagery and numbers could not be stopped and the fact that they could leave without a trace made them an unstoppable force.

Once their 'top sider' recruit had established themselves over a territory, they supplied the Na'gee with technology and resources that helped them attempt to balance the scales of power in a world of dangers that were unlike anything on the 'top side'. It had been this way for centuries as far as Camacho could tell. It was a good plan too. The Na'gee controlled most of North and South America's underworld and had smaller setups in key parts of Asia, Africa, and the Middle East. Camacho didn't know for sure, but he suspected there were more than that.

As Camacho and Primo walked toward their destination on the 'other side' path, Camacho sneered at Primo subtly, as he often did. Although the man had saved his life countless times, Camacho despised the man. He despised anyone that he thought was weak and he knew Primo had only made it as a recruit because of his gift. "He was too weak, too soft to have made it the real way." Camacho thought.

Primo had been with the Na'gee much longer than Camacho. Camacho remembered that Primo was already an adult when he was recruited as boy after he lost his family. Primo was assigned to Camacho though. They said it was a gift to give him someone with such power, but he knew what they really thought. "They really think I'm too aggressive and too careless to stay alive without his little tricks." Camacho thought as he often did.

Despite how often Primo had indeed saved him. Despite the fact that less than an hour ago Primo had actually saved him again. Camacho still refused to believe that he needed this soft older man.

Camacho stopped his mental brooding as they approached their destination. Olo stood in front of the green hut. It almost appeared to be built out of the side of the hill, was covered in moss and could be easily mistaken as just a hill if you didn't know what to look for. The door blended right in with the rest of it and would have been undetectable even to the trained eye, had it not stood open.

In front of it stood Olo. Olo, like all the native Na'gee warriors had a shaved head and was completely covered from head to toe, including his face, in some sort of tribal tattoos. Like all the warriors he wore leather pants, a leather vest with no shirt underneath and boots. The colors of leather did vary from warrior to warrior, but that's about all that did. Olo's leather was all black. He wore a very large knife, that looked almost more like a small sword than a knife, in a black leather sheath hanging from his belt. On the other side of his belt hung a large .50 caliber pistol in a black leather holster. The back of his belt was covered in extra clips for the large pistol.

Olo's ears were adorned up and down with large black stone earrings and he wore two leather straps around his neck, one held the circular stone talisman that all warriors wore, and one held a claw that looked like it belonged to a giant eagle.

He nodded at the two men and led them inside. Once inside the hut, Olo surveyed the landscape outside as if ensuring they had not been seen and then pulled the door shut and secured it with two log cross bars. He rubbed his talisman and the blur appeared. They all stepped through 'the path' and appeared in the basement of Camacho's hide away house.

As soon as the three men stepped through into the basement, they went to work. Well, Primo went to work while Olo and Camacho hovered. Primo went directly to the keyboard in front of the large screen on the wall and with a few clicks pulled up video footage of the governor's house exploding. They all nodded. They knew that was needed and part of the plan.

"As if I need them to give their approval to do my job." Primo thought bitterly. He didn't like Camacho. Didn't like him at all. Camacho was the third 'top sider' they had assigned him too and while he didn't like any of them, he liked Camacho the least.

"Doesn't matter what they say or if they approve, my honor is true. I shall fulfill my responsibilities." Primo thought proudly. The older man was always bitter. He despised the fact that he was never given a chance to run a 'top side' territory. He always had to help some careless hot headed young fool who just wanted to show everyone he knew how to kill. That's what the Na'gee thought the "soft top siders" needed, so that's who got the job. To them Primo was too thoughtful, too cautious to do what needed to be done. They wanted savagery, even if it came with stupidity. Although he hated it, Primo accepted it. He was loyal. He was honorable. He would do what he was told to do to support his tribe in any way they saw fit.

With a few more clicks of the keypad Primo pulled up Vic's house and then pulled up the path Vic's vehicle had taken that day. He went one place after he left his house, then he headed to 'The Spot', where he was pulling up now. Primo switched to the cameras strategically located across from 'the spot' and they showed Vic pulling up and parking in his usual spot. He walked towards the door and a moment later they watched him shoot the door man in the face.

"Think we have time to make it there before he leaves? If we catch him, we could work him in the basement for days." Camacho said with a vicious snarl. "Only if we move fast and then we still may not make it, we don't have warriors in position to come through the path there right now. They are preoccupied." Olo said ominously. After a brief second of thought he continued. "We have him, we can track him, or we can just end him remotely. Your men there are nothing. Let us continue to watch and learn about our prey, while we send warriors to the place he went. We have warriors not far from there on our side. Undoubtedly, he has attempted to hide his family and anyone else he was working with there." Olo said it all with no emotion, just firm monotone instructions that he clearly expected to be followed. "Let us make the bodies of his beloved, decorations for his hideaway before we confiscate his life." Olo said.

They all nodded in agreement. It wasn't that Olo necessarily had authority over either of them. It could even be argued that Camacho was the one in charge here, but the Na'gee warriors were fierce and did not take kindly to being challenged. Unless it made no sense at all, which it rarely did, they were deferred to when it came to battle plans… hell battle planning is how they survive every day on the 'other side'.

With the men in agreement, Olo once again rubbed his talisman in that peculiar way that created the blur or the 'path' to the 'other side'. He stepped through, leaving it open this time, and walked across the same moss hut they had left just moments earlier. He picked up what looked like an old Nextel device and communicated coordinates to someone on the other end. When he finished, he put the device down and stepped back through the blur into the basement, closing the path behind him.

With the orders given, all three men watched video footage of the assault on 'the spot'. None of them seemed to react emotionally, they just seemed to be learning, processing, downloading everything they could about who their adversaries were, how they moved and how they fought. The only sounds in the basement were the occasional remark from Camacho cursing the assailants.

Chapter 8:
"Always Go Right"

"Finally." Eva said with an exhausted sigh. She had been working on Vic's instructions since she put the kids down to sleep a few hours ago and had just finished. She didn't like it, but she knew it was the right thing to do. Vic had been clear about the camping pack and the instructions for her and the kids if he wasn't back by the morning. He'd also much more discreetly been clear about the tracks. Vic knew how dangerous the men he worked for were and he clearly knew that he had no idea how dangerous the man he was working with now was, so he gave Eva clear instructions.

"As soon as we leave" he had said. "Go play with the kids in the woods around the house and get a clear idea of your three routes. Once you put them down to sleep, make three trails, try to send them towards a road or some form of water. Then walk backward all the way back. Know where the one you plan to take is just in case you need to go the camping route babe." He had said it all so seriously but couldn't help but break into a smile and embrace her at the end of it. Despite the danger. Despite the uncertainty of it all. He was still so happy when he was with her.

She knew it was a good idea. She also knew that they both knew what route she'd take, right. It was always the one on the right. She and Vic had agreed to that long ago. It really just made sense, pursuers always gravitated towards the middle and then it left a fifty-fifty chance on them picking the left or right. In most circumstances people tended to go left. Right was always the way she went. It was always the way Vic went. They always knew which way the other would go.

She'd been through her training, in what seemed like another life it was so long ago. So, Eva knew what to do, knew how to do it and well… laid the tracks and backed back down each one. Now she was finally done. "Now I can get some rest too." She thought. Then she openly laughed at the idea.

"Yeah right". She said to herself. Her man was out there risking his life to save hers and she was in some strange house that obviously didn't belong to the creepy stranger that left her with it. "No. No sleep for Eva tonight." She thought as she casually checked the clip of the 9mm pistol she carried for the third time. Staring out the window thinking these same thoughts over and over and then she saw it. She didn't know what "it" was, but it was something. In the distance where the road met the driveway. "What is that she thought?" as she squinted to try to get a better view.

She had the lights in the kitchen already turned off, and as she peered towards the strange blurry light or glimmer or whatever it was, she saw a booted leg begin to come through until it turned into a man stepping out of the blur. She couldn't see much detail at the end of the long driveway where it met the road, but she could definitely tell it was a man. It looked like he was wearing boots, pants and a vest and he was definitely shaved bald. Then a second man began to step through. Eva didn't wait to see what this man looked like, she removed the string that she had taped to the wall earlier, in case Samuel didn't come back friendly with Vic, and tied it to the doorknob. She looked up to ensure everything she had secured to the ceiling was still in place. After a quick review of her handy work, she ran to the couch, shook Mila awake and grabbed Steph in one arm. They headed to the back door as fast as they could, she grabbed the pack with her other hand, threw it over her shoulder and out the back door they went. The only sound that any of them made at all was Eva's faint whisper to Mila "We're taking the right trail Mila, you'll be able to see it. Don't stop until we get to the stream and don't make a sound."

"I know mom" Mila whispered back "Always take the one on the right." Those were the last words, the last sounds that they made as they headed through the yard and down the trail.

As the third Na'gee warrior stepped through 'the path' from the 'other side' they let it close behind them and surveyed the area. They stood at the end of a long driveway where it met the road. There were woods all around them. The men traded silent looks that communicated satisfaction that they were in a wooded area and not those nightmarish city landscapes. They wondered how these 'top sider' even breathed on top of each other with no plant lights and all the gasses and fumes from their motorized inventions. The three warriors could see the house. They saw that the downstairs lights were off, but the upstairs lights were still on. This pleased the warriors, as it was much more satisfying to kill prey that was awake, that could fight. Killing sleeping prey was easier, it was faster but it easy and fast wasn't what a warrior craved.

The men spread out and silently moved towards the house. They weren't really sure what they were hunting, but they knew that there was nothing on the 'top side' world, that compared to what they hunted on the 'other side'. All they knew was that they were to kill anyone and everyone they found, then they were to display their corpses of their victims to make a statement.

As they neared the house, the warrior on the left peeled away to circle the house. The warrior on the right leaped up to grab the roof hanging over the porch and pulled himself up. From there he began to climb his way towards the upstairs window. The warrior who had been in the center, continued up the porch to the door. He tried the knob and found it locked. The warrior wore brown leather pants, a brown leather vest and had a wide brown leather belt with a large knife in a sheath on one side and large pistol in a holster on the other side, just like his two comrades. On this warrior's belt there was also a small bag that was tied shut. He swiftly opened the bag, pulled out a small bone pin and worked the lock for not more than a second. "click" the lock gave way and he replaced the bone pin as fast as he had produced it. He eased his knife out and stepped in through the door.

As soon as the door swung open the string pulled and set off the makeshift pipe bomb that Eva had secured to the ceiling earlier that day. Her plan had been simple, if Vic and Samuel weren't on the same page when she asked Vic on the porch she would simply walk inside and then yank the string as soon as Samuel stepped under it. "See how well your freezing bullshit works with a full of nails" she had thought when installing her contraption. There proved to be no need then, but it seemed it would be useful now. As the makeshift pipe bomb exploded it shot directly down, spraying a couple dozen large framing nails down towards the warrior's head.

There was no doubt that this trap of Eva's design would have killed most men, but Na'gee warriors weren't most men. Most men wouldn't last one night on the 'other side'. The warrior heard a faint noise, right when the bomb was starting to go off and leaned his body from the waist backwards in a fluid motion like a snake and as fast as a snake striking. The result was that the nails missed his head and his upper body, but his legs didn't move. Several nails protruded from the tops of both his feet and the thigh of his left leg and knee that had been slightly bent forward.

Pain shot through the warrior's body, but anger coupled with surprise seemed to drown it out. Despite the pain he felt he didn't make a sound, not a gasp or peep. He just seethed for a moment and began to proceed through the house, when he noticed the warrior that had come through the window standing at the bottom of the stairs at the other end of the hall. The warrior gave the signal that the upstairs was clear and also gave a silent chuckle at his comrade's misfortune.

It lasted only a second, but it was enough embarrassment to fuel the fires of anger burning inside the nail riddled warrior even more. Yet there was still work to be done, so the two, one of them limping, quickly surveyed the rest of the house and then stepped out the back door.

The third warrior that had circled the house, was

crouched by the wood line, and turned to face his fellow warriors as they approached. He gestured towards the woods, specifically towards the three trails. "Three trails." He said in plain English. All the 'other side' warriors had adopted the language of the 'top side' region opposite them. It had served them two purposes, for one it allowed them to practice the language that they needed to use when taking 'the path' to the 'top side' for resources or work and two it gave them an alternate language to use on the 'other side' that wasn't as well known to some of the more nefarious predators that hunted them from time to time.

"The one on the left and in the middle were laid earlier and back traced to deceive a fool." the warrior said in a harsh deep voice. "The one on the right, was used the same way, but two people from the house used it again not long ago. One of them is a child."

The other two warriors nodded and all three began to slowly head down the trail on the right, closely surveying the woods surrounding the trail looking for signs of someone hiding. They assumed, with a child in tow, they would try to hide sooner or later and avoid attempting to outrun their pursuers.

Eva, still carrying the pack and Steph who was wide awake now, hurried down the trail as fast as she could. Mila followed closely. They had moved much slower when they started down the trail, trying to match the footprints they had laid earlier, but once they got a quarter mile down the trail, they figured there was no need in wasting time with that. "If someone follows us this far, they're not likely to turn around. We either lose them or we confront them." Eva thought. Although the thought of losing anyone that could find and follow her trail this far was very unlikely with her two children in tow. All she could do now was keep moving and think. "Dammit Eva, you've got to think of something." She told herself.

As the children and her topped the slight hill, they saw that it sloped steeply towards a stream. This was new territory to her, as she hadn't made her trail this far earlier. There were several large trees that had fallen and littered the way down. Two large trees crossed the stream and made somewhat of an X shape where they crossed each other at the opposite side of the stream. On the other side, the brush was thick and it inclined back up to a much higher hill. She knew she had to pick a spot to either hide or make a stand soon. It wasn't that she heard anyone pursuing her, on the contrary, the woods were eerily silent. It was more that she could feel that someone was chasing, no hunting her and her children. Call it mother's intuition, call it instinct, she didn't know what it was, but she knew it was real. Someone was coming after her.

Eva made her decision. She walked to the edge of the stream, that could barely be made out from the top of the hill she had just walked down, due to the thick brush and the fallen trees. She put Steph down and crouched in front of both her children. Before she could speak, Mila said "why are we stopping mom. They're not far behind us and they're coming mom." She gave her mother a pleading look.

Surprised at what Mila had said, Eva responded "how do you know they're behind us Mila and how do you know there's more than one of them?"

Mila just looked at her mother and said, "I don't know,

but there are three of them mom and they're coming." Eva shook off her surprise "it doesn't matter" she thought.

"Mila, Steph" she said. "Take the pack" as she was talking, she was pulling the pack off her shoulder, removing the small camping hatchet, and closing it back "cross the logs and go up to the top of that hill as fast as you can. Mila, take my gun. Do you still remember how your daddy and I taught you to shoot?"

Mila didn't want to leave her mom, but she saw the look in her mother's eyes and sensed the danger, so she said nothing. She even laid a hand on Steph's shoulder when he started to speak, which instantly silenced him. Steph listened to his parents, but he always followed his big sister's lead. He trusted she knew best, no matter what.

"Yes" Mila said. "Make sure the safety is off, look through the sites and breath out when I pull the trigger. I remember."

"Good girl." Eva said. "You go to the top of the hill and hide at the top. If you see anyone coming up that hill besides me, you shoot them. They won't be able to dodge or take cover, when you have the advantage of the hill."

"What about you Mom?" Mila asked. "There are three of them mom. There really are."

"That's ok Mila." Eva said with a forced smile. "Your mom has a plan. Now hurry. GO!" Eva said in a whispered shout. With their mother's final instruction, the two children hurried across the log. Eva didn't wait to see if they made it. She knew her children could cross a log and climb up a hill. She had to worry about keeping them safe from real dangers and maybe staying alive in the process. "Damn, three of them." She thought.

Eva quickly climbed halfway up the hill to where the large fallen tree lay, preciously on its side ready to roll down the hill at just the hint of an earthquake. "With any luck, I can be the earthquake" Eva thought. She swiftly used the hatchet to chop away at the base of the tree up and down, the more she chopped away overgrowth and debris, the more the large tree slightly wobbled. She jammed a large stone under what she thought was the center most point on the teetering tree and then dug away the last few areas that seemed to hold it in place. Suddenly the tree shifted, its full weight on the long-angled rock that she had jammed under it. She sped up her pace, silently praying thanks that this crazy plan seemed like it might work. She untied the para cord that was wrapped around the hatchet handle, tied it firmly around the base of the long-angled rock and ran it down the hill to the large fallen tree that lay be the shore.

Her plan was simple, somewhat crazy and relied on a degree of hope.

Wait for the three men to come over the log and head down the hill. She'd yank the rock and hope the tree crushed them all while she hid safely behind an equally large tree at the bottom of the hill, so as not to crush herself in the process.

Anyone that made it out still breathing wood get the hatchet. "Yeah, maybe I shouldn't have given Mila my 9mm." Eva thought. Still, even though she thought it, she knew that the odds were against her and that leaving the children unarmed wasn't an option. At least on the high ground they would have a chance at taking out anyone coming up after them. "And I still have the 22 pistol in my boot holster" Eva thought. It only carried five bullets, but five bullets were better than just a hatchet.

Her thoughts stopped and she crouched lower as she noticed the three men clearing the top of the hill.

Before they started down though, there was a beeping noise, like an old ancient Nextel that construction workers used to use. "The man is heading back to the house. Finish him. The others are dead." were the instructions that came screeching out of the Nextel looking radio. The three men looked at each other and two headed back the way they had come, one of them noticeably limping.

Eva was flooded with mixed emotions. While on one hand, she was relieved that her outrageous plan now had a chance of working. Three men were definitely different than one. On the other hand, who was dead and who was coming back to be ambushed unknowingly by those other two.

"Have to worry about that if I survive" Eva thought as she noticed the remaining man coming down the hill. He hopped over the large log she had rigged without even touching it and prowled down the side of the hill like some sort of mountain lion. Eva waited until he'd taken six more steps and then yanked the cord with everything she had. It didn't move.

She yanked again, this time planting both feet against the log in front of her and pulling with her entire body, she crashed backward as it gave way. The rock flung forward, and the log propelled down the hill much faster than she dreamed it would. Just before the log steamrolled the man, he leaped five feet straight up in the air and landed safely behind it. He looked at Eva who had stood up, she looked at him and he smiled.

The warrior slowly approached, as Eva, fearing the worst, backed into the flat area of pebbles and gravel by the edge of the stream. She had spotted this area as the most level ground for a last resort standoff. The warrior noticed the terrain and nodded approval. Eva didn't wait, she quickly pulled the 22 caliber pistol from her boot holster and fired. She intended to empty the clip, but didn't get but two shots off, before the man had pulled his own very large pistol and shot the gun right out of her hand. He hadn't even hit her at all, just literally shot the gun out of her hand. "What the hell kind of man is this?" she wondered. She noticed that she'd grazed his right arm and it seemed deep the way that blood flowed from his arm, but he didn't seem to notice.

He pointed his gun at her, stared in her eyes and then holstered it. He removed the large knife and started to approach. "Sick bastard, wants to toy with me. Either that or the psycho just likes cutting people up." Eva thought as she pulled up the hatchet preparing to defend herself.

As the man neared and Eva saw the tattoos covering his face and the rest of his body, saw the look in his eyes, saw the way he carried the knife, she immediately decided that defense would be a slow death.

"No, I need to attack. Need to try to throw him off and hope I get lucky. It's the only way." She thought.

Without another thought, Eva swung the hatchet in her right hand at his head with all of her force. The warrior was definitely caught of guard, but he still was able to swiftly step left out of the way of the swing. Eva counted on it and continued in one fluid motion spinning around backwards and catching the man with her left elbow in his nose. She felt the crunch of bone and knew she had broken his nose.

She spun back the other way crouching as she spun and swept the man's legs out from under him, just like she'd been taught all the years ago during her military days. The man landed flat on his back, hard. With that she jumped up and swung the hatchet down with two hands toward his exposed chest as he lay on his back. She was no longer thinking, she was just moving.

The man rolled right, and the hatchet sank into the ground. He didn't get up though, instead he immediately rolled back left and crushed the side of her face with his fist. He leaped to his feet, blood pouring from his arm and his nose. Eva was staggering trying to get her balance and shake off the stars she was seeing when she was kicked in her side. The kick sent her flying into a tree and she felt her back crunch. She was hurt. Before she could take a breath, he had hit her in her ribs, cracking at least two.

The man grabbed her neck with his right hand and lifted her off the ground, holding her against the tree with a grip like a steel clamp. Eva fought to maintain consciousness and breath through this death grip. Then she heard the man speak for the first time. He spoke through the blood pouring down his face, but his words were clear and cold.

"You fought courageously Top Sider. Now I will break you before I take your life." He said. Then, still holding her in the air by her throat with his right hand, he dropped the knife he held in his left. With his left hand he ripped her shirt off. The horror stopped with a loud shot that rang through the air and Eva instantly dropped to the ground. She found herself laying on the ground staring face to face with the man that had just held her and saw the bullet hole in his head.

Eva looked up and saw Mila standing there holding the 9mm in her hand. "Sorry I took so long mom. I had to make sure I had a clean shot." Said Mila. "Can you get up mom? We've got to hurry. Daddy needs our help."

Chapter 9:

"Our Prized Knife Fighter"

Camacho and Olo stood over Primo's shoulders watching the monitor that Primo sat in front of. On the monitor they watched the fire fight that took place at 'the spot'. The men watched the tall man, Vic, that was supposed to take the blame for the governor's mansion and then later appear to have blown up himself and his family, infiltrate their facility and take out half the lieutenants there in mere seconds. Camacho became more and more enraged as he watched how easily his men were dispatched, but Olo did not seem surprised. He shared his lack of respect for Camacho's men, by merely muttering "Weak Top Siders".

What did surprise all three men was when they witnessed a new man appear in the doorway and immediately engage in the gun fight, with knives of all things. This man's arrival not only shifted the tide of the battle, which despite heavy losses looked as though it was about to end with Vic on the floor dead, but he then disappeared from the doorway and appeared behind the closest upturned table. The men stared in shock, momentarily not believing what they had seen.

"Did he just take a path?" Camacho asked. "Is this a rebel from the 'other side' Olo?"

It was Primo, not Olo that responded in his soft raspy voice "He's not wearing a talisman, he couldn't have taken a path and besides it was too fast. No, Camacho, this man disappeared from one location and appeared in another. We have witnessed some sort of teleportation."

The men continued to watch the fight and then, Primo spoke up with just the slightest degree of excitement in his voice. "I know this man!"

Olo and Camacho both shifted their eyes from the monitor screen to Primo. With the silent questions in their eyes, being clear enough for Primo, he continued.

"Look at the leather straps he wears across his chest holding the daggers Camacho. This is our prized knife fighter." Primo said it with a hint of pride in how fast he had identified the attacker.

"Why the fuck would our knife fighter be with Vic attacking 'the spot'?!" Camacho yelled.

It all came together for Primo in an instant. "The guys cut his pay in exchange for letting his family run the kitchen at the club. They should've all been there tonight. Actually, he should've been there too." Primo paused for effect and then continued. "He obviously survived. He must blame the organization for their deaths."

"Damn." Camacho said. Camacho wasn't in his position of power for his intelligence, but he wasn't a complete fool. There could be another connection, but this made the most sense.

"Did we know he could do that? That teleporting shit?" Camacho asked.

"No." Primo said. "Had we known, we would've found other uses for him. He is a skilled fighter without teleporting, he never lost a fight Camacho, and we pitted him against the best." Primo paused as his words sunk in. "With this teleportation he is more than formidable. Let's hope he doesn't make it out of 'the spot' tonight."

Camacho grunted in response.

The men spoke as they were watching the fight unfold on the screen before them and for a moment, they thought that neither man would make it out of 'the spot' alive, that was until they saw the third man walk in. They watched him almost casually, no not casually, calmly walk in the door and head straight towards the gun fire. He didn't run, he didn't duck or dodge, he simply gunned down each man as they popped up from cover to take a shot. He ended the fight quickly. Too quickly. All three men with nerves of steel, were slightly unnerved at what they had just witnessed, although none of them would ever admit it to each other.

From there the men sat in silence watching, brooding as the three men on the monitors raided their facility. As they watched, Primo typed away furiously on the keyboard connected to a different monitor to his left. He searched police records, military data bases, even DOT records for any images resembling the third man, but ultimately came up with nothing. Whoever this man was, it seemed he was from another country and here illegally, either that or he was a ghost.

As they watched the men on the monitor breach the data room, they became more tense.

"They cannot disrupt the migration Camacho." Olo said sternly. "We have invested to much into this plan, these fools will not jeopardize it. The future of the Na'gee depends on it."

"I understand how important it is Olo. Don't worry, the information won't make any sense to them and even if they do ever manage to figure it out, it will be too late." Camacho said as he uncomfortably watched the man taking pictures of the critical locations they had targeted. Before either man could say anything else, Primo spoke up.

"Look at Vic." Primo said. "The fool has figured out the tracker on his vehicle. He sees that we know where he went. Look at his face! He knows what is to become, or has become, of his people there." Although they could not hear the men they watched, they could tell from the frantic actions of Vic on the monitor that Primo was right. They watched Vic race to the elevator and out the door.

"Good. He is going to join his people and become one of the slaughtered. We have four more warriors in the hunting party on the 'other side' of that location. I will send them all to be sure." Olo said coldly.

Camacho spoke up next "Those other two bastards have transported or teleported or whatever our knife fighter's doing, a significant amount of our plans, money and weapons to the parking lot. At least we'll recover something from 'the spot'. Primo, set off the explosives and finish them." Camacho gave a crooked smile when he gave the order.

In truth he felt relieved. He couldn't afford to waste time with some irrelevant war with these fools and he damn sure didn't need an enemy out there that could teleport. "This is a good turn of events." Camacho thought. "I need to be focused on the migration. I need it to go smoothly and secure my place of power as chief of the Na'gee on the 'top side'. That is my true purpose. I have no time for these distractions." He thought to himself.

Olo nodded, satisfied with the instructions Camacho had given Primo. He knew this 'Top Sider' Warrior 'Camacho' that they had chosen was power hungry and would need to be humbled at some point, but until then his knowledge of the 'top side' and his savagery would serve the Na'gee well. He would be vital for the migration. "After that, well we'll see. He's still a 'top sider'." Olo thought.

Olo waited until he saw Primo remotely activate the explosives at 'the spot' and then watched with satisfaction as the building exploded with both men inside. That left only the man they called "Vic" who would be handled by real warriors. With that final thought, Olo grasped the stone circular talisman he wore and opened a 'path' directly behind him. In traditional fashion, the 'path' made a sort of vertical blur line that looked to be something like a mirage in the desert. Olo stepped into the 'blur' and was in the hut that the men had previously been in on the 'other side'. The Olo spoke once again into the old Nextel looking device that he carried. He quicky contacted the remaining warriors positioned at the location on the 'other side', opposite the greenwell house, that he'd contacted earlier. He instructed them all to take the 'path' and kill the tall man Vic, along with anyone else they found.

Once the instructions were given. Olo turned off the Nextel device, stepped back through the blur into the room with Camacho and Primo and closed the blur behind him.

"It is done." Olo said. "Let us waste no more time on these fools. They fought well for 'Top Siders', but now they are all dead." Olo said. Olo then turned to face Camacho and said "Camacho are the gangs you command in the designated positions?"

"They're ready. We've got the 'Gridlox' ready to move on the north side of the city and the 'Hellions' in the designated positions on the south side. They'll move in as soon as I give them the word." Camacho replied arrogantly.

"Good." Olo said. "Let us proceed with the plan then. Ignite the other buildings, have your people ready to take out the first responders when we give them the word." Olo paused and stared deeply into Camacho's eyes before continuing. "And Camacho, make sure they're ready to infiltrate the military bases and the patrol stations. I do not wish for the Na'gee to be forced to take these locations by themselves, the distractions are vital." Olo said it all with cold and stern authority. He was more passionate about this than the stoic warrior usually was about anything. Olo was honored among the Na'gee tribes. He was considered one of their greatest warriors, if not the greatest. Despite his status among his people, there was no arrogance about else great warrior. He was firm, to the point and confident, always. Olo cared for nothing, but his people and this migration was meant to provide a future for his people. "Nothing can go wrong" Olo thought to himself with conviction.

Camacho nodded to Primo, clearly passing along the instructions as if the man had not clearly heard Olo, or maybe Camacho thought that until it came from him Primo would not act. Whatever drove the action, Primo hated him more than ever for it. Once again Primo thought "I hate this fool. Those ignorant Na'gee placed a man of my intelligence and experience under a fool like this just because the gene allows him the gift of battle prowess." As they often did, the bitter thoughts just fueled Primo's inner turmoil. "The Na'gee's world of violence and a struggle to survive has corrupted their minds. They place too much emphasis on physical power and not enough on intelligence, it will be their downfall here. This migration will fail." Primo thought. He knew he could never dare speak any of these thoughts or it would mean a traitor's death pure and simple. He just dwelled on these thoughts and the idea he held onto deep inside that he should be the chief of the 'top side' and that the Na'gee should remain on the 'other side' and let resources continue to be funneled to them. "They don't belong here." Primo thought bitterly.

Regardless of his feelings and ideals, Primo pulled up the various screens to remotely detonate the various explosives at the key positions. For now, all he could do was his part. For now.

With the two men behind him having diverted their attention to the TV screens on the opposite wall, Primo proceeded with discretely accessing CCTV camera footage from the street across the from where the club stood before it was destroyed. He navigated to the appropriate time right before the explosion and scrolled through footage until he found it. Clear as day, he had an image that captured that same mysterious man who ended the fight at 'the spot'. The video clip he chose, showed the man pull up in a black luxury sedan, stop in front of the club, step out with what appeared to be an RPG and blast a rocket directly through the propped open front doors of the club.

Primo sent the video clip to his phone. He said nothing to other men, but he knew that a video clearly showing this man blowing up the club, could easily incriminate him for setting off all of the explosions. If for any reason the migration wasn't successful, and Primo desperately hoped it would not be. This video would shift blame to the deceased mystery man, which could prove useful. If the migration was successful, well then it didn't matter. Either way, for now it just wasted a little storage on his phone.

Primo, stood up and turned to other men, whose full attention was on the TV's on the opposite wall. All three men stood watching the various news feeds and waited for the breaking reports they knew would be coming. That would be their signal to release the gangs and the migration would officially begin. Primo knew that if it was successful, he'd be serving Camacho or someone else just like him, until he died. He'd never achieve any power if the migration took place, in truth he doubted any 'top sider' would ever achieve power again, once the Na'gee were established here. For now, there was nothing he could do, he knew this to be true. "For now." He thought. "Just don't take too long or it will be too late." Primo told himself.

Chapter 10:
"I Never Get Kicked in the Face"

Vic drove faster than he'd ever driven before in his life. Where he was going wasn't far, but he'd seen how quickly Camacho could send people to take out everyone at a location and they knew his location, that was clear. As he drove, he figured that they were tracking his vehicle, it was the only thing that made any sense. That meant that they would know he was going back, he knew that could make things even more dangerous for his family, but the way Vic saw it, better for them to face more danger with him there, than any danger with him not there.

It didn't take him long at all before he was approaching the hidden driveway to house. The place wasn't far from 'the spot'. "Obviously one of the reasons Samuel had chosen it." Vic thought.

He stopped a hundred yards from the driveway and pulled his SUV off the road into the woods. He drove the vehicle as far as he could into the woods to minimize the chance that it would be seen from the road. He didn't care if it got stuck.

Vic knew that if he made it out of here alive, he never be driving that SUV again. Not with them tracking it. "Damn, I loved this ride." Vic thought. "Oh well. No time for that. Eva and the kids need me."

Vic eased out of the vehicle and closed the door very quietly behind his so as not to make a sound. There were still a couple hours of darkness left and he planned to use it to his advantage. He hurried through the woods, fast and yet deadly silent.

Vic clung onto the idea that he would run through the woods and find Eva and the kids sleeping safely at the house. It didn't feel right though. He just felt something was wrong. He felt it in his gut, but he clung to the hopeful idea nonetheless and he ran. He ran as fast as he could possibly run without making a noise.

The way Vic figured it, it didn't matter if he was right or wrong. Even if things were fine, they wouldn't be for long. He had to get his family out of here. "It just isn't safe" Vic thought.

Vic slowed to a walk as he began to make out the house through the woods. The walk evolved into a stealthy creep as he neared the edge of the woods. Vic stopped just shy of the tree line and observed the house. He looked towards the windows, hoping to see Eva pacing about, but he saw nothing. That is until he noticed what appeared to be the top half of a bald head pop up, peer out of the farthest window to the left on the second story and then disappear again. It happened so fast and was so subtle that he wondered if he'd actually seen what he thought he saw.

Vic was off to the right side of the house in the woods. He could barely make out some of the front of the house and could see the entire right side. There was one large window on the first floor and three small windows on the second floor of the right side of the house. The motion Vic thought he saw was at the farthest window to the left on the second floor. Still hidden just beyond the tree line, Vic strained his eyes staring at the windows and then after a minute or two he saw it again. From the same window, it was just a split second, but he was sure of what he saw this time. There was definitely someone crouched by that window who was peeking out every now and then. "Probably making rounds between that window and the windows at the front of the house." Vic thought.

As he contemplated his next move, he heard a faint "thud" behind him. To an unsuspecting ear, it would go unnoticed, but Vic was on high alert, and he knew what it was or at least what he thought it was as soon as he heard it. To Vic it sounded like someone hopping out of tree behind him, attempting to take him by surprise. "No one's freezing Vic twice in twenty-four hours." Vic thought.

Less than a second after the noise directly behind him, Vic made his move. The noise was close enough that he had barely felt a vibration in his feet, to Vic that meant good odds that he could reach the sneaky would-be assailant. He kicked back with his right foot, hard and fast. It connected with the man's leg directly above his knee. In all actuality, it connected with a handful of large nails that were protruding from the man's leg just above his knee. Vic didn't think, he'd thought enough today. He just continued in one fluid motion and turning as fast as he had kicked, he swung his left fist with full force and connected with the man's throat. Before the man could even gasp from the impact of the hit, Vic punched his throat again with his right hand, then again with the left. Knocking the man back against the tree that he had apparently jumped out of, with a crushed windpipe.

Without slowing down at all, Vic grabbed the man's head in both of his hands and twisted fast and hard. The loud "snap" of the man's neck breaking was the only noise that broke the silence of the night throughout the entire exchange.

Still holding the man's head, Vic softly laid him on the ground. He looked at the man that he had just killed and instantly recognized the bald head, the tribal looking tattoos that covered head, face, arms, and all. The strange leather vest and pants.

"This is one of Camacho's creepy family members, that's for sure. Not good. There will be more of them. There were always more of them." Vic thought.

With that thought, Vic shifted his attention back to the second story window, concerned that the 'lookout' may have noticed the scuffle just past the tree line. He stared for a moment and didn't see the head. He was about to make his dash to the side of the house, where he planned to go in through the downstairs window and with any luck, creep upstairs and catch the lookout unaware. It was at that moment that Vic saw Eva and Mila appear from the woods behind the house, just to the right. "Always the trail on the right" Vic thought pleased. He was instantly flooded with relief, thankful that they were alive. Thankful that they weren't hurt.

On second glance, he noticed Eva was limping. She appeared to barely be making the walk with some assistance from Mila. He glanced once more at the upstairs window and with no sign of the lookout, he made his dash to the house.

He yelled in a hushed whisper, "Eva, go back! Go back! It's not safe!"

As soon as he got the words out a nightstand came crashing out from the 'lookout's' window. Vic jumped backwards, just in time to dodge the falling nightstand. It crashed to the ground in front of him. Right behind the nightstand came a bald, tattooed man in brown leather pants and vest. The man had apparently leaped from the second story window but landed gracefully as if he had hopped off a small porch. Vic immediately noticed the large pistol on one hip and the giant knife on the man's other hip. He knew he had to move quick, so he pulled his .45 caliber pistol intent on ending the fight before it began, but the man was on him, before he could even aim the gun.

The Na'gee warrior moved with the speed of a wildcat. He leaped, kicked the pistol out of Vic's hand and without touching the ground, continued his spin kicking Vic in the face and sending him flying several feet backwards. The warrior landed and rushed Vic, swinging his right hand at Vic's head, Vic blocked the swing, then blocked the left swing that followed. The exchange continued like this for what seemed like a dozen swings and then out of nowhere the warrior switched tactics and swept Vic's feet out from under him.

Vic hit the ground hard, just in time to get kicked directly in his face by the warrior's booted foot.

"That's twice!" Vic roared. "I never get kicked in the face and that's twice in one day!" As Vic roared in frustration, he caught the man's foot when the warrior attempted a second kick. He did the exact same thing to this warrior that he had done to Samuel earlier that day. Twisting the warrior's foot, hitting him in the knee and then in the groin, with a flurry of lighting fast strikes that ended with him flipping the warrior backwards off his feet.

The skirmish and the backward flip had landed the warrior in the brush on the tree line that separated the woods from the clearing around the house. The warrior's eyes instantly shifted to the body of his comrade that lay just past the wood line. He turned his gaze back towards Vic who was cautiously approaching.

The warrior quickly pulled his pistol from the holster on his side, but Vic saw the move coming and was on him. He wasn't fast enough to knock the pistol out of the warrior's strong grip, so he did the next best thing, he placed his hand firmly over the hand that the warrior held the pistol with and grabbed the warrior's other wrist with his free hand. As the warrior struggled to wrench himself free from Vic's grip, Vic repositioned his finger over the man's finger that was on the trigger and began squeezing.

The gun exploded over and over until there was just a clicking noise that replaced the sound of gunfire.

Both men recognized the noise for what it was, and the focus shifted from control of the pistol to the fight at hand.

The man did exactly what Vic would've done with his

arms being held, he swung his head forward attempting to break Vic's nose with a vicious head butt. Vic was waiting for it.

As soon as the warrior reared his head back and began the forward motion, Vic released both hands slightly crouched and then leaped straight up, catching the man's face with the top of his head, and sending the man stagging backward with what appeared to be a broken nose.

Eva and Mila watched the fight from the back corner of the house. Eva had the pistol in her hand but feared taking a shot. "They're just moving so damn fast." She thought. "I can't risk hitting Vic."

Then as Vic caught the man's incoming headbutt and used his own head and a kind of leap to send the man staggering backwards, Milla tugged frantically at her mother's arm.

Eva, looked down at her daughter who was pointing at a tree to the far left of both men with her other hand. "Shoot there mom. Shoot there now mom!" Mila didn't say it, she screamed it.

The scream from her daughter caught her completely off guard. It startled her so much that she just did as she was told and fired at the nothingness in front of the tree that Mila pointed at.

At the moment she pulled the trigger, she saw the blur appear. It appeared right where she had been aiming. Right where Mila told her to shoot. The shot went right into the blur and the roar of a deep voiced man screaming in pain shocked everyone there, including Vic and the warrior he was battling. They all looked and watched the blur quickly disappear. No one had emerged from it, but someone was definitely on the other side when the bullet went through.

The men's battle continued, Mila and Eva continued to watch on. Unbeknownst to them, a minute later a similar blur appeared at the end of the long driveway. Four Na'gee warriors stepped out of the blur and onto the driveway. One of the men had a bullet wound in his left arm.

CHAPTER 11:

"YOU'RE HOLDING YOURSELF BACK"

O h shit!" Samuel yelled as he saw the last light on the transmitter light up. He knew that was it. Regrets flooded his mind. He should've known to vacate the place as soon as he learned from Dante that Camacho was still alive. He should've expected the place to be wired with explosives.

Then the thought that he had failed to avenge his family hit him like a sledgehammer. That realization felt like he was getting physically assaulted, it hurt so bad. The bright lights from the explosion burned his eyes. The heat hit his face.

Samuel felt these pains, felt the sorrow in his heart at failing to avenge his family and then wondered why he was still feeling the pain. Why wasn't it over. "Is this death? Just feeling the last sensations over and over?" Samuel thought.

As Samuel squinted past the bright lights, he realized he was looking at the explosion from the parking lot. He was standing by piles of cash, weapons, and documents. He was looking at the explosion, he was feeling the heat from the explosion, and he was half blinded by the explosion, but he wasn't IN the explosion.

Samuel turned his head and noticed Dante beside him, covering his face with his arm. It instantly made sense. Dante's quick thinking had saved them both. "Well, his quick thinking and the fact that the guy can teleport." Thought Samuel.

Dante coughed from the explosion and looked at Samuel. "You alright man?" Dante asked.

"Yeah. Just a little shaken up. I'm fine." Samuel replied. Then he thought twice and added "thank you Dante."

"Sure thing." Dante said. "Sorry, I didn't get us farther away. This was the only place I could picture in the parking lot."

"Is that how it works?" Samuel asked. "You have to picture the place?"

"Yeah, sort of." Dante replied. "I have to see it, you know, in my mind. I can't just go somewhere if I can't see it in my mind."

Samuel didn't reply. He was thinking through the implications of this talent and how he could use Dante to further his mission of vengeance, since apparently, he had another shot at it thanks to this guy.

"Stay here. I'll pull the car up. We'll load what we can of this stuff quickly and then we've got to help Vic. They know where we were, that means Vic and his family are either in danger or will be soon." Samuel said. Dante nodded and

Samuel took off across the parking lot where his black sedan was parked.

In no time at all, the two men had loaded about half of what they had removed from the building. Samuel had told Dante that the bomb could have been something they had triggered, or it could have been remotely detonated. If it was the latter, then odds were someone had been watching them.

"If they were watching us, let's leave some of this behind and hope they think we didn't make it" Samuel had said to Dante.

In no time, the men were in the car racing towards the house that they had left Vic's family at. On the way, Samuel broke the silence by handing a pistol from the driver's side door to Dante. "Here. There's fifteen in the clip." Samuel said.

To Samuel's surprise Dante refused the weapon. "No thanks man. I don't do guns." Dante said.

Dante didn't know what else to say. He didn't want to tell this man that he had no idea how to use a gun, but he knew that he didn't. The stakes seemed too high to try to figure it out now and he didn't trust telling this man anything about what he didn't know.

Instead, Dante continued with "I use these." And he patted the knives strapped across his chest.

"You ever hear the saying about bringing a knife to a gun fight man?" Samuel replied, still holding out the gun, offering it to Dante.

Dante half laughed and said, "People don't fight knives

like me. Besides, I don't do guns."

With that Samuel put the gun back into the door compartment.

Intrigued, Samuel asked Dante "Do you use it to fight?" "The knives? Hell yeah I do and I do it well." Dante replied.

"No." Samuel said. "Not the knives. It." he said.

"Oh, the teleporting?" Dante replied. "No, I never have." Dante paused for a moment wondering how much he should trust this man, but then figuring they were fighting for their lives against the same evil bastards that killed his family, he decided to continue.

"I fight with knives in underground fights. Or at least I did until I saved enough money with my winnings to get a place for my family and bring them here to the states." Dante continued. "couldn't use my gift in the fights or, well you know, I don't think they would've paid me or let me keep fighting."

"No, I keep fighting and teleporting separate. It'd be tough anyway. In fighting I kind of clear my mind and enter, I don't know, some kind of primal state. To teleport I must clearly picture where I'm going. They're really different states of mind. Does that make any sense?" Dante asked at the end of his explanation.

"Yes." Samuel said and then added "but you're holding yourself back."

The men sat in silence for the next few minutes until they were almost at the house.

"Look" Samuel said pointing to what was just the tail end of Vic's SUV poking out the woods about one hundred yards before the driveway.

"Did they run him off the road or you think he was trying to hide it?" Dante asked.

"No telling, but I think the time for stealth has passed Dante. We're going straight in, fast and loud. You sure you don't want the gun?" Samuel asked one last time.

"I told you Samuel. I don't do guns. I'm ready" Dante said. Although inside he was terrified. He wanted to avenge his family more than anything, but this was all way more than what he'd ever experienced. He pushed away the fear filled thoughts and steeled himself as the car swerved onto the driveway without slowing down.

The luxury sedan hit the driveway going way too fast, it fishtailed from side to side. Samuel kept control of the vehicle though and kept his foot on the gas, even when he noticed the four oddly dressed men halfway down the driveway.

Dante, saw the men too. "You're going to hit those weird guys!" Dante yelled.

"That's the idea Dante, they don't belong here." Samuel replied.

The luxury sedan barreled down the driveway towards the four Na'gee warriors and almost hit them, but they all leaped to the side just before the impact. Two men leaping left and two men leaping right.

With the men out of the way there was nothing between the car and the house, but half the driveway and they were going fast, very fast. Samuel hit the brakes and jerked the wheel, which sent the car to a sideways slide, stopping just feet from the front porch.

The driver's side was toward the old house and the front of the car faced the right side of the house. Without taking a breath, Samuel opened his door and rolled out yelling at Dante in the process. "This way! My side!" Samuel yelled.

Samuel's harsh words snapped Dante out of the shock he was in. He just knew they were about to drive through an old house. "What just happened?" Dante thought as he mindlessly followed Samuel's instructions and climbed over the seats exiting out the driver's side door.

Dante had just barely made it out of the door when he felt Samuel grab him and yank him down into a crouch next to him. Then they heard the gunshots and the sound of the car getting murdered with a hail of bullets that seemed to rock and shake the vehicle they used as cover.

Samuel popped his head up, a 9mm pistol in each hand and shot back. He only fired a handful of shots, before quickly ducking back down as the car endured another wave of bullets.

"These guys aren't like the ones at 'the spot'." Samuel commented gravely to Dante. "This isn't going to be easy." As soon as he spoke the words, Samuel turned to Dante with a look in his eyes that sent chills down Dante's spine.

"Can you teleport behind them and take one of them out?" Samuel asked Dante.

"I don't know this driveway, I can't even see behind them,

let alone picture it man. I told you it doesn't work like that." Dante replied.

"I'll cover you. Peek over the hood of the car and look at the spot behind one man. It doesn't matter which one. Just stare at it, then duck back down, picture it in your damn head and go stab the bastard. Then come back. You can do this Dante!" Samuel shouted the instructions over the wave of bullets that were peppering the car they used as cover. The impact of the bullets was harsher. The men were walking side by side down the driveway firing, and they were getting closer.

"Ok, man. I'll try, but if these assholes kill me, you gotta promise you'll murder that son of bitch Camacho! Promise me man! My family must be avenged!" Dante said with passion in his eyes.

"I promise, dammit! Now get ready!" Samuel yelled. Despite his promise, Samuel thought that if this didn't work, he may not have the chance. With that assuring thought in his mind, Samuel stood and opened fire on the men.

The warriors didn't leap for cover when he fired, but they shifted from side to side in some type of formation as they approached that made hitting them damn near impossible.

While Samuel fired, Dante did as he was told. He peeked over the hood of the car and stared. He stared at the man on the far left, really, he stared at the driveway just behind the man. He memorized the look of that spot, crouched back down pulled out a dagger in each hand and readied himself.

A split second later, Dante appeared behind the warrior. His plan was simple, appear behind him, move as fast as he could to take this one warrior out and then teleport right back to the safe cover behind the car where he just came from. "I got this!" Dante thought.

When he appeared behind the warrior, however, the warrior instantly turned around and swung his left hand, punching Dante in the face. Dante went flying backwards and as he flew; he saw the warrior raising his pistol towards him. Dante squeezed his eyes closed and concentrated as he flew backwards. He concentrated on the spot of cover behind the car where he had just been moments ago. When he opened his eyes, he was there. Instead of crashing to the ground and taking a bullet, he was back behind the car, right next to Samuel.

Samuel looked at him and asked, "Did you get him?"

"No!" Dante yelled. "It didn't work! They're too damn fast! He almost killed me!" Then more calmly Dante said "Sorry Samuel, but I told you teleporting and fighting don't work together. They're different things man."

As he spoke, Dante could tell the from the impact of the bullets hitting the car and the sound of the gun fire that the men were much closer. They would be on top of them soon. Very soon.

He could tell from the look in Samuel's eyes that he knew it too.

"Do it again." Samuel said. "This time take me with you."

"No way!" Dante said. "You know what it felt like after the explosion Samuel. It disorients other people when I take them with me. They'll kill us both before you get your bearings."

"They're about to kill us both right here Dante. What do you think does us in first, the men flanking both sides of the car and filling us up with holes or one of their damn bullets hitting the explosives we loaded in the truck and blowing us to pieces?!" Samuel didn't yell, but it was obvious he was angry when he spoke.

"Now. Do it again and take me with you Dante. Don't even look again, just take us right back to the spot you just went. Now!" Samuel said it so harshly and forcefully, that Dante didn't even respond. He just thought to himself that he would teleport back to his apartment as soon as Samuel was shot and killed by these men. Preparing himself with this grim thought in his mind, he grabbed Samuel's arm and did as he was told.

The two men appeared right back in the same spot that Dante had previously appeared at. They were further behind the warriors than Dante had been, due to the warrior's steady advance on the car they had been using for cover.

Samuel was dizzy, disoriented, but he had counted on that. He didn't try to focus, he just lifted both arms, each holding a 9mm pistol and fired. He fired where he knew the men would be, where he knew they were before. He didn't worry about what he saw or the dizziness in his head.

The two warriors in the middle, one with a bullet wound in his arm from Eva's shot into the blur earlier, were gunned down before they could even turn around. Samuel emptied what was left of his clips into them. He had not trusted the precision of his memory-based aim enough to only take a few shots. He knew the risk of this plan, but he also counted on Dante being able to take them back to the cover behind the car and give him time to reload.

Dante saw Samuel fill the two warriors with bullets and stepped back. Shocked at what had just happened. He was two steps away from Samuel when he heard the clicking sound of empty guns trying to fire. Both remaining warriors, who had turned around heard it too.

The two remaining Na'gee seemed not to notice their fallen comrades, instead they shared crooked smiles at the sound of Samuel's empty guns. Both men holstered their firearms and pulled out the large knives that they wore on their hips. They had obviously also noticed that Dante held no gun and for some crazy reason seemed intent on killing their opponents up close and personal.

Samuel revised his plan of taking cover. Filled with rage and anger, he threw both pistols down. He didn't even look at Dante as he started towards the warrior ahead of him on the left, he just spoke as he walked away. "The one on the right is yours." Samuel said grimly.

Surprised and stunned at the entire situation and the way it was playing out, Dante replied "What do you mean he's mine. What do I do?"

"You don't use guns, remember Dante? So, use your damn knives." Samuel said calmly and with that he focused his attention on the warrior ahead of him.

The Na'gee warrior saw Samuel approach. He sized the man up and down and for a brief second, thought about sheathing his knife and beating the weak 'top sider' to death with his bare hands. Then he shook that thought off. He didn't know how these 'top siders' had gotten behind them and that meant he didn't know what other tricks they might have up their sleeves. The Na'gee warrior decided that carving up this 'top sider' and taking his head was the better way to go. He advanced.

For just a moment Samuel thought the warrior might choose to forego the knife and engage him in hand-to-hand combat, but as the warrior advanced with knife in hand Samuel knew that wasn't going to happen. Suddenly the warrior went from a steady walk to a wild leap, slashing at Samuel with the large knife. Despite the warrior's ferocity and speed, Samuel side stepped the wild attack.

The Na'gee warrior didn't slow down, he spun and swung the large knife sideways aiming to take Samuel's head off in one vicious swing. Samuel stepped back, dodging the attack once again.

The warrior stepped in towards Samuel and kicked him with his right leg, followed quickly by a swing of the knife he held in his right arm. This time, Samuel sidestepped the kick but instead of stepping back to avoid the swing, he stepped in, ducked, and came up with a powerful uppercut catching the warrior under the jaw. As the impact from Samuel's uppercut connected with the warrior's chin, he froze the warrior. The Na'gee warrior went flying into the air, his body remaining frozen in its last position throughout its flight and as it landed on the ground.

Samuel approached the 'frozen' fallen warrior, pulled the warrior's knife from his frozen hand and slit his throat. He ripped the talisman from the warrior's neck and laid the knife on his chest. Then Samuel turned to see how Dante was fairing.

"The one on the right is yours" he says. "Use your damn knives", he says. Dante thought to himself as the warrior approached with a large knife in hand.

Dante was scared, the vengeance filled rage that had carried him into the shootout at 'the spot' had dissipated with the realization that he was in way over his head. All this shooting and death was unlike anything Dante had ever seen before. He didn't even watch movies with this kind of stuff in them.

As the warrior neared with bloodlust in his eyes, Dante knew he had to do something, or his family would never be avenged. He failed to protect them. He had even unknowingly led them to their deaths, he had to make it right. Those thoughts led way to his next thoughts. The thoughts that brought him back to the moment at hand. The thoughts that helped him recognize that the man approaching him carried a knife.

"I know how to fight with knives." He thought. "I've never been beaten in a knife fight." He thought as his confidence built. "There's never been anyone better than me at fighting with knives!"

With this final thought, Dante made his move. His moves would have been lethal regardless of 'the gene's' enhancing effect on his agility, but with them, they were unstoppable.

With a dagger in each hand, he crouched low and slashed open each of the warrior's legs right above his knees. The warrior swung his large knife straight down and Dante, still crouching, side stepped the blow, stepped back in front of him and leapt up with both knives, slashing the man open from his waist to his shoulders on each side of his belly button. Dante ended the motion by coming back down with both hands and stabbing a dagger into each of the warrior's shoulders.

The warrior didn't ever have a chance to attempt a second strike at Dante. With what Dante had described as a 'primal rage' he spun around behind the warrior and pulled two more daggers as he spun. He was behind the warrior before the man had even realized he had been stabbed in the shoulders.

Now directly behind his opponent, Dante stabbed him in the kidney with one hand, while he slit the warrior's throat with the other hand at the same time. He let out a low growl as the warrior's lifeless body hit the ground. Dante looked up to see Samuel watching him.

Samuel observed the violence and savagery of Dante and once again thought of how he could use this man in his mission of vengeance. The only comment he made was, "Quickly to the side of the house, I hear more."

Both men ran towards the right side of the house and rounded the corner to see Vic and another warrior in flurry of strikes and blocks. Back and forth, back and forth. The men appeared evenly matched and neither appeared severely injured.

As they rounded the corner, the warrior who was facing towards them looked up and saw them coming. The slight distraction was immediately taken advantage of by Vic who drove his fist into the center of the warrior's face, knocking him backwards a couple steps.

Rather than countering, the warrior stepped back two more steps and grabbed the stone circular talisman he wore on his neck. A 'blur' started to appear behind him, and Vic instantly leaped at the warrior yelling "No you don't!" in the process. He crashed into the warrior, snatching the talisman out of his hand, and tackling him in one motion.

The blur disappeared as quickly as it had appeared. The warrior was visibly shocked, and Vic was visibly enraged. From his position on top of the man, he wrapped his arms around the warrior's neck rolled to his side where the warrior's back was on top of him and wrapped his legs around the warrior's mid-section. He squeezed the warrior's neck with his arms holding the powerful chokehold in place, while he squeezed his legs around the man's mid-section with similar force.

As the life visibly drained out of the warrior, Samuel yelled "We need him alive Vic! Don't kill him!".

Vic didn't listen, he just kept squeezing. Vic squeezed the life out of the warrior and kept on squeezing until he felt Eva's hand touch his arm and heard her voice say "It's over babe. He's dead."

Vic seemed to come back to reality from wherever he was and looked up into Eva's eyes. He slowly released the dead warrior and shoved him off him. Then standing he looked at Eva and said "What happened to you? Are you ok?"

Eva said "I'll be ok. There's another dead one in the woods. Steph's hiding near his body. Mila's getting Steph now."

"You killed one of these guys?!" Vic asked surprised. Samuel and Dante who were standing by watching the exchange were equally surprised.

Eva pretended not to notice the surprised looks and responded nonchalantly "Yeah, pretty quick too babe. What the hell took you so long? Were you playing with him?"

The men all stood shocked, staring at Eva.

Chapter 12:
Plans Unfold

It didn't take long for the group to collect themselves. They dragged all the bodies behind the house, taking the stone circular talisman that each of them wore. They quickly cleaned themselves up, pulled the old van out of the shed that sat behind the house to the right and parked it next to the bullet ridden luxury sedan. Samuel had spread out the maps with markings that he'd taken from 'the spot', across the hood of the sedan and was comparing the maps to the photo's he'd taken with his phone. Dante hovered over the hood as well, trying to piece together some sense of the information without getting in Samuel's way.

Vic wasn't far away; he had the children settled in the van with the sliding door open. Eva sat in the doorway of the van, with her feet on the ground and the children behind her. Vic was tenderly caring for her wounds and listening intently as she filled him on what had really happened. As Vic heard Eva recap the earlier events and how Mila had saved her, he was flooded with conflicting emotions.

Anger that someone had hurt the woman he loved was the first emotion that hit him, but shock at what his daughter had done to save her came closely after. He was proud of Mila, but it broke his heart that his sweet little girl had to kill a man, even if it was to save her mother's life. It hurt him inside even more, when he looked Mila in the eyes and said "Mila, I'm so proud of you for saving your mom and so sorry I wasn't there to do it. Are you ok?"

It wasn't Mila's words that chilled him and tugged at his broken heart, it was the unemotional monotone way she said them "It's ok Dad. Sorry I took so long to save her. I just couldn't get back across the stream and get a clean shot any faster." She said it like she'd do better next time, but also like she didn't care at all about killing the man. Vic left it alone and thought "she's only ten. She shouldn't have to go through this at ten."

Vic's eyes met Eva's and they locked. In that silent look they shared their heartbreak for their daughter, they shared their concerns about what was next and where they would go from here and then their silent communications were abruptly interrupted by Samuel's outburst "That's it! The news reports tie directly to the locations on the maps!"

Everyone's eyes shifted to Samuel. He seemed uncharacteristically frantic and kept switching his gaze from his phone to the spread-out maps. Finally, in what appeared to be frustration, he looked up at Dante. "Do you have your phone on you?" Samuel asked.

"Sure, and I know you said no phones on the way and that we had to get rid of them, but there wasn't time because as soon as we got here…" Dante's words were cut off as Samuel harshly interrupted him.

"I don't care about that now! Pull up the news reports, quick!" Samuel said.

"Which report? What station are you looking at?" Dante asked as he pulled his phone out and started fiddling with it.

"Any of them! All of them! It doesn't matter!" Samuel yelled, while still switching his gaze from the maps to his phone, but even faster than before.

"Ok, ok, oh shit!" Dante exclaimed. "Both hospitals have been blown up man!"

"Keep watching, there's more. Tell us all what you're seeing and be specific about where it's happening Dante!" Samuel said urgently. "Vic, what do you know about the street gangs Camacho controls?" Samuel asked.

"The street gangs?" Vic's question seemed more rhetorical than anything. He obviously didn't know what was going on or where Samuel was going with all of it. He slowly stood and turned away from Eva and made his way over to Samuel and the sedan hood turned tactical planning station.

"Well, he controls them all Samuel. Even the ones that war with each other. The drugs and the guns all come from Camacho, which means he calls the shots when he wants too." Vic said. Then Vic added "Of course, none of them are really anything to pay attention to except the 'Gridlox' and the 'Hellions'. Those two have wiped out most of the smaller gangs, have an uneasy truce in place and have graduated to more organized crime than street hustling."

Vic paused to see if he had shared too much, but as soon as he did Samuel looked up at him and said "Come here, what does that symbol mean to you?" The symbol was a diamond shape with three vertical lines in the center, it was purple and shown in various locations on the north side of the map.

"That's the 'Gridlox' symbol." Vic said. Then Vic added "and that red one all over the south side of the map that looks like a skull with three horns, that's the 'Hellions'." Vic stared at the map with Samuel, now interested in figuring out what was going on.

Dante spoke up "Oh shit guys! There are gangbangers parked outside the hospitals that blew up shooting at the cops and fire fighters. They've got two cars with fifty caliber guns mounted on the rooves."

Samuel nodded and pointed at each hospital on the map. One was on the north side with a large X drawn over it in purple and a small 'Gridlox' symbol next to it. The 'Gridlox' symbol was at the hospital location on the map, but it had a line of arrows that seemed to lead it there. When the men traced the arrows back to the originating location on the map it was an industrial park of warehouses.

"That's the 'Gridlox' Northside hang out. Well one of the two. Looks like they clearly sent them from there to start gunning people down at the hospital." Vic said. Then followed it with "But why?"

Then Vic pointed to the south side of the map. "Look it's the same for the Hospital on the south side but with the 'Hellions'. They moved them from one of their two main bases of operations to the hospital explosion!" Vic shouted.

"Look at the other locations marked on the map Vic.

The other lines coming from the same bases of operations Vic! The 'Hellions' one is headed to the I-10 interstate where it enters the city on the southside and the 'Gridlox' one is headed to I-85 interstate where it enters the city from the Northside." Samuel finished looking up at Vic.

"They're taking out the hospitals, trying to take out the first responders and cutting off the primary access to the city, but why Samuel? What the hell does it mean? It's too organized and it's both major gangs, so it must be Camacho, but what's his end game?" Vic asked.

"Guys, reports are starting to come in, there are multi car explosions that blocked off both interstates leading into the city. It looks like over twenty cars in each one." Dante said. Then Dante went on "You might want to figure this out a little quicker, because at this rate we're just guessing the news a couple minutes before it happens."

"He's right Vic." Samuel said. "Look here." Samuel indicated another purple 'Gridlox' symbol on the north side that had 2 lines coming from it and at the same time pointed to another 'Hellions' symbol on the south side that one line coming from it. "Are these the other two main bases of operations for the gangs?" Samuel asked.

"Yeah, that's them." Vic said. "Oh wow. Is that the two main police stations for the city the purple lines are headed towards?" he asked with surprise in his voice.

"Yes and look at where the south side one is headed. It's the military base." Samuel said gravely.

"Look Samuel, there are other symbols marked smaller at specific spots of the police stations and the military base.

Those aren't any gangs I know of." Vic said.

Samuel looked at the symbols too. He wondered what they indicated as well. Then he moved on following the colored lines that went from gang bases of operations to the gang symbol on police stations and the military base and from there all the lines converged on the largest high-rise hotel in the center of the city. "The Deluxe". Well, they actually marked key positions surrounding "The Deluxe" Hotel and on the center of the hotel itself, was a larger version of that same strange symbol.

"What is that?!" Vic asked again.

Samuel was thinking the same thing and then it hit him. He looked up and pulled out the stone circular talisman he had taken from a dead Na'gee warrior. The design on the talisman matched the strange symbols perfectly.

"More of these warriors are going to come through these blurs or whatever they are. Look at how they're positioned." Samuel said pointing. Vic leaned in and so did Dante, who was too caught up in the discovery unfolding to pay attention to the news feeds any longer.

"Those bastards are trying to take over the whole damn city!" Vic said.

"What?! What do you mean take over the city?" Dante asked as if that were the most far-fetched thing he'd ever heard.

Samuel didn't speak, looking momentarily lost in thought, so Vic shared what he and Samuel had obviously figured out already.

"Look. They've got gangs taking out hospitals and attacking first responders. They've blocked off the major access points to the city and they're also heading to take out police stations and the military base. It is a rudimentary battle plan Dante. Create distractions that spread out the resistance, block access points and then take out their troops. If the symbols mean anything, their planning to have the gangs hit the police stations and military bases from the outside, while these bald-headed tattooed warriors appear through one of those crazy blurs and take them out from the inside." Vic finished, seeming almost proud at how he put it all together.

"Then they're preparing to defend the most centralized location in the city and occupy it by what appears to be moving in the rest of their forces, if these symbols mean what they look like they do." Samuel added pointing at the large symbol on Hotel "The Deluxe".

"Uh guys, how long do you think it's safe to stay here?" Eva interrupted. "Don't you think they'll send more of these bastards to finish what the first group couldn't?"

"I think they've stopped worrying about us Eva." Samuel said then added "but you're right, we need to move."

Samuel looked at both men crowded around the hood of the sedan. Then gestured to the map as he spoke. "We've got to stop them now or we'll never stop Camacho. He'll be too insulated once he brings the rest of his weird family members over and takes control of the city. We know how these guys fight and with everyone focused on the gangs outside their facilities, the warriors coming through the blur are likely to make short work of the police stations and the military base."

"The locations are too spread-out Samuel and you're right, we do know how they fight, so we know we can't split up and take out a large force of them." Vic said. "We have to pick the most important location to help defend. If you ask me, it's the military base. We can't let them get a hold of that kind of fire power." Vic concluded by staring at both men around the hood of the sedan, obviously waiting for them to debate the suggestion.

"Dante, have you ever been to any of these locations?" Samuel asked.

"Nah man. I don't even have a visa, Samuel. I stay way clear of cops and soldiers. Shit, the closest I've ever been to the damn military base is the park down the street, they used to do knife fights there late at night, you know the amateur stuff." Dante stopped talking when he noticed Vic and Samuel looking at each other, almost silently communicating and most definitely ignoring him.

"Ok. What's the closest you've ever been to this police station here?" Samuel asked pointing to one of the two police stations on the map.

"I don't know man. I guess the bus stop around the corner from it." Dante asked. He was starting to understand where Samuel was going with all of this. So he immediately jumped ahead and looked at the location of the next police station.

"I've been to the bus stop by that one too! It's almost directly across the street!" Dante exclaimed.

"Perfect." Samuel said. "Load up any weapons and ammo you want Vic. Dante, if you ever considered changing your mind on guns, now might be the time?" Samuel said questioningly.

"Nah, I'm good with my knives Samuel." Dante replied proudly.

"I'm with you Samuel. The little mohawked bastard Camacho's gotta die, but what about Eva and the kids? I can't leave them here." Vic said.

Samuel looked over at Vic's family in the van. He thought on it for a moment and then ripped off a corner of the map and began writing on it with a pen he produced from his pocket. When he finished, he handed it to Vic and said "That's the address to a spot I secured near the city. It's about six blocks from Hotel 'The Deluxe', which is probably closer than you want them to the action, but it's safe and its stocked." Samuel said.

"There's food and guns. It's located in the basement below an antique shop. They can get in by punching that code into the keypad on the back door in the alley. They can take the van; Dante will get us where we need to go." Samuel finished and looked at Vic, then at Eva who obviously was listening to it all.

Before either of them spoke, Mila broke the silence. "It's the right place for us to go now Dad."

Both of Mila's parents were unnerved at how she said it. It was cold and matter of fact, like she just knew things they didn't. They both knew they needed to dig into this more, but they also both knew it wasn't the time or place.

"You good with this babe?" Vic asked Eva.

"Yeah. Don't you dare die though." Eva said in response

and then kissed her husband passionately, took the paper from his hand and headed towards the van.

Vic didn't respond, he just followed her to the van and approached the open sliding door. He stared at Steph and Mila. They stared back. Steph looked angrier the longer the stare lasted and finally blurted out "No Dad! I want to go with you! I can help you fight Dad!" the young boy yelled.

Vic was stunned, proud and his heart to hear it. He never doubted that he'd survive. He truly didn't believe anyone could take him, but he hated to leave his family again, especially with everything that had happened in such a short amount of time.

"I want you to too Steph, but you've got to keep your mom and Mila safe. You're the man while I'm gone. I'm counting on you." Vic said compassionately.

"Ok Dad. I'll keep them safe, but please hurry back." Steph said, seemingly consoled and refocused on this serious responsibility his father had tasked him with.

"I will son. I love you man." Vic said in response and then leaned in past Mila and hugged his son tightly.

After the warm embrace between father and son, Vic leaned back and looked Mila in her eyes.

"I'm so proud of you for how you helped your mom, Mila. Are you sure you're, ok?" Vic said softly.

"I'm good Dad. I think we'll be ok, but hurry." Mila said. Then Mila added "Dad, don't feel bad about leaving. This has to be done to save everyone. It's not just about us. Samuel needs your help. I don't like him, but he's right Dad." She said it all coldly and with a faraway look in her eyes.

"How do you know Mila?" Vic asked earnestly.

"Huh? I don't know Dad. I just know things sometimes." Mila said, obviously uncomfortable at being questioned about something she clearly didn't understand.

"Ok Mila. I love you. Look out for your mom and your brother." Vic said and he hugged his girl with all the love in the world.

He stood back, shut the van door, and walked to the open driver's window where Eva sat, ready to go.

"Be careful babe." Vic said.

"We'll be fine. Do what Mila said and watch your back." Eva said.

They kissed once more, and Eva started the old van and started down the driveway. Vic turned around to face the two men who witnessed the entire exchange but said nothing out of respect.

Vic could tell that Samuel wanted to talk about Mila and how she knew things, but he refrained and instead looked at his two counterparts and said "Military base first then. Let's talk about how we want to do this. I think I have a plan".

"Of course, you do." Vic said with a half-smile. Then he added "If you two gene freaks want to take the weirdo warriors, I'll take on every damn gang banger. Fair trade?"

They ignored his obviously sarcastic comment, and all gathered closely around the maps on the hood of the Sedan.

CHAPTER 13:
POLO

Polo was ready to go. He hated waiting. He could tell his crew was getting stir crazy, they hated waiting too. Polo checked his watch for the fourth time "Still not time." He thought.

Polo hadn't earned his place as leader of the 'Hellions' from having patience. No, he earned his place as head of the large gang by being aggressive, taking chances and, well being built like a diesel truck didn't hurt either. Polo was a "retired" professional defensive end. He stood six foot eight inches tall and weighed 315lbs. He was built like a monster and often behaved like one too. He "retired" or was kicked out of professional football for repeated acts of violence on and off the field. Even when he played by the rules, he was too violent for the sport. Polo was widely known for killing two different quarterbacks by breaking their necks when he sacked them.

Now this huge maniac led one of the largest gangs in the city… the 'Hellions'. With over two hundred members, the 'Hellions' controlled the trafficking of guns and drugs on the south side of not just the city, but the entire state. It was really the violent nature of the gang that generated the most profit for them and had built their notorious reputation. They ran underground fight rings, had an extensive network of extortion, and profited generously off their "murder for hire" business. It was Polo and the 'Hellions' that had taken out the last two governors and through extorting various state officials had paved the way for the current governor to take the position. Well, current until him and his family had blown up in his house the day before. "That's what happens when you cross Camacho fool." Polo thought to himself.

It was of course Camacho that had orchestrated and paid for all the moves to control the governor. Polo couldn't stand Camacho, but he paid well and controlled the supply of guns, drugs and well, everything. No one had ever been able to figure out how he was able to ship so much into the city without ever being detected by authorities or rivals, although many had died trying to figure it out. Polo was content with the prices and loved the availability of anything he needed, but he firmly believed the only thing better than a good supplier was to have direct access to a good supplier's manufacturer and distribution model. So far, no one had been able to figure out how Camacho did it. It was like his shipments just appeared in his safe houses out of nowhere.

This job, however, held much more appeal than just a big payout. This was big. Camacho was taking over the entire city. He had laid the entire plan out. It required a truce between the 'Hellions' and the 'Gridlox', but that was a small price to pay for complete control of the entire south side of the city. Sure, Camacho would call the shots from Hotel 'The Deluxe', but as long as he got his cut of the profits, he'd stay out of the way like he usually did. "Yeah, once this job is done, I'll be a king!" Polo thought to himself.

He relished the idea of having complete control of half the city. No hiding, no underground anything. This would be their world. Other states and federal governments would have to treat them as their own entity. Other gangs may even follow their example. This would change the world and Polo loved the idea of being a king in the new world.

As he rolled these thoughts around in his head for what had to be the hundredth time, he felt stir crazy again. He didn't want to wait anymore. He wanted to get on with it. Yet, despite his feelings, he waited. He knew that this was the most critical part of the entire plan. This part would determine success or failure. The military base was the key. Control of the military base meant tanks, helicopters and critical ammunition and gear. It wasn't just more weapons, the 'Hellions' were armed to the teeth already. It was the fact that once they took control of the military base these weapons couldn't be used against them. "Yeah, the base is the key." Polo thought. "That's why they've got my 'Hellions' taking it out and sending those weak ass 'Gridlox' to attack petty street cops" he thought proudly.

Polo checked his watch again and was excited to see it was time. "Finally!" He exclaimed out loud. Then he reached into the old school lowrider he was leaning against and held the horn down for what seemed like forever. The park that was filled with one hundred 'Hellion' gang members when silent. Six men began running towards him. These were the bosses that answered directly to Polo.

"It's time boys." Polo said with a vicious sneer. "Remember

the plan. Four men to a car. Fifteen cars with me right up to the front of the base, you two take the other ten to the back of the base. When you get to the back of the base mow down the fence and pour in. Everyone there dies. If it moves kill it." The men all nodded. There was no fear or concern on their faces, instead they appeared eager and bloodthirsty. These men knew what success here meant. They knew that as Polo's underbosses, they would have more power than they ever dreamed of after they pulled this off. They were ready.

"Remember dammit. We don't give them time to think, just light them up and whatever you do keep all gunfire away from the main building. We take them out on the outside. Exactly ten minutes after we engage, Camacho's creepy dudes are going to hit them from inside the main building." Polo said the last part sternly and looked at each of his underbosses threateningly.

"We leave in ten minutes sharp. Make sure the guys are ready. Timing is key." Polo said.

They all nodded and with a gesture from Polo that looked like waving them away, they were gone. Running back to their groups and emphasizing the same orders.

"Ten minutes and we begin our conquest" Polo thought.

CHAPTER 14:
"WE'LL JUST TAKE TWO."

Samuel, Vic, and Dante heard the horn blare and then the loud commotion in the park went silent. At once at least one hundred gang bangers turned their attention to one car with one extremely large man standing beside it. Six men ran up to the large man and everyone else stood silently watching.

"Now's are chance. Move." Samuel said.

Almost an hour earlier the three men had decided to defend the military base first. They hoped to make short work of it and then leverage Dante's convenient means of travel to move on to defending the police stations. They figured amongst themselves that they had decent odds of protecting the military base and at least one police station. They knew that if the attacks were initiated at the same time, then it would be very tough to get to both police stations. The plan was vague, but it was all they had. Vic and Dante would attack the 'Hellions' approaching the front gates and keep them engaged long enough for the soldiers at the base to muster up a counterattack.

Samuel would warn the base soldiers, work to get them organized and prepare them for the warriors from the 'blur' that would undoubtably appear in the main building at the location marked on the map.

Samuel didn't say "how" he would pull off warning the soldiers and defending the main building. He just said that he would do his part and they had enough to worry about with their part. The men couldn't argue with that logic, so they didn't press for more details. They both wondered though. Once the plans, if you could call them that were agreed on, the men loaded up the weapons that Samuel had taken from 'the spot' and placed in his trunk, into a large duffel bag. Vic threw the bag over his shoulder and grabbed the rocket launcher out of the back seat and carried it in his free arm. Dante still refused to take any guns, but they had convinced him to take the eight grenades that they had found and secure them to his belt.

Samuel carried only his two pistols that he wore in his shoulder holsters under his black jacket and loaded his belt with several extra clips.

"This is going to be a fire fight guys. These gangbangers are going to be equipped with fully automatic assault rifles, you can count on it. You sure you don't want to be equipped with the same guys? There's several in the bag?" Vic asked both men, with evident concern on his face. To him it just made sense. It didn't matter what kind of gene freak ability these guys had, bullets were bullets.

Both men declined. Samuel just patting his pistols and saying "I've got bullets Vic."

Dante just shook his head 'no'.

Vic had exhaled loudly and said "Ok. Don't say I didn't warn you. Now I'm going to have to be the one that covers both of your asses."

Samuel had then told Dante to teleport him to the park by the military base. The closest place to the base that Dante had been to before. In a flash both men and disappeared. Moments later Dante appeared back before Vic, grabbed his arm and the next thing Vic knew he was dizzy as hell and being dragged down behind a row of bushes.

"What the hell?" Vic blurted out trying to get his bearings and figure out why he was being drug to the ground.

"Shhhhh!" was the response he got from both Samuel and Dante at the same time.

It only took a couple seconds for Vic to shake off the disorientation. When he did, he immediately realized why they were hiding behind bushes. Not ten feet from them were lines of cars parked and in front of the cars further towards the center of the park, were tons of gang bangers. More than Vic had ever seen together at once.

"Holy shit! That's way more than we thought there'd be!" Vic whispered to his companions hiding behind the bushes. Then he followed with, "Why the hell did you teleport us right on top of them Dante?"

"I didn't know they were here, and I can't just go anywhere Vic. I have to know the place. Have to have been there before and be able to picture it in my mind." Dante replied defensively.

"Well, I'm sure glad you didn't visit the center of the park, or we'd really be screwed right now." Vic said.

"What do you think Samuel?" Vic asked. "It's not only a heck of a lot more gang bangers then we thought there'd be, but we still got to figure out how to get to the base ahead of them."

Samuel thought about Vic's question. Then he pointed at the two cars closest to them. "They're running." Samuel said softly in a 'I've got it all under control tone'. Then he added "All the cars are running. We'll just take two and head to the base. By the time they get there, you'll be waiting for them."

"Just take two?" Dante asked. "There's like a hundred guys with guns out there Samuel. Half of them look like they're carrying uzis or assault rifles."

Vic interrupted Dante from continuing to point out the obvious and said, "I told you guys they'd have assault rifles."

Samuel and Dante both gave Vic annoyed looks.

"As soon as there's a chance, I'm taking one and heading to the base. I'll drive it through the back half of the park over the grass and away from them, instead of through the center parking lot. You two, can either take one and set up a position closer to the base, or you can start killing the bastards right here. It's up to you." Samuel gave them both a dead stare, that let them know he was completely serious and then continued talking. "Just remember, if you don't attack them closer to the base, it will be much harder for soldiers to back you up. You may be on your own." Samuel said, laying out his intent and their options clearly.

Dante looked at Vic, obviously deferring to the older more experienced man.

"Well shit." Vic said considering his options. "I sure like having a place right here to make a stand behind the cars more than driving closer to the base and hoping I find a good place, but you're right Samuel. Some damn support would be nice."

Vic surveyed the lot full of 'Hellions' once more, obviously weighing his options and then broke the momentary silence by casually saying "I guess we'll do both."

Samuel and Dante both looked at Vic with obvious confusion. So, Vic continued.

"Dante, all you have to do is picture where you're going and you can teleport there right?" Vic asked.

"Yeah, that's how it works." Dante said.

"So, what if you don't try to picture it in your head and instead you just look at it? That's picturing it too and would be faster right?" Vic asked.

Dante appeared to think on it for a moment, then without answering he turned away and looked at a spot further down behind the bushes and in a flash, he was gone. Dante reappeared still crouching behind the bushes, several bushes away. Then he was gone from there, and right back in front of them.

"Yeah, that does work. Wow! It's way faster than thinking about it." Dante exclaimed with genuine excitement at this new revelation.

"Great! So, as soon as Samuel is ready to go. I want you to look as far down the line of bushes as you can and teleport there. Then start working your way around away from us, placing a grenade behind each car you come to, until you run out of grenades. You got eight of them, right?" Vic asked.

"Great call Vic." Samuel said. "That will be our distraction and create a little confusion."

"Got it. Tell me when you're ready." Dante said.

Just then the three men were startled by the loud blaring of a horn.

"Now's our chance. Move" Samuel said.

Dante immediately disappeared and was back in less than one minute.

The six men that ran up to the large man by the lowrider, were running back to other groups of men, obviously passing along whatever instructions they had been given.

Then cars started exploding. Everyone in the park jumped and looked towards the exploding vehicles, while Vic and Dante scrambled towards one of the two closest cars and Samuel headed for the other one.

When the cars started exploding, Polo jumped back, instinctively raising the sub machine gun that was hanging from a strap on his shoulder. Eight cars on the far end of the parking lot blew up almost simultaneously. At least fifteen 'Hellions' were laying on the concrete dead or severely injured.

Several other 'Hellions' were holding their heads or their

arms, bleeding from what must have been shrapnel flying through the air. If that weren't enough, two cars far away from the explosion took off across the park in the opposite direction.

For just a second, Polo thought that some of his men were deserting after seeing the explosions. Then he realized that whoever blew up the cars must be stealing the other two to get away.

Enraged and torn, Polo knew he had to make a decision quick. Pursue and kill the fools that had the nerve to attack a gathering of one hundred 'Hellions' or stick to the timetable and hit the base with the troops he had left. His anger made it hard for him to think rationally. "Who the hell would have the balls to attack us?!" He yelled.

"Fuck it. We'll have to find out later. The stakes are just too high to blow this opportunity." Polo thought. He had made his decision, but he wasn't happy about it.

"Forget the crazy bastards! We'll find them and kill them later! Time to take the city!" Polo yelled over the mass confusion and noise in the park.

"Let's go show these military clowns who the real soldiers are! Let's show them who the Hellions are!" Polo cried at the top of his voice.

The remaining 'Hellions' roared back and began scrambling to the remaining vehicles.

In less than five minutes fifteen vehicles packed with 'Hellions' poured out of the park in the direction of the military base.

CHAPTER 15: THE BASE

Samuel drove fast. Vic and Dante stayed right behind him. As he approached the base, he noticed the large fenced in acreage around it. He saw that the buildings were at least one hundred yards from the fence in all directions and felt better about the odds of holding back the remaining 'Hellions'. He didn't slow down as he headed to the split in the fences.

They opened at what was the front center of the large base, allowing a two lane road to go down about a quarter mile with fences and trees lining both sides. Samuel knew instantly that Vic would take advantage of the sort of bottle neck layout of the entrance to make his stand. Despite only working directly with the man for the last twenty-four hours, Samuel felt a strange sense of comradery towards Vic. They were very different, but Vic had proven himself formidable and reliable. He was decisive and willing to take whatever actions needed to be taken, yet still dedicated to his family in a way that brought back painful memories of the family that Samuel had lost.

"I chose well with Vic, he's even more than I hoped for." Samuel thought. "It will be quite disappointing if he dies here today."

As Samuel approached the end of the quarter mile two lane road and the barricade and guard tower that was positioned at the end, he saw in the distance in his rear view mirror Vic and Dante's car parking sideways. They were blocking the entrance to the two lane road, just like he knew Vic would do.

Samuel half smiled for a split second and then focused on the task at hand as he pulled the vehicle to a stop at the guard tower that was in front of the barricade.

The two lane road actually split around the guard tower, one lane going to each side. The lanes on each side were blocked by steel barriers that were on some sort of lifting mechanism, that was controlled from inside the tower.

Two soldiers with assault rifles stood in front of the tower, one man stood inside the window of the ground floor of the tower. As he stopped the car, one of the two soldiers in front approached Samuel's door.

As the man was approaching Samuel looked up and noticed that two more soldiers with assault rifles were positioned on top of the twenty-foot-high guard tower.

"Hardly a tower. More like a tall toll booth." Samuel thought.

The soldier that approached Samuel's driver's side, leaned in towards the open driver side window as he looked at the odd lowrider suspiciously. "What's your business here sir?

You sure you in the right place?" the soldier asked Samuel.

In response, Samuel handed the soldier a business card that only had a phone number on it across the middle and nothing else. Then he said "Call this number now soldier. It will reach an emergency room at the pentagon. When they answer, tell them a Ghost Agent is at the gate to take control of the base, agent number 17. Tell them the password is phoenix-alpha-black. Do it quickly! We don't have much time!"

The soldier did not move. He just stared at Samuel and then finally said, "whoa, whoa, whoa. Who are you now?"

"Do what I said now Soldier, or I won't have time to defend this base from what's coming, not to mention you'll be stripped of your rank and court-martialed. That's an order!" Samuel replied harshly.

The soldier stepped back, obviously startled, and then hurried inside the tower. Samuel watched him speak rapidly to the man inside the tower window and then the man picked up the phone and put it to his ear. Within seconds the soldier hurried back towards Samuel's window and the gate was being raised.

"I don't know who you are, but the secretary of defense just said that this base is under your command sir. He's calling the general inside the main building now. What the hell is going on sir?" the soldier said, sounding much more unsure of himself than he had just moments ago.

"Call the general on your radio and hand it to me now." Samuel said. Then he went on as the man started working the radio "Then you and the men at this tower radio for support and help those two men blocking the entrance! They're with me and they're going to be the best line of defense you have against that caravan approaching!" Samuel yelled the last part and then snatched the radio out of the man's hand just as someone on the other end started saying "what is it soldier?". Then Samuel drove through the open gate towards the main building as fast as he could, giving the general orders on the way.

The soldier looked at Samuel speed away and then looked back towards the front entrance to the base drive. He did see a car parked sideways and two men positioned behind the side towards the base, appearing to be intent on using the car as cover. He also saw several vehicles rapidly approaching.

The soldier turned and started yelling orders to the men stationed at the tower with him.

"Here they come!" Vic said, sounding more excited than anything. This was his favorite part, not thinking, not waiting, just acting and reacting. This is what he felt he was built for. He didn't need any freak genes to be an unstoppable force. "I'm the grim reaper after all. Hope they're ready." Vic thought.

Vic had two assault rifles leaning against the car between them and held the rocket launcher in his hands. It was loaded with a rocket and there was one more rocket by his feet. He intended to finish them as quickly as possible. That was the plan. Speed was critical if they had any hopes of getting to either of the police stations.

"That's not enough cars." Vic said suddenly concerned. "Where the hell did the rest of them go?"

"Something isn't right. They must be splitting their forces and going to try to hit the base from two sides at once." Vic said. Then in a rushed voice he said "Change of plans Dante. Do what you did at the park. Look ahead of you and teleport there. Do it fast and work your way around the base until you see where the other 'Hellions' are headed. Then come back and do what we talked about. I'll keep these guys busy, they should be in position for you when you get back. Once we finish them, we'll take out the other ones. Got it?" Vic stared at Dante waiting for a response, for anything to indicate that the young man had captured and understood the rushed instructions.

Dante froze for a second and then visibly steeled himself and said "Finish them? I thought we were just holding them off until we got support from the troops at the base Vic?"

Vic just smiled at Dante and said, you really think one hundred gangbangers are going to hold out against us that long? You're working with the Grim Reaper now Dante!"

Dante could've sworn that Vic even chuckled after saying that ridiculous line. He chose to ignore it, as he ignored the concerning feeling that flooded through him at the thought that Vic was going to try to take them all on without any help. He tried to hide back his lack of confidence and just said "Ok, got it Vic. Be careful man."

"You too." Vic said, but it was too late for Dante to hear it. The man was already gone.

By himself, Vic looked up and saw the cars swerving to stop sideways, making a kind of half circle wall of vehicles across from him. He laughed to himself at the confusion he imagined them in, when they saw one of their own cars blocking their path to the base. Then he glanced back at the tower. He saw Samuel speeding ahead towards the main building through an open gate and no soldiers appeared to be frozen or injured.

"How the hell did he manage that?" Vic wondered. He told himself he needed to learn more about this mysterious man he was working with. Then he refocused himself on the task at hand.

As four of the soldiers from the barricade started the quarter mile run towards the front entrance to the base they noticed there was only one man there now. As they ran, they saw the man stand up holding what appeared to be a rocket launcher and fire it at the car parked sideways directly across from him. The explosion blinded them and was followed by a hail of gunfire, which was obviously aimed at the man behind the car.

They kept running, all wishing they had sent the fifth soldier on foot to get reinforcements and taken the jeep up to the front. Then they saw the man reload the rocket launcher and take out the other center most vehicle in front of him.

One of the soldiers yelled to the soldier that had spoken to Samuel. "You sure this guy needs our help?".

Vic saw the soldiers approaching. He didn't know if they were coming to attack him for firing rockets in front of the base or if they were coming to help him defend the base. The way they opened the gate for Samuel made him wonder if they had somehow been convinced of the real threat. He noticed that they didn't lower their weapons and they weren't shouting at him, so he chose to ignore them for now.

"Time to rain more hell on these 'Hellions'" he thought chuckling at how bad the play on words was in his head and thinking how much grief Eva would have given him if she'd heard it.

He smiled, set down the rocket launcher, grabbed the closest assault rifle and stood firing at the cars to the right and left sides of the ones he had exploded. He shifted his shots back and forth from the left side of the burning cars to the right side, hitting a 'Hellion' more times than not. Vic knew that this approach was riskier than just taking the cars out on one side, but he wanted to split their troops. It was part of the plan, and the plan wasn't for him to have to shoot all these guys.

As Vic ducked back down to take cover from the return fire, he saw that the soldiers were just about to him. He readied himself just in case this wasn't a friendly visit.

The four soldiers ran crouching to join him behind the car and on the way one of them took a bullet to the head and dropped in his tracks. The other three instinctively dove for the cover of the car.

They looked at their fallen comrade and then looked at Vic. "We have orders to help you defend the front sir. More troops are on the way." The lead soldier said to Vic.

Before Vic could respond, Dante appeared next to him. The soldiers looked terrified. One of them pulled his pistol fast, but Vic was faster, knocking the gun out of the man's hand and grabbing him by the throat in a motion so fast that it seemed like a blur. "He's with us." Vic growled, then released the man.

Dante, looked surprised, but maintained his focus and kept his attention on Vic. "They're approaching the back side of the base. They drove through the fences and are heading to the hangars." Dante said.

Vic looked past Dante to the soldiers. "Did you hear him?" Vic asked. The soldiers nodded.

"Then you" Vic said pointing at one soldier "get on your damn radio and redirect all the reinforcements headed this way to the hangars to defend the rear of the base. We'll defend this side on our own!"

The soldier didn't question, he just did as he was told and began talking into the radio. Vic turned to the other soldiers and said, "When my friend here disappears, start shooting at the cars they're using for cover. Whatever you do don't shoot at the guys behind the cars, just shoot at the cars. Shoot low."

When they all nodded, Vic added "You don't have to understand, just follow orders."

Then Vic turned to Dante and said. "You ready?"

In response, Dante looked up over the trunk of the car and stared at the spot behind the vehicle to the far left. "Let's do it!" He said in a kind of growling tone as he pulled out a dagger with each hand.

Upon hearing Dante's words, Vic signaled to the two soldiers next to him, while the third still talked to what sounded like frantic voices on the radio. Vic and the two soldiers stood and opened fire on the vehicles in front of their attackers. After a brief moment of firing, they ducked back down behind the cover of the vehicle and Dante disappeared.

Dante instantly appeared in the spot behind the car furthest to the left. He was directly behind four 'Hellions' who were standing from their cover position and starting to fire their automatic weapons back at Vic and the soldiers. They didn't even see Dante appear.

With a low growl, that he let out subconsciously, Dante rushed to the closest two men in a blink of an eye. He slit their throats from behind, then slashed at the side of the neck of third 'Hellion' down the line with one hand and stabbed him in the gut with the other.

All three of them fell dead, but the fourth noticed the movement and started to turn his weapon towards Dante, still firing. Rather than use his enhanced agility to try to take the man out before being shot, Dante just looked behind the man and teleported there in a blink of an eye. He slashed the fourth man's throat from behind. Dante snapped out of his rage and thought "That was way easier than dodging and fighting."

Then Dante said to himself "Ok, Dante. One group down. Let's finish it."

Excited about this new way to use his ability and a chance to help Vic who seemed to be fighting the 'Hellions' all on his own up to this point, Dante looked at the next car and repeated his move. What followed was a flurry of slashing and stabbing, of disappearing and reappearing. It was all done with a kind of fluid precision, like a ballet dancer performing for a crowd. A perfect rhythmic masterpiece of violence and bloodshed.

In Minutes Dante had dispatched all the 'Hellions' positioned on the left side of the two burning vehicles. Over twenty men dead, with their throats slashed or stabbed and most never saw it coming. After finishing the last of them, Dante paused and looked at the blood and bodies around him. He was struck by the gravity of what he had done.

"So many dead. So fast. What have I become?" Dante thought. "What would my family think of me?"

As soon as Dante thought of his family his feelings changed. He was flooded with that same initial rage and anger that he had felt when he had first lost them. "Camacho took my family. They don't have the chance to think of what I've become. He forced me to this! I will make sure his people never hurt anyone again!" Dante was alone, but he said this out loud with a harsh trembling voice. He had no more second thoughts, no more regrets. He was ready, even eager to kill everyone even remotely associated with Camacho. With anger pulsing through his veins, he refocused his mind on Vic's plan and teleported himself back to the cover of the vehicle Vic and the soldiers crouched behind while gunfire from the right side of the burning cars filled the air.

Dante appeared next to Vic and said "Done. Left side's clear. You ready?"

Vic paused for a split second before barking instructions to the soldiers. He noticed the change in Dante's eyes. The change in his face and voice. The young man in front of him wasn't the same man that had teleported away just moments ago. Vic saw the blood streaming from Dante's hands, where he still held a dagger in each. He also noticed that despite the fire in Dante's eyes and change in his demeanor, his hands didn't shake or tremble in the slightest. No, he was steady and appeared ready. The sudden change in the young man unnerved Vic. He'd seen a lot in his life, he'd seen good men lose it and turn to vicious monsters upon being exposed to violence on a large scale. He worried about Dante. He worried if the man could handle this and all the bloodshed to come. He also worried at what this man was capable of if he lost it completely.

Vic shook off the uneasy thoughts going through his mind and addressed the soldiers next to him.

"You get troops heading to cover the breach by the hangar?" Vic asked the solider that had been on the radio.

"Yeah, they're getting everyone they can. The new guy in charge has a lot of soldiers barricading the large room in the main building and taking positions aimed at the center of the room, not sure what that's all about but it doesn't leave a ton of guys to go cover the hangars. We're sending who we can." The soldier said.

"The new guy in charge?" Vic thought. "If he's having them get ready for the warriors who would undoubtably be coming through the 'blur' in the main building, then it had to be Samuel. How the hell is he 'in charge'?" Vic thought this was as unnerving as Dante's demeanor.

"Ok. Good enough. Let's finish this first. Take out the front line of guys firing if you can. Dante here is taking me with him and I'm going to cut through the flames and mow these bastards down, while they're shooting at you." Vic landed his instructions intensely and all four soldiers clearly understood.

They replied in unison "yes sir!"

Then Vic added "Don't you fucking shoot us!"

Once again, his intense instruction earned a chorus of "Yes sir!" from the soldiers.

Vic reloaded the rifle he'd been using, then grabbed one of the ones leaning against the car with his other hand and looked at Dante. "Well. Let's go finish this!" he said.

Dante grabbed him by the arm, and they were instantly behind the cars on the left side of the burning vehicles. Dante crouched with Vic, holding him steady as the tall man tried to orient himself.

Polo stared at his men firing at the car blocking the entrance to the base and cursed under his breath. "This wasn't how this was supposed to happen." He thought. "Who the hell knew what we were doing and attacked us before we got here? Then the bastards cut us off and now we're fighting in damn near the street, instead of taking the base." These frustrating thoughts were fueled every time he glanced at the burning vehicles that divided his forces. "One damn car and they're holding us all off!" he thought. "Who the hell are these guys?!"

The vehicles being rocketed had kept him from being able to lead all his men and get a good view of how the battle was going. He had to admit it was a great move, but he hated it nonetheless.

"This wasn't how this was supposed to happen!" Polo thought again. He needed to end it. Needed to end it quickly. He had no idea how his guys on the other side of the burning vehicles were doing, but he knew they were making no progress on this side. He also knew that these mystery men, now had some of the soldiers supporting them.

"We're letting them bring the damn fight to us and we're supposed to be raiding the base!" This Polo yelled out loud for everyone around him to hear. He knew if they just kept trading gunfire back and forth that he'd eventually lose more men and that they'd eventually get more support from soldiers in the base.

The only hope he had was that although it wasn't going according to plan, there was still a chance that this would be enough of a distraction to pave the way for Camacho's guys to take the base from the inside. "It doesn't matter. We got to do something extreme to end this shit and get to the base." Polo thought. Then he made his decision. They'd just do what he always did best. They'd go straight for them.

Polo yelled for the three men closest to him. The men ran to him quickly, listened closely, nodded, and took off to the cars on the far end of the line. Polo followed closely behind them.

In seconds the men had two cars started and ready to go. The smallest man sat behind the driver seat of one car positioned in front of the second car. The second car had another man in the driver seat and Polo and five other men they had gathered, crouched behind it. All the other men, about fifteen in total, kept firing from the front line of cars.

There was no signal, no warning, the first car just took off. It drove from the far-right side of the line of cars forming a barricade, the furthest away from the burning vehicles and headed straight for the car blocking their path to the base. Slowly the second car followed, with Polo and five men crouching, trotting behind it.

The soldiers saw the car heading for them fast. They didn't need experience to know what was about to happen. The car headed their way was nothing more than a motorized battering ram and they were about to feel the impact.

All three soldiers fired at the driver of the car headed straight towards them. The man was crouching low behind the wheel, not looking where he was going, just going straight. They didn't know if they could hit him or not, but deep down all of the soldiers knew it didn't matter. He was too close and coming too fast. Impact was inevitable. The only thing they could do was keep firing and try to leap out of the way when the car hit.

A second later the lowrider plowed into the car the soldiers were using as a barricade. A loud crashing noise filled the air and momentarily drowned out the sound of gunfire. Two soldiers successfully leaped out of the way, while the other one was hit by the force of the car being pushed back and thrown across the concrete, all losing their rifles in the leap or the flight.

The second car pulled up to the crash and Polo led his men around at a full run. Polo crashed full force into the closest soldier that had leaped out of the way of the crash. He hit the man so hard in the mid-section that he felt the man's ribs shatter. The two men crashed to the ground. Polo crushed the man's skull with a powerful blow to the face. He stood up and saw his 'Hellions' unloading on the one injured soldier that had not leapt away successfully and then saw the other soldier that had leapt out of the way from the corner of his eye.

The soldier had lost his rifle while leaping to safety and was frantically trying to pull his sidearm. He was staring at Polo, having just witnessed the large man kill his comrade. He was terrified and the fear made his hand tremble while he tried to pull his pistol. Polo didn't even think about the sub-machine gun he wore hanging across his chest from the left shoulder strap. He just charged the man.

As the soldier finally managed to get his gun out, he was hit. The man was tackled to the ground instantly having the breath knocked completely out of him, before he ever got a shot off. Polo used both hands to bash the soldiers head against the concrete until he felt the skull crush.

The large leader of the 'Hellions' stood up and saw that his men weren't watching him. They hadn't even witnessed his savagery. They were staring back at the direction they'd all come from, with looks of shock and surprise on their faces. Polo tried to see what had caught their attention and heard the gunfire. He saw his men on the frontline were gone and it immediately hit him "Where the hell were the initial attackers. These were just soldiers from the base." The thoughts not only fueled his anger, but they triggered a feeling that the large man rarely felt. Polo was afraid.

Polo knew he'd lost his defensive position and now, he'd spread his men even thinner, while their enemy had flanked him and was undoubtably firing upon his remaining 'Hellions' from behind the line. He knew this could be the end of it all. This could wipe out his attack. This could end his chances at running half the city. It could end his chance to be a king. He hoped the other half of his men attacking the hangars were faring better than this.

Finally, Polo decided he didn't care about any of it. All he cared about was killing these men that had ruined everything for him. He wanted to take their lives with his bare hands. Nothing else mattered anymore.

Polo shouted at the five 'Hellions' that had run behind the car with him and the one man that had driven the second car (the man in the first car, was killed from the soldier's bullets). "They went behind us from the left side. They're killing our brothers. We're going to follow the same way they went and kill these bastards from behind! Hurry!" With that Polo took off running for the barricade of cars on the left side of the burning vehicles. The six 'Hellions' followed.

Vic finally got his bearings and stood up. He saw all the bodies around him from Dante's previous attack but chose not to think about that right now. He had work to do. Holding an assault rifle in each hand, he looked at Dante and said "stay behind me and watch. If you see anyone taking aim at me from a direction I'm not looking, teleport over there and do your thing. Whatever you do Dante, yell the direction to me before you go. I don't want to shoot you on accident. Got it?" Vic said it all in a hurry and looked Dante in the eyes waiting for a response.

"Let's go. I understand." Dante said coldly.

"Yeah, he's definitely changed." Vic thought.

Then Vic took off, running further away from the base around the flames of the burning vehicles. As soon as Vic had made his way around, he saw about fifteen 'Hellions' gathered by the front barricade, but they weren't shooting. They were just watching. He decided he'd wonder about what had caught their attention later and pulling the trigger of the assault rifles he held in each hand he mowed down all fifteen of the 'Hellions' in seconds. Dante stood behind him watching the bloodbath.

Vic stopped firing when the last man fell. A few had managed to turn around and fire back, but their aim was wild. They didn't have a chance to see where they were being shot from. They just randomly fired, until Vic's bullets got to them.

Then it was silent. Dante and Vic stared at the bodies of the 'Hellions' that Vic had just shot. They didn't say a word. They just listened to the silence and stood close to one another while they stared for a moment. It had all happened so fast.

They snapped out of the momentary trance, by the feeling of being hit by a truck.

Polo was faster than all of the six 'Hellions' with him by a large margin. As they ran for the barricaded cars, he quickly distanced himself from the other men. He didn't care. He was going to kill these saboteurs if it's the last thing he did. He gained speed as ran, cleared the cars that formed the barricade and quickly made his way around the back of the flames from the burning cars. He saw the two men in front of him staring and the bodies of his 'Hellions' and he just ran faster.

He leaped and caught each man with one arm. Hitting them with everything he had, like he was still playing professional football. The collision sent Polo and the two men he hit flying to the ground. He knew he'd hurt them, but taking two at once, one with each arm, diminished his impact from the life taking blow it would have been if he'd used all of his body to hit one man.

Still, they were down, and they were his now, he thought.

Vic didn't know what the hell hit him, but he knew it him hard. Real hard. He'd let go of both guns he held when he was hit and was now lying on the concrete with what felt like a giant's arm across him. The arm was moving. Giant or not Vic knew that the pounding of fists always followed a hit like that, so he swung first.

The large man on top of Vic had hit him with his right arm. So, Vic swung his left hand at the man's face and shoved with his legs.

The punch didn't seem to faze the large man at all, but shoving with his feet pushed the man backwards, off of him. Vic rolled to his left and jumped to his feet. He was wobbly and his ribs hurt from the tackle, but he was up. "You don't fight a guy that big laying on the ground." Vic thought.

He saw Dante lying on the ground and knew he had been hit at the same time. He hoped Dante was alright but knew he couldn't worry about that right now. The man before him was barely a couple inches shorter than Vic, which made him a very tall man and he had to be at least 300lbs. He was a massive man that had rage in his eyes. Vic expected the man to go for the sub-machine gun he wore and was prepared to kick the gun into the man's chest as soon as he started to raise it.

Instead, the large man looked at Vic, then looked at Dante who was still laying on the ground moaning and took the sub-machine gun off of his shoulders and threw it on the ground. He faced Vic with a murderous look and rushed him.

Vic knew how bad he hurt from this man's previous tackle and knew he might not make it through another one. So, he side-stepped the charge, but left his foot out tripping the man and sending him crashing to the concrete.

Polo jumped up, face bleeding from the crash into the concrete yet still seemingly unphased. He turned and rushed Vic again. Vic once again, quickly side-stepped Polo and tripped him, sending him crashing to the concrete.

This time Vic didn't wait for Polo to rush him again. He jumped forward and kicked Polo in the face as the man was starting to stand up. Then he spun and kicked the side of Polo's left knee with all the force he could muster. There was a loud popping sound and the man's knee shot sideways, very out of place.

Polo roared and swung viciously at Vic's head. Vic ducked, punched the man in the groin and then hit the side of Polo's other knee with his elbow, the full force of his body's momentum was packed into the hit. Another loud popping noise and the right knee shifted visibly out of place. Vic continued his movement with a leap straight up with both fists extended above him, catching Polo in the jaw with the full force of his body jumping upward. The big man fell on his back. Legs appearing useless, jaw broken, yet still somehow immediately began rolling to his feet.

Vic noticed six 'Hellions' rounding the corner with guns raised as he was in mid leap kicking Polo in the face again. He also noticed Dante was no longer on the ground and hoped the man would keep him from getting filled with lead while he battled the giant before him.

Dante rolled to his feet. Dizziness filled his head and pain filled his body. He saw Vic fighting a monster of a man and amazingly seemed to be handling the enormous man with relative ease. Dante couldn't understand how Vic was already up and fighting after the hit they had both taken. Despite his pain, he was slightly amazed and truly inspired by what Vic was capable of.

"He doesn't have the gene. He doesn't have any special abilities like me or Samuel, yet this man faces any odds without hesitation." Dante thought in admiration. Then Dante noticed several 'Hellions' rounding the corner of the flames with guns raised. He knew this was his part.

Too dizzy to picture anything in his mind, he just looked at the spots behind them and them and was there in an instant. The two men closest to him fell with slashed throats before they knew what hit them. The other men turned, and Dante dipped low. He stabbed two men in the groins at the same time, leaving a dagger in each of them while he spun towards the next two still crouching. As Dante kept the fluid motion going, spinning to the next two men, he pulled two more daggers out and leaped up. Both men fell with daggers in their throats.

Dante pulled two more daggers and finished off the two men that he had stabbed in the groin. Not one of the six men got a single shot off.

Dante looked up and saw Vic land a kick flying kick on the giant's face. The large man fell back and Vic stomped his head over and over with such speed and power that Dante was unnerved at the ferocity.

"After what I just did, I'm unnerved at Vic's ferocity?" Dante wondered to himself.

Vic finally stopped. The large man wasn't moving. Vic reached down and picked up the sub-machine gun the man had dropped and looked at Dante.

"Thanks. You ready? Take us to the other side where the rest of the 'Hellions' are attacking the hangar. We're not done yet." Vic said.

CHAPTER 16:
AGENT 17

As Samuel had raced through the open gate, he glanced in his review mirror one more time. He saw where Vic and Dante had blocked the end of the quarter mile entry road with their car parked sideways. He couldn't make out what exactly they were doing, but he knew Vic had the rocket launcher ready. The odds weren't good, but he trusted Vic to handle himself.

Samuel swerved the lowrider in front of the main building and quickly leaped out. Running towards the front doors. Two armed soldiers started to step together and block his path into the building. Samuel yelled while he ran towards them "You got your orders, now step aside, and follow me. I'm in command of this base now!" His shout startled them, but it had its desired effect. He saw the recognition wash over the men's faces. Instead of barring his way, they stepped back and held open the double doors. Samuel ran through and both soldiers followed their new commander.

Once inside he slowed to halt, taking in the place. It was one level, with several conference rooms on the sides. An admin's desk right at the front by where he stood and doors opposite him at the back of the large open room that he assumed led towards either warehoused supplies and/or a weapons room. "Probably both." Samuel thought.

To the back left of the room was a large office. He saw an older gentleman who wore a general's uniform and hat and sported a thick grey mustache approaching him from the office, flanked by six armed soldiers.

'What's the meaning of this and who the hell are you?" The general barked at Samuel.

The general carried on, not giving Samuel a chance to respond. "I don't take kindly to getting calls from the pentagon saying that me and all my men have to take orders from some mysterious damn civilian!"

Samuel didn't know how much time they had, but he knew they didn't have time for this. Not now. They had to prepare while they still could. It wasn't a bunch of untrained gang bangers coming for them. He knew they'd be fortunate to hold off the weird warriors from the blur even if they were prepared.

"If I was a civilian, I wouldn't have been given command of you and your men general." Samuel replied curtly. Then he went on "Now, if you wouldn't mind quitting your bitching about how everyone didn't take your feelings into consideration, I have orders to give that will hopefully save the lives of you and your men. Do you understand me general?" Samuel stepped towards the general as he spoke firmly and stared the general in his eyes.

Despite a look of outrage and embarrassment on his face,

that he was poorly trying to hide, the general responded with a salute and said "Sir, yes sir!".

All of the soldiers gathered in the main building stared in shock. To most of them, the general was the highest ranking official they'd ever seen and now some mystery man, wearing a black sports coat, black jeans and boots walks in their base and just takes over. It seemed unreal. They didn't have time to dwell on it though, because as soon as the confrontation with the general was over, Samuel started shouting orders.

"Take all the desks and drag them back towards the walls and upend them to form a barricade. Upend the desks in all the offices on the perimeter of the room and shove them against the glass windows. Now!" Samuel roared. When he saw a handful of people start scrambling, he addressed the general who was staring at him, obviously assuming these tasks were for others.

"I need sandbags or whatever you've got reenforcing these desk made barricades and I need assault rifles lining the outside of the barricades every few feet. Get as many men positioned behind the barricades while a few keep working to reenforce them." Samuel paused and stepped closer to the general and stared him in his eyes. Then he spoke again, this time in a lower voice "General, our enemy will have high caliber weapons and will appear somewhere in the center of this room. They are well trained, fast and no soldier here is likely to survive any hand-to-hand combat with them. They could be here any second general. Moving fast and doing what I say is the only chance we've got at saving your men's lives and the city."

The general visibly pushed his feelings away and started

barking orders at his men. Rushing them, calling out specific orders and soldier names, all of which were reenforcing Samuel's instructions. Then the radios started chirping.

"We've got a breach in the back fence by the hangars!!! We need reinforcements! Several civilian vehicles and approximately thirty or forty civilians with automatic weapons have crashed through the gates and are attacking the hangar and surrounding buildings! We need help!"

The radio stopped chirping, and everyone paused, waiting on the orders that would send them to support their fellow soldiers being attacked.

"Shit! They've divided their forces." Samuel thought. Then he looked up and addressed the general in a loud voice, that while directed toward the general was clearly meant for everyone in the room to hear.

"Jump on the radio general and organize whatever support or counterattack you can from here, using only the soldiers already posted on that side of the base. We DO NOT leave this building!" Samuel noticed the surprise and mutinous looks on the faces of all the soldiers in the room with him. "I guess I better give them more or they're going to end up dying in here halfheartedly" he thought.

"Listen to me now troops! The attack on the back of the base and the one that my associates are holding off at the front of this base are distractions! They are meant to spread you out and turn your backs on the real threat that will be coming from inside this room! Now you have your orders, move fast if you want to save your own lives!" Samuel shouted this and the men started moving.

Samuel looked around to survey what had already been done. He saw several tables making shoddy barricades in more of a half circle defending the front of the room from the back half. Most of them had sandbags in front of them already. There were four soldiers crouching behind them, staring at about twelve of their comrades working hard to make the back of the room match the front. Samuel didn't like it. Technically they were doing what they were told, but he would've much preferred they scattered the desks into a spotty full circle around the middle of the room and then filled in the gaps then doing one half at a time. He knew it was his fault. He'd never been very involved with the basic troops, even in his past days before he lost his family, but he knew enough to know that you had to specify what you wanted, or you were likely to get something else.

"I just hope we have enough time" He thought. The thought was interrupted as he noticed the large blur from the corner of his eye. It was appearing in the center of the room and the only soldiers that noticed it were the four in position behind him, the rest were too busy hauling sandbags and guns.

"Get down!" Samuel screamed as he leaped over the closest barricade to him. He landed near the four soldiers. They had their backs to the front doors and were facing the center of the room opposite the double doors at the back of the large main building room that led to the supply rooms.

Before they even saw bodies emerging from the 'blur', bullets started flying. These weren't the large pistols that Samuel had seen the other warriors use, no, these were clearly automatic rifles.

The soldiers that were hauling sandbags and guns through the double doors started taking fire and dropping like flies, as several lean dark-skinned men stepped out of the blur, still firing the automatic weapons they held.

There were eight of them so far. All were bald and completely covered with some type strange tribal tattoos, just like the ones Samuel had faced before. They all wore the same brown color leather pants with matching leather vests and held automatic assault rifles. They formed a line aiming at the now scrambling soldiers at the back of the room.

While the six Na'gee warriors in the middle kept firing, the one on either end of the line formation, started turning in a circle laying down gun fire across the rest of the room. They hadn't seen the barricaded half yet and it appeared the general and at least two of his men had leaped behind the far end of the barricade.

The soldiers near Samuel didn't move. He didn't know if they were just shocked at witnessing these weird warriors appear out of nowhere or if they were concerned about hitting their friends across the room with bullets if they shot back. "Probably both." Samuel thought as he pulled both of his pistols out from the shoulder holsters under his jacket and began firing back.

Samuel wasn't surprised, he knew the warriors were coming and he didn't care if he hit soldiers in the crossfire "Necessary sacrifices." He told himself as he kept firing.

Samuel didn't aim for the warriors that were turning towards him on the ends of the line, no, he aimed for the two in the middle, next to the blur. His thoughts were simple.

Take out the ones that don't have a chance to see it coming and dodge, not to mention hit the damn blur in case more are working their way through.

His plan worked. The two Na'gee warriors in the middle dropped dead. As soon as they fell the two soldiers on the ends aimed at Samuel and he ducked down just in time to avoid catching all of their bullets. As he ducked, he yelled "Shoot back dammit!"

That did it. The soldiers down the line from him started shooting back and so did the general and the two soldiers near him.

The Na'gee were ready this time though. They all leaped at once into the air, straight up about seven or eight feet and aimed down behind the barricades while in the air. Half of them aimed for the general and his men, while the other half aimed for the soldiers past Samuel.

Samuel, still crouching, kicked back off the barricade propelling himself across the floor towards the front doors on his back. He aimed up and took out two more Na'gee, who dropped out of the air.

The Na'gee finally landed after what seemed like a forever of floating in the air, at the same time that Samuel crashed into the front doors behind him. The tables had instantly turned. Now the remaining four Na'gee had the advantage of the barricades while Samuel was out in the open. It also looked like all of the soldiers and the general had been killed.

Samuel leaped back through the front doors he had crashed into and dove into the bushes to the right side of the glass doors as they exploded behind him from gunfire. He was outside now and the Na'gee would undoubtably pursue him.

With this in mind, he leaped to his feet and ran staying close to the large building. He didn't really hear them, but he knew they had come outside moments later. He assumed they would split up with two going one way and two going the other way around the building, but he hoped they would all follow him. His plan counted on them not catching up to him before he made it to the back door of the building where the soldiers had been bringing in supplies. If he could just get there, he could duck in and then pop back out and hopefully catch them mid run.

Samuel ran with everything he had.

The four remaining Na'gee warriors walked outside rifles ready. They clearly saw the bushes the man in black had dove into and the matted down grass where he'd ran around the building. They had hunted and been hunted by far fiercer and more cunning predators on the 'Other side'. This one man was of little concern to them, they did notice that he had slain four members of their hunting party though.

The warriors paused. Two electing to follow this strange top sider, while the other two went back inside to finish what they were here for. They seemed to all agree on this course of action without uttering a word.

Samuel ran. As he was turning the corner going from the side of the building to the back of the building he caught a glimpse of two warriors rounding the front corner behind him. He also heard gun shots coming from inside the building and knew that at least some of them had gone inside to finish off any soldiers still breathing. Samuel made a quick decision and slid to a stop. He didn't like how exposed he was, but his options were limited. Now on the back side of the building, he eased back to the corner he had just ran around. Samuel steadied himself, counted to three and turned the corner firing both pistols.

He had hoped he would catch the warriors running in pursuit about halfway down the side of the building heading his way. If so, he felt confident that in mid stride with limited cover he'd be able to take them both out quickly.

When he turned the corner, however, he realized these strange warriors were much, much, faster than he had given them credit for being. He turned firing, and his guns were literally touching the warrior in the lead. "Another second and they would've been on top of me!" Samuel thought, shocked that they could cover that amount of distance so fast. He didn't have much time to think though, because while his firing guns touched the first warrior, the warrior that closely followed the first quickly reacted.

The second warrior's reaction was lighting fast, he dove into the lower back of his partner that was being shot at close range, knocking the man into Samuel who was still firing. The three men crashed to the ground in a heap.

The second warrior was on top of what had become a dog pile of sorts. He had obviously forfeited his assault rifle when he chose the diving tackle move, but it didn't slow him down. He reared back and punched right past the head of the warrior between them, catching Samuel in the face.

Samuel was stuck laying with his back on the ground. His

hands were pinned between him and the dead warrior on top of him and with the added weight of the second warrior who sat half on top of the dog pile, he struggled to wrench them free. He endured a second powerful punch to the face, still unable to get his hands free. He saw the warrior rear back to hit him again and knew that two or three more of the hits and he'd lose consciousness. That would be the end. He knew if this man knocked him out, he'd never be waking up again.

With this harsh realization in mind, Samuel stopped trying to pull his arms out from under the man on top of and quickly reached straight down instead, feeling around near the dead warrior's waist. "Got it!" Samuel thought as he took the third powerful punch to the face. He saw stars, his head was spinning, but he didn't slow down. He knew his life depended on it. What he had found was the large knife the warrior, like all of them, wore around his waist. Samuel slid the knife out of the sheath and with his arms still somewhat trapped between him and the dead warrior he shoved the sharp, large knife straight up through the dead man's mid-section and into the groin of the warrior that sat on top of the dog pile punching him.

The warrior howled in pain and rolled off the side, holding himself where he had been stabbed. Despite being dizzy Samuel forced himself to keep moving. He shoved the dead man off of him rolled sideways to the fallen warrior that had been stabbed in the groin and without even standing he reached out and grabbed the warrior's arm, instantly 'freezing' him in place.

Samuel exhaled. Gave himself a moment to lay in the grass and gather his bearings. "Damn, these guys pack a punch!" Samuel thought, face and head pounding from the three direct blows he'd taken to the face. He slowly stood and looked back towards the front corner of the building. He was once again shocked at how quickly the warriors had caught up to him. "They're damn fast too. We cannot let these men take the city or we may never get it back." Samuel thought grimly.

He nonchalantly shot the warrior he had 'frozen' on the ground in the head and began to trot towards the back doors of the main building. He knew there were still two more of these hardened warriors inside as he could still hear random gunshots.

Samuel made it to the double doors at the back of the building and peered into the warehouse area in the back of the building through one of the small square windows that was at the top of each door. He saw one of the two warriors throwing another automatic rifle over his shoulder with the attached strap and leaning down to pick up extra clips. Samuel didn't know where the other warrior was, but he knew he wouldn't get too many opportunities with these warriors, so he burst through the doors firing.

He caught the warrior three times in the side, before the warrior leapt for the cover of a stack of crates. Samuel ran directly at the crates and jumped on top of the stack as the warrior was sliding to a crouching position behind them and beginning to ready his weapon. As Samuel landed on top of the crates the warrior looked up and was shot twice in the face.

Samuel jumped behind the crates landing next to the warrior and leaned down to take the assault rifle when he heard the doors open from the main room into the back room, he was in. He stayed down.

Slowly and silently reading the rifle he had taken from the dead warrior, Samuel peered around the corner of the crates. He saw the last warrior walking around the opposite side of the room, peering here and there, head on a swivel. Samuel didn't know if he was looking for survivors to kill or looking for his fellow warrior, but to Samuel it didn't matter.

As soon as the warrior's head turned to the other side of the room Samuel stepped out from the cover of the crates and emptied the clip of the automatic rifle into the body of the last warrior. Samuel dropped the rifle on the ground and reloaded his pistols. He glanced at the doors the warrior had come from leading into the main room of the building. He was tempted to search for survivors but decided against it. "This warrior wouldn't have made his way back here if he hadn't finished everyone off in there." He thought. "Damn. Didn't even save one of them." These thoughts made Samuel momentarily mad at himself for his failure. Then a familiar cold calm ran through him as he thought "They were necessary sacrifices."

"I need to help Vic and Dante finish off the 'Hellions' and then get to the police station before it's too late." Samuel thought as he headed for the back doors of the building. As Samuel exited the building, he started towards the back of the base and then had second thoughts and changed his direction. Still running, he now headed the opposite way of the hangars. He ran towards the large garage buildings behind the main building. "No sense in running down there, when I can grab a jeep or something to drive." Samuel said to himself as he ran towards the garages.

When Samuel got to the garage buildings he walked around to the front where the large garage doors stood open. Inside he saw two military jeeps, one of which had a large heavy artillery gun mounted to the top. He started towards it, but then stopped and looked to his left. In the next bay over he saw something he liked much better. "This will do nicely" Samuel thought as he half grinned and hurried to the vehicle.

Chapter 17: Sous Chef

Dante looked at Vic, who appeared hurt and winded after his scuffle with the giant 'Hellion'. Dante's body still ached from being tackled by the big man. He hesitated, not feeling confident about questioning Vic's directions. The fact that Vic had dispatched the extremely large man without any weapons or gene abilities, made Dante less confident in questioning him, but he went on anyway and said. "Vic are you sure you don't need a minute? We don't know what we're going to be teleporting into over there."

Vic looked at Dante as if he would be the tall man's next victim and said harshly "We don't have a damn minute Dante! If you're worried about what we're beaming into, then grab a damn gun, they're laying everywhere around us!" Vic finished his harsh statement seeming on the verge of saying more, then instead walked over to a dead 'Hellion' and picked up another sub-machine gun, similar to the one he had confiscated from the giant 'Hellion' he had fought. He checked the clips, felt around on the body near him for extra clips and found two. He placed the clips in his pockets and looked up at Dante.

"Still no guns, huh? Your choice man. Remember, Samuel's taking the creepy outer space warriors or wherever the hell they're appearing here from. You and me get the damn gang bangers. Our jobs only half-done Dante. You did well here. Now let's do it again." Vic said this part calmly, almost supportively.

Dante knew he was right. He was encouraged by this older yet extraordinary man and respected him. Dante nodded, walked over to Vic and grabbed him by the arm and then said "You ready? Remember, you'll be disoriented for a few minutes."

"You just do your thing and sous chef these assholes until I can see straight. I'll take it from there brother." Vic said curtly.

A second later they were standing by a twelve-foot-tall chain link fence with barbwire on the top. About ten feet of it had been crashed inwards and obviously driven over. They looked ahead and about one hundred yards in front of them, they saw the closest hangar. Several vehicles that clearly belonged to the 'Hellions' were on either side of the hangar. Gunshots rang through the air.

"Dante, get us to the back of the building so we don't have run across this damn field. From there we'll go to the right and take that group out first." Vic said.

"Why the right side?" Dante asked wondering if there was some advantage he was overlooking.

Vic responded with "We always take the path to the right

Dante. It's just what we do."

Dante hesitated for a moment and then said "but Vic, we just attacked the left side first out front."

Vic thought for a moment and then said "Would you forget that shit Dante, we always go right dammit! Now let's go."

Thoroughly confused and thinking that maybe the big 'Hellion' had hit Vic harder than he realized, Dante shrugged and grabbed Vic by the arm saying "Whatever you say Vic." An instant later both men stood directly behind the large hangar that was being attacked from both sides.

As Vic struggled to get his bearings Dante heard him mumble "wow. It gets worse when you do it a couple times in a row."

Dante left Vic leaning against the back of the building and made his way to the corner at the right side. He peered around and saw about five 'Hellions' shooting at running soldiers who were holding their side arms and trying to find cover in the wide open space in front of the hangars that looked like it served as a runway for planes and jets. The 'Hellions' laughed as they gunned down the running soldiers.

Dante looked back at Vic, who had pushed himself away from the support of the hangar back wall and was slowly making his way to the corner. He decided not to wait for Vic. He decided he couldn't stand here and watch these evil men kill these soldiers in cold blood and laugh about it. Then Dante disappeared.

Vic looked up and saw Dante vanish. He knew what that

meant. His first thought was that Dante should've waited on him, but then he thought twice "The young guys got as much reason to want to take out Camacho's guys as any of us do. Let him get them." Vic thought to himself as he approached the corner. He peered around to see exactly that... Dante 'getting them'.

The five 'Hellions' were spread out. They had car lengths between them and weren't in a straight line. Dante knew it wouldn't be quite as easy as what he'd done out front when his adversaries were packed in more condensed spaces. He appeared behind the closest one and slashed his throat. The other four instantly saw it and turned their guns towards him, firing.

In a flash Dante was gone, behind the next man. He slashed this man's throat from behind as well but was thrown backward from bullets hitting the man's body before he fell. The bullets had come from the others, who upon seeing Dante appear behind another of their members, had apparently chosen to gun them both down. Dante and the body in front of him came crashing to the ground. The man whose throat he had slashed had served as a shield, protecting Dante from the bullets, but now this heavy shield lay on top of him, and he was between two cars. He couldn't get a good look at anywhere to teleport to and he heard the three other men approaching. Dante, pushed with everything he had and rolled the heavyset gangbanger off him. He started to rise, and bullets hit the car beside him. He ducked back down, trying to crouch and run back between the cars, away from the gunfire that was hitting everything around him.

When he got to the back of the car, he circled it and

looked around. He couldn't look up at his attackers or he risked being shot. Everywhere else around him was wide open space, with no signs of cover. "If I teleport anywhere that I can see, I'll get gunned down like the soldiers." Dante thought. So, he did the only thing he could think of, he teleported back to behind the hangar where he had just taken him and Vic minutes before.

Vic peered around the corner. He saw three 'Hellions' shooting at Dante, who was crouched behind a car. He saw Dante vanish and then heard a faint noise behind him. Vic whipped around pointing a sub-machine gun at whoever was sneaking up on him. He stopped himself, just in time, when he noticed it was Dante.

"What the hell are you doing back here? I almost shot you man!" Vic exclaimed.

Dante was rattled. He seemed slightly out of breath and simply said "They had me pinned. I didn't know what else to do man."

"Ah hell." Vic grumbled. "Let's do this kid!" and with that Vic rolled around the side of the building, the sub-machine he held in each hand exploded with gun fire and the three 'Hellions' who were still firing at the back of the car Dante had used for cover, were immediately gunned down.

Vic looked back at Dante and yelled "Now come on, we don't have time to be going backwards man!"

Vic took off running towards the front of the hangar, Dante quickly followed.

As they approached the front of the hangar, Vic saw a

handful of 'Hellions' firing on more scattering soldiers. As he surveyed the chaos, his eyes swept over one 'Hellion' holding a rocket launcher who was staring directly at him. The man grinned and fired the rocket.

Vic screamed "Get down!" and dove back behind the corner, crashing into Dante who had been running to catch up with him. The two hit the ground as the cars near them exploded, knocking them across the ground and into the side of the hangar building.

Dante's ears rang. He didn't feel like he could move. It was the second time in less than thirty minutes that he felt like he had been hit by a truck. He saw Vic moaning on the ground to his right, holding his head. Dante, started to sit up and was able to see the man with the rocket launcher come around the corner of the building. He saw that there was another rocket loaded. He saw the man see him. The two made eye contact and the 'Hellion' grinned and fired again.

Dante saw the rocket flying towards them and grabbed Vic by the arm.

Still laying on the ground, Vic and Dante stared at the explosion on the side of the building where they had just been. Everything was destroyed.

Dante had taken them all the way back to the broken fence this time a hundred yards away. He knew that if he saw the 'Hellion' come around the flames with another rocket then they'd be completely exposed. He prepared himself to teleport Vic and him back to the front of the base, where they had successfully defended the other 'Hellion' attack.

Vic began to rise. He looked at Dante, nodded a silent

thanks and then said with a smile "It's a good thing they didn't have rocket launchers at the front attack, huh Dante?"

Dante didn't laugh, but instead was once again amazed at the tall man's composure. Vic now standing, looked at Dante and reached his arm out to help the young man up.

Dante took his hand and as Vic pulled him to his feet he said "How about you take me back over there, so I can kill that trigger happy son of bitch?"

Before Dante could answer, the entire right side of the hangar exploded. Despite being at a safe distance, both men jumped, startled by the explosion.

Vic stared and said, "What the hell is he shooting at now?" A moment after he got the words out, the vehicles on the left side of the hangar exploded. Then seconds later the hangar itself exploded.

Dante and Vic stared in confusion. This time it was Dante who broke the silence by saying "Maybe the soldiers are firing rockets back at them?"

"Maybe. Let's jog over there this time. We don't know what the hell we're teleporting into. Stay close though and be prepared to get us out of here, if they turn those rockets on us." Vic said and he started jogging to the left of the decimated hangar.

Dante started jogging closely behind the tall man and said, "Hey Vic, I thought we always go right?"

Vic replied without slowing down or looking back, he just yelled out "We do, but that shit didn't work out so good. So, now we go left." Then he added, "but Dante, we always go right."

Dante didn't respond, he just followed closely behind Vic thinking "yep, that big guy hit him way too hard in the head."

It didn't take long for the men to cross the open field and make their way around the right side of the burning building. As they neared, they saw three 'Hellions' running away further to the right, about fifty yards from them. As the men ran, they were exploded by a blast so large that it left what appeared to be car sized crater in the ground.

"Oh shit!" Vic shouted in shock. "Guess you were right Dante, the soldiers did pull their crap together. About time they did some of the work to defend this place."

The two men casually walked around the corner, keeping a large distance between themselves, the burning hangar and the exploded 'Hellion' vehicles. The men stayed close together, neither needing to verbalize what they knew they were both thinking. They knew that the soldiers could easily aim at them next, so they needed to be ready for Dante to get them out of there.

As they cleared the corner and got a good view of the front of the hangar, they immediately saw what had apparently destroyed all of the 'Hellion' forces.

A large tank sat in front of the hangar, still aiming its cannon at the remnants of the burning building.

As they stared, they saw the top open and Samuel climbed out onto the roof of the tank. He surveyed the destruction around him and then his eyes rested on Vic and Dante.

He waved for them to come on and yelled "Quit standing around staring! We've got to try to save the police station!" He paused for a moment and then shouted "Hurry up. I've got a plan!"

Chapter 18:
It's Too Big!

ante and Vic looked at each other, both once again amazed at this mysterious man and both not sure they were really excited about another one of Samuel's plans. They simultaneously shook their heads and then started jogging towards the massive tank.

When the men got to the tank, Samuel who had still been sitting on top of it, jumped down to meet them. He looked at both of the battered men and asked, "Are you both alright?"

Vic answered for them both, "We're good Samuel. How about you? Looks like someone hit you in the face with a hammer man."

"I could say the same to you Vic. I'm good." Samuel said, as he thought to himself "The way that warrior hit me in the face, it might as well have been a hammer."

Samuel looked both men over once more and then began to talk.

"Dante, what's the largest thing you've ever teleported?"

Samuel said.

Dante thought for a moment, then answered, "I've carried some big boxes and well, my mom wasn't real small if you know what I mean. I guess nothing too big."

Samuel stared at him and then looked at the tank. He waited for the implication to hit Dante.

He knew it did when Dante exclaimed "I can't teleport a giant tank man! It's too big Samuel!"

Samuel responded to Dante's outrage with a calm level tone, asking "How do you know you can't? Has it been harder to teleport things or people that are bigger?"

Dante shifted his wild gaze back and forth from Dante to the massive tank. Thinking now more than ever, that Samuel was a complete lunatic. Then he slowly answered, "well no, but Samuel, it's huge."

"Try it." Samuel said. "If it doesn't work, you'll know. Try to take it to the bus stop by the northern most police station."

Dante looked anything but confident and responded meekly saying, "Ok, man. I'll try."

The young man, with blue jeans that were torn and dirty, a t-shirt that seemed so covered in soot and dirt that it was impossible to tell what color it used to be and two large leather straps crisscrossed over his chest filled with daggers, approached the large tank.

He took a deep breath then reached out and put his hand on the tank. Just like that, the entire tank was gone. A split second later, Dante was standing before them smiling ear to ear. He shouted "Holy crap Samuel! It worked! I teleported a freaking tank man!"

"Take us to it." Samuel said.

Minutes later, Dante stared around at all the wild stares aimed at them as Vic and Samuel leaned against the tank, getting their bearings.

The giant tank sat in the middle of the street in front of the bus stop less than a block from the police station. Cars skidded to a stop, people walking had all stopped to stare and the people that had been at the stop waiting for the bus were cautiously moving away.

Samuel shook off the dizziness first and began climbing up to the top of the tank. He yelled back "Come on Vic, shake it off and get in here. We've got to go."

Vic did as he was told and quickly began climbing up to the top of the tank, with Dante following closely behind. Once they all were inside, Samuel reached past them and pulled the top hatch shut. He settled behind what appeared to be the controls to drive the tank and the massive machine started moving.

As he drove, he began talking "At this point, I think we're only going to manage saving one of the precincts. We'll do what we can for the other, but it depends on how long it takes us here." Samuel waited for a reply or a protest, but after a few seconds of silence he continued.

"The goal is to end it quickly and the most important thing is that we don't let these mysterious warriors survive the assault. The way I see it we have two options. One, we use the tank to dispatch the 'Gridlox' that will be or already are, attacking the station from the outside and Dante, you teleport you and Vic inside and take out the warriors as they come through." Samuel paused for what seemed to be effect and then went on. "Option number two, we take out the 'Gridlox' and the entire station with the tank. This would of course kill the officers and the warriors, but at least it would take out Camacho's guys. It's less risky than option one. What do you think?"

"Samuel, we got to save these officers if we can? If not, we're just as bad as Camacho!" Dante said with passion and conviction.

Vic and Samuel traded looks and then Vic spoke up "Look Samuel, I've got no love for cops, but Dante's not wrong. Give us chance to save some of them, you handle the gang bangers this time."

"You remember how these mysterious warriors fight guys? I barely made it out of the base building alive and none of the soldiers there survived. You sure you want to take this risk?" Samuel said it coldly and matter of fact.

This time it was Vic and Dante that traded looks. Both men were flooded with memories of their last encounter with these tattooed warriors. Then Vic looked back at Samuel and smiled "Yeah, we're sure. They're about to learn the same lesson their buddies learned; you don't fuck with the grim reaper." Then Vic added with a smirk, "Besides, I got one hell of a sous chef backing me up Samuel. Ain't that right Dante?"

Dante did not wear a similar smile, he seemed to still be thinking about his last encounter with the strange fighters from the 'blur'. He just said "Yeah, yeah, whatever Vic."

CHAPTER 19:
"YOU FORGET YOUR PLACE TOP-SIDER"

Camacho, Primo and Olo watched as breaking news alerts filled the multiple screens in front of them. They were still at Camacho's hide away, watching their plans unfold via the media's coverage of the strategically planned catastrophes. Camacho now sat in the center of a large leather couch facing the screens, while Primo observed from a office chair with wheels on it, that he used to roll over to the control monitors periodically. Olo stood rigidly watching all the news feeds displayed before him without expression.

They witnessed the two interstates that accessed the city get successfully obstructed and the demolition of the two major hospitals. They watched the standoffs in spotty, yet still live coverage as their gang affiliates gunned down as many first responders as they could before ultimately falling victim to swat team bullets. This did not bother them, this was, after all, part of the plan.

As was the assault on the police stations which had just

begun.

What did bother them though, was that they did not see anything about the military base falling yet.

"Maybe they're trying to cover it up or keep it under wraps. You know how Washington does?" Camacho had speculated loudly. "Primo, see if you can pick up anything on the back channels."

Primo remained silent, but he rolled his chair over to the computer monitors, put headphones on and began clicking away at the keyboard. A few minutes later Primo took the headphones off and set them down next to the keyboard. He turned to face the other two men across the room as he picked up a remote control from the other side of the keyboard.

"We've got a problem." Primo said. Standing and looking at both of the other men. "I intercepted an encrypted communication about the military base. It was sent to a special force's unit being deployed. It does not good. Look." As Primo finished he pointed to the middle screen, which he switched from a live broadcast near one of the hospitals, to something that looked like a classified military file.

The classified document was titled "Potential Rouge Ghost Agent" and showed a picture of a bald-headed, dark-skinned man that wore a black sports coat and black jeans. All three men recognized him as the same man from the footage they had watched of 'the spot' being raided.

The next picture showed the same man, sitting on top of a tank at a completely destroyed military base.

The document went on to describe this Ghost Agent taking command of the military base and then leaving with a specialized tank. The general and everyone else inside the central command building were left dead and last seen with this man, this 'Ghost Agent' entering the building and assuming command.

There was speculation that he used street gangs as a distraction to kill the general and steal the tank.

The document showed another picture toward the bottom of the page of what appeared to be the same tank in the middle of the street, not two blocks from the northern most police station that was being attacked by gang members.

The orders on the document were clear. This special forces unit was to stop the tank from attacking the police station with the gangs it appeared to be affiliated with and bring in the 'Ghost Agent', dead or alive.

Camacho was the first to break the silence. "I thought you had a hunting party take this fool out Olo!" he screamed.

Olo, turned calmly and stared coldly into Camacho's eyes. The stare lasted only a minute or two, but it felt like a lifetime of tension rising in the room. Then Olo said "You forget your place 'Top Sider'. Do not presume that your 'special gifts' of strength and speed allow you the authority to speak challengingly to a warrior of my status. I will not remind you again, regardless of the value you provide in this world." Olo said it all calmly as he continued to stare at Camacho.

Camacho's eyes blazed with fury, but he did not speak. Primo half expected the smaller man to leap at Olo and attack him. Primo half hoped he would and that Olo would finish the fool and spare him any more of the misery of working with Camacho.

However, despite his hopes, Primo could not help but offer a solution to the situation. He often offered solutions to these people he worked for, when it would be in his best interests for them to fail. He didn't know why he did it. Primo often told himself it was loyalty, but deep down he relished the opportunity to remind them that they were all fools compared to him.

So Primo broke the rising tension in the room and said "This may still work out for us. For the migration."

Camacho and Olo both shifted their angry stares from each other to Primo and Primo continued.

"I have downloaded street camera footage of that same man firing the rocket into the club. If I leak that to the media stations and say that he has been responsible for all the explosions and the chaos, not only the military, but every remaining law enforcement agency will be after him. Afterall, he's driving around in a tank over half the city away from Hotel 'The Deluxe'."

As he paused to gauge their reactions, he realized they were not following, so he elaborated.

"Don't you see. If every remaining form of resistance is after him, we can move the Na'gee into the designated positions around the Hotel and commence. Let the gangs and the cops and soldiers fight each other and this Ghost Agent, while we secure our position. I suggest we reroute the current Na'gee headed to take the police stations. That will no longer be necessary. They'll do more good here." Primo said it all with a hint of arrogance. He was proud of his intelligence and struggled to hide this pride when he shared ideas that he felt should be obvious to others.

Neither man said a word in response to Primo's suggested plans. After long moments of silence, Olo spoke.

"Leak your video and your propaganda to the press Primo. Let our enemies focus on each other. However, we still need to take the police stations. In light of these new developments, maybe we don't need to take the stations, as much as we need to immobilize them. I will still send warriors, but I will only send two to each location. They will place explosives through the path and leave the buildings worthless to the 'Top Sider' resistance." Olo said it all more like he was speaking to himself or thinking out loud, then as if he was speaking to them and maybe he was. It didn't matter, plans were changing.

Primo felt proud that he had once again shown his worth, while Camacho still steamed with anger at being challenged by Olo.

Olo, once again rubbed the strange stone talisman he wore on his neck and the 'blur' appeared in the middle of the room. He stepped through and began talking in the Nextel looking device. Moments later Olo stepped back and said "They are working on getting the necessary explosives to the locations. Instructions have been given. Let us proceed to the Hotel and prepare for the arrival of the Na'gee people."

As they all started to head for the door, Olo stopped and addressed Primo.

"You stay. See what else you can learn about these men, all of them, their families, the locations they have visited, their past. Everything Primo. Any adversaries that cause this much chaos deserve to be better known. Provide me updates as you learn more about all three of the men that attacked 'the spot'." Olo finished his instructions and waited for a response.

Primo nodded and turned back towards the monitors that he had just stepped away from. He didn't like it. He didn't like Camacho and Primo going to usher in the full migration of the Na'gee to this world, while he was told to stay away and do research. He also didn't understand why Olo wanted him to look into all three of them. "Sure, if this man in black survived then it's feasible to think that our knife fighter did too, but why look into Vic and his family when the Na'gee hunting party slaughtered them the previous day?" Primo thought.

Olo turned and headed towards the door heading out. The same door Camacho had stormed through as soon as he'd Olo's instructions to Primo. Olo was greatly disturbed by what he had chosen not to share with his companions, the fact that he could not reach the hunting party he had sent to take out Vic and his family. They hadn't arrived at their designated location and were no longer responding to radio communications.

Olo believed in signs, in fate, in destiny. These 'Top Siders' had proven more than formidable on multiple occasions now. They had kept surviving and finding ways to interrupt the Na'gee's migration efforts.

"These Top Siders seem different from the other soft people of this world, and they somehow seemed destined to be pitted against my people." Olo thought to himself as he walked out.

Chapter 20:
Halbred

Special Agent Halbred had received the encrypted communications. He had never heard of Ghost Agent going rouge before. Hell, he hadn't even known that more than a couple even existed. He had already sent word to his unit as soon as he received his orders and knew they would be there soon.

Halbred was a large red-haired, bearded man, in what appeared to be his forties. He had broad shoulders, a thick build and stood just over six feet tall. Halbred led a very unique special forces unit for the government.

What made it so unique is that his team was comprised of soldiers that had the 'gene', which was largely frowned upon in the military, at least officially it was. He had the 'gene' too and had proven his valor on many occasions for the government, which allowed him special privileges. One of those privileges was that they 'allowed' him to recruit and train his own unit of soldiers with the 'gene'. They had been deployed several times and never failed to accomplish a mission, but they had never been deployed to take action on their own country's soil. Halbred didn't like it.

He didn't like the thought of civilians being around when his team engaged. "Matter of fact, I don't like any of this. It doesn't smell right." He grumbled to himself. Halbred had logged into the camera footage at the base, and while all the footage was destroyed from the main building and the hangar. He had seen this Ghost Agent appear to fight against the gangs. "Well, I saw him fight in close range with two other men, who definitely weren't soldiers outside the hangar and I saw the destruction from the satellite views of what appeared the be the aftermath of this man using the tank against the gangs" He thought to himself. To Halbred, it just didn't add up.

Like it or not, he'd do his job, but he just wished he could make sense of it. "Why?" he mumbled to himself. "What does he get out of announcing himself after years off the grid, then wiping out a military base and stealing a tank? Which, oh by the way he just appears across town with and starts driving down the street. Not a bit of damn sense." Halbred thought to himself.

His thoughts were interrupted by the chirping of the communication device in his ear. The voice from the device said "They're all here sir. Everyone is ready and waiting on the helipad."

"I'm on my way." Halbred replied back. He stood up, collected the files he had spread across his desk and headed for the door. Still thinking to himself how he wanted to handle this situation.

Halbred, left his small office, made his way across the

wide-open floor and to the elevator. He hit the button labeled 'rooftop' and this old elevator began to creak and moan as it took him to his desired destination. The creaking and moaning seemed to grow louder on the way up and ended with the doors opening with a loud screeching noise. Halbred thought of all the money the government poured into so many ops and so many experiments and wondered why it took an act of congress to fix an elevator.

"All the damn dangerous ops and that death trap of an elevator is going to be what kills me" he thought to himself as he walked out of the old elevator and onto the roof.

He instinctively surveyed the scene as he always did. Too many years of service to turn it off. He saw the large helicopter on the helipad across from him. The pilot was already in position and had the chopper started and ready to go.

Halbred knew the pilot well. Her call sign was 'Bird'. Unlike the others on his team, 'Bird' had no enhanced abilities, she didn't have the 'gene', but she was a damn good pilot who had piloted them in and out of more than a few tight spots. Halbred trusted his life and the lives of his team in her hands.

On the rooftop stood the rest of his team. He looked them over, assessing how they arrived. It was just for show, just to keep them on their toes. He knew these soldiers well and knew that they would all be on point and ready. "Still, can't let them get comfortable." Halbred thought.

Halbred looked them up and down from right to left. To the far right was 'Diggs'. He was a short, stocky man with grayish looking skin. He wore his gray hair slicked back and wore his dark blue fatigues, as did the rest of the unit. Diggs, had the unique ability to, well, dig. He could kind of wave his against the surface in front of him and dig about a car's depth into the ground with each swing. It had come in handy for tunneling behind enemy lines and providing immediate barricades in the middle of the battlefield on many occasions. The fact that it didn't matter what substance the ground was made of, made his unique ability all the more valuable.

The next down the line was the skinny solider they all called 'Fuse'. Fuse wasn't much taller than Diggs but was far skinnier than his stocky teammate. He wasn't out of shape, no, Halbred wouldn't tolerate that from anyone in his unit, the pale man was just lean. Fuse had brown hair that hung almost to his shoulders, but he always kept it pulled back in a ponytail. His abilities were just as valuable to the team as Diggs' were. Fuse could touch anything and turn it into a bomb of sorts. He kind of charged it up to explode. The larger the object the longer it took and well, the larger he wanted the explosion the larger it took to charge. Others on the team had described it as charging a phone or an electric car on multiple occasions, especially when they had been forced to hold of enemy troops for what had seemed like forever, waiting on Fuse to finish charging something to explode and cover their escape.

Then there was 'Radio'. He was the weirdest of the bunch by far. The man had a brown hair with a buzz cut, was of medium build and average height. His eyes made him stand out though. They had no color, instead they looked like static on a TV screen all the time. Radio was able to somehow intercept communications of any kind. It didn't matter if it was an email, a radio or a satellite. "Hell, unless they're sending a letter with a pigeon, he can pick it up." Halbred had said on many occasions to the team. The man just had to kind of focus on the subject, and he was able to intercept any comms being transmitted on it. This was probably the most advantageous ability to have in the unit and had saved all their asses on more than one occasion.

The last two members of his special unit were 'Roid' and 'Flutter'. Roid was a very large, abnormally large man, he stood almost seven feet tall and weighed well over 350lbs. His only ability was strength, but damn he had a lot of it. Roid was a walking, oversized, muscled, tank of a man that could lift a car with ease, and showed this skill off to anyone willing to watch. He'd earned the nickname 'Roids' long before his military days and it just stuck.

Flutter on the other hand was a muscular woman, with short blonde hair and dark green eyes. She could fly, which came in handy, but she could also touch people, objects, well anything really and make it float. She often teased the oversized teammate Roid when he started his bragging and would send him floating in the air like a balloon that escaped a child's hand.

Yes, this was his unit. They had been officially named "Special Unit; Gene 6". Halbred loved his squad, but he hated the name. He hated that because tasked with recruiting and training 'gene' soldiers, that it had almost been the reverse of what he hated about the military. They forced him to discriminate against soldiers, good damn soldiers, that didn't have the 'gene'. "It isn't right. It shouldn't be a damn 'gene' that qualifies us." He thought, as he often did.

Halbred had been discriminated against for a long time because he had the 'gene' and he passionately hated discrimination in any form because of it. His ability made him damn near invulnerable. His skin was like steel. Sure, he looked normal, but his skin didn't feel normal. He could withstand bullets and blades. He would dent and bruise and was sure that enough force could probably kill him or crush him one day, but for the most part he was indestructible it seemed. In his earlier years in the armed forces, he had been a part of losing battles and was the only soldier left alive. This didn't earn him honor or respect, it earned him resentment and hatred from other soldiers. For some reason they often didn't see it as him not being able to die, they saw it as him leaving the men around him to die.

Halbred had shaken those perceptions, and his feats and accomplishments had earned him much respect across many branches of the military over the years, but none of it diminished his bitterness towards them all. Not only did his experiences make him bitter, but they made him very sensitive to people being labeled, especially soldiers or special agents. He'd experienced firsthand how quickly the armed forces can mislabel someone. This mission stirred up these deep-rooted feelings. "It just doesn't make sense. Why? What's the point?" he thought again, thinking of the current assignment and the Ghost Agent he was sent to bring in.

Halbred, finally addressed his unit. "Radio, did you fill them in?"

"Yes sir. There are more than just the files we were sent though boss. The local media just aired a report saying that there were videos linking him to all the explosions across the city today and that he just took out the entire North Precinct with the tank sir." Radio stopped and just stared at Halbred, with the static waves moving across his eyes.

"How the hell does the local media have info that the state department doesn't Radio and how the hell can one person be blowing up several different locations across all ends of the city at once?!" Halbred shouted.

No one responded to Halbred's rant. They just watched him silently and waited for their orders.

Halbred looked up and stared each one of them in the eyes, going down the line from right to left. Then Roid addressed him "We got the official orders, but what's the word boss?"

This was common in the unit. They had been on many missions following Halbred's lead. They trusted him, would die for him, and knew that sometimes his orders slightly varied from the official orders. They didn't ever question it, and all kind of liked it. They knew they followed a man that would get shit done, but they also knew he had a strong moral compass and would do his best to make sure they didn't go home with a heavy conscious' if it could be avoided.

Halbred understood the question. He spoke loudly to the entire unit in response.

"Orders are to take this Ghost Agent, dead or alive team. I want to talk to the man before he takes his last breath, so the dead part is only if your life or the life of your teammates is at risk. We'll do our job, but none of it smells right team, so be alert and pay attention to everything. There could be others at play here." He paused for effect. They all nodded, so he concluded with. "Alright then. That's it. Load up!"

In seconds, they had all boarded the helicopter and it was airborne headed for the North Precinct.

Chapter 21:
Framed

Samuel cautiously maneuvered the massive tank through the busy streets, destroying street lights, mailboxes, and countless vehicles in the process. It didn't really matter how hard people tried to get their cars out of the way, the street was just too small, and the tank was way too big.

Vic laughed to himself at the damage it caused, and the audacity that they were really driving a tank down the street. Dante, on the other hand cringed at just about every impact.

By the time the precinct came into view, they had pretty much destroyed an entire block. They saw immediately that the assault on the precinct was already underway. There appeared to be about twenty vehicles in front of the precinct forming a half circle. Most of the vehicles were pickup trucks with large caliber guns mounted to the roof and a man standing in the back using it to fire on the precinct.

Within seconds of their arrival, they were noticed.

"Kind of hard to miss a giant tank." Vic mumbled.

The 'Gridlox' gang members stirred in panic, some turning their mounted weapons around and opening fire on the tank. They obviously weren't prepared for this unlikely turn of events.

Then before Samuel fired a shot from the tank, the entire precinct exploded. The three men in the tank were taken by surprise, but unharmed inside the protection of the large armored tank. The 'Gridlox' however weren't so fortunate.

Every vehicle forming the half circle around the building had been decimated from the explosion. There didn't appear to be a single gang member left breathing.

A news helicopter was circling overhead, obviously filming the entire course of events. Samuel cursed, "How the hell did that happen?! We didn't even fire a single shot!"

He noticed the news chopper above them circling and looked gravely at Vic. "They're going to think we did it. All they're going to see is this massive tank and the precinct explode. Everyone's going to think we're the reason." Samuel paused, letting his words sink in and then shouted again. "How the hell did it explode?!"

There was no way that Samuel could've seen the blur appear in the middle of the precinct while the 'Gridlox' were attacking it. No way, that he could've seen the lone warrior step out and place the large device in the middle of the floor, before stepping back into the blur and disappearing. All Samuel could've seen is the building erupt moments after he arrived on the scene.

He knew he had been framed. He knew that this likely meant that the pentagon thought he was somehow behind the military attack and had stolen the tank. He doubted he could change their minds once they latched onto a theory like that, but he pulled out his phone and decided he'd try.

Before dialing he looked at the two men with him. They had barely said a word, the implications of the event weighing heavily on them. They had not only failed to save anyone, but now they looked like the culprits.

Samuel addressed them both. "This is bad guys. Don't say anything. I'll explain later." With that said, he began dialing numbers on the phone.

Vic and Dante could only hear one side of the conversation, but it was enough to completely confuse both men. They didn't hear Samuel say 'hello' or anything of the sort. They just heard their mysterious friend say "Ghost Agent. Number 17. Password: Pheonix-Alpha-Black. Connect me with the secretary of defense now."

The two men were stunned, both wondering more than ever who the hell this strange man was that they had somehow ended up working with. They listened closely, trying to learn more and hoping that something would be said that would make sense of it all.

"Secretary, it's not what it looks like. The street gangs were organized to attack the precincts and the base. We did what we could to organize a counterattack at the base and procured the tank to stop them here." Samuel paused to the sound of someone shouting on the other end of the phone. Neither Vic or Dante could hear what was being said, they could just tell it was being said loud.

Then Samuel continued. "Sir, we did not attack the

precinct. I know what it looks like, but the tank did not fire. As for the general, I tried to help them defend the main hall. He did not survive." More yelling seemed to follow Samuel's response.

Then after a moment Samuel began again. "Yes sir, I was the only survivor again. Regardless and with all due respect sir, I cannot do that. The attack is being coordinated by Camacho. It isn't over. They'll be attempting to commandeer Hotel 'The Deluxe' and move foreign bodies onto our soil. They must be stopped." Samuel stopped talking, there didn't seem to be any response and he grew visibly angry. This time he shouted into the phone "I will not turn myself over sir! I don't give a shit how long I've been off the grid! I didn't do this and I'm going to stop the man that did! The same mad man that had my family killed!"

His words were intense. He was steaming with anger and frustration. They heard the voice on the other end talking back, although it seemed quieter now. They had no idea what was being said, but they saw that whatever it was, it only enraged Samuel more.

"It's not a vendetta, it's justice dammit! How the fuck could I have blown everything up on every end of town! That's Ludacris sir and you know it!" Samuel paused, obviously getting an ear full in return.

"A video of me at the club?! That monsters club?!" Samuel exclaimed. "That's totally unrelated sir."

"Oh fuck it! Anyone you send for me dies. You know this sir. You can thank me for saving the city later, right now you can kiss my ass!" Samuel yelled and hung the phone up.

As soon as he hung up, he started typing away on his phone and in seconds had tapped into the local news feeds. He saw his face in the top right corner of the screen and the words 'Domestic Terrorist' labeled in bold on the bottom of the screen. The rest of the screen flashed from picture to picture.

Vic and Dante leaned in, looking over his shoulder.

The pictures went from him on top of the tank at the military base, to the tank in front of the decimated precinct, to the exploded hospitals, the interstate destruction, to the governor's destroyed home and then to a picture of him with a rocket launcher aimed at the club.

"Shit!" Samuel cursed. "They're framing me for all of it."

Dante was the one who yelled next, "You blew up the club?! You killed my family?!" He screamed the words and then vanished, only to appear directly behind Samuel with a dagger to the man's throat.

"You told me it was Camacho! It was you the entire time! You killed them! You killed them!" Dante shouted. Tears began streaking down his eyes and he shook with rage.

As Samuel started to move, Dante dug the dagger further into his next slightly cutting into his flesh and said "You move, you die. I know what you can do, and you won't have the chance."

Vic watched silently. Not sure if he should intervene or not. As he debated internally on the best course of action, Samuel spoke.

"I didn't do it. Just like I didn't murder the general or

attack the base or blow up this damn police station Dante. They're framing me. You've witnessed have the lies yourself, why believe this one?" Samuel said it all so calmly, so coolly.

Vic was shocked at how Samuel could go from steaming with rage only seconds before to being so utterly calm now. He was also shocked, although he told himself he shouldn't be, at how smoothly Samuel had completely lied to the young man. Vic knew Samuel blew up the club. It was part of the plan from the beginning. Not to kill off Dante's family of course, but to take out Camacho then and there.

When Samuel had gone over the plan with Vic, he had never thought about the innocent people that would die. He had been too worked up about his own family's safety and the fact that Camacho had betrayed him. He understood Dante's rage and knew that although he had formed a bond with Samuel, that Dante had every right to kill him and likely would if he didn't believe Samuel "or even if he does believe him and finds out differently later." Vic thought.

Dante slowly removed the knife from Samuel's throat. He moved around to stare at Samuel, standing just out of reach of the man. Staring Samuel in the eyes, Dante said "You're right. You did not do these other things. We did not do these other things they're accusing you of. I will ask only once, Samuel, did you kill my family?"

Samuel stared back at the young man and lied without hesitation "No Dante."

Vic was shocked and thought that this wouldn't be the end of it. Dante sheathed his knife, but still stared at Samuel.

"Are we done here Dante, or have you chosen to be another

victim of Camacho's manipulation? You told us he blew the club up, remember?" Samuel said sternly to the young man.

Dante looked like he calmed down, just slightly, and then said coldly to Samuel "You're right Samuel. I'm with you, but please know I speak the truth when I say that if I find out you" the young man paused and shifted his gaze to Vic and then back to Samuel and continued "either of you were behind the bombing, I'll kill you both before you know what hit you. It won't matter how much I've come to respect you." The young man finished his cold statement with glassy eyes. He sounded like he was talking about putting his dog down.

Vic knew what Dante was capable of and knew from that moment on, he'd better keep and eye on the young man.

Samuel on the other hand just nodded, seemingly unphased by Dante's emotions or his words and said "Fair enough."

The tension in the tank was broken by the tank rocking like it had been hit by a bomb.

CHAPTER 22:
SPECIAL UNIT: GENE 6

Hit em' again Roid!" Halbred yelled over the roar of the helicopter. His unit was hovering about one hundred yards over the tank and Roid was leaning in the open doorway of the chopper holding a rocket launcher.

Roid grinned at the command, then looked back and said, "thought you didn't want him dead boss?"

Halbred's look made it clear that he didn't share Roid's sense of amusement at the situation. "You see the size of that tank?! This ain't killing them. No, the best thing we can hope for is to rattle them out of their shell. Now hit em' again soldier!" Halbred yelled.

Roid began chuckling and fired another rocket at the large tank, hitting it right at the hatch on top. He aimed there on purpose. He'd follow Halbred's orders no matter what, but he figured it wouldn't be his fault if he 'accidentally' blew the top hatch open and roasted the bastards.

As soon as Roid fired, he pointed the front end of the launcher back inside the helicopter, where Flutter immediately reloaded it. As she was loading the next rocket, he and Halbred locked eyes for just a second.

A second was all it took. Halbred knew what he had tried to do and that look meant it would be his ass if he 'accidentally' toasted them.

As he aimed the reloaded rocket launcher at the tank again and awaited orders.

"How about you aim for the damn tank tread and see if you can immobilize instead of trying to do the one thing I said not to do dammit?!" Halbred yelled to Roid.

Roid shrugged and said, "Sure thing Chief." Then he fired the third rocket and landed a direct hit on the right side's tank tread. The tank shuddered and the tread looked like it almost came off entirely. The tank, that had started moving after the first blast, kept moving, but it was more like a slow crawl or a car with a flat tire now.

"Again?" Roid asked Halbred as Flutter was loading another rocket for him.

"Yeah, shut that damn thing down. We're not going to be chasing a tank across town." Halbred said in response.

As soon as the words left Halbred's mouth, the next rocket was on its way. This one hit in almost the same spot as the last one and managed to do what the last rocket had almost done. The entire tread on the right side was destroyed and came off the tank.

The tank shuddered and twisted, but its forward motion

was successfully stopped.

As the tank stopped moving, the cannon started moving, aiming upwards, directly overhead.

The unit in the helicopter all saw it, they had been waiting for it.

"Time to go to work! Flutter, get Fuse and Roid down there on top of that tank before he gets lucky and shoots us out of the air!" Halbred yelled.

With the command given, Flutter touched Roid's arm with one hand and Fuse's arm with the other hand. Both men started floating ever so slightly and Flutter took off. She flew right out of the open door on the helicopter, holding each man with one hand. It was like she was pulling a weightless balloon through the air with each hand.

She moved fast, towing them with her and let go a few feet above the tank. Both men landed on the top of the tank, on either side of the large cannon.

Fuse reached out and touched a part of the cannon. He knew he didn't need to blow the entire thing up, that would take a while to charge and Halbred wouldn't want to wait that long. So instead, he just charged a small hand size portion where the cannon started emerging from the tank.

The charged area glowed a bright blue, like it always did and then he looked up grinning at Roid. Roid grinned back and both men jumped off the top of the motionless tank. By the time they hit the ground, they heard the loud explosion, followed by a clattering sound and the entire barrel of the cannon fell of the side of the tank, clanging loudly on the ground.

With that the helicopter lowered itself about twenty yards away from the tank and landed gently in the street.

Halbred spoke through the loud speaker on the chopper "Agent 17! We know you're in there. We know what they're accusing you of! I'm Commander Halbred and this is Special Unit Gene 6. If you've heard of me and my unit, you know we're the best chance you've got of staying alive and clearing your name. Time to come out and talk soldier!"

Halbred wasn't sure there was anything to clear up. He didn't like the entire situation; it just didn't make sense and Halbred liked things to make sense. Regardless, the way he figured it, a dangerous man that was cornered was more likely to come out and play nice of he felt he'd be heard. Halbred waited for a response and moments later he got one.

"I know who you are Halbred, but you don't know me. There is an enemy force that has disabled the primary means into the city. They used the bombing and concurrent attacks on first responders as distractions to spread out resistance. Then they organized simultaneous attacks on the military base and the two major precincts to take out resistance. They did what you would of done. Think about it. I stopped them at the base and didn't make it hear in time. I'm just another distraction Halbred, their primary target is to commandeer Hotel 'The Deluxe' and take the city as their own." The words coming through the tanks loud speaker were Samuel's.

"I'm going to stop them. Help would be appreciated. See you there solider." Samuel said and then there was silence. Well, until Halbred responded.

"It doesn't work like that 17. You ain't going anywhere. Not yet anyway. Come on out and let's talk through this." Halbred said in response, still talking through the helicopter's loudspeaker.

There was no response.

"I'm not going to count to ten or warn you again 17! If there's any truth to your story, come out now and let's talk about it. If we have to come in there and drag you out… well, that's a different road all together!" Halbred said.

Still no response.

Finally, Halbred put down the controls to the loudspeaker he'd been talking through and addressed his team. "Fuse! Roid! Crack that damn tank open like an egg and let me through. This fool chose the hard way!"

Roid and Fuse grinned at each other once again and Fuse placed both hands against the side of the tank, they were still standing next too. A section on the side of the tank about the size of a full-grown man started faintly glowing blue. It slowly grew brighter and brighter.

Halbred was stalking towards the two men, with a large baseball bat in his hand. He still had his assault rifle over his shoulder and his sidearm on his hip, but the bat was in his hands. This wasn't new for him or for the unit to see. Halbred was indestructible as far as they knew. Sure, bullets hurt him, but nothing seemed to penetrate his skin, so when he wanted to take someone alive, he always pulled out his old metal bat and, well, went to work.

Halbred stopped when he was about ten feet from the

tank, directly next to Roid, who had eased away as the spot on the tank began to glow very brightly.

Fuse finally let go and walked over to meet the two men. He nodded and Halbred stepped in front of them, while the two men tried to crouch behind him.

BOOM!!!

The side of the tank that had been glowing erupted, sending shrapnel flying everywhere. The two men heard several pieces bouncing off Halbred and then the man was walking away from them to the newly formed hole in the side of the tank.

Roid and Fuse immediately pulled their assault rifles and posted themselves on either side of the outside of the opening and Halbred stepped through.

In moments they heard Halbred yelling a wide array of profanity. They looked at each other knowing, that this wasn't good.

Halbred stepped back out through the same hole he'd initially come through and stopped his rant. He looked at both men, then the rest of his unit at the chopper.

"He's bloody gone dammit! I don't know how the lucky damn magician did it, but he's gone!" Halbred yelled.

This time it was Flutter that responded. She had been airborne since dropping her teammates onto the top of the tank. Now she lightly landed in front of Halbred and said "Doesn't really matter. The dumbass just told us all where he was going over the loudspeaker, right?"

Chapter 23:
Primo

Primo hung up the phone. It was his first call to Olo since Camacho and the tall warrior had left him hours ago. Despite hours of research, he had found little more than what he already knew about Vic and Dante, and there was nothing he could find in any government servers about this man in black. He did, however, have luck when he searched all the city's street camera data. He had specifically looked for images of the man in black and the black sedan he had seen the man step out of when he blew up the club. The searches hadn't produced a lot of results, but it did seem to show an old antique store just blocks from Hotel 'The Deluxe' that either the man or his car had been at several times. The man never actually went into the antique shop, but he parked near it on several occasions and was caught walking into the ally that ran beside the building and to the back of the building.

There were no cameras in the ally, so where exactly he went from there wasn't entirely clear, but the fact that he came and went from the ally so often, was telling enough. He had reported his findings to Olo and was told to keep them between the two of them and to keep researching.

Primo wasn't happy that he was still forced to stay so far removed from the migration and had suspicious thoughts that this would be the norm after the migration took place. Top Siders like himself, had proved useful navigating this world and supplying resources the 'Other Side' would be nothing more than administrative assistants at best once the migration was successful.

Despite all of the frustrating thoughts running through his mind, Primo still found that he was very curious at what Olo might be up to. "Why have me do research like this when the migration is at hand? Why does this man matter and why would he want me to look into Vic and his family if they were dead?"

Primo found it intriguing because he couldn't figure it out. As he wondered at the implications, he continued running image searches into the city's street cameras. This time he looked for Vic and narrowed his search to the timeframe after the Na'gee hunting party had supposedly dispatched him and his family. He found nothing and instantly thought that Vic must be dead, like he expected.

"Of course, the fool is dead. No one survives a Na'gee hunting party." Primo thought.

Next Primo ran the same search, but this time looked for images of Dante and found nothing, since the explosion at 'the spot'. "Whoever this man in black is, he must've been the only survivor." Primo thought to himself.

He lost interest in his work but continued to do what Olo asked regardless. He may be disgruntled, but Primo was still thorough. He carelessly ran another image search in city street camera data base, this time looking for images captured of Vic's wife since the explosion at 'the spot'.

Primo's attention was caught when it surprisingly showed one result. It showed Vic's wife parking in front of the same antique shop that the man in black had frequented. He watched the recorded footage closely and saw her get Vic's two children out of the old van, look around suspiciously and then head quickly down the same ally, that the man in black had been seen taking in previous footage.

"How did the family survive?" Primo thought.

He once again dialed Olo's number and shared what he had seen with the warrior. Olo told him to say nothing of what he had found to anyone else and to keep monitoring that camera. He said to notify him immediately if they were seen on camera again and then he hung up.

Primo sat before the monitors, feeling confused about what was going on and insulted at having to stay put all at once. He thought that something must be done to stop the migration if he ever had hopes of achieving a position of power. With his mind made up, Primo began typing furiously at the keys of the keyboard in front of him.

When he stopped, he reread his work. He hesitated, knowing that if discovered his punishment would be far more severe than simply being put to death. The Na'gee were a brutal tribe, the most feared of the human tribes on the other side. They prided themselves on torture and human sacrifices and Primo believed that they actually worked with the dark ones that hunted and fed off of humans, although that was widely disputed amongst the whispers of the Na'gee people.

Primo knew that if he proceeded with this act of betrayal, it would either pave the way to his ascension of power or mean a slow torturous death. He stared at the screen, feeling the pressure of this monumental decision before him.

He skimmed back over the words that if sent would alert the top officials in the government of an enemy force aiming to take the Hotel, the city and then the entire eastern half of the country. The details that the enemy would be coming through at portal on the roof. The details that would put a stop to the migration or end up ending everything for Primo.

He took a deep breath, hit the 'send' button, and then sat back in his seat with an evil grin. He had finally made his move. This might end the migration, but he knew he'd still have to deal with Camacho, if he wanted to be in charge of the Na'gee infrastructure on the 'Top Side'.

"How to deal with Camacho?" he thought to himself.

CHAPTER 24:
PRIMARY OBJECTIVE

ommander! We just got new orders." Radio shouted to Halbred over the roar of the chopper that was headed towards Hotel 'The Deluxe'.

"Sounds like they said the Ghost Agent is now our secondary objective. The primary objective is reconnaissance of the same damn hotel we're headed towards. They received an anonymous notification through a secure channel only available to department of defense officials. It says that a foreign force will be coming in through a portal on the roof and working towards taking of the city and possibly half the country. We're supposed to surveil the situation and let them know if the mysterious source provided accurate intel or not sir." Radio finished rushing all the words out, into what seemed like one long run on sentence, as he often did.

Halbred looked thoughtful but didn't respond.

Flutter did speak, however and when she did, she addressed the entire unit in the helicopter. "That sounds an awful lot like what that Agent said over the tank's loudspeaker guys."

Halbred, looked like the comment snapped him back to the present from wherever his thoughts had taken him and addressed his unit.

"Doesn't matter Team, not yet anyway. We've got our orders, let's go see what the hell is going on. Bird, head towards the Tech Firm building next to the Hotel. Land us on the roof and keep your distance from the hotel on the way" Halbred shouted his orders to ensure that everyone heard, and the helicopter slightly changed course.

"Flutter, when we get close, take Roid and Diggs with you to the street level. I want you three in the sewers, coming up into the basement of the hotel and I want you to move quickly. We're going to check the place out from the top and the bottom. Everyone understand?" Halbred asked firmly.

The entire team shouted, "Yes sir!"

Chapter 25:
Eva

Eva parked on the street in front of the antique shop. She looked out the windows of the van, scanning up and down the street. It seemed quiet here. "At least its quiet for now." Eva thought.

On the drive through the city, she had witnessed chaos. There was simply no other word for it. It seemed the explosions across the city and the assaults on first responders and police stations had instigated a full blown riot. She had seen people breaking into buildings, looting and setting fires.

"The city has gone freaking crazy!" Eva thought to herself. She glanced into the review mirror at her children in the back of the van. She saw the looks on the faces of Mila and Steph and knew that they had witnessed it all as well. She saw fear and confusion on the face of Steph, but Mila's face was expressionless. It was obvious that she had witnessed the chaos and she looked out the windows, seeming to scan the street for signs of danger here, like Eva did, but she was not confused or scared.

Eva pushed aside the concerns for her daughter. She tried

not to think of what the horrors of the past twenty-four hours had done to Mila. She tried not to think of the amazing things that her daughter had done in the past day and half.

"There's too much to unpack there. Now is not the time." Eva thought as she cautiously stepped out of the van and eased her way to the sliding door of the van.

Eva opened the door and waved for the children to follow her.

"Come on. Hurry. We need to move fast." Eva told them in a hushed voice.

"Are the crazy people going to come here too Mom?" Steph asked, looking about nervously as he exited the van.

"I don't know Steph, but they're not here now. Let's hurry up in case they are coming this way." Eva said in a loud whisper to the young boy.

Mila got out of the van last and shut the door behind her. She looked up and down the street and then looked at Eva, as if silently asking which way they should go.

As if responding to the silent question, Eva said "Come on. This way. We're going into the ally on the side of the building." She took off and both children ran quietly behind her.

They ran past the large windows in the front of the antique shop and then turned the corner into the ally on the side of the building. Despite it being the middle of the day, the alley was dark, stuck in a everlasting shadow, cast by the tall buildings to either side.

The three of them hurried down the alley until they got to the chain link fence that separated this ally from the ones behind it. They could go either left or right unless they wanted to climb the fence.

They went right, following the directions that Samuel had given them and after just a few steps they saw the door. The doorway was at the foot of a very small concrete staircase going down below street level in the back of the building.

Eva waved for Steph and Mila to follow and hurried down the steps. Once there, she looked over the door and found a keypad to the side of it. She entered the code that Samuel had given her and the door slowly swung inward. She rushed the children into the darkness beyond the door and then stepped in herself, pulling the door shut behind her.

Once inside, Eva felt around for the lights and before she found the switch, they came on and illuminated the small basement room. Eva nervously looked around the room as she pulled her pistol out. She quickly scanned from one end of the room to the other, to see who had been waiting for them and had turned the lights on when they entered. Then her eyes landed on her son Steph standing in front of a light switch on the opposite side of the room.

The young boy was grinning proudly. Eva let out a sigh of relief and tucked the pistol back into the waistband of her jeans. The children and their mother looked around, taking in everything they could about this strange place. The basement room wasn't big. It was one open space with what appeared to be a bathroom off to the side and a couple closets on the other side of the room. No other rooms seemed to branch off from the open floor. There was a small table with two chairs off to the left, in front of a free-standing old stove and a large warehouse style sink.

On the opposite side of the small room was a small couch facing a wall that was covered with pictures and files and newspaper clippings. Behind the couch was a small cot, with two blankets on it.

Eva walked over to stare at the covered wall. She saw several locations marked on maps that were posted on the wall and newspaper clippings about murders, politicians, new laws and Camacho. To Eva, it looked like Samuel had captured every moment that the media had mentioned Camacho or one of his businesses and had pasted them on the wall.

As she stared at all of the information, trying to soak it all up, she thought to herself that everything on the wall must be related to Camacho in some way. She noticed that the adjacent wall had one small rectangular window towards the top of the wall and beneath the window was a lone end table that had a lone framed picture, resting on top of it.

Eva walked to the wall and stood on her tip toes to try to peer out the window. She was able to make out the side alley they had just walked through. The window seemed to be sitting just barely above ground level in the alley. It would allow her to see the feet of anyone walking down the alley, but not much more.

She turned her attention to the picture on the end table. It was Samuel, but he was wearing a black suit, with a white shirt and a black tie. It the picture there was a beautiful dark-skinned woman with bright green eyes that was standing next to him, wearing a formal black gown. He had his arm around the woman's waist and in front of them both stood two children. There was one boy and one girl, that appeared to be close to the same ages as Mila and Steph. The children were dressed like their parents in the picture, with the older daughter wearing a black formal gown and the younger son wearing a black suit, with a white shirt and black tie, just like Samuel wore in the picture. All four of them were smiling in the picture.

Under the framed picture that stood on the end table, was a folded newspaper clipping. Eva, gently lifted the framed family photo and picked up the newspaper clipping. She set the picture back on the end table and unfolded the piece of newspaper.

The headline itself startled her as she read it. It said 'Woman and her two children found dismembered in an abandoned warehouse that exploded. The remains of their body parts were found nailed to what was left of the walls of the warehouse.' At this time, they remain unidentified.

The article went on to describe that the warehouse had exploded, from what was originally thought to be gas leak, until the flames were put out and the bodies were found.

Eva gasped and put her hand to her mouth. She set the article down and stared at her children. She was terrified by what had apparently happened to Samuel's family. It made her terrified for the safety of her own family. It also made her wonder, what had Samuel been involved in to make them come after his family like that.

She tried not to think about it, but what she had read had scarred her. It had terrified her. It also helped her realize why

Samuel had gone out of his way to save them. The similarities between her family and the family he lost were too much alike to be overlooked.

Eva walked over to the other side of the room where the small table sat near the stove and sink and noticed two old filing cabinets. She opened the top drawer on one of them and found a tea pot and a box of tea. She went on to inspect the other drawers and found some dishes, pots and pans, some dry noodles, and the bottom drawer under an old cutting board, she found a large pistol.

She left everything in place except the tea pot. That she pulled out, filled with water from the sink and set on the stove. She figured a hot cup of tea would be good for all three of them.

As she sat on one of the two chairs waiting on the water to boil, she noticed both her children staring at the picture. She heard Mila talking to Steph in hushed tones and listened in.

"That's Samuel's family Steph. They're all dead now." Mila said.

"Why? What happened to them?" Steph asked his older sister with compassion in his eyes.

"Samuel stopped the bad men's illegal operations in another country Steph. That's what Samuel used to do, he stopped bad men from doing bad things in other countries before those things hurt people here, in our country. The bad men found out and hurt his family." Mila said it all in not much more of whisper and stared into her younger brother's eyes to ensure he understood.

Eva gasped from across the room.

"How do you know all that Mila?" Eva said out loud.

Mila jumped slightly startled by not just her mother's abrupt question, but also because she obviously thought that she had spoken quietly enough to keep her mother from hearing.

Mila took a deep breath, seeming to calm herself from the start and turned around to face her mother. "I don't know mom, I just do. I'm sorry mom, I can't explain it. Sometimes I just know things and feel things mom." Mila said it all with a hint of frustration, like she had been questioned numerous times about this.

Then Steph turned around and spoke up. "She always knows things mom. Mila knows everything. She knows when things will happen, before they happen mom. She knows when Dads coming home late or not at all. She just always knows mom." Steph said it all so earnestly and with a tone that suggested that he had known this for some time.

"Why haven't either of you told me and your dad about this?" Eva asked her children.

"Just, well, I knew you'd ask how, and I don't know how mom. I just know things. Sometimes I know scary things and I wish that I didn't, but I do mom. I can't turn it off." Mila said it was a sadness in her voice that made Eva stop with her questions.

Eva just sat, staring at her children with love in her eyes and reached out her arms, still sitting in the chair. In response to their mothers, gesture, both children walked across the room and hugged their mom.

Eva embraced them both and thought to herself "How did I miss this before now? How long has she had to deal with this on her own?"

The three of them hugged for what seemed like forever and then the teapot started to whistle. Eva stood, and sat Steph in the chair she had been sitting in. She gestured for Mila to take the other chair at the small table. She fished two old coffee mugs and one glass out of the file cabinets and poured boiling water into each cup. She put the pot, still over half full of boiling water back onto the hot burner of the stove and dropped tea bag into each cup. Then she squeezed honey into the cups from a half empty plastic bottle of honey that she'd found in the drawer with the tea.

None of them said a word, they just waited for their tea to cool, and all stared across the room at the picture.

A few minutes later they were sipping their tea in silence. When they had finished their tea, Eva got the children comfortable on the small couch, with one of the blankets from the cot.

She sat back across the room in one of the chairs and continued to study the papers covering the wall. About an hour later, Steph had fallen asleep, and it looked as though Mila was dozing off, until her eye's suddenly popped open wide and she jumped up from the couch. She looked over at Eva with wide eyes that seemed to be filled with tears and said "Mom, the bad people are here."

Eva looked from the painful expression on her daughter's face to the small window just in time to see two pairs of booted feet pass by. She frantically looked around the room, trying to come up with some type of plan that would save her and her children. As she racked her brain to come up with something, she found herself thinking the same thought over and over. "Damn you Vic. You should be here with us! We need you Vic!"

CHAPTER 26:
HOTEL 'THE DELUXE'

Camacho and Olo, along with four heavily armed members of Camacho's security detail, pulled up to Hotel 'The Deluxe' in the large white SUV. As the SUV pulled up in front of the doors and stopped, the six heavily armed men in front of the building stiffened to attention.

These men, like the men that rode with Camacho and Olo were not members of street gangs. These were Camacho's personal men. He had dozens of them working for him, most were ex-mercenaries. They all wore black military style uniforms and were always heavily armed.

The two men in the front of the SUV got out and opened the doors to the back, letting Olo, Camacho and the other two security officers out of the vehicle. The men started towards the front doors, when Olo stopped and grabbed Camacho by the arm.

Camacho turned around, to see why the Na'gee warrior had stopped him and Olo said "You go ahead. I will be 'checking on something' first. Make sure the accommodations are ready to welcome the Na'gee tribe to their new home." As Olo finished speaking, two Na'gee warriors walked out of the front of the Hotel. They ignored everyone there and just looked at Olo.

Olo gestured to the large white SUV they had all just got out of, and the warriors walked past everyone and got into the driver's seat and the passenger seat of the vehicle. They seemed not to even realize that anyone else in front of the Hotel existed.

Olo looked back at Camacho again and said "I will take this transportation. Ensure we are ready for the tribe Camacho!."

With that Olo turned and got into the back of the SUV and it sped away. Camacho grumbled under his breath, obviously frustrated that he had just been assigned 'host duty', while Olo attended to other secretive matters that he hadn't bothered to share with Camacho. For a split second, Camacho wondered would his rank and power be yanked away from him after the Na'gee had secured their position in this world, but he quickly blew the thoughts off.

"I'm too valuable. They couldn't run this world without me. They wouldn't dream of cutting me out." Camacho thought to himself. He then turned to the men with him and said "Well let's go dammit! To the roof." He directed this to the four men that had ridden with him and Olo. Then as the four men started to head inside, Camacho turned to one of the six men in front of the building.

"No one comes in, no matter what. Let the gangs setup a

perimeter, but you and your men are the real defense, they're just distractions. Is everyone in positions around the building already?"

The large man, with a blond flat top and a goatee that covered his square jaw responded to Camacho's barrage of questions. "Yes sir. We've got them at all critical points around the building and positioned in the basement, parking deck and key locations across various floors sir."

"Good. Who's running point on securing the building?" Camacho asked the man.

"Captain Vinco, sir. He took the liberty of cleaning out the tenants and taking command of the existing building staff. Well, most of them, a few examples had to be made." The security officer stopped talking, with a look on his face like he thought that he may have said too much.

Camacho seemed to contemplate the update for a moment and then said. "Cleaned out the tenants huh? What'd he do with the 'trash'?"

"We stored it in the boiler room for now sir." The man said in response.

"Good enough. Is the roof secure? Anyone coming through yet?" Camacho asked.

At this question, the security officer seemed to hesitate. After a moments pause, and look of impatience that had appeared on Camacho's face, he answered. "A handful of them have 'come through' sir. They've got huge sniper rifles and took positions around the roof. None of them said a word." The security officer looked very uncomfortable when talking about the Na'gee.

These were hardened mercenaries. Most had seen battle in multiple countries. Very little unnerved them, but the Na'gee warriors definitely seemed to have them on edge.

Camacho didn't mind. He liked everyone on edge. He felt it kept them all sharper.

"Good enough. Tell Captain Vinco to meet me on the roof. We're heading up to greet our guests." Camacho said. As he started to walk away with the four men he had arrived with, he stopped and turned back. "Oh and tell him to bring a few members of the staff with him. These visitors are big on ritual, we'll need to greet them with a sacrifice."

Camacho didn't wait for a response, although he did enjoy the disturbed look he saw on the security officer's face as he walked into the front doors of the hotel.

As Camacho and his entourage made their way through the massive lobby of the hotel, he looked around, silently judging the security detail. He caught glimpses of at least twelve men, and assumed there were more that he didn't see.

While Camacho noticed a handful of bullet holes here and there and a few blood streaks on the floor, where bodies had been drug out of the room, he was overall pleased that his men had taken the hotel and left very little signs of the hostile takeover.

"It makes things a lot smoother when all the damn cops are tied up." He thought to himself as he approached the elevator.

When the grand elevator doors opened he was greeted by

Captain Vinco and two of his men. Camacho referred to all of these men as 'security', but there was no doubt that these were soldiers. Captain Vinco was a lean man that looked to be from the islands. He had light brown skin and wore his hair in tightly pulled back braids. He had a pencil thin mustache and a goatee that also extended into a long tight braid.

To Camacho the man looked more like a pirate than a mercenary, but Vinco ran a tight ship and kept his men in line. He lashed out violently for any breaks in protocol or carelessness.

Camacho generally let his private security ranks decide for themselves who would run what jobs and who would be point. On a few occasions he knew that leadership had been taken through bloodshed, not given, but he didn't much care. He almost preferred it this way. As long as they did what he said and handled the jobs the way he said to handle them, he was good with them running their interpersonal affairs however they saw fit.

Camacho was always a fan of the 'survival of the fittest' motto, so he appreciated their approach to hierarchy. Despite his comfort with letting them choose who would be assigned which of his jobs, he was pleased that Vinco was running point on this one. This one was too important for just anyone.

"Pleasure to see you sir. We have the roof covered to protect against internal and external interruptions and have strategically placed assets in several key locations. We are prepared to greet your guests and keep them safe or… otherwise sir." Captain Vinco said. He made it clear that all Camacho had to do was give the word and his men would take out the Na'gee just as quick as they'd protect them. Camacho liked this. He enjoyed his position of power that the Na'gee had helped him achieve, but he also enjoyed having his own force that was loyal to him.

"Good. We will greet them and ensure they can adjust to their new accommodations Vinco." Camacho said with an evil grin that seemed to suggest 'for now'.

Then Camacho added. "Did you get a few members of the staff for me?" We will need them on the roof Vinco.

"Yes sir. My men are holding two up there now. Wasn't sure what you were looking for with a sacrifice, but I figured young and vibrant was better. That's what you got sir. One man and one woman." Vinco said respectfully. He, unlike his man at the front door, wasn't bothered at all about a sacrifice. Based on his reasoning behind the selection of staff members, it sounded like Vinco may have done things like this before.

"I knew I liked this one." Camacho thought. Then he said "Nice Vinco. Let's go to the roof and greet our guests then."

Vinco nodded at his man that had been holding the elevator doors open during the discussion and the man selected the roof top button. Camacho and his four-man entourage boarded the elevator and the eight men headed to the roof.

The elevators opened to a massive roof. The roof had one very large flat level and then an elevated platform that was a helipad on the opposite side from the elevator. Directly to the right of the elevator doors was the door to the stairs. There was another stairway on the opposite side of the roof by the helipad, but only one elevator.

In the center of the roof, there were four Na'gee warriors holding their circular stone looking talisman together forming a large blur. Camacho knew this to be a path to the 'other side'. He knew that time was limited, as it would not be safe for the Na'gee to gather and attempt to migrate through the path in the dark. The 'other side' was not like this world. It could not be traversed after dark by human tribes.

Even in the daytime, there were risks gathering this many Na'gee together in the open. There were other human tribes they warred with, the ancient ones and the predators of the 'other side' that all stayed very active during the daylight hours.

Camacho looked at his watch and figured they had about four hours or so, to get the tribe through the path. He knew there would be days of migration to follow, but the key families and warriors were to come through first, to ensure their new home was secured.

Camacho surveyed the roof and counted about ten Na'gee warriors with large sniper rifles, posted in strategic positions around the roof. They seemed to be looking diligently for anything that may attack them from the air.

"They're scarred from the terrors of the 'other side'. They'll go crazy here without having to constantly fight to survive." Camacho thought.

There were about ten of his men scattered about the edges of the roof. They seemed to be positioned in between each Na'gee warrior. Camacho knew this was not accidental and found it humorous. His men also had sniper rifles, and at least two of them had rocket launchers leaning up against the wall of the roof edge next to them.

In the middle of the roof, were four more of Camachos men and two more Na'gee warriors that weren't part of the efforts to keep the large path open. The four soldiers were holding staff members by the arms, each pair held one staff member, who seemed to too scared to struggle.

There was a young man that couldn't have been much older than his mid-twenties. He had dark well combed hair, dark eyes a clean-shaven face and seemed fit. He wore a well pressed concierge uniform. The other staff member was a young woman of similar age. She was dressed in maid's garments, was young, vibrant and had long blond hair. She held tears in her eyes and shook with fear.

Again, Camacho found himself pleased with Vinco and his selections.

The Na'gee approached Camacho and he made a slight hand gesture to them, which they returned. He pointed to the two staff members and said, "we shall honor the Na'gee and let their first footsteps in this new world be trekked through the blood of sacrifice!" Camacho addressed the two Na'gee in front of him but shouted it loud enough for everyone on the large roof to hear.

The two warriors in front of him nodded, as did every other Na'gee who was posted around the edges of the roof. The only Na'gee that didn't acknowledge Camacho's loud statement, were the four holding the path open. Those four were covered in beads of sweat and seemed to be weakening.

This was natural. Camacho knew, as did the other warriors, that traveling a path was simple enough to a Na'gee trained on the use of the talisman, but holding a path open for extended periods of time, especially a large path, would slowly drain the life out of a human. No one knew why, it just did. These men would not be expected to make it. They were sacrificing their lives to migrate their people to safer lands.

Camacho knew there would be more like them in the days to come, until the full migration was complete.

He shook these thoughts from his head and approached the two staff members, who started squirming as he got nearer. The two Na'gee warriors walked with him on either side.

Camacho reached under his untucked silk shirt and pulled a long dagger from a sheath, that remained hidden beneath his shirt. In slicing motion that was so fast, it appeared as nothing more than a blur, he slit both their throats.

The two Na'gee warriors approached, and each took one of the victims from the soldiers still holding the bodies and they drug them over before the blur. They each held a body under one arm and used their other arm to point the bleeding neck wound to the ground.

In unison they almost did a slow ritualistic dance as they painted the ground with blood. They did not stop until the bodies stopped leaking blood from their necks. Then, still holding the bodies under their arms, like a tucked football, they walked to the edge of the roof and hurled them over carelessly.

"You have honored the Na'gee adopted one. You have done well. Stay and greet our brothers and sisters with us."

One of the warriors said to Camacho. With that, Camacho and the two warriors stepped onto the blood in front of the blur and waited together.

Chapter 27:
"What Have You Got Us Into?"

"Where the hell did you take us Dante?" Vic said loudly as he looked around the small, cluttered apartment building hallway that the three men stood in.

"Samuel said get us as close to the Hotel as I could, but to stay out of the street. This was the first place I thought of Vic. It's only a couple blocks from the Hotel… I think." Dante said, trying to explain himself.

"This is the only freaking place you could think of?! Where the hell are we? Did you take us to freaking crack house Dante?" Vic said, assaulting the young man with questions as he paced in the dirty hallway.

A homeless man who had been laying in the corner of the hallway sat up and said "Why all the yelling man? Hey, do you have a dollar?" He was looking at Vic whose pacing had taken him closest to the man.

"A dollar?! How about a freaking boot?! Vic shouted.

The man scurried further down the hall and didn't look back.

Before Vic could continue his rant, Samuel who had been looking over the edge of the hallway railing, up and down at the floors above and below them turned and addressed Dante.

"You did good Dante. This is perfect." Samuel said. Then he turned to Vic "He took us to the abandoned building on 31st Ave. It's scheduled to be demolished. We're only two blocks from the Hotel and there's no one here to see us."

Vic nodded, with realization washing over his face and looked around with what appeared to be a fresh perspective, until his eyes rested on the homeless man that had scurried to the far end of the hallway. The man had his manhood in his hand and was pissing over the banister down to the ground level.

Vic turned back to Samuel and said "Well, that son of bitch saw us."

Samuel ignored Vic and the peeing homeless man and started heading to the stairs. Dante and Vic followed, and the three men made their way down to the ground floor and out of the old ran down building.

Once outside, the men hit the sidewalk and headed towards Hotel 'The Deluxe'. No one had to say a word about it, but they all kept their heads on a swivel, looking this way and that way constantly.

The city was in turmoil. It seemed that the explosions across town and the attacks on the police had instigated a full-blown riot. People were looting shops and destroying everything in sight. Several cars were on fire in the middle of the street.

As the trio passed the next alley, they saw three men dragging a screaming woman back towards the dark shadows at the end of the alley, every now and then one of them would kick her.

"Fuck this! I'll be back." Vic said in a voice that sounded like his bottled-up anger at the chaos around him had reached its boiling point. The tall man took off running down the alley and leaped in the air, using his momentum and his entire body to throw a flying punch at the closest man. His fist connected with the man's face and Vic felt bone shatter under his knuckles. The man collapsed instantly. Vic didn't know if he was dead or alive, and he didn't care.

The sudden attack caught the other two off guard for a moment, but now they had their eyes on Vic. They let go of the woman, who ran off screaming and faced Vic.

"We were gonna have fun with her fool! Now we gonna have fun with you instead!" One of the men yelled as he swung his right fist towards Vic's face. Vic stepped to his left, easily dodging the wild punch and then caught the man's arm with both hands and broke it over his knee.

The man screamed in pain, as his sidekick pulled a long knife. In a speed of movement, Vic lunged at the man and grabbed the hand he held the knife in. Using both his hands, Vic turned the knife back towards the man holding it and shoved it into his chest. As the man, slumped lifeless to the ground, Vic heard the man whose arm he had broken running away, back toward the street.

"No you don't, you sick degenerate!" Vic yelled, as he reached down, pulled the knife from the now dead man's chest and threw it at the running man. The knife sunk into the middle of the fleeing man's back and hit the ground, sliding to a stop in front of Dante and Samuel who stood watching.

Vic walked back up to the two men, who had apparently watched the entire incident and said "Alright, lets go. I know we got bigger fish to fry, I just can't watch sick shit like that without doing something."

Samuel glanced at Vic and the dead man at their feet and without a word, he turned and continued walking down the street. Dante and Vic followed. Dante seeming unphased at the violence he'd just witnessed.

As they walked, Vic leaned over and said quietly to Dante "You thought you were the only one who did knives, didn't ya?"

Dante just shook his head and cracked a half smile in response.

The three men didn't make it much further before they noticed that the chaos and violence around them had intensified. They seemed to be in the heart of the riot. People fought around them. Then one large man, who wore no shirt and was beating another man with a baseball bat in the middle of the street looked up at the three of them and pointed with his bat.

"Looks like we got a few wise guys walking our streets

boys!" The large shirtless man yelled.

He had a huge belly and giant arms to match, with bushy curly hair and a thick beard. When he yelled, four other equally large men stopped the various acts of violence they had been preoccupied with and all begin walking towards the three companions.

Vic turned to face them, with an evil grin and Dante pulled a dagger out in each hand. Both men jumped at the gunfire that rang out dangerously close to their ears. They looked back in unison, to see Samuel re-holstering his two pistols. Both men calmed at the realization that it was Samuel that had fired. They turned back to the men that had been approaching and all five, lay dead in the street, each had a single bullet in the center of their foreheads.

Samuel kept walking and Vic and Dante hurried to keep up.

The chaos around them didn't stop, but no one seemed to pay them attention again. As they walked, Vic spoke up. "Samuel, what's this ghost agent stuff? What are you man?" he asked.

Samuel glanced back over his shoulder, just long enough to look Vic in the eyes, then turned his head back and kept walking as he responded "I'm exactly what I told you I was Vic. I'm a man whose family was murdered, and I intend to murder the man responsible, and everyone associated with him." Samuel paused, then continued "That is all I am now. That is all that matters Vic."

"Yeah, I believe you Samuel and I'm with you man, but the way they let you into the military base. This special unit attacking us, calling you ghost agent 17 or whatever. What have you got us into?" Vic asked, trying once more to get Samuel to talk.

"They remember who I once was Vic. That is not me anymore. You've gotten yourself into the same mission that I have. You agreed to this, and you did it to keep your family from the same dreadful fate that mine endured. We're in the same thing now that we were in when this started. We just haven't finished it yet." Samuel said it all cold and monotone. It wasn't much of an explanation, but it was enough for Vic. It made him remember exactly what the stakes were. It reminded him that these evil bastards they were heading to face had tried to murder his family too.

The reminder made Vic not care so much about Samuel or his past. Samuel was right. He knew what he was in the middle of, and he knew he could count on Samuel to carry his weight. Vic decided that was good enough for him and kept walking.

As the three men rounded the corner, the saw the chaos that had surrounded them before, did not extend itself to the perimeter of the hotel. There were at least twenty cars in view parked every ten feet or so and they looked like they circled the entire building. Around each vehicle was a handful of gangbangers, that looked to be 'Gridlox'.

Samuel, Dante and Vic, stopped in their tracks and slightly eased back to the corner, they had just rounded. Outside of this apparent guard around the hotel, the streets were completely empty.

Closer to the buildings entrance, there were heavily armed

men in black military style uniforms.

"Those are all ex mercs. They're Camacho's personal security. They know what they're doing." Vic said quietly.

"We need to avoid wasting time with these men and alerting our key targets to our arrival. The main entrances will be a fire fight and re enforcements will keep coming. We'll try to get into the parking deck. Each level there accesses the corresponding floor on the building." Samuel said it in hushed tones, still staring around the corner. It was hard for the other men, to know if was actually talking to them or just talking through his plan to himself.

Samuel finally tore his gaze away from the hotel to face Vic and Dante. "Lets circle around the back of this building and come back to the street. It should take us towards the front left of the parking deck, we'll figure out how to get in from there. Come on." Samuel said it and took off back the way they had come, staying close to the building they intended to circle.

He never looked back to see if the other men were following, but he knew they were. They were all in this together now. "At least for now we're together." Samuel thought as he rubbed the cut on his neck from where Dante had held the knife.

As the three men came around the other side of the building, they saw the parking deck to the hotel. The parking deck attached to the hotel on the back and wrapped around about a quarter of the sides of the large building.

The parking deck was ten stories high, and each floor had an entrance to the corresponding floor of the hotel. Between the three companions and the parking deck were more of the 'Gridlox' gang members leaning on their cars that were spaced evenly around the building.

All three men stood in the shadows of the neighboring building watching the gang members across the street. They watched and waited, looking for an opening that would allow them to get to the parking deck undetected. After several long moments, Samuel's deep voice broke the silence.

"It doesn't look like we're going to be able to sneak past them, unless you can teleport into the parking deck from here Dante." Samuel said. At this comment, Samuel and Vic both looked at Dante, who had been strangely quiet ever since they left the tank.

Dante looked up at them and seemed to snap back to the present from whatever deep thoughts he had been lost in. "Huh? What?" Dante asked.

"He asked if you can zap us over to the parking deck from here man." Vic said impatiently.

Dante looked at the parking deck across the street as if seeing it for the first time. Then shook his head as he responded. "The side walls are too high, I can't see where I need to go."

The side walls he was referring to ran about three feet tall all around the open-air parking deck. It still left wide openings between the wall and the ceiling of each floor but was clearly built high enough to prevent someone from leaning over and falling to an unfortunate end. They also clearly prevented Dante from getting a good enough look at the parking deck to be able to see where he needed to teleport them to. They could get a glimpse of the parking deck ceilings that were covered with steel rafters, but they couldn't see the floor at all.

Samuel turned back to face the other two men and said "Ok. It doesn't look like we've got a way to sneak past them from what I can tell. Unless you see something different Vic, I think we're going to have to take one post out quick and quiet and try to get to the deck before the surrounding groups notice us. What do you think?"

At this, Vic turned back towards the building. He paused only a second before responding. "They're on it. Too tight and the streets too quiet. We'll definitely have to take one group out to make it Samuel and if we're not quick, we could be fighting our way through the lot of them." Vic said it all casually.

"Ok. The closest group has two men leaning on the hood of the car and two other men inside. Dante can you get inside the car?" Samuel asked.

Dante, who was still peering at the gang members on guard duty, shook his head and answered softly. "I can't see inside the car to get in there Samuel. Even with the windows down, I can't see what I'd be teleporting into. I can get to the two men on the hood though. I'd have to appear in front of them, but I can take them out before they know what hit them." Dante said it more coldly then he usually sounded and both Vic and Samuel noticed it.

This time it was Vic that spoke up. "If we used guns every gang banger around the building will hear us, not to mention the damn mercs up front. We got to move quick and quiet.

Give me one of those fancy knives Dante. I'll take the guy leaning out the passenger side window as soon as you appear in front of the two on the hood. We'll both go for the guy in the driver seat as quick as we can. If he gets a shot of or yells, we're fighting our way in through all of them." Vic said it like there was no discussion and then abruptly stopped and stared at both of the men with him.

"Ok." Samuel said.

"Shit." Dante mumbled as he handed Vic one of his daggers. "I want that back Vic." He added.

"Sure thing bud, I'll even wipe the gangbanger guts off it for ya." Vic said with a smile.

With the plan agreed upon, Dante and Vic eased around the corner.

"You ready Vic?" Dante asked in a cold shallow voice.

"Damn the kid has definitely changed" Vic thought. Despite his thoughts, he said "Let's get em' Dante."

In an instant Dante was gone and Vic was running towards the car with the knife in his hand. Dante appeared in front of the two men leaning on the hood and slashed both their throats at the same time, with the knife he held in each hand.

Has Dante slashed, Vic hurled the knife in his hand catching the passenger who had his arm hanging out the passenger window, in the neck. The man clutched at his throat and then fell forward.

Dante was moving around the driver's side, as Vic reached

the passenger door and ripped the knife free from the dead passengers neck.

They were both too slow. The man in the driver's seat didn't start shooting or yelling, he just hit the horn on the steering wheel and held it in. By the time Dante got to the open widow and slashed the man's throat, there were several 'Gridlox' running to the car from the down the street on both sides.

The first couple men in each group dropped clutching their chests as an eruption of gun fire came from Samuel running across the street with a pistol in each hand.

"To the parking deck! Move! Move! Move!" Samuel yelled.

Dante turned towards the deck and teleported to the doorway into the parking deck about twelve feet away from them. As soon as he disappeared from the spot by the car a large caliber bullet struck the vehicle in the exact spot where he had been standing. Vic looked up from the other side of the car and saw the glint of the sunlight off of the sniper's rifles on the roof.

"Snipers!" Vic yelled as he leaped over the hood of the car. A bullet struck the spot where he had been standing. Vic hit the other side of the vehicle and ran towards the entrance, leaving Samuel who was running about ten feet behind him and still firing at the gang bangers, who were now shooting back.

Samuel made it to the doorway and dove inside, landing next to Dante who was standing there.

"What the fuck Dante?! Get him out of there before a

sniper takes him out man!" Vic yelled.

Dante looked like Vic had snapped him out of a trance again and said "Oh shit".

Dante quickly peeked around the corner and was gone. He appeared right in front of Samuel, grabbed his arm and both men were instantly back inside the entrance to the parking deck, leaving a snipers bullet imbedded in the street where Samuel had been only seconds before.

As the men appeared inside, Vic rolled into the doorway and let his large .45 caliber pistol explode into the ranks of quickly approaching 'Gridlox'. Several men fell and the others dover for cover, forgoing their pursuit for the moment.

Vic rolled back inside the parking deck and saw that Samuel was shaking off the dizzy spell from teleporting.

Vic yelled "The stairs! Across the deck! Let's move!"

All three men ran for the stairs.

Chapter 28:
Intercepting the Target

That's him, Agent 17, and he's in a damn fire fight with the damn gang bangers on patrol." Halbred said. At the sound of gunfire, he had shifted his binoculars towards the side of the hotel they were surveilling.

"Wasn't he supposed to be working with the gang bangers blowing shit up Commander?" Fuse asked with clear confusion.

"Yeah, well he sure as shit ain't with them now. Time to get to the bottom of this. We're sticking to the mission and getting to this Agent 17. Then we're freeing any hostages in the hotel and taking out these damn terrorists." Halbred with his normal intensity. Most people thought the large red headed man was always angry, his unit just thought he was Halbred.

"Fuse, grab the ropes we're going down there and catching them in the parking decks. Radio, Bird, keep watch, keep us posted and be ready to get airborne and cover that roof full of snipers with lead. Everybody got it?!" Halbred asked sharply.

He was answered by a chorus of "Yes sir".

In no time, Halbred and Fuse were repelling down the side of the building headed straight for the street that the companions had just run across. As they made their way down, Halbred barked into earpiece comms unit he wore.

"Flutter, you, Diggs and Roid need to hurry your asses up! We're engaging these gangbangers and headed to parking deck to intercept our target. There's nothing stealth about this mission now, so make your way up through the basement, securing floors on the way. We'll try to stop them on the second or third floor of the parking deck. Hurry!" As soon as Halbred stopped shouting orders, the comms unit crackled, and he heard Flutter reply.

"Diggs is getting us through the wall into the boiler room below the basement now boss. We'll be in asap. See you pronto sir" she said.

Halbred quit talking into the comms unit, seconds before his feet hit the concrete. Fuse landed at almost the same exact time as him. The two men simultaneously shook their long ropes free, from the anchors they had set at the top of the building that made it safer to repel down.

As the ropes fell, both men rapidly wrapped them around their arms. Neither rope ever touched the ground. They fastened them to their belts and took off at a run towards the front of the building, directly across from where the three companions had entered the parking deck. It was actually the same path that the companions had taken. They both rounded the corner with their assault rifles ready and saw what appeared to be roughly a dozen 'Gridlox' surrounding the entrance to the parking deck. The gang members were all easing forward with guns ready.

Fuse, waited to follow Halbred's lead, but he didn't have to wait long. Halbred, didn't hesitate. He opened fire with his automatic assault rifle and began dropping the gang bangers from behind.

As soon as Fuse saw Halbred open fire, he joined. Squeezing the trigger of his large assault rifle. In seconds there were no 'Gridlox' left standing near the parking deck entrance.

The two men surveyed the street and noticed large groups of 'Gridlox' rushing towards them from about one hundred yards out on either side. Fuse looked questioningly at Halbred.

Halbred quickly responded to the wordless question. "No time. Primary objective first." He was running through the entrance to the parking deck, before he finished speaking with Fuse on his heels.

The two men immediately noticed the door to the staircase closing across the parking deck. It was clear that the door led to the stairs that would lead to the multiple levels of the parking deck. Neither man spoke and neither slowed down. There was not need, they'd been through too many missions together. It was clear where they would be going and what needed to be done. They often knew what the other one would do before they did it. It was the same for the entire unit. They all knew each other inside and out.

The men hit the door, and bolted up the steps, clearing several at a time. As they arrived at the second-floor door, they slowed down drastically and eased out the door cautiously. They saw the three men heading across the floor towards the door that entered the hotel's second floor.

The three men were about fifteen feet in front of them, moving cautiously across the lot. Fuse once again waited to follow Halbred's lead.

"Agent 17!" Halbred shouted with his rifle aimed at the backs of the three men. They all stopped in their tracks and turned around to face him in unison.

"You see what's going on around you Halbred. Don't be a fool. I'm not the threat. That must be clear now." Samuel said calmly in his deep voice.

"It's not that simple 17!" Halbred barked. "We're going to take care of these terrorists, but you've got some explaining to do. Starting with, if this isn't your doing than how are you involved?" Halbred.

"Fuck this! We don't have time for this shit!" Vic said.

Vic's comment was all it took. Dante was no longer standing next to them; he was suddenly behind Halbred dragging a dagger across the large man's throat. Despite Halbred's skin looking normal, it wasn't. As the knife drug across his throat, it made a screeching sound like metal on metal.

Fuse, cringed at the noise and stared at his commander being attacked. Knowing a knife couldn't hurt Halbred, but still feeling obligated to intervene. His hesitation and momentary distraction was all Samuel needed.

Samuel cleared the fifteen feet between them in a flash

and crashed into Fuse, knocking him to the ground and leaving him frozen there. Samuel stood to face Halbred and was shocked to see, that the old bearded, red-haired soldier had not only survived the throat slashing maneuver from Dante, but he had quickly turned and punched Dante in the face so hard that the small man went flying into the closed staircase door behind him.

Vic leaped at Halbred, in an attempt to catch him off guard, but the seasoned soldier was ready. He pivoted clear of the attempted tackle and swung his right knee up, catching Vic in the gut as the tall man came down.

As Vic landed doubled over and at a loss of breath, Halbred finished the swift movement with a heavy two-handed blow to the back of Vic's head.

Samuel touched Halbred's arm. "We don't have time for this, and I'd prefer not to kill these men." Samuel thought as he touched the soldier to freeze him in place.

Halbred turned to face him with a surprised look on his face. "Did you just fucking poke me with your finger?!" He yelled at Samuel as he swung his right fist and punched Samuel in the face.

Samuel staggered backward, seeing stars and shocked at the turn of events. He had never run into anyone he couldn't freeze before. This was new territory. He didn't understand why it didn't work. He didn't have time to figure it out though, as his thoughts were interrupted by a powerful right hook to the side of his head. Everything went black and Samuel crumpled to the ground.

CHAPTER 29:
THE SAME SIDE

"What the hell happened?" Samuel thought as he opened his eyes and attempted to get a sense of his surroundings. He was propped against the tire of a car. Vic and Dante were to the left of him, peering over the trunk of the vehicle and to his right were Fuse and Halbred peering over the hood of the vehicle.

Vic noticed him looking around first and put a finger to his lips, signaling for Samuel to remain quiet.

Then in a hushed whisper, Vic said. "There's at least twenty of them out there. The red-haired soldier threw you over his shoulder and bolted behind the car, when they started coming through from inside the building. The skinny soldier with him rushed us over here with him fast. We don't think anyone saw us."

"These aren't the gang bangers, these are the mercs. This is serious Samuel." Vic added, still whispering.

Samuel glanced around, pulling himself together and then looked strangely at Halbred and Fuse to his right.

In a hushed voice, he addressed Halbred "How did he move?" He nodded towards Fuse when he asked the question.

Halbred, looked Samuel in the eyes, seeming to decide if he would answer the question or not and then replied. "Not sure what you did to him 17, but once I KO'd you, he jumped to his feet."

Then Halbred added. "You and your friends would be toast if we didn't get you to cover as they we're pouring in. The way I see it, you and me aren't finished 17, but we're all on the same side until we free the hostages and take this building back."

Samuel stared back at the large red-haired man, still baffled by the fact that he had been unable to freeze him. Samuel was also angry that he let himself be so surprised, that he was taken off guard and knocked out.

"Well, I guess now I know that if I'm knocked out, anyone I froze is freed. Interesting that it doesn't free them when I sleep, but it does this way." Samuel thought to himself.

His thoughts were interrupted by Halbred. "Well? What say you 17?" Halbred asked impatiently.

"It's Samuel, I'm not 17 anymore and I agree." Samuel said coldly as he turned to peer over the car they were all using as a hiding spot.

He saw what Vic had described. At least twenty of the mercenaries who were dressed in black fatigues. They were combing the deck. They were communicating on radios and based on what Samuel could hear, they had men combing multiple decks at the same time.

As if that hadn't been enough, Samuel watched about ten 'Gridlox' pour in from the staircase door.

A lean, pale skinned man addressed them harshly. "You all, stay with us and send the rest of your guys to the third and fourth floors! We're combing three at a time."

The large muscular 'Gridlox' in front of all the others, wore a white tank top, and baggy black pants. He carried a sub machine gun and had a pistol tucked into his waist band. He stared at the lean mercenary coldly, evidently unimpressed with the smaller man and said, "who the fuck are you?"

In response the lean man, covered the distance between them and was in the gang members face. "I'm fucking Lieutenant Riker and I'm in charge of everything here!" The lean soldier screamed into the face of the large 'Gridlox'.

"You ain't shit. We work for Vinco or Camacho." The gang member said challengingly.

The lean man was visibly infuriated. He yelled harshly again "Vinco is running point for now. He's the one that ain't shit! This should be my unit! This will be my unit... and Camacho is just a mark paying us!!!" Lieutenant Riker shouting it so close to the gang members face that spit splattered the forehead of the larger man.

Riker turned and started to storm away and then abruptly stopped, turned around and shot the gang member in the face. The man dropped dead at his feet and by the time he hit the floor, several mercenaries had their weapons pointed at the remaining gang members.

One of the gang members put his hands in the air and

said "Hey, hey. We on the same side man. We getting paid just like you. He was a dumbass, we're on it." He motioned towards the dead gang member when he spoke.

Riker nodded, apparently accepting that the rest of the 'Gridlox' would fall into line, but was obviously still irate at being challenged.

He looked at a few of the mercenaries around him and said, "I'm checking on our teams on the other floors, clear this one and move up." With the instructions given, Riker was through the stairwell doors and gone.

"He's a touchy little prick ain't he?" Vic said in a whisper as his companions and the two soldiers with them watched the event play out.

Chapter 30: Reinforcements

"Come on Diggs, you heard the Commander." Flutter said, rushing the short stocky man along. The three soldiers, Flutter, Roid and Diggs were in the sewer tunnels that ran under the streets. They stood at a wall that they believed was on the other side of the boiler room beneath the hotel's basement.

"I'm on it." Diggs grumbled. The short stocky man always grumbled, it was just his way. He stood in front of the wall and rubbed his hand over it. His hand stayed approximately three inches away from the wall and as he moved it in a waving motion, the entire area of wall in front of him came away and was tossed in the direction of where his hand ended up pointing at the end of his waving motion.

It's what he did. He could 'dig' through anything, anywhere as far as the unit could tell. On a couple occasions, he made good use of his ability to effortlessly hurl the material he had 'dug out'.

"About time." Roid said with a chuckle.

In fact, they had just walked up to the wall and Diggs immediately did his thing, but the entire unit gave Diggs a rough time. The way they all figured it, if the man insisted on grumbling all the time, then they would give him something to grumble about and that's how it went.

The oversized and incredibly muscular solider Roid, stepped through the hole in the wall first, machine gun up and ready. Diggs followed and Flutter took the rear position.

The smell of decay took all of their breath away almost instantly. The three soldiers gasped and flicked on the lights attached to their rifles. As soon as the lights were on, they saw what created the smell that filled the air.

The large boiler room was filled with huge piles of bodies.

"Holy shit! There's got to be over a hundred bodies in here!" Roid exclaimed.

"They must've killed everyone staying in the hotel." Flutter said, disgusted at the sight of so many bodies.

In front of them were indeed stacks of what amounted to well over one hundred bodies. Old and young, man and woman, even children. The people that had done this had been indiscriminate in their slaughtering.

"Not just guests. Look at the uniforms. No telling how many of the staff they killed as well." Diggs grumbled.

"Enough. We see what they've done. You both heard the boss. Find the door and let's move." Flutter said.

"Already found it. You guys ready?" Roid said as he started walking towards a large door that was illuminated from the light on his rifle.

Diggs and Flutter didn't respond. They just positioned themselves on either side of the door, as Roid opened it up. The door led to a small hallway with a stairwell at the end, that apparently led to the basement and on up to each of the hotel's floors.

As they made their way down the hallway, Flutter radioed Halbred.

"I don't think there's any hostages left Commander. It looks like they've killed them all and stashed the bodies in the boiler room. We're hitting the stairs now, want us to clear the first floor?" Flutter said into the comms unit.

"Negative!" She heard Halbred say in response, in what sounded like a harsh whisper. "We're pinned down on the second-floor parking deck. Head straight to the second floor, radio me before you make entry and we'll lay down cover."

"10-4 Commander" Flutter said in response. Then she looked at the two soldiers with her, who had heard the entire conversation through the open channel comms that they wore on their ears like all of the unit members.

"Well, you heard the boss. Let's get them out of a jam and kill some of these sick bastards!" Flutter shouted as she passed both men and began to hurry up the steps.

Roid and Diggs followed, matching her pace.

The three soldiers quickly made it to the second-floor door and this time, it was Roid and Diggs who positioned themselves on the sides of the doorway, while Flutter opened it and entered the well-lit second floor of the hotel.

She immediately saw three men in all black fatigues on the other end of the hall and opened fire on them. Two of them fell dead, but the third managed to slip around the corner at the end of the hallway. She saw directional signs at the end of the hall. Pointing to the right, the direction the man had ran, was a sign with an arrow that said, 'Parking Deck'.

Flutter started running down the hall, towards the deck and uncoincidentally towards the man that got away. She didn't hear them, but she knew Roid and Diggs were on her heels.

The three soldiers stopped at the corner and Flutter peered around. She barely pulled her head back, before the entire corner of the wall was shot to pieces.

As Flutter jumped back, while gunfire still ripped away at the corner wall, Roid dove on the floor into the opening. He had the trigger on his automatic weapon squeezed and had dived low, beneath the bullets coming in their direction. The result was that he shot the legs and the falling bodies that followed of at least four men dressed in black fatigues.

The gunfire aimed at Flutter, Diggs and Roid instantly stopped and apparently just for safe measure, Diggs rolled around and shot holes into the door at the end of the hall that they had been standing in front of.

Roid jumped to his feet and glanced at Diggs. "Yeah, brother. Damn that door." Roid said to the short man and chuckled.

All three of them ran towards the doorway that had a sign over it which said, 'Parking Deck'.

Halbred and Samuel were the first to notice the sounds of gunfire coming from the door to the hotel's second floor. Quickly, all the mercenaries and gangbangers looked at the door and aimed their weapons.

"Now!" Halbred said as he began firing at the backs of several of the closest men.

"Go Dante. The far side of the deck!" Vic said to the young man next to him.

Dante's eyes were red, his face was angry and then he was gone. A moment later he appeared on the farthest side of the parking deck from where they had taken cover. He had appeared behind two 'Gridlox' and quickly slit their throats. Two other gang members that stood nearby, aimed their weapons, but they were too slow for Dante. He spun, crouching at the same time and rotated to the two men, quickly slicing open their thighs, then their stomachs, then his upward motion ripped open their chests before ending them with throats slashed.

The men fell before him. Ten feet away, two more men turned and before they could fire, they each caught one of Dante's thrown daggers in the neck and fell to the ground. Dante pulled two more knives and disappeared. Heading to more of the 'Gridlox' that were spread out on the far side of the parking deck. He was in a furious rage and wanted to kill as many as possible, but he was still careful to keep his slicing and dicing away from the shootout, his companions and the soldiers were having with the mercenaries.

As soon as Dante disappeared, Vic dove to the next car down, separating himself from Halbred and Samuel who were exchanging gunfire with the mercenaries who had mostly found cover of their own.

From the corner of his eye, Vic noticed that Fuse did the same thing going the other direction.

Vic dove to the next vehicle, trying to position himself to flank the enemy and noticed Fuse doing the same thing. "Nice to work with people that know what they're doing." He thought as he opened fire on the side of a mercenary whose position was exposed as Vic had maneuvered around the cars.

A split second later the doors to the second floor of the hotel burst open and Roid and Flutter laid down fire on the backs of several mercenaries that had taken cover with their backs to the doors.

That was the moment that Halbred had been waiting for. He leapt over the car and rushed the two closest mercenaries. They had jumped on the other side of the car they were using as cover when Flutter and Roid had burst into the lot shooting. This left their backs to Samuel and Halbred.

Halbred slammed into both men and the same time, crushing them against the car. One man managed to get a shot off and fired into Halbreds chest.

The red-haired soldier jerked back as if he'd been punched and then furiously slammed the shooter's head against the car at least six time, before the man's fell limp. The entire time, Halbred held the other man by the neck. When he looked back at the man, he noticed that he had bullet hole in his forehead.

He looked to see who had shot him and saw Samuel walking openly through the center drive path of the parking deck with a pistol in each hand. He was firing here and there, and every shot seemed to catch a target poking its head out to shoot back.

Halbred, looked around the deck. Fuse was finishing off three mercs that had tried to run to the far-left corner.

Flutter, Roid and Diggs had apparently cleared the entire area near the hotel doors. Vic had just finished off two mercs who had run to the far-right corner for cover and on the opposite end of the deck and young Hispanic man, stood breathing heavily around over a dozen dead bodies. He had blood splattered all over himself and from his forearms down he was completely covered in blood. He held a dagger in each hand and kept looking around from side to side quickly, in search of his next victim.

"We'll have to watch that one." Halbred thought to himself.

The Halbred shouted so loudly that his voice echoed through the parking deck. "Clear! Gather at the doors to the hotel floor! Everyone!" Halbred made it a point to glance back at Vic and over at Dante to emphasize that 'everyone', meant them too.

The group gathered together quickly. Dante giving the soldiers a start as he just appeared in front of the doors. Halbred had grabbed a radio device off one of the dead mercenaries and stood before the group. Before he started talking, the radio beat him to it.

"Multiple targets have taken the second-floor parking

deck. All lobby and parking deck squads move to the second-floor stairs. Units 3 and 6 head to the second floor of the hotel. We'll bottle them in and kill them all. No survivors." The radio screeched and then went silent. They had all heard what was coming.

"Sounds like they're coming from both sides. Some of us will need to make a stand, while the rest of us need to hit the roof. They've got some way that they're bringing in more troops up there. We'll be overrun eventually if we don't stop it." Halbred said it all fast and loud.

"I'm going to the roof. Camacho will be there. We'll have to try to shoot our way through to make it up." Samuel said.

"We're not going that way 17, or uh, Samuel." Halbred said. "Flutter can take us all straight up the outside." Then Halbred turned to the rest of the gathered group and said "Alright, Samuel, flutter and I are going up. Roid, you're with us. Fuse, Diggs, you stay put with Samuel's guys and hold this floor. We'll be back to flank them as soon as we clear the roof." Halbred said it all with authority and started to head towards the exterior half wall on the edge of the parking deck, but stopped when he heard someone say "No."

It was Dante who had spoken. He looked at Halbred and then at Samuel, seeming to blow off the older soldier as if Halbred meant nothing to him.

"I'm going to the roof too. I'm going for Camacho too Samuel." Dante said with a cold distant tone to his voice.

"Shit." Halbred said. He looked at Fuse and Diggs and asked, "you need one more or you think you can hold the floor with what you've got?"

It was Vic who answered him, not his two soldiers though. Vic was casually confiscating assault rifles and clips from two dead mercenaries when he spoke up.

"We got this without my sous-chef, soldier. Go kill that little mohawk bastard and be quick about it, so I don't have to come do it for you after I clear this floor." Vic said it all with the arrogant confidence that made him who he was. Then Vic mumbled seemingly to himself, but obviously loud enough for everyone to hear. "Hold the floor… what kind of sissy shit you soldiers on. I clear floors dammit."

"I like that one." Roid said with a smile as the huge man kept walking toward the outside wall.

Halbred, Samuel, Flutter and Dante followed him.

Vic turned to Fuse and Diggs and said "The names Vic and I'm the damn grim reaper fellas. Time to man up boys!" He said it with a vicious smile.

"If you're half as good as you think you are, we should be alright." Fuse said. Diggs just grumbled "Take your positions and quit jabbering. We got us three against a hell of lot."

All three men spread out, taking cover behind cars that gave fuse a clear line of sight on the hotel floor door. Diggs a line of sight on the parking deck stairway door and Vic positioned behind a car towards the center, so he could provide support fire in either direction.

Halbred and his group all approached the wall at the back of the building and flutter touched each of them. As soon as she touched them, they started to slightly float, weightless.

"Everyone grab hands." Flutter said. "We're heading up."

They all did as they were told and Flutter grabbed hold of Samuel and Halbred who were the closest to her and leapt over the half wall on the east side of the building's parking deck, pulling the group behind her like a weightless bundle of balloons.

Chapter 31:
Mila

"H ide quick!" Eva said in a loud whisper. Eva stood in the center of the room with her pistol in her hand as she watched Mila and Steph scramble. Steph ran to the kitchen and tucked himself down beside the old free-standing stove. Mila ducked into the closest closet, leaving the door barely cracked open.

"I need to move this couch around to try to provide some form of cover or maybe I should flip the table over." Eva thought frantically, knowing that she didn't have much time before the men outside entered the basement room. "Maybe, they were just randomly passing by. Maybe Mila's wrong and they're not coming for us." Eva thought, but she knew neither were true.

She was immediately distracted from her panicked thoughts by Steph's hiding spot.

"Steph, that's too open and it's the same direction as the front door. Go the closet with Mila." Eva said in rushed words that were still full of a type of patience and love that only a parent could muster up in the most intense of situations like this.

Steph started to rise, but before he got all the way up, the front door burst open. Two Na'gee warriors came rushing in behind the door that had been kicked off its hinges and flew into the room.

Eva screamed "Get down Steph!" and opened fire. The warriors were fast, never slowing down. As they burst in, they made immediate use of the small room, processing its size and features as they ran. One warrior bolted to the left and one the right, they jumped after two quick steps and in unison each bounced their feet off the wall halfway up and dove towards Eva from either side.

One of Eva's bullets caught the man on left in his right arm, before his wild leap to the wall, but no other shots connected. The warriors were just too fast.

As the warriors kicked off the walls on either side and dove towards Eva, she shifted her aim to the man on the right. She didn't dare fire towards the left wall, in fear that a bullet would miss the fast assailant and catch Steph, who was still ducked down by the stove.

She figured, she'd take one of the men and out and then take her chances fighting the other in close proximity. "Yeah, because that worked out so great last time, I ran into one of these weird, tattooed guys." Eva thought.

Ultimately, it didn't matter. She aimed for the right, but she wasn't nearly fast enough. The warrior slammed into her before the gun was pointing in the right direction. As they crashed towards the ground, their falling bodies were hit from the other warrior diving into them from her left.

Eva felt her already sore ribs crack from the impact. As the three of them fell into a heap in the middle of the room, the second warrior from the left, who was on top, jumped up, standing over them. The one who had hit her first and was directly on top of her. He reared back and swung. Hist fist connected with the side of Eva's face, hard, and she started seeing stars.

He hit her a second time and the dizziness intensified. She knew she had to do something quick or this would be the end of her and her children. "Dammit Vic! Where are you?!" She thought.

That was her last thought, she turned her brain off and instinctively fell back on her training that seemed like a lifetime ago. All the female soldiers had been taught several ways to get out of a situation like this. A situation where a stronger male was on top of them. She applied her training and quickly pulled both legs up placing a foot on either side of his ribs. She dug her heels in, finding the bone and twisted hard and fast. An audible "cracking" noise filled the room, and she knew she cracked ribs on both sides of her attacker's body. As soon as she heard the "cracking" noise, the man reared back in pain. She anticipated this. Her training told her this would always happen. So that was the moment she slipped her bent legs in front of her, planting her feet on his chest and kicked hard. The man flew backwards crashing into the kitchen table.

Despite the pain in her side from broken ribs of her own and a head full of stars, Eva started to jump to her feet to face the other attacker. She didn't make it far. Just as she started to rise, the other warrior who had stood over them and watched his companion get thrown past him, kicked her in the face with the bottom of his booted foot.

Eva's head flew backwards and hit the floor. The man, still standing over her, stomped her ankle and she felt a pop. He kicked her knee, and she felt another pop. He seemed to be working his way up towards her head, injuring her along the way. It was almost like he preferred to punish her for fighting back, then to just finish her. Eva, tried to roll and kick with her other foot, but the man was prepared for this. He caught her foot and slung it away from him casually.

He stared into Eva's eyes with evil amusement and slowly pulled his large knife out of its sheath.

Fear flooded through Eva. Fear for herself as she knew she could not stop this man, but more fear for her children that would be helpless once this man killed her. She kicked again and again, and each time, the warrior who was still staring at her, just caught her leg and threw it away from him.

After several failed kicks and a several moments of staring at her, letting the fear of the inevitable build up, he raised the knife over his head, preparing to swing it down into her chest, ending her life.

The warrior that had been kicked across the room had gotten to his feet and was easing closer behind the warrior with the knife, apparently leaning in for a good view of the kill.

The Na'gee warrior swung down with the knife, but before it got to its target the room lit up in a painfully bright white light and the word "Stop!" echoed through the room in an ominous otherworldly type of voice.

The word sounded like it came from a crackling megaphone that someone with deep, yet shallow and distant voice had yelled into.

Both warriors went flying across the room and crashed into the wall so hard that their bodies cracked the concrete wall. The room was still so bright that it was hard to see. The warrior who had held the knife, lay crumpled against the wall in a heap. Blood streamed from his eyes, his ears, and his mouth. He had taken the brunt of whatever force had hit them. The second warrior that had been behind him, had been forcefully thrown into the wall, but didn't look like he had been hit the same way as the other.

Eva, still laying on her back on the floor, rolled her head away from the warriors to see the source of the light and saw Mila standing in front of the closet she had been hiding in.

Mila had a brilliant bright white light glowing from her, that made her skin look transparent. Her eyes shined brightly showing nothing but light and she stared in the direction of the two warriors.

From the shadows just outside the open doorway of the basement room, Olo watched the events take place. He watched the two warriors he had brought with him attack the traitor's wife. He watched the emergence of a 'Brite' and their defeat that followed.

Even from the shadows outside the basement room, Olo knew the warrior that had taken a direct blow from the 'Brite' was dead. The other would survive unless the 'Brite' attacked again or unless the warrior was foolish enough to try to attack the 'Brite', in which case the light would consume him.

Olo also noticed the whimpering of silent fear from the kitchen and knew it must be the traitor's little boy. Swiftly, Olo rubbed his pendant stepped into the blur and seconds later reached out of blur that appeared beside the living warrior on the floor. He pulled the warrior into the blur, and it disappeared. Then across the room by the stove, another blur appeared and Olo stepped out.

He looked at the glowing girl and her mother on the floor as he grabbed the boy by the neck and lifted him into the air.

In a deep voice Olo spoke to the girl and her mother. "The boy is mine. He will be bathed in the aging waters and come back to kill you all as a Na'gee! I will break your traitorous man first and tell him the same! You will die by your family's hand Brite!" Once the words were said, Olo stepped into the blur and disappeared with Steph, who he still held by the neck.

Mila screamed "No!" in the same otherworldly voice and her body filled the room with blinding light. The entire wall and doorway exploded. Eva saw the brightness and the explosion, but for some reason could see through it and wasn't affected by the impact of the force that came from her daughter's presence. She looked at Mila in wonder, watched the glow fade and saw the tears streaming from her eyes.

Mila just mumbled "I couldn't save him mom. I couldn't save Steph." And she collapsed.

"I couldn't either Mila. I couldn't either." Eva said as she laid her head on the floor and began to weep uncontrollably.

Chapter 32:
Steph

Olo stepped out of the blur, or 'the path' as it was called by the Na'gee. He was still holding the young boy by the neck and as the blur faded away, he gently set the boy down on the ground. Olo looked around the area closely. He scanned the sky first, then the tree line surrounding the small clearing they had appeared in. About ten feet from them both, the warrior that survived and that he had pulled out of the basement sat on the ground. The warrior was still visibly hurt and shaken up.

The boy and warrior several feet away sat on green grass that was littered with dead leaves of all shapes and sizes. It seemed they were in a small clearing in the woods. Trees of various sizes were on all sides of them.

The sky was bright and clear and the sun that seemed more orange than yellow shined brightly.

Steph was trembling with fear. He did not know what had happened. One minute these weird, tattooed men were coming through the door attacking his mother and the next moment, everything flashed brightly. He had felt a strong hand on his throat and then was here, wherever here was.

Olo finally stopped scanning the area around him and looked back at his companion who still sat on the ground.

"Pick yourself up Ansai. We have much to do. We barely saved this child from the demon's attack. Come let us explain what has happened to the young boy." Olo said in his deep gruff voice.

At this, the other warrior began rising from the ground, although he appeared to be very stiff and confused by Olo's choice of words. He got up and slowly walked over to where Olo stood by Steph. As he got near, Olo crouched down making himself as close to eye level as he could with the small boy.

"Young one, your name is Stephan, is it not?" Olo asked.

Steph looked up at the man still terrified and mustered up a shaky reply "Steph" he said.

"Very well Steph. I know you are afraid, and you should be. We are the Na'gee. We are great warriors that battle with monsters and demons to keep our world and your world safe. Your sister is dead young Steph. She was killed by a demon long ago that your father and mother made a deal with. This demon has taken over her body and rules your parents. The demon is called 'Brite' and it will kill everyone in both worlds. We tried to stop it and your parents attacked us. They serve the demon. All I could do was save you young Steph." Olo finished his explanation and stared at the boy, waiting for a reaction. Ansai stood over them both watching the exchange, still visibly confused.

"No. Mila is not dead. I was just with her. You're wrong! You didn't save me, you tried to kill my mom!" Steph said, his voice rising as he spoke.

"I understand your confusion young Steph. I understand the pain you must feel knowing that your sibling has fallen victim to a great demon, but it is true Steph. Think of how your sister has been acting. Think of how she made the bright light and killed my friend. Think of her voice shouting in the room. Is that the sister you have always known?" Olo asked, still staring into the boy's eyes.

Steph looked away, visibly thinking through what Olo had said to him. He looked back at Olo and softly said "No. Mila is not the same anymore. She barely speaks and she says weird things. She knew you were coming before you came. It was the same in the woods behind that weird house."

"That is because the demon knows we hunt it. Your parents work for the demon now Steph. They want the world to die. I am sorry to have to tell you this. I am sure, like all children that love their parents, that you don't want to hear that they have chosen the path of evil, but it is true young Steph. Now I must ask you, have you chosen to serve this evil demon that murdered your sister?" Olo said it all gravely, continuing to stare into the boy's eyes the entire time.

"No!" Steph yelled at him. "I hate the demon that took my sister! I want it to die!" The boy yelled.

"Ok Steph. We believe you. It will be hard for us to trust you though because we know you must still love your parents. It is hard for a child to accept that their parents are evil, even if they chose to sacrifice their own daughter to raise a demon." Olo finished and waited for Steph to respond.

"They sacrificed Mila? No, they wouldn't ever. They love us." Steph said.

"The did Steph. A 'Brite' demon can only take over the body of human if the humans parents sacrifice and kill the body for the demon. It's the only way it works. They wanted this to happen. They knew we would come to stop the demon, that's why they took you to hide. That's why they are working with the strange men." Olo stopped talking and sniffed the air. He quickly stood and looked at Ansai.

"Protect the child." Olo said as he slowly pulled his large knife with one hand and his large pistol with the other hand. Olo turned very slowly to face the tree line behind them.

Suddenly a large reptile that stood on two large legs and had short arms in front of it, rushed through the trees at Olo. The reptile stood about eight feet tall and had a massive head and long tail. It moved fast rushing Olo, while opening its huge jaws that showed rows of razor sharp teeth.

Olo fired three shots into the chest of the large reptile and then flipped over the beast sinking his large knife into the back of the creature's neck, where it connected with the head.

Olo landed smoothly on his feet behind the reptile, as it collapsed into the ground sliding forward before coming to a stop directly in front of Ansai and Steph.

Steph gasped and shouted "A dinosaur! You killed a dinosaur!"

Olo calmly turned to face the child and said, "We kill

many monsters young Steph. Just like we hunt demons. The Na'gee warriors are heroes."

"But I thought all the dinosaurs were dead?" Steph asked, still in shock and staring at the dead beast within an arms length of him.

"Many of the things your people think are dead or are myths and story book legends are really just creatures from my world Steph. They used to be able to slip through to your world more frequently when there were organic paths to take between the worlds. As our worlds age, they grow further apart, and your people choose to believe that they never existed or have all perished." Olo finished and then approached the boy and crouched near him again.

"Steph, there are scarier things in my world than creatures like this. Things that your world believes are just legends and things that your world has never dreamed of. We cannot stay here long, it isn't safe. If you believe me and trust me about your parents and the demon, I will teach you our ways and train you to kill the monster that murdered your sister. I will train you to kill the parents that let her die. I will teach you to be Na'gee, young Steph." As Olo finished, he stood and reached out his hand to Steph.

Tears streamed down Steph's face, and he looked away. For several long moments Steph stared into the distance and wept. Then the boy looked back at the dead creature in front of him and back at Olo. He sniffed, wiped the tears away and grabbed Olo's hand. Olo pulled the boy to his feet and the two stared at each other.

"I want to kill the demon that murdered my sister! I hate

it! I loved Mila, I hate my parents for doing this to her. For doing this to both of us, we loved them. I will kill them for this." Steph said firmly.

Olo nodded and said, "you must do as I say. It will not be easy, but you are strong Steph. First, we must make you big like a man though."

At this Olo turned to Ansai and said "Take the boy to our local outpost. Gather two warriors and take the child to the aging waters. I will return before long. Keep him safe."

Instead of nodding Ansai looked hesitantly at Steph and then back at Olo.

"Olo we must speak." Ansai finally said. The warrior who usually followed orders without question, uncharacteristically turned his back on Olo and walked a few feet away then stopped, keeping his back turned.

Olo stalked over to him and looked at him without saying a word.

Ansai looked back at the boy to ensure they wouldn't be overheard and then said. "Why would we save this soft top sider child and why would we age him and train him like a Na'gee Olo?"

"Did you not see the 'Brite' that almost killed you fool? Do you not remember what you were taught? A 'Brite' can only be killed by someone of its own blood. This boy is that someone. A 'Brite' is too powerful to leave unchecked with the top siders, especially ones that have made themselves enemies of the Na'gee." Olo finished his statement with evident impatience.

"Olo, 'Brites' are just made-up stories that the wise ones tell. They are not real, and why does it matter if we are migrating to the new world?" Ansai said.

As soon as Ansai got the words out, Olo backhanded him across the face with tremendous force. Ansai staggered back a step and Olo stepped up to his face with clear anger in his eyes.

"You sound like a foolish top sider Ansai! Have you grown soft like one too? I have studied the top side. All of the creatures from our world are thought to be made up stories to them, but they are real here.

Are you too stupid to think that stories from our world are real in theirs?!" Olo seemed to get angrier as he said it all yet understanding seemed to brighten in Ansai's eyes.

Then Olo struck him with another back hand and again stepped closer to his face "and don't speak to me of the migration! We watch and keep our people safe, but this is our home! We will ravage the top side for resources, we will even send the old and weak to live their final days there, but Na'gee warriors will always remain here! Always Ansai!" Olo said firmly.

"Yes Olo." Ansai said. "I mean no disrespect great one. It's just that the wise ones have said the top side will be the new home of our people."

"The wise ones, rule the weak and soft in our tribe Ansai. It is I, Olo, who rules the warriors. We will never grow soft in that world! We will never give up our world to the predators we fight!" Olo said the last statement with passion and conviction.

Ansai, did not say another word, he just nodded.

"Get the boy to the aging waters and then begin his training. I hold you responsible for his safety, Ansai. If the boy dies, you will be stripped of your honor and tortured while witnessing the slaughter of your family. Keep him safe and train him well though, and you will achieve great honor as the Na'gee warrior that forged the weapon to kill a 'Brite'." Olo's voice elevated as he spoke of great honor and Ansai was inspired.

"Yes Olo. I will make this soft top sider a great warrior. You will think he is of this world when I am finished. I will make you proud great one!" Ansai said and then he rushed over to Steph.

Olo did not move from his spot, he merely turned and said to Steph.

"Go with Ansai. He will protect you and teach you to be a great warrior Steph. I will return and we will avenge your beloved sister together." When he finished talking, Olo scanned the tree line again and then took off running with incredible speed.

Ansai grabbed Steph by the arm and rushed the boy into the woods, going in the opposite direction.

Olo turned and ran through the woods with the grace and speed of a wildcat. Before long, he could see his destination on the hilltop in the distance. On the hill he saw the large pathway to the top side open and could make out many of his tribesman gathering around it and slowly making their way through.

"It is too many gathered at once. It will attract trouble. The wise one's are fools!" Olo thought to himself as he ran.

It didn't take long for Olo to make it to the hilltop. He knew that his wild run there, would have undoubtably alerted predators or worse to the gathering, but he did not care. He considered it reckless to have that many people gathered at once anyway and figured they would learn one way or another.

It wasn't that Olo was against the migration. He actually thought it made sense to send the old ones and the wise ones. He thought that the soft top side world would allow some Na'gee to grow naturally instead of having to be bathed in the aging waters to survive. It was just that he didn't think it made sense for anyone else, especially his warriors. He would not give up this world. Olo believed the constant fight for survival is what made the Na'gee warriors strong and fierce.

Once on top of the hill, Olo walked past the Na'gee lined up to go through the path and made his way straight up to the blur or the pathway. Before he entered, Olo turned and spoke loudly to the Na'gee gathered on the hilltop.

"You gather as if you forget the dangers of our world. Be cautious my people and go to the outpost long before dark. We do not need to all travel in one day." Olo said it and the people gathered nodded. Then Olo turned and walked into the path.

Camacho stood before the open pathway on the roof front and center. The man wanted each Na'gee that came through to see him first as the ruler of the top side world. He wanted them to associate him with their escape to safer lands. He wanted to be the one they revered and thought of when they slept peacefully at night.

As Na'gee slowly came through one at a time, he nodded to them. Silently letting them know he was in charge of this new world. He was shocked when he saw Olo come through and walk right up to him.

Before Olo spoke a word, Captain Venco ran up to Camacho and said "We've got trouble sir. The same group that were attacking the east side have made their way into the parking deck. We have them trapped on the second floor of the parking deck and are sending squads from the deck stairs and from inside the building."

Camacho turned from Olo, still shocked that the warrior who had driven away from in front of the hotel, was now walking through the migration path and standing before him. He waved it from his mind and addressed Captain Venco, the head of his private security, instead of pondering what Olo had been up to.

"It's just three of them, right? How fucking hard can it be to kill three men?!" Camacho shouted.

"They've got some type of military unit with them now sir. We'll take them though, don't worry." Captain Venco said sternly.

Olo chose this moment to address both men. "You send who you were sending top sider and let us see who kills them first. I will handle this myself." With that Olo began walking to the west side of the roof and using hand gestures, he summoned five Na'gee warriors who had been positioned with sniper rifles to join him.

When they arrived to the edge of the roof, the warriors set down the large rifles and picked up a rope that had been laying next to the closest sniper. They secured it to the roof top and threw it over the edge. In a blink of an eye, Olo and the five warriors he had summoned were over the edge climbing down the rope on the west side of the building towards the second floor.

As they arrived at the second floor Olo and the five Na'gee warriors skillfully slipped from the rope to the side of the building and into the rafters of the ceiling of the second floor of the parking deck. They started to make their way from rafter to rafter like spiders, never noticing the group of companions that seemed to float off over the eastside wall opposite them.

Chapter 33:
The Rooftop

Bird! Radio! You're up! We're coming up the eastern perimeter from the outside. Need you to get that chopper moving and start laying down some fire on the west side asap! It wouldn't hurt my feelings a bit if you actually took some of them damn snipers out while you're at it!" Halbred screamed into the comms unit he wore on his ear.

"10-4 Commander. We're on our way. Hurry up or there won't be anyone left for you sir!" Bird responded through the radio.

As soon as the words stopped, the group heard the sound of the helicopter in the air not far from their location.

"Slow us down Flutter! Give Bird a sec to get over there before we clear the top wall!" Halbred barked at Flutter who was still pulling him and Samuel through the air like weightless balloons. Halbred's other hand was locked onto Roid, who looked oddly casual about being pulled through the air weightlessly. This seemed extremely odd to Samuel based on how large the man was. Samuel similarly pulled

Dante and was shocked at how effortlessly he was able to pull him along. It seemed that if he let Dante go, the young man would go flying off in the air.

"Quite an interesting ability. Could come in handy in the future if we survive the roof." Samuel thought.

Samuel noticed Dante's grim look. He noticed the cold, darkness in the young man's eyes. Dante wasn't the same at all. Despite them being so close to these strange soldiers, Samuel decided he needed to say something before he hit the roof and depended on this man to watch his back.

"Dante, you alright? You look troubled." Samuel asked quietly.

Despite his hushed tone, the entire group, with the exception of Flutter, shifted their eyes to Dante. Dante noticed. He scowled at them all as he turned his head to face Samuel. He stared silently, almost hatefully at Samuel for an awkward moment and then responded.

"I just murdered over a dozen men Samuel." Dante half growled. "You and these damn soldiers may like killing, but it's not normal for me! I'm only here because my entire family was murdered a day ago and working with you psychos is my best shot at revenge. No, I'm NOT fucking alright!" Dante never raised his voice, he just half growled the entire response in a low, vicious tone.

"It doesn't matter though. When we get to the roof, I'll kill every bastard up there. I'll do my job, just don't let these trigger-happy soldiers shoot me while I'm doing it." Dante added in a cold shallow voice.

No one said a word. The sound of the approaching helicopter got louder and louder. They heard people start shouting on the roof and then the day was filled with the sound of automatic gunfire coming from the other side of the building.

"Now Flutter!" Halbred shouted.

Seemingly out of nowhere the slow floating sensation was replaced with a high-speed dart through the air. As they cleared the top, Flutter swung her hands forward slinging Halbred, Samuel and the men they had in tow flying onto the roof. As soon as her hands let go, their full weight came returned, and they went crashing onto the roof.

They landed and all bounced to their feet as Flutter came down softly to stand behind them. There was still a huge blur opening of some sort in the middle of the roof, and dozens of armed soldiers. About half of them were Camacho's private security or Mercenaries and the other half were Na'gee warriors. All of them had their full attention on the helicopter firing upon them on the other side of the roof.

"Let them have it!" Halbred shouted. However, his command was only heard by Roid and Flutter, as Samuel had darted off towards the nearest group of mercenaries and Dante had disappeared, only to appear in the middle of a group of Na'gee The young knife fighter instantly begun slicing throats with his dagger and disappearing only to reappear right behind the next closest men.

Samuel's attack was completely opposite from Dante's. He ran through men without having even pulled his pistols yet. He just moved with the speed of a professional athlete running, rolling, side stepping, through a crowd of at least six soldiers touching each one and leaving them instantly frozen in whatever position they had been in when touched.

"Holy shit! Look at those guys go Commander." Roid said as the three soldiers stood momentarily mesmerized by not just the unique fighting skills Samuel and Dante possessed, but also by the bravado they exhibited.

They were jerked out of their momentary roles as spectators when Flutter screamed "Bird!!!" and opened fire on the west side of the roof.

Halbred and Roid looked up to see that a sniper's bullet had gone through the windshield of the helicopter and hit Bird in the neck. The special unit's pilot, their friend who had flown them in and out of so many dangerous situations, was instantly dead. The chopper started twirling erratically and Radio made a wild leap for the roof out the side of the helicopter.

The man almost made it to the edge, might have even made it, if it hadn't been for the speed of the Na'gee warrior that leaped over his companion, landed on the edge of the roof and shot Radio with his large .50 caliber pistol. The bullet hit Radio in the chest and the impact sent his body backwards in midair. He began falling the twenty plus stories to the ground and the helicopter fell behind him, still spinning like crazy.

"Noooo!!!!" Both Halbred and Roid yelled. They squeezed the triggers on their automatic assault rifles with fury in their eyes and began dropping Na'gee and Mercenary alike.

Camacho ducked back towards the cover of the doorway

to the elevators on the roof when the helicopter started shooting. He noticed a man appear behind a group of distracted Na'gee warriors and start cutting their throats, before they knew what had happened. He recognized the man as the young knife fighter that had attacked 'the spot'.

"Fools! They're used to the quite of the 'Otherside', they fail to stay alert over the roar of gunfire and a helicopter!" Camacho thought.

Then Camacho noticed the other man, with no weapon at all, leaving men standing still. "They're somehow unable to move, once he touches them." Camacho thought to himself as he observed the man freeze several members of his private security.

Camacho saw the soldiers, who had arrived with them, but cared little for them. It was these two that had caused him so many problems. It was these two he needed to deal with once and for all.

He was so caught up observing every detail of the battle before him that he hardly noticed that Captain Venco and two of his men had joined him in the doorway.

He looked at the two mercenaries with Captain Venco and said "Keep the soldiers busy, I'll throw them off for you. Venco, meet me by the other two. We'll take the knife fighter first. He teleports and he always pops up behind your back and tries to slash your throat. You know what's coming now, so don't let him kill you." Camacho said it all fast and harshly, obviously expecting them to ask no questions and do as they were told.

As soon as he finished giving the men their orders, he

took off, fast.

Camacho loved to use his gifts of speed and strength and it was a sight to see when he did use them. In the blink of an eye, he covered the distance to the large solider and struck him so hard in the middle of the chest that the man folded over and went flying backwards about three feet, gagging for breath. Despite Camacho's surprise that it didn't send the large man flying off the roof, he didn't slow down. He was moving now and didn't intend to stop until he had finished.

Camacho turned backwards toward the female soldier he had passed and darted towards her leaving a blurry array of color behind him as he moved with incredible speed. He never slowed down, striking her in the head with his right fist and all of his momentum as he ran by. She went flying almost seven feet across the roof and collapsed.

The red-haired soldier that looked to be in command started firing his rifle at him, so Camacho darted away towards the knife fighter across the roof. "I've got more important people to deal with, let the damn mercenaries earn their money." Camacho thought as he ran towards the area whered Dante was fighting at.

With Camacho out of the way the two mercenaries that were still in the doorway unloaded on the red-haired soldier. Their trained eye's hit him with every shot, but instead of falling the man jerked from the impact and then looked up at them. Their surprise at the ineffectiveness of their weapons distracted them from moving before being gunned down in the doorway, by the same soldier they had just shot.

Halbred was angry. Well, he was always angry, now he

was irate. He had just witnessed two of his unit die. He didn't know if Flutter was alive after the hit she'd taken. To Halbred this was his fault. He tried to shoot the man that had hit Roid and Flutter, but the man darted off in a blur.

"How the hell can he move that fast?" Halbred thought as bullets hit him from the other direction. He turned to see two men in the entryway to elevator firing at him and he gunned them down. Then he was struck in the back of the head by what felt like a sword.

Halbred turned to see the Na'gee warrior who had him with what was actually a large knife. He swung the butt of his rifle at the man, but the warrior bent in half backwards dodging the swing. As soon as the rifle passed over the bent warrior bounced back up and hit Halbred again with the knife, this time in the neck.

The clanging sound of metal bouncing off metal rang through the air, and the warrior looked shocked. Halbred took advantage of the moment and slammed his left fist into the warrior's nose, while still clutching his rifle with his right hand. Bone crushed under the hard skin of his fist. The warrior looked dizzy as he staggered backward, with blood pouring from his face. In one smooth movement, Halbred lifted his rifle and shot the warrior in the chest three times. Then a barrage of automatic gun fire flew past Halbred. He quickly looked to see it's source and saw that it was Roid who was shooting.

Halbred looked back behind him and saw the bodies of two Na'gee warriors falling dead. With three more quickly approaching.

"Leave them to me Roid! More of these weird, tattooed fighters keep coming through that opening. I don't know what it is, and I don't care! Shut that thing down solider!" Halbred roared.

Roid didn't respond, he just took off towards the center of the roof where the pathway was held open by the Na'gee who were now squatting on the roof floor. Seeming to lose strength the longer they held the path open. Roid saw two warriors that had apparently just come through the blur look in his direction and begin to run towards him.

"Oh, these fellas think they're gonna cut me off, huh." Roid thought amused. The big man was now in his element. He pushed the loss of his friends out of his mind and immersed himself in the battle before him. This is what he believed he was made for. This was his sport and he loved it.

Roid began firing his rifle at the two men. Despite his accuracy, they zigged and zagged out of the way of his shots, with incredible speed and agility. In seconds the two Na'gee were on him, with their large knives pulled.

The first warrior swung his knife at Roids chest. Despite his enormous build, Roid wasn't slow. He nimbly stepped backwards and then jumped right back forward kicking his attacker hard in the middle of the chest. Roid felt the breastplate and rib cage shatter beneath his powerful kick and the Na'gee warrior collapsed.

The other warrior took advantage of Roid's attention being diverted and swung his knife at the large man's back. Roid tried to dance out of the way, but he didn't notice in time and still took a large slice across his back. Roid felt the sting of the blade and for at least the hundredth time, he envied Halbreds impenetrable skin.

The warrior swung again and this time, Roid saw it coming. He caught the man's wrist before the knife came down and crushed the warrior's wrist with his strong grip. Then Roid yanked the arm he held towards him, while he kicked the warrior's body away from him. The result was the warrior's crushed body flying several feet away, while Roid was left still holding an arm that was no longer attached to the warrior's body.

Roid dropped the arm and picked up the rifle he had dropped. He opened fire on the Na'gee who were holding the path open. Their bodies were peppered with bullet holes, and they died where they had squatted. Then the blur simply disappeared.

The resistance on the roof was almost wiped out. There were a handful of Na'gee and three mercenaries on the far end of the roof where Samuel and Dante fought, but it looked to Roid like this side was clear.

He saw Halbred, had killed one of the three and caught a hold of another one. "Ahh, can't nobody kill the Bossman. Guess I'll help those other two." Roid said to himself as he started to make his way towards Samuel and Dante.

CHAPTER 34:
THE PARKING DECK

The doorway that led inside the hotel from the second story parking deck, burst open and a hail of bullets came with it.

Fuse who was ducked down behind a nearby car, chuckled to himself. "Nothing like shooting without looking. That's a hell of a strategy. These mercenaries may be less trained than the damn gang bangers." Fuse thought to himself as he continued his silent chuckling.

Halfway across the parking deck, Vic had similar thoughts. "These idiots don't even know what the hell their shooting at! This ain't going to be too hard. Morons!" Vic thought to himself, from the safe cover of the large SUV he hid behind.

Diggs, who was positioned on the other side of the parking deck, near the door that led to the exterior parking deck stairs, did not share their amusement. He just grumbled to himself and waited on the door near him to burst open.

"Leaving me, Fuse, and some damn untrained maniac to fight an army. Great freaking strategy boss. Glad you got confidence in us." Diggs grumbled quietly to himself, like he often did.

Then the door near Diggs burst open. No gunfire followed this kicked open door, but several 'Gridlox' gang members did. The 'Gridlox' all had their weapons ready as they slowly came through the doorway and began to fan out.

Diggs had initially planned to wait to see how many of them their were before he gave away his position behind the large pickup truck he used for cover, but after seeing them start to spread out he changed his mind.

"You're not spreading out on me dammit." Diggs grumbled as he began to aim his assault rifle at the doorway. Then Diggs opened fire and the battle began.

He moved his automatic weapon from left to right, spraying down the men that had begun to spread out. He stopped his movement when his rifle's aim had made it to the doorway, but he didn't stop firing. All the 'Gridlox' gang members in view of the parking deck, dropped with fatal bullet wounds.

Diggs stopped firing when he noticed that however many were still in the stairwell, had moved back and were well clear of the doorway.

"Your pinned now assholes. Poke your heads out and old Diggs is gonna get you." Diggs yelled.

Fuse could barely see the fire fight that had begun on Digg's side of the parking deck, but he could see enough to tell what was happening.

"The gang bangers are smarter than the damn mercs!

Who would've guessed." Fuse thought. Then he decided he'd wait no more.

"No point letting Diggs have all the fun." Fuse said to himself as he popped up to stand over the car he had been using for cover and began firing his rifle at the mercenaries who were making their way into the parking deck.

Despite his previous thoughts, the mercenaries did not go down as easily as the 'Gridlox' had for Diggs. Two men were hit and with swift diving movements, the rest of the six men that had already made it through the doorway quickly took cover behind nearby vehicles.

Two men began returning fire from the vehicles they hid behind, while the others used the cover to make their way further into the garage. No doubt with plans to circle around their attacker.

Vic cursed to himself "Damn trigger-happy soldiers. All you had to do was let them get further in unscathed, think we'd already left and then treat it like a firing squad when they were all huddled up bitching about the waste of time, but no, they had to make this shit difficult."

Overly frustrated at the soldiers and aware that the mercs were slowly making their way deeper into the garage, Vic decided the waiting game was over. Instead of standing up and firing over the SUV he used for cover, he laid on his stomach and began shooting the ankles of the mercenaries moving from vehicle to vehicle. As the men fell, he shot the rest of their bodies.

In second Vic had killed three of them and had seen that the fourth was hidden behind the tire of an old sports car.

Vic stood and looked over the hood of the SUV to notice that more mercenaries were trying to make their way into the parking deck from the hotel, but Fuse was doing an admirable job of laying down fire on the doorway and the two men shooting at him from nearby vehicles. Vic knew he wouldn't be able to hold both groups at bay for too much longer.

Vic glanced at Diggs and noticed that the short stocky soldier was having no such problems. He'd managed to pin all the 'Gridlox' in the stairwell quite effectively.

Vic turned his attention to the doorway that led into the hotel, not forgetting about the man still hiding behind the sports car across from him and started shooting. Men trying to get a shot off at Fuse, never saw it coming and were hit in the doorway.

From Vic's position, one of the two men across from Fuse was exposed. He quickly took advantage of this and filled the man with lead. As soon as Vic shot him, he ducked out of instinct and the SUV rattled with the impact of gunfire, coming from the man ducked behind the sports car across from him.

Vic waited and as soon as the gunfire stopped, he jumped up and started firing at the sport car, while he ran towards it. He knew he'd be exposed to the men in the doorway of the hotel, but he also knew that the man across from him would not look up as long as he was shooting, so he took his chance.

In seconds Vic was leaping over the trunk of the car still firing. The man who had taken cover there was killed with several shots to the head.

Vic landed on his feet, and kept running, this time towards the man across from Fuse. The man never saw him coming, he just kept shooting at Fuse until he was dropped by bullets from Vic's assault rifle.

Vic took the man's position and joined Fuse in shooting at the men in the doorway to the hotel.

The first of Olo's warriors dropped silently from the parking deck rafters behind Diggs. He stabbed the man in the back with his large knife and then left it in him, while he broke the stocky man's neck. The warrior then slowly started making his way towards Fuse, darting from vehicle to vehicle, crouching the entire time.

The second warrior made his way in the rafters to Fuse. He hovered over the man, unseen, waiting for the break in the return gunfire that would allow him to safely drop behind the man and dispatch him.

While he waited, Olo made his way for Vic. Olo had made it clear that the tall traitor was his and his alone. His men did not question him.

The three other Na'gee warriors that had accompanied Olo, made their way straight down the middle rafters of the parking deck, headed towards the doorway leading to the hotel.

Vic's peripheral vision caught something flying by to his right, towards the outside of the western wall of parking deck. He stopped firing and surveyed that area of the parking deck.

"Was that a person flying by?" Vic thought. "Wait a second, there's no gunfire. Why isn't Digg's shooting?" Vic wondered as he noticed the lack of movement or noise coming from that direction.

Before another thought could cross his mind, Vic saw the huge helicopter crashing down past the outside western wall. He noticed it spinning erratically as it fell past the opening air of the outer half wall. Vic was shocked, "Holy shit what's happening up there?" He wondered.

With the thought, he half glanced upwards and noticed the three warriors, crawling from rafter to rafter, right down the center of the parking deck. They were headed towards the doorway that Vic and Fuse had the mercenaries pinned at.

"Sneaky fuckers!" Vic thought as he raised his rifle and unloaded on the center rafters and warriors alike.

Vic hit all three several times and their bodies fell into the center of the parking deck.

Vic changed his clip and took off heading for Diggs position. "Something isn't right." The tall man thought. After a few feet, he began scanning the rafters in front of him while he ran. He had almost made it to the doorway at the western side of the deck, that led to the exterior staircase of the large garage, when he noticed 'Gridlox' gang members, start coming out of the doorway.

Vic didn't slow down, he just started shooting as he continued to run towards them. What Vic had not noticed is Olo who had dropped behind him, right before he started running in this direction. He also had not noticed Olo silently running behind him.

Vic cleared the doorway, or at least he figured he did.

He'd either killed all the men there or scared them back into the stairwell for cover. He kept moving and scanning everything in the direction he ran. While he didn't see any other falling men or helicopters, he noticed a rope that was hanging outside the garage. The rope came from above and kept going as far as he could see.

"They must be where the damn tattooed and creepy came from." Vic thought.

Then he was struck in the center of the back by what felt like a strong kick. Vic went staggering forward but managed to stay on his feet.

The tall man, whipped around with his assault rifle, only to receive another hard kick right on the wrist of his right hand. The same hand that held the rifle's grip. He felt a sharp pain in his wrist and the rifle went flying out of his hands.

Vic glimpsed the warrior in front of him. He saw the fearsome warrior's right arm swinging a fist towards his head, and let instinct take over.

Fuse stopped firing at the doorway when he noticed the three creepy tattooed bald men fall from the rafters in the center of the ceiling.

"Oh, shit! They're coming from everywhere!" Fuse said to himself.

He saw Vic, who had seen them and gunned them down, start running towards Diggs position and instantly was flooded with worry for his friend. Diggs and Fuse had fought together for many years and he always worried about the grumpy short soldier.

Fuse started to scan the ceiling to see if any more adversaries had taken the rafter route, and caught a blur of motion slightly behind him.

He flipped around to see a Na'gee warrior land behind him. Fuse saw the man's feet hit the ground, without making a noise. Without thinking Fuse, leaned sideways and kicked the man as he rose. He didn't have to think, Fuse was well trained. If an enemy gets too close, you use your feet to push them back and give yourself space to swing your rifle around to dispatch them. He done it before, he didn't think twice about doing it now. Only now, it didn't quite work like it had in the past.

Despite still being in the process of rising from his drop to the floor, the warrior wasn't caught off guard. He caught Fuse's foot, swept his other leg out from under him and elbowed Fuse in the face as he came crashing down. Fuse hit the ground in front of him hard and rolled to his right, in an attempt to avoid the following blow from the warrior that he guessed was coming.

The warrior held his position and slowly pulled the large knife out of the sheath on his belt. He watched Fuse roll out of the way, and he watched him rising to his feet. The warrior watched it all with the patience and precision of skilled predatory, stalking it's prey.

As soon as Fuse made it to his feet, the warrior struck. He grabbed the end of the rifle with his left, while he simultaneously used the knife in his right hand. The quick motion ended with Fuse taking the oversized knife right into his gut. The large knife protruded from his back as it stuck all the way through the soldier. Fuse gagged and blood began coming out of his mouth.

The warrior held Fuse up and stared into his eyes for a long moment, then shoved the man off his knife and watched him collapse onto the floor. The warrior looked up and saw the mercenaries pouring through the doorway. He stepped from around the vehicle and halted them in their tracks. The other Na'gee who had been heading towards him, silently dropped from the ceiling next to him. They stopped the mercenaries from going any further into the parking deck and then they turned and watched the fight that had begun between Olo and the tall man. They knew they were not to let anyone interfere. Olo had made it clear that this one was his. The seasoned warriors had experienced this in battles on the 'otherside' before. Olo was in charge of the Na'gee hunting parties and often picked the largest predator or adversary as 'his'. They watched and they waited, while Fuse lay on the ground on the other side of the car, he only minutes before used as cover. He wasn't dead, but he was bleeding out quickly. He knew this was it. He decided this would be it for everyone if he had a say in it.

As he lay on the ground, Fuse placed one hand flat on the ground and reached the other hand towards the support column next to him. He closed his eyes and held onto life while he charged the floor and the column with his gift. He began charging them with everything he had. He figured if he could hang on long enough, he could take the whole damn building out with every one of these bastards in it.

As the fist swung towards Vic's head, he dipped down slightly and stepped into his attacker. Swinging a hard left hook towards the warrior's mid-section, he knocked the man backwards.

Before Vic could flow into his next move however, the warrior responded by swinging his left knee up and into Vic's ribs. The warrior, Olo, followed the movement with a leaping punch with his left hand. Vic sidestepped the punch and caught the warrior's arm, throwing the warrior over his body towards the wall.

Olo, felt the grip on his arm and momentum of his body being flung by the tall man so he locked his hand onto the arm of the man that was flinging him. The result was that as Vic hurled the warrior over his shoulder, it built momentum, the warrior hung onto his arm and landed flinging Vic instead over his body. To the Na'gee and the Mercs observing, it looked like a wild acrobatic, two man cartwheel or something to that effect. Regardless of how it appeared, they all saw that it ended with Vic crashing into the concrete half wall that ran around the perimeter of the parking deck.

Vic crashed into the wall hard. His shoulder felt tweaked from the throw. He started to jump to his feet and met a booted heel to the face. It was followed by a hard overhanded right fist to the head. Then a left hook to the jaw. Vic was being pummeled, he couldn't get to his feet and had the concrete wall to his back. The forcefulness of each blow was astonishing to Vic. He had been hit, a lot, but had never been hit this hard. The tall man did the only thing he could think of, he dove forward crashing into his attacker's mid-section.

The diving tackle knocked Olo on his back and Vic immediately began rocking from left to right hitting Olo in the face with everything he had. About four hard blows connected, before Olo was able to throw his forearms up to block the hail of punches. Vic didn't care, he didn't let up. He just kept swinging. Then he was flying.

Olo slid his feet under him and kicked himself in a backwards type of flip or somersault, sending Vic who was on top of him flying over his head and crashing to the ground. Olo jumped to his feet and flipped over Vic's head, while Vic was rising. As soon as Olo landed on the other side of Vic, he jumped and kicked Vic with both feet in the back, sending him crashing into the concrete half wall again. Olo then ran towards Vic and leapt right past the tall man over the wall, off the parking deck floor. He dove for the hanging rope, caught it with both hands and swung back in towards the wall.

Olo swung back into the parking deck, past Vic on the opposite side of him from where he had initially leapt over the wall, still holding the rope. Instead of landing the warrior, simply hit the ground running and leapt off again, doing the same move, diving out into the open air on one side of Vic and swinging back into the parking deck on the other side of Vic. This time when he swung in, he dove as far inside the garage as he could, and the rope sinched tight around Vic's neck.

Vic hadn't caught on to what the man had been working towards, he had waited for his moment to strike the man that was jumping on and off the parking deck on either side of him, for seemingly no reason. By the time Vic figured out what the warrior was up to, the rope was choking him. The warrior had gotten to his feet and pulled hard. Vic had both hands on the rope that was wrapped around his neck. As the warrior pulled harder Vic choked for breath more. He couldn't get the rope free and knew that he was slowly being choked out, the rope was pulled too tightly for him to move.

Then the warrior who was facing him, the warrior that was using his entire body to keep sinching the rope around Vic's neck tighter and tighter, spoke in a deep an authoritative tone.

"I am Olo, traitor. I have visited your wife, your son Steph, and your daughter Mila." Olo paused and let the words sink into the choking man's brain. He waited for Vic to not only understand what he had said, but to realize that he had used his children's names.

Then Olo continued "Your son Steph is mine now. He will be bathed in the aging waters, taught to fight like the Na'gee and then he will come back to kill your family. You have my word, top sider, your wife, and your retched daughter will die by your son's hands, while I, Olo, watch over. Take this knowledge to your grave traitor!"

Olo did not speak again, he simply pulled on the rope with greater force.

Vic heard the terrifying words, he was flooded with fear, rage, sadness and guilt all at once.

"How? How could he get to them? I should've been there!" Vic thought, as he struggled to maintain the consciousness that was slowly slipping away from him. He started seeing stars and felt himself blacking out, then suddenly the pressure around his neck loosened.

His blurry, disoriented vision caught glimpses of the warrior he had battled, dropping the rope, running towards him and then leaping with both feet out in front of him.

Vic was suddenly struck in the chest with the incredible force of both Olo's legs and went flying over the edge of the second story of the parking deck. He blacked out, before his body came crashing down from its two-story drop, right into the top of the 'Gridlox', large lowrider sedan that was parked outside the hotel. The impact crushed the vehicle.

Behind Olo the two Na'gee warriors and the large group of Mercenaries had watched the entire fight. Lieutenant Riker was standing by the two Na'gee while the rest of the mercs stood further behind. They'd witnessed, not only Olo's fighting skills, but his quick thinking and use of his surroundings to take on the formidable tall man. They had heard the strange words that Olo had said to the man. To the Na'gee, the words were slightly confusing and very concerning. They knew there must be a reason that Olo hadn't murdered the man's family that he had spoken of but did not understand what it could be. To Lieutenant Riker, the words sounded like nonsense, meant only to torment his opponent on his way to death. Riker did not try to hide the vicious smile on his face. Emotionally tormenting his opponent before killing him, made him like this Olo even more.

Olo slowly turned around and looked at the gathered audience, with an evil triumphant look in his eyes.

"I have much to do. Go help them on the roof." As Olo gave the instructions, he rubbed the stone circular talisman that hung around his neck, as it did with all Na'gee warriors, and the blur appeared behind him. Olo, stepped through the blur, or the path to the 'otherside' as the Na'gee called it and then he was gone and the blur disappeared.

CHAPTER 35:
THE ESCAPE ROUTE

amacho halted a couple feet before the massacre before him, stopping right next to Venco who watched the bloodbath. He saw the knife fighter continue to disappear and then appear behind trained Na'gee warriors only to slash their throats. Captain Venco, the head of his private security, was not a Na'gee warrior by any means, but he was a well-trained fighter and a battle tested soldier. You had to be to lead Camacho's private security.

The mercenary group had previously been known as 'The Plague'. They were one of the largest and most notorious mercenary groups in the world. They hand branches or cells in several different countries. Each of which had its own leader. They did not all roll up to one over-arching authority, it was more like each cell had a leader that would coordinate with other cell leaders. This approach had led to their longevity as taking out one commanding officer, did nothing to rattle their organization.

In all actuality, various cells fairly frequently took out their own commanding officers. Their code was clear, survival of the fittest. If you killed the commanding officer, you took command. Clear and simple. The belief was that this kept 'The Plague' strong.

Captain Venco, led the U.S. cell of 'The Plague' and to hold that rank for any amount of time, was a testament to his competence and his capacity for violence. For quite a while now, the U.S. cell had focused on working for Camacho. The shorter man paid better than most small countries and warlords and kept them busy with far more than just his security detail.

After a moment of watching, all the Na'gee surrounding Dante had been killed and the young knife fighter with the gift of teleportation, turned his eyes on Camacho and Venco.

Neither man said a word, they just silently moved a couple steps away from each other, giving themselves distance to move freely without the other being in their way. Both Camacho and Venco had observed enough to know what they were facing and where the attack would come from. Words were not needed. They knew what they needed to do and knew that they would either time their moves correctly or they would die. It was as simple as that.

As soon as Dante, disappeared each man that now stood facing one another, swung their elbows hard behind them at seemingly nothing.

Camacho's body whirled around, swung in a circle, his elbow hitting nothing but air. Venco's elbow however, went from swinging at the open air behind him to smashing into Dante's face that was suddenly behind him. As soon as his elbow connected, he reversed his momentum as fast as he could and swung backwards with the other elbow. Venco's right elbow connected with Dante's head, just like his left elbow had seconds before.

Camacho saw the captain of his security catch the knife fighter in the head. He saw the younger, smaller knife fighter stagger from the impact of the two hard hits he had taken to the head. Camacho took off, using every bit of the unnatural speed that he'd gotten from the effects of the 'gene' and landed a powerful running punch to Dante's chest. The hit sent the young mad flying across the roof.

Dante was in a rage, he moved faster than he had ever moved before. He focused on slicing men open, while always looking at the next spot he would appear. It resulted in a kind of elegant ballet dance of teleporting and slashing and teleporting and slashing. Trained Na'gee warriors died all around him. Dante didn't think, he didn't care what the men were doing. He didn't care what weapons they held. None of it mattered. He was too fast, one second here and then one second there. Every reappearance resulting in another body dropping to the ground.

When the last of the warriors around fell, Dante looked up to see a soldier in all black and Camacho himself standing side by side watching him. Dante knew this was his moment for vengeance. He didn't have to think, he teleported to kill the man by Camacho, so he could relish killing Camacho last, without any distractions. When he appeared behind the man though, he was instantly hit. Then Dante was hit again. He didn't know what had happened. He didn't know what had even hit him. He saw stars. He couldn't focus, he couldn't think, he couldn't teleport away. He was just dizzy and then something hit him in the chest so hard that he felt ribs on both sides crack, before everything went black.

"Make sure he's finished. I'll deal with the other one." Camacho said to Venco. Captain Venco only nodded and began walking towards Dante's collapsed body across the roof.

Camacho turned his attention to Samuel, who had watched it all, as he had been slowly making his way towards Camacho. There were eight mercenaries left, frozen in odd positions behind Samuel.

The two men's eyes locked, then Camacho took off, running towards Samuel with incredible speed. One thought ran through Camacho's mind as he ran "Can't let him touch me."

Samuel had seen what Camacho and his mercenary had done to Dante. Samuel had noticed that they were thoughtful about their defense. He also noticed that Camacho had incredible speed. The speed he expected, the intelligent approach to fighting was a surprise to him. Samuel had hunted Camacho for years and he knew that the effect of the 'gene' had given Camacho incredible speed and strength. He had always known the man to be violent and irrational though, not intelligent and patient.

He recalculated his strategy based on this observation and pulled out both of his pistols.

"If the fool noticed how to combat Dante's gifts, then he'll be focused on not letting me touch him. Guess we'll do this without the intimacy of touch." Samuel thought to himself, still walking towards Camacho.

He saw Camacho's companion head off towards Dante, knowing this meant that the man intended to kill Dante before he recovered. Samuel felt a rare feeling of guilt. He felt responsible for Dante. He wanted to help the young man, to save the young man, but knew there was nothing he could do. Not while he faced Camacho. Then all thoughts stopped, when he saw Camacho take off for him.

Samuel barely saw the man take off. "Damn, he's fast." Samuel thought as he instinctively spun to his right firing both pistols at the ground where he just stood.

The fuzzy image of Camacho speeding by running, turned into a wild uncoordinated crash into the frozen bodies of the mercenaries that Samuel had left behind.

Camacho got to his feet, very unsteadily, and Samuel noticed blood pouring from his left calf. Camacho stared at him, face red with rage. He took off back towards Samuel, this time zigging and zagging. Camacho was still fast, but he was nowhere near as fast as he was before Samuel's shot had injured his leg.

Instead of firing his pistols this time, Samuel counted to three as the zigging and zagging man flew in his direction. On three, and with the man almost upon him, Samuel dropped to crouch and did a sweeping spin move with his right leg extended. Before he even saw Camacho on him, he felt his leg connect and the fast man crashed to the ground hard, sliding several feet away.

Samuel didn't wait for him to recover; he came up out of the crouching spin move and opened fire on the spot Camacho had come sliding to a stop at. Camacho still spread out, from his crashing slide, just rolled across the roof, side over side, almost as fast as he had run. Then he jumped to his feet, albeit quite unsteady, with the bullet wound in left calf. He stared at Samuel; Samuel stared back.

As Roid made his way towards Dante and Samuel, he saw Dante finish off the weird, tattooed warriors surrounding him. He saw Dante get caught off guard and he saw the battle begin between Samuel and the amazingly fast smaller man that had hit him with incredible force earlier.

Roid was shocked at how well this Samuel, or the 'Ghost Agent' that his unit had been sent for handled himself against an opponent so much faster and stronger. The big man was impressed and made a mental note to watch this Samuel character closely, if they made it out of this alive.

Roid saw the mercenary stalking towards the body of Dante. The large man didn't know if Dante was still alive or not, but he knew he wouldn't be for long if that mercenary got to him. Roid pulled up his rifle and started shooting at the merc, Venco, who approached Dante.

Venco, saw the big man running towards Camacho, stop and shift his attention to him. As soon as the large man raised his rifle, Venco dove behind a large rooftop HVAC unit for cover. He crouched behind it as he heard the bullets beat into the other side of the HVAC unit. He popped up to return fire, knowing that there was nothing near the big man that he could use for cover.

"This will be quick. Damn oversized fool started a fire fight without any cover. Surprised he's survived long enough to get the privilege of dying by my hands." Venco thought to himself.

As Venco jumped up and opened fire though, he found himself shooting a very different man. This was not the same enormous solider that he had intended to kill. This man was a completely different solider with red hair and broad shoulders and the bullets seemed to only piss the man off and shred his clothing. The man was running at him fast. His body positioned in between Venco and the large soldier, catching all the gun fire, like a human shield. A human shield that was propelling towards him quickly Venco thought.

"Nope. Not getting into hand-to-hand combat with somebody that's freaking bullet proof." Venco thought as he jumped up. Venco turned away from the rapidly approaching solider and quickly covered the few feet between him and the edge of the roof. Then he just place both hands of the edge and hand vaulted himself off the roof.

Halbred skidded to a stop, when he saw the mercenary vault himself over the side of the roof and thought "coward" to himself.

He turned back to Roid and said, "check on Flutter, Roid!"

"Yes sir!" Roid shouted back and took off towards his fallen his companion, who had still not moved since being hit.

Halbred looked up and saw Samuel facing off against the smaller man with the incredible speed and strength and took off running in their direction without hesitation. He intended to make sure this little speedster who might have killed Flutter was taken care of. From what Halbred could tell, the small man appeared to be in charge here, which made him responsible for the deaths of Bird and Radio too. Enraged and driven by an overwhelming desire for vengeance, he cleared the distance between them in no time.

Halbred, saw Samuel holding his own. He noticed that Samuel had injured the man's left leg, which had slowed him down some. He saw Samuel try to end it with his pistols and watched the man roll on his side with lighting quickness avoiding the gunfire. He watched the man jump to his feet and stare at Samuel. Samuel stared back. Halbred, kept on running completely unnoticed by the smaller man with the mohawk and slammed his fist into the side of the man's head with everything he had.

The blow sent Camacho staggering and Samuel fired again. He caught Camacho in the side, before the man took off towards the other side of the roof. Samuel began to follow. Halbred, pulled his own sidearm and headed towards Camacho too. Both men intent on not letting the smaller man leave the roof alive.

Camacho felt the bullet hit his side and took off running, head still spinning from the hit he'd taken to the head. He didn't know who or what hit him, but he knew this was suddenly not going at all like he had intended it to go. As he ran, he noticed two, Na'gee warriors hop onto the roof from where the rope that Olo had taken earlier, hung over the edge. Camacho skidded to a stop next to the men.

Halbred and Samuel weren't far behind him, both jogging towards the three of them.

As they ran, Halbred's comms unit came to life crackling

in his ear. "It's over guys. Diggs is dead… Vic's dead….I'm done… buildings about to blow…. Get your ass's out of there… you …. Got…. Three minutes."

The voice sounded like it was choking or gurgling, and the words were broken up, but it was clearly Fuse. Halbred wanted to ask what happened. He wanted order the man to get up and get out alive, but Halbred was a seasoned solider. He knew there was nothing to say. He knew from the sound of the voice and what it had said, that Fuse was gone. He also knew that Fuse was taking this entire building with him.

"Building's gonna blow! Everyone else is dead! We gotta get outta here!" Halbred yelled to Samuel as the two ran towards Camacho, who had been joined with two of the weird, tattooed warriors that had appeared from the side of the roof.

Roid had Flutter in his arms, she was alive, but was still unconcious. He was heading towards Halbred when he heard Fuse through the open communications channel in his comms unit. The big man's heart broke. In an instant the unit had gone from an unstoppable force to half of them dead. These were his friends, his family. He loved them all and now had lost almost all of them. He noticed the two warriors come up from the edge of the roof and saw the rope hanging over the edge.

Roid started running, connecting the straps and clips he had on his uniform to the ones on Flutter's uniform. The big man figured that repelling down the side of the building would be the fastest way out of this time bomb and intended to bring Flutter with him.

"No way I'm losing anyone else today!" Roid thought passionately.

Camacho made it to the two Na'gee warriors and almost collapsed into one of them. He knew he was losing way too much blood, way too fast. The bullet wound in his side screamed with pain. The closest warrior caught hold of him and held him up, looking at the wound in his side and then in his leg.

"We've got to get out of here" Camacho said. "Open a path now!"

Neither warrior responded, but the one that was not holding him up, immediately started rubbing the talisman he wore around his neck and the blur appeared before them. Camacho and the warrior who helped hold him up stepped through. The second warrior followed.

Halbred and Samuel both saw their target escaping through the weird blur that appeared to be some sort of gateway or transportation method. Both men sped up.

Halbred, seeing Roid running towards them yelled "Follow them! We're going in!"

As the second warrior stepped through, Samuel dove through the portal behind him. Halbred followed him, almost crashing into Samuel as they dove at almost the same time. As the pathway started to close, Roid dove through, still carrying the body of flutter.

In an instant, Camacho, the two Na'gee, Samuel, Roid and Flutter were gone.

Chapter 36:
Aftermath

Captain Venco, who had appeared to hand vault off the top of the roof, but had really just hung onto the outside edge, hanging for several minutes until he felt confident the soldiers had moved on. Pulled himself back up onto the roof.

He saw the blur in the air appear across the roof. He was familiar with this, as the tattooed bald men referred to as 'Camacho's Family' often appeared from these blurry breaks or openings in the air. He watched Camacho, the Na'gee and the men they fought disappear into the blur. He saw the blur vanish and was left alone on the roof.

Captain Venco shrugged, pulled his sidearm and began walking towards the body of Dante, that had still not moved. As he slowly walked towards the unconscious man, he saw the doors to the stairs open up to a large group of his men, led by Lieutenant Riker.

Venco noticed Riker's hand to the comms unit on his ear. He noticed the man talking, but he didn't hear anything in his comms unit. This seemed strange to Venco, as they were all on the same open communications channel. Anything that Riker heard, he should be hearing too.

He made a mental note, to confront to the him after he'd finished killing the fallen young man he was nearing. Riker, motioned for the men with him to stay behind and began walking to meet Venco at the body of the young Hispanic man lying on the roof. None of the men, seemed aware that they were minutes away from the entire building exploding.

Vic awoke to the sound of an incredible explosion and the feeling of heat searing his skin. He struggled to move his body, that roared out in pain from every part of him. He didn't know where he was and struggled to remember what had happened to him.

As he slowly opened his eyes, he saw the entire hotel blowing up in a massive explosion. Flames and debris shot out in every direction. Vic gave it everything he had and managed to roll off the top of the crushed roof of the vehicle he was laying on. The roll sent him off the roof and crashing his face and chest into the asphalt. Despite the pain and the difficulty, he was having trying to move, he forced himself to slide his stiff body over, tucked himself as far under the crushed vehicle as he could. He laid there in agony, trying to collect his thoughts as debris from the explosion rained down all around him.

As Vic lay there, it all slowly came back to him. He remembered his fight with the warrior who had called himself Olo. He remembered failing to catch on to what the warrior was doing leaping around with the rope, until it was too late. Then he remembered the words the warrior had said to him, as this Olo was choking the life out of him.

"Steph! He said Steph was his! He knew my son's name. He knew Mila's name." The thoughts came pouring into Vic's mind. It filled him with panic, but also with adrenaline. He lay there, worrying frantically about his children and his wife. Tears began to streak down his face.

After what seemed like forever, the explosion seemed to stop. Debris and wreckage stopped raining down all around him. Vic began to slide out from under the cover of the crushed vehicle, feeling pain everywhere in his body.

The tall man struggled to his feet. Despite the pain, he didn't feel like anything was broken, but he didn't know for sure. He slowly started walking. Every step hurt like hell. He was wobbly and unbalanced, but he kept moving, walking away from the destruction and devastation that was left from the hotel explosion. He didn't care about it. He didn't care how it was destroyed. He didn't care who had made it and who hadn't. Nothing but his family mattered right now, so Vic kept walking, gaining speed and balance as he went along.

It seemed like it took hours to make it the few blocks to the old antique shop. Vic made his way to the alley that ran down the side of the building and noticed the chunks of brick everywhere when he rounded the corner. He noticed the huge missing piece of wall at the far corner of the building, where the entrance to the basement hideaway was supposed to be and fear for the worst flooded him.

Limping, but still moving, Vic made his way to huge gap where a wall obviously used to be. He could see rubble and debris inside the building. More tears streamed from his eyes as he stared at what was left of the place he had sent his family too.

"They were supposed to be safe here!" Vic thought. Self-blaming thoughts overtook him, and the tall man almost fell to his knees to weep, when he heard the word "Daddy?"

Vic looked up, wondering if he had imagined it. He started to climb through the opening into the debris and rubble of what was left of the basement room. Then he saw them. Eva and Mila, sobbing and holding each other. They were huddled together in the far corner of the basement room. Mila's eye's caught Vic's. Both pairs of eyes full of tears. Eva had not looked up.

Vic hurried across the destroyed room and half collapsed next to them. He wrapped his arms around them. As the tears poured down his eyes, Vic found himself unable to speak. He was so overwhelmed with emotion that the words would not form in mouth. He just squeezed his wife and daughter and cried with joy that he had found them alive.

After several moments Eva looked up into her husband's eyes, seeming to notice him for the first time. She was clearly distraught and had a crazed look in her eyes. She seemed to struggle to speak and then finally managed to get the words out. "He took Steph! He took our son Vic!"

Vic didn't need to ask who. The words that the warrior Olo had spoken to him coursed through his mind.

"I know Eva. I know." Vic said as he squeezed his wife even tighter. Then Vic sat back a little, pulling himself together and looked at Eva and Mila with some degree of his composure having returned.

"He's not dead. Whatever the hell they're doing to him, they're not killing him. I fought the man that took him, he said he was training him. Training him to come back and kill both of you." Vic said solemnly to both his wife and daughter.

The words were even more confusing to him when he heard himself say it out loud. "How the hell can a little child be trained to come kill his mother and sister." Vic thought to himself.

What he said was very different though. "He's a small child. If they're intent on training him as one of their own for any purpose, regardless of what it is, it means we have time Eva. We have time to get him back." Vic said it with passion. His words that were meant to reassure his wife, oddly inspired him at the same time.

"We just have to figure out where those weird blurry paths take them and how to get there." Vic said, starting to shake the emotions, as he shifted his focus to what needed to be done.

"They lead to their world Dad." Mila said. Then seeing the look on her father's face, she added "I don't know how I know. I just do Dad. There's a lot I don't understand about myself now, but you must believe me."

As Mila finished talking, she stood and began to make her way across what remained of the basement room. With both parents watching her, wondering what she was doing, she began digging through the debris on the other side of the room. They saw her move several chunks of concrete and brick. They saw the body of the dead Na'gee warrior she uncovered. Then they watched as Mila carefully removed the long leather strap from over the dead warrior's head.

The strap had a circular talisman that appeared to be made from stone hanging on it. Holding it out before her, Mila slowly ran her hand across it in a circular motion and a blur appeared in the middle of the room. She stared at the blur, then looked back at her parents who had been watching in awe then entire time.

Her eyes were filled with a bright white light and her body had a faint strange glow coming from it. She stared at her parents and then spoke in a voice that did not seem to be her own.

"This is the way to their world Dad. Let's go get Steph back." Mila said in an distant ominous voice.

Vic and Eva stared at the blur that had appeared. They stared at what had become of the daughter, filled with confusion and worry, then they looked at each other.

Vic stood up slowly, staring at his wife while he rose. "We'll get him back Eva. I promise we'll get him back." He turned and began moving towards the blur or the path that Mila held open near her and heard Eva speak behind him.

"Oh, no you don't Vic! We're not splitting up again! We're all going to get our son!" Eva said loudly and aggressively as she began limping across the room behind Vic.

The tall man stopped and reached out his arm for Eva to lean on and together the two hobbled over to the their daughter who seemed to glow brighter than she had moments ago.

The three of them walked through the path together and the blur disappeared.

PART 2
THE "OTHER SIDE"

Chapter 37: Arrival

Samuel's dive ended with him hitting soft grass and quickly rolling to his feet. He was on a grassy hill, that seemed to peek out of the top of a dense wooded forest. From his vantage point on the hill, he could see that the forest covered as far as the eye could see, only broken up by small lakes and patches of grassy fields or plains.

The sky here had a slightly orange tint to it, but Samuel couldn't tell if that was this place, wherever it was or if it was because it was evening time here and the sun was on its way down. He caught flashes of people running from the bottom of the hill to disappear into the dense forest. They seemed to be Na'gee, though only a few that he saw seemed to have the same shaved head and tattooed look. Others just seemed to be similarly indigenous looking people.

As Samuel got his bearings, he caught a blur of motion from over his right shoulder and quickly spun out of the way. The move allowed him to barely dodge the large knife that swung downward towards him.

One of the two Na'gee had swung it and the other was

slowly creeping around behind him with his own knife drawn.

"Hurry! The sun is near setting you fools! And don't let that one touch you!" He heard Camacho yell from a few feet away.

"I don't fucking think so!" Halbred yelled as dove into the Na'gee that was creeping behind Samuel, tackling the warrior into the grass. Halbred's tackling movement instantly transitioned into a death grip, as he wrapped his powerful legs around the warrior's neck and used each arm to tug tightly on each of the warrior's arms. He executed the move with trained efficiency, and it looked like nothing but torture to the Na'gee warrior who struggled to break free and to breathe.

The other warrior saw Samuel watching and swung downward at Samuel's head with the massive knife again. Samuel saw it coming and this time he did more than just dodge the attack. Samuel stepped under the warrior's arm and swung upwards with his left hand into the warriors elbow. A loud 'cracking' noise filled the air and the warrior howled with pain and his entire elbow reversed its position and his bones protruded from his arm. As the 'cracking' noise and the warrior's howl filled the air, Samuel was swinging his right hand hard into the warrior's gut.

As the warrior bent over, from the impact of the gut punch, Samuel turned his back to him, wrapped his right arm around the warrior's neck that was bent forward in a sort of bow and dropped to the ground, breaking the Na'gee's neck.

The 'crunching' sound of the neck breaking sounded like it echoed from across the hill. When Samuel jumped back to his feet, he noticed Halbred jumping to his feet at the same time and saw the other Na'gee lying on the ground with a broken neck of his own.

Camacho watched it all. He watched the events unfold and end quickly, while he stood debating whether he dared get involved again with two bullet wounds, the one his side bleeding profusely. He watched both of these men turn their attention on him, while the large stood behind them, still holding the unconscious woman.

Despite the odds and his injury, his pride still had him deciding whether to attack them or not. He still felt he could kill them all with his bare hands. "But at what cost?" He thought.

Then Camacho noticed the sky. He noticed the sun beginning to set and then looked down at the blood on his hands and pouring from his side. A fearful realization washed over Camacho, his face turned as white as a ghost and he took off down the hill and into the woods, with all of the speed he could still muster.

Samuel saw him run and knew there was no way he could catch the speedster. He also saw the blood trail and felt confident he could track him, with relative ease. What he couldn't understand was where the sudden look of fear on Camacho's face had come from.

As Samuel begin to look around, trying to figure out what had frightened the man so bad, on his own turf, he heard Halbred speak.

"I don't know this place and I know most places. What I do know is that when a native gets that scared in their own land, you take cover quick. Everyone move! Get off this damn open hill and into the cover of the trees! Now!!!" Halbred yelled it all.

He was a trained soldier and had been in many strange places, his words made too much sense to ignore. Roid, still holding Flutter, began running with Halbred closely behind him looking this way and that way, while he ran. Samuel only delayed long enough to snatch the strange circular stone talisman off of each dead Na'gee's neck before running quickly behind the two soldiers.

As the group made it to the tree line, they quickly found cover in a thicket of bushes, several feet into the think forest, just outside the clearing at the bottom of the hill. Roid laid down Flutter, who was breathing, but still unconscious. It was hard to tell how bad her injuries were just yet, there just hadn't been time. Halbred looked at her and then quietly motioned for Roid to go gather some nearby fallen branches to make a stretcher of some sort.

Without a word being spoken, the instructions were clear to Samuel who barely knew these men. The way Roid took off, made it evident that they were just as clear to him. The big man, moved silently and much faster than Samuel would have thought a man of his size could move. With trained stealth, Roid was off moving around the tree line in the shadow's, gathering branches. Samuel and Halbred stayed crouched in the thicket by Flutter, who they had gently laid on the ground near them. Both men surveyed the land, looking for whatever unknown dangers had terrified Camacho, as they watched the sun set and darkness fall.

It was mere seconds after the sun set, when they noticed the two shapes appear at the top of the hill. They had obviously come from the far side of the hill and had seemed to arrive at the top of the grassy hill at incredible speeds, based on the way they skidded to a stop.

They wore black tattered cloaks of some sort, with hoods that were thrown back from their fast movements. Even from the tree line at the bottom of the hill, Samuel and Halbred could clearly make out their pale, almost translucent looking skin. They seemed shaped like men, just very tall and lanky and without a sign of hair on their bodies.

Samuel tapped Halbred and whispered, "look at their hands and feet."

Halbred peered closely and saw fingers and toes that seemed almost three times longer than a normal person. They seemed to end in pointy claw like features. The more they looked at them, the less they looked like men at all, this was emphasized as they started sniffing the air and oddly jerking their bodies this way and that way as they moved. The creatures seemed to gravitate to the spot where Camacho had stood and then they both dropped to all fours, sniffed, and then began licking the ground, like dogs licking up something that spilled.

An instant later, their heads jerked up and they started sniffing the air. Both of the creatures sniffing motions, aimed them in the direction of the tree line where Roid had stopped his collection of branches and hid behind a large tree. Apparently, the large man had seen them too.

The creatures rose from all fours, back to standing, somewhat hunched over on two feet and slowly began creeping down the hill, sniffing the air as the moved. As they neared the bottom of the hill, the two creatures began to separate themselves from each other. One of the creatures slowed it's pace and moved directly towards Roid's location, while the other creature looked around like a wild animal and then took off into the woods about fifteen feet further down the tree line from where Roid hid.

The speed at which the second creature took off, unnerved Samuel as he watched them. The closer they got, the more it was clear that whatever these things were, it definitely wasn't human. Their large eyes shined a glossy black. They had no pupils from what he could tell, they had pointed ears and their skin was such a pale white that it was almost translucent. Their incredibly long fingers and toes were tipped in pointed claws. The creatures looked very predatory, and Samuel figured that if they were the reason that Camacho had ran off, then they were undoubtedly formidable. He continued to watch from behind the brush where he crouched next to Halbred and Flutter, who still lay unconscious on the ground.

He watched the creature approach the tree that Roid hid behind. He watched Roid slowly moved around the giant tree, as the creature started to circle it. They saw Roid pull a long knife from his belt and start to speed up his silent movements around the tree. The large man's intentions were obvious to the observers, he intended to circle behind the creature and end it silently, hoping not to alert its counterpart that had disappeared somewhere into the woods.

As they circled the tree, Samuel saw a blur of movement

in the branches above them. He stared closely, wondering if he was seeing things and then saw it again. As he peered into the tree branches that hung a good twenty feet above Roid and the creature, Samuel made out the shape of the other creature. It was crouching on a branch, hidden well by the way its black tattered cloak blended in with the darkness of the night and shadows in the branches. The creature was looking down and it had caused the hood of the tattered cloak to fall over its head, making it even harder to make out. Despite the camouflage, Samuel clearly saw what was happening… they were hunting Roid. He knew that as soon as Roid walked under the creature, it would pounce. He began to suspect that the other creature knew exactly where Roid was and was setting him up for the surprise attack.

Samuel didn't know if Halbred noticed what was happening or not, but he decided he didn't care. He felt the guilt weighing heavily on him for the deaths of Vic and Dante. He felt the guilt weighing on him for Dante's family. Samuel knew that it was the cost had that to be paid for vengeance, but that cold logic didn't alleviate the responsibility he felt for these good men losing their lives. He had grown attached to them both in a very short amount of time and blamed himself for what had happened to them. Samuel decided that he would not let another good man die today.

Samuel jumped to his feet, leaped over the thicket that they hid behind and ran towards the clearing, pulling one of his pistols in the process. In three long strides, Samuel had emerged from the tree line into the clearing at the bottom of the hill and began firing his pistol at the creature in the tree, who was almost directly over Roid by now.

The creature leaped through the air, dodging the bullets, and landed in the clearing about five feet in front of Samuel. Not only was it twenty feet in the air only moments ago, but it was also at least twenty feet away. Despite the distance, the creature made the leap towards its new target with relative ease.

It hissed at Samuel, revealing jagged teeth and two incredibly long fangs. Then it dove for Samuel. Samuel tried to shoot it, while it dove but the creature twisted its body in the air evading the gunfire and crashed into Samuel. When it hit him, Samuel went crashing to the ground on his back with the creature on top of him. Its mouth was wide open and it looked like it was about to bite Samuel's head off. It held that look as it stayed frozen in place from Samuel's touch.

Samuel shoved the sinister looking frozen creature off of him and saw Halbred running past him with a furious look in his eyes.

"Think you gonna sneak up on me, do you?" Roid thought to himself as he creeped around the large tree. The big man knew that the creature was behind him, stalking him. Roid pulled out his long belt knife and sped up his pace around the tree without making a sound.

"We'll see who ends up being predator and prey, you creepy bastard." Roid thought as he moved. He was intent on catching the creature from behind with the knife before it ever knew what hit it. He failed to notice the other creature in the branches above, waiting for him to walk under it.

It was then that Roid saw Samuel dart into the clearing

and begin shooting into he tree above him. Roid looked up to see the creature that had been over him leap an incredible distance, only to land directly in front of Samuel across the clearing.

Then Roid was hit from behind. The large man, with strength enhanced by 'the gene', hit the ground face first and felt a terrible pain come from the large open slice on his back that had been given to him by his rooftop battle with the Na'gee.

The creature had slammed into Roids back, hitting him hard with both hands and feet at the same time. As soon as Roid hit the ground the creature dug both of its clawed feet and both of its clawed hands into the large slice across Roid's back. It tore the wound open using all four of its limbs and dove it's head and massive teeth into the center of the wound.

Roid howled in pain, which quickly diminished into gurgling murmurs as the creature tore into his insides from the wound on his back.

Halbred was running for them, he saw it all happen. To him it looked like the creature was eating Roid alive, he was almost to them when the creature looked up and stared at him. Its face was completely covered in Roid's blood, which it licked clean with one swipe of its extremely long black tongue.

Halbred was almost to them, afraid to shoot because of how close to Roid the creature was crouching. It didn't end up mattering. The thing cleared the distance between them with one leap and smashed itself into Halbred. Before the soldier could react, the creature was biting at his neck.

Despite the powerful force of its bite, the creature couldn't penetrate Halbred's skin. In what seemed similar to a feeding frenzy that a shark experiences, it continued trying to bite at his neck again and again.

This gave Halbred all the time he needed. He pulled his side arm and started firing his large pistol into the creature's body at point blank range. The beast fell off him to the side and then rose to its feet leaning over low to the ground.

Halbred saw black blood pouring out of the creature's wounds and then watched as the wounds started closing and bullet shells fell out of the creature onto the ground.

The two faced off with one another and before either moved, the creature's wounds completely healed. Halbred fired again, this time running straight at the creature as he shot it. The creature took three bullets to the chest, before it started to dodge around to the left of Halbred, despite its tremendous speed, Halbred cut off the attempt to catch him on the side with a strong right-handed punch to the things face. He followed the punch by swinging his left arm, holding the pistol to the creature's throat, and fired three more times at point blank range.

The beast staggered backwards, Halbred pulled his knife with his right hand and dove onto the creature frantically stabbing and tearing at the healing bullet wounds in the creature's neck. The beast flailed and jerked and Halbred, who now straddled the creature just cut away more furiously.

By the time Samuel made it over to the two, to help Halbred, the old, seasoned soldier had cut the creatures head off and was holding it in front of him staring at it, still straddling the creature's body.

Roid was motionless, lying face down just past the tree line, blanketed by the shadows of the massive trees. Samuel walked towards the large man and heard Halbred's raspy voice.

"It's too late Samuel. This damn thing had its entire head inside Roids body. The soldier, my friend is gone. No one could've survived that." Halbred said it all with a distant sorrow in his voice.

Samuel was not an empathetic person, but he felt for the Solider. The man had led a legendary unit, whose notoriety had reached every branch of the military and then some. He had forged these people into being a collective force to be reckoned with. Samuel knew that did not happen without building an incredible bond, a family type bond, and in a few short hours he'd lost almost all of them.

Samuel knew the guilt and responsibility he felt for letting Vic and Dante die, couldn't compare to what this man was feeling right now.

He glanced back at Halbred, trying to be discreet and not intrude on the man's moment of grief. He saw the glazed look in Halbred's eyes, he saw the way his hands slightly trembled, and he saw the aura of hatred surrounding the man as he continued to straddle the creature's headless body and stare at the head he held out in front him.

Samuel averted his eyes and walked over to where Roid lay. It was obvious that Halbred was right. Roid's back was completely ripped open. His skin was spread out to either side of his body like wings and he was a pale blue all over.

Despite the savage display his body was left in, Samuel noticed that all the organs appeared to be inside of him. At least from what he could tell at a glance. He also noticed that there was hardly any blood anywhere.

"So, the thing didn't try to eat him." Samuel thought. "Where is the blood? There should be blood everywhere." Samuel thoughts haunted him. He was pulled back from his wandering thoughts when he heard Halbred's rough voice directly behind him.

"Doesn't make a bit of damn sense." Halbred said. "Where's the fucking blood? This entire area should be drowning in Roid's blood. What the hell man, we went from dealing with damn teleporting tribal warriors to fucking vampire monsters or some shit?! Get the hell out of here!" Halbred seemed to just angrily rant all this to himself.

Despite the fact that the man was just complaining, the far-off possibility that he might actually be on to something unnerved Samuel greatly. "What is this place?" Samuel thought.

Instead of sharing any of his concerns, he instead said "Doesn't matter Halbred. You've got one solider still counting on you, and she's not going to last long if more of these come. Let's get her and get deeper in the woods. We need to find cover for the night. We'll track Camacho tomorrow and figure out where the hell we are along the way." Samuel didn't say it forcefully, but it was clear that he expected Halbred to go along with it when he said it.

Halbred stared at Samuel for a moment then huffed and stomped his way over to where Flutter was lying behind the nearby bushes, still unconscious. He picked her up delicately, and began to make his way deeper into the dark forest. Samuel followed closely behind, not failing to notice that Halbred had seemingly removed the head of the creature that Samuel had frozen.

"Must've done that while I was staring at the big soldier's body." Samuel thought.

Both men constantly looked in every direction, they were obviously on high alert. Despite their cautious behavior, neither man noticed the pair of large eyes staring at them from a patch of bushes roughly twenty feet away.

As the men walked deeper into the woods, the eyes evolved into a large shadowy shape that followed them silently, staying well-hidden and keeping back at least twenty feet.

After what seemed like a mile or two, they found a spot where two large boulders leaned against one another and massive tree. It created a confined area, with the two boulders forming makeshift walls on either side and the massive tree that had to be at least ten feet around in diameter served as the back wall. It created a sort of 'U' shape and the large low hanging branches gave it a sort of ceiling. Neither man spoke, as they both headed into the darkness of the natural shelter. Words were not needed; they knew they weren't likely to find a better spot then this.

It was pitch black in the shadows of the tree and the boulders. As their eyes adjusted, they saw that it gave them about a twelve-foot half circle to move in. They noticed strange markings in the center of the boulder on the right.

The markings were in almost a strange spiral shape, with stars or dots circling the outside of the spiral and the entire design had a faint greenish glow to it.

As Samuel looked at the design it seemed strangely familiar to him. He stared at it, trying to figure out where he'd seen it before.

Meanwhile, Halbred laid Flutter down against the tree as far back into the cover as he could get her. The seasoned Solider kept looking up into the thick branches, obviously not trusting their ceiling after the maneuver he'd seen the creatures pull on Roid earlier.

Halbred, look over at Samuel when he heard the man say "That's it. It's all the same." The soldier stepped closer to Samuel to figure out what the man could be talking about and saw him holding up the two circular stone pendants that he'd taken from the dead Na'gee.

The designs on the pendants were almost identical to the design on the boulder.

"What do you think it means Samuel?" Halbred asked gruffly, in hushed tone.

"No clue, but look, as you hold the talisman or pendant or whatever it is, closer to the design on the boulder it starts to glow the same greenish color." Samuel said as he held the Talisman closer, demonstrating what he had described.

Halbred watched then said, "it's making the design on the boulder glow brighter too."

Samuel took one of the two talisman he had held and touched the design to the design on the boulder, trying to match the shapes exactly. When he did, the front of the boulder surrounding the design opened up into a large eight-foot-tall doorway. Both men slightly gasped as they stared at the doorway that had appeared.

Samuel reached his hand into the blackness that seemed to form this large doorway and then pulled it back. He looked at Halbred, as if to silently ask the man what he thought.

Their wordless dialogue was suddenly interrupted by the sounds of light footsteps coming from both sides of the boulder.

Halbred, held four fingers up, then motioned two fingers left and two fingers right. Samuel could tell the veteran Solider was right. The footsteps were barely audible, but it was clear that there were two sets coming from each side, slowly closing in on the opening to their shelter.

The two men looked at the doorway on the boulder and then looked at the back of the shelter where Flutter lay. They realized the footsteps were too close. They wouldn't have time to get her and get through before whoever was stalking them burst through the opening.

Each man eased just inside the doorway, one hiding behind the right corner and one hiding behind the left corner.

Four of the black cloaked creatures slowly entered, sniffing the air and eyeing Flutter who was laid down at the back of the 'U' shaped shelter.

Samuel grabbed the two closest to him as they started to walk past, freezing them both instantly. Halbred drove his knife straight into the throat of the closest one to him and jerked back hard, slashing the creatures throat open. He pulled the knife free, then drove it forward again, jamming it deeply into the creature's open wound on its neck and jerked again. His quick movements had cut through half of the creature's neck. It wrenched and gasped at the air.

The second creature on Halbreds side, came down with its large teeth and fangs on Halbreds arm, trying to tear through the limb and free it's companion. It had no luck getting through Halbreds skin but kept chomping down over and over. Samuel started to move towards them to freeze this creature and was cut off by a giant wooded club that came crashing through the doorway, crushing the biting creature into the ground.

A large shape emerged from the shadows outside the opening, holding the massive club. It was at least eight feet tall and covered in black hair. It looked like a cross between a man and giant ape. It looked at Halbred, still fighting the creature he held and was still working to saw the creatures head off with his knife while struggled. Then the creature looked at Samuel who eased back a step.

With one swift motion, the creature lifted up the massive club and slammed it down on the head of the creature it had just smashed. Turning the creatures head into nothing more than a chunky black puddle.

It turned quickly towards Samuel, swung its club past Samuel and smashed one of the frozen creatures the same way. Then the large hairy thing did the same to the other frozen creature.

Samuel backed away. Not sure if this thing was friend or

foe yet and calculating, how he would get past the large club to touch the beast if it came to that.

The beast looked into Samuel eyes and then it spoke. "More come. You kill dark one's like T'kche. You warrior. Come. Safe." It said it in broken, choppy words that came out somewhat like a growl, but Samuel understood it, nonetheless.

Before Samuel could respond, he heard Halbred's voice. "Is this thing helping us or hurting us Samuel? I can't see its face, but I hear it growling at you man."

"It said for us to come with it, to safety. Can't you understand it Halbred?" Samuel asked.

"Understand what man?! It's just growling." Halbred replied frustrated.

The large beast looked at Samuel and then at Halbred. It pointed to the two talisman that Samuel held and gestured towards Halbred. Samuel followed the beast's motions and tossed a talisman to Halbred.

Then the beast spoke again. "Now you hear. More coming. Must leave now." As the beast spoke, it walked past Samuel and through the doorway in the boulder.

Samuel looked at Halbred questioningly. "Well, I understood it that time. Let's go man. Can't be worse than here, with these damn things." Halbred said as he moved towards Flutter and picked her up.

Samuel looked eerily at the Talisman that he held, wondering how it seemed to let them understand this giant, hairy manlike beast.

"I'm guessing there will be a lot more questions than answers in this strange place. Where the hell are we?" Samuel thought.

Halbred passed Samuel, carrying Flutter in his arms and they all made their way into the opening in the boulder, that closed shut behind them. Following the strange beast that so far seemed to be ok with them enough to get them out of these woods crawling with the weird creatures that looked like some sort of twisted version of a demon or vampire from a low budget movie.

As they entered the dark tunnel, they noticed more drawings and weird shapes on the walls. They all glowed brightly, providing just enough light for them to see. The tunnel seemed to be going down, further underground. It smelled like the dusk and dank smells that generally fill large underground caverns, but it was coupled with the strong smells of wild animals.

The large beast was leading them, walking at a slow pace in front of them. Samuel realized that at any moment, this massive thing could turn on them with the deadly club that he wielded, so he tapped Halbred who was in front of him on the shoulder.

"Give her to me." Samuel said. "You may not be able to get smashed by this thing, but I'm assuming she can."

Halbred nodded and handed Flutter to Samuel gently. As they started walking again, with Halbred in the lead, his hands now free, he spoke softly over his shoulder. "Just because they can't penetrate my skin with knives, bullets or apparently fangs, it doesn't mean old bigfoot here can't smash me dammit."

As soon as he finished speaking, they heard a gurgling kind of growl coming from the beast in front of them, but it kept walking, so they continued to follow.

"Is that thing laughing at him?" Samuel thought.

Chapter 38:
From Child to Warrior

As Ansai emerged from the woods, still holding Steph's little hand he looked at the large crevasse in the side of the tall mountain in front of them, put his free hand to his mouth and made a loud series of whistles that echoed in the open area.

The sounds seemed to be repeated from very high up on each side of the large crack running up the extremely tall mountain, that seemed to rise hundreds of feet into the air. When the whistles were repeated back, Ansai tugged on Steph's hand and said, "we are cleared to proceed, little Steph."

They walked closer to what seemed to be a flat stone wall and entered the crevasse or crack that looked like it split the mountain in half. It made a path that was about six feet wide. There were ledges and small caves scattered about at various heights on either side. The path itself seemed to stretch out about fifty yards before it opened up to the other side.

The two walked through at a brisk pace. Steph noticed shadows and shapes moving on the ledges overlooking the path.

"Whose up there?" Steph asked Ansai.

"They are Na'gee guards. They ensure that nothing comes down the pass, to the aging waters." Ansai said.

As the two emerged from the mountain pass, Steph gasped. The mountain surrounded them on all sides. It looked like it had been hollowed out to form this clearing in the middle that held a small lake of sorts. There were small trees and bushes scattered around the perimeter of the lake, but they were all at least six feet back from the water. The ground seemed to be stone, like the walls of the mountain and the trees and bushes seemed to grow directly out of the stone.

What had made Steph gasp, wasn't the strange landscape as much as the color of the lake. Its waters were a bright pinkish red, that created an eerie pink glow across the entire clearing in the middle of the mountain.

There were about a dozen Na'gee warriors standing on ledges overlooking the small lake. Two older Na'gee with braids of white hair and long white braided beards stood under the shade of a tree before them. When they saw Ansai and Steph approach, they stepped out from under the tree and walked towards them.

They each held a long staff, that had a massive, curved blade at the top. After walking a few feet towards them, they stopped and planted their staffs in the ground firmly.

Ansai, let go of Steph's hand and walked towards the two old men. He took a knee and bowed before them.

While still bowing he spoke. "Olo has sent me. We must bathe the top sider in the aging waters like we do the young of our people and teach him the ways of the Na'gee warrior. He is kin to a 'Brite' and must be equipped to kill it, lest it threaten the control the Na'gee have over the land." Ansai said.

The two old men looked at each other, then back at Ansai. Then the one on the right spoke.

"You are sure it is a 'Brite' Ansai?" the older man asked.

"Yes. It almost killed me, Olo saved me and 'retrieved' the boy." Ansai said carefully, knowing that Steph was listening.

The two old men looked at Steph then at each other. They seemed to want to ask more questions but were cognizant about the boy listening.

Finally, the one on the left spoke. "Bathe the top sider boy and begin his training as you were told to do Ansai. Olo, will need to come to us and explain more. The appearance of a 'Brite' and this strange request, leaves much to discuss."

Once he finished speaking, the two men turned their backs to Ansai and Steph and walked back over to the shade of tree.

Ansai rose and waved for Steph to come to him. The two walked towards the lake, ignoring the older men under the tree. They stopped about six feet from the water and Ansai crouched next to Steph, looking at him in the eyes.

"You must proceed on your own, young one." Ansai said. "I cannot touch the waters again. I was bathed at about your age as well though. It is safe, but it will not be pleasant."

Steph looked at the strangely colored lake suspiciously and then back at Ansai.

"What do I do?" Steph asked.

"Walk into the waters. Keep going until you are fully submerged. The waters will do the rest." Ansai said and he gave Steph a light push on the back to get him going.

Steph started towards the water but paused after a few steps and looked back at Ansai. The boy was terrified.

Ansai looked at him, still crouching and yelled firmly "The demon killed your sister little one! The demon made your parents sacrifice her. This is the only way to stop it! This is the only way to avenge your family Steph!"

The young child heard the words and tears began streaming down from his eyes. He sniffed, stood straighter and continued to the water's edge. Once Steph got to the edge of the pinkish red waters, he paused for only a moment, then he proceeded to walk into the lake. After a few steps he was knee deep and then gasped out loudly and went under as if pulled down by some unseen force.

He remained below the water for almost an hour, while Ansai watched and waited, without moving an inch. The two old Na'gee watched as well, from under the shade of the tree. No one moved and no words were spoken while they waited.

Then a body floated to the top of the water, near the edge closest to them. It was not the body of the boy that had waded in an hour ago. This was the body of a full-grown man. The body floated on its back and on top of the water, with its eyes closed and the waters seemed to take it to the edge. The body washed up onto the stone shoreline and laid there without moving.

The man that laid on his back on the shore, wasn't dark skinned like the Na'gee, he was actually very pale, with blonde hair and seemed to be very tall, lean and muscular. His eyes slowly opened and he rolled onto his side, where he began choking and coughing up the pinkish water.

Ansai rose from his crouching position, but did not approach the man, he just stared at him.

The man choked and coughed for several minutes and then slowly rose to his feet and looked around as if seeing the clearing for the first time. He slowly turned in a circle taking it all in, and then his eyes fell on the lake. He was left to stare at the strange waters for several minutes and then the two older men who had been watching from the shade of the nearby tree, walked over to him.

One of the older men, touched this strangely tall and pale man on the shoulder and the man turned to face the old Na'gee. The other old Na'gee man stood directly behind him.

The old man that faced him stared into the tall man's eyes and then struck him in the center of the forehead with the flat side of the curved blade at the end of his staff. A large bright blue light flared from the contact and momentarily lit up the entire clearing.

The tall man fell backwards, into the awaiting arms of the other older Na'gee, who caught him and gently laid him on the stone ground. The two men, stood over the unconscious tall man and using the sharp tips on the blades of their staffs begin to cut small tribal designs into the pale man's skin.

Each time they seemingly finished a marking, it glowed bright blue and turned from a bleeding cut in the skin to a tattoo that appeared to have been there forever. They did not cover the man completely, but they did tattoo several of the markings on his face, arms, chest and legs. Every time they finished marking, it flashed a bright blue and turned into what appeared to be a tattoo.

Ansai patiently watched this go on for several long minutes. He had witnessed this many times, but it was strange to see this take place with a top sider boy. Not all Na'gee went through the process, some children of chieftains or wise ones were allowed to age naturally, but very few. Not many children survived the predators of this world, the aging process gave the Na'gee a chance to be the predators instead of the prey in many cases. Still, to do this with a top sider, felt wrong to Ansai.

Ansai, was shaken from his thoughts by the harsh voice of one of the older Na'gee men. They were now both standing over the tall pale man, who was partially covered in tattoos now and still laying on his back unconscious.

"We have done our part. He is ready to be tested young warrior." The old Na'gee said.

Ansai looked at the pale man on the ground and then back at the old Na'gee who had spoken to him.

"Wise one, please forgive my ignorance, but I have witnessed the aging of many young warriors. He does not appear to be complete. He only has some of the markings." Ansai said as respectfully as he could.

He knew that in every ageing, the person was completely

covered in markings from head to toe. If not, they would fail to understand what they needed to survive. Aging the body without educating the mind was even more dangerous than letting a child run about.

"He is a top sider, he does not need to know all of our ways. He simply needs to know how to stay alive long enough in this world to kill the 'Brite'. If Olo wants the Top Sider to know more, tell him to teach him, but we will not give him all the knowledge of our people young warrior." Once the old man finished his harsh explanation, he turned and walked back to the shade of the tree with his companion.

Ansai guessed it made sense, but wondered how he would know what they had taught the boy and what these old wise ones had decided to leave out. He figured he'd just have to proceed as usual, knowing that if the boy died, Olo would kill him next.

Ansai approached the tall, pale man and crouched down next to him. He slapped him hard across the face once and then followed it with a backhand from the same hand.

The tall man's eyes opened widely, and he gasped. He coughed and choked and grabbed at his head as if dealing with a massive headache. Ansai knew that this too was usual, after the ageing.

He slapped the man again and this time got his attention.

The man stopped coughing and narrowed his eyes at Ansai.

"Young Steph, it is I Ansai. You have been through the aging process, now your life will not be as long as it once would've been, but you are strong and have learned much. Stand up and we will test your new knowledge and skills." Ansai said as he stood and reached his hand out offering Steph a hand up.

Steph paused for a moment, obviously taking it all in and then grabbed the offered hand and allowed it to help him to his feet.

He felt incredibly strong and agile. He knew things that he didn't understand. He looked at Ansai and spoke in a deep voice that he did not recognize as his own. "How old am I now Ansai?" he asked.

"The wise ones would say you are old enough to survive like a warrior now Steph." Ansai said.

Steph looked over at the old men standing in the shade of the tree and then looked back at Ansai. "I have not asked the wise ones. How old would Ansai say that I am?" Steph said in a voice that still didn't seem his own.

Ansai smiled at the boldness of the top sider. It was unusual for anyone to come out of aging and have any amount of confidence, at least until the training exercises. This top sider was different. He seemed perplexed, but not rattled. His nerves were solid.

"You are about twenty-five years of age now Steph. In body and …" Ansai paused and glanced back where the old Na'gee stood, then he continued. "Most of your mind."

Ansai waited for Steph to respond, and when he didn't, Ansai continued. "Come Steph, follow me and see what you have learned."

With that Ansai, began walking around the eerie lake, leaving plenty of space between him and the lake. He stopped over at a stone face of the inner wall about a quarter way around the lake and two warriors appeared on a ledge about fifteen feet above him.

One of them tossed down and large knife, identical to the ones that all the Na'gee warriors carried.

Ansai picked it up from the stone floor and tossed it to Steph who had followed him.

"Prepare yourself. Don't think, you know what to do. Just do it Steph. You now face a 'Ragu'." Ansai said and then he quickly moved to the side pressing his back firmly against the stone wall.

The two warriors on the ledge made some movements and the face of the stone wall opened up. When it did a creature came roaring out.

The creature was a grayish green color and stood about four feet tall. It had thick muscular arms, legs and a slightly round body. Its eyes were beady and red, almost reptilian and its ears were pointed. Steph noticed that it wore a rag cloth over its groin area, held in place by a crudely made brown leather belt, that had what appeared to be a sheath for a weapon of some sort on each side, although both were empty. It was holding a long spear though, that appeared to be made completely from one piece of stone.

The creature or the 'Ragu' as Ansai had called it, skidded to a stop about three feet in front of Steph and growled and gurgled strangely. The noises suddenly made sense to Steph. He understood them. He listened closely to the noises, and they became words in his mind.

"I kill you damned Na'gee! You torture and kill too many! I kill you and all your families as you have done to the Ragu!" The beast roared.

Though Steph was momentarily overwhelmed with excitement that he could understand this strange monstrosity, as the words sunk in, he grew concerned.

"Why would this creature want to kill the Na'gee for the terrible things it raved about if the Na'gee were good people? The Na'gee saved him from a demon that his parents tried to sacrifice him too, like his sister after all." Steph thought. He was trying to make sense of it all in his mind when the Ragu attacked.

Despite its shorter, stocky build, the Ragu moved with incredible speed. It covered the feet between Steph and where the creature had stood in seconds, lunging with the stone spear.

Steph whirled to the side and kicked the creature in the back, sending it stumbling along.

The Ragu turned quickly and lunged back with the spear again roaring.

"No, it's not roaring, its screaming something at me." Steph thought. He listened to the words that the growls made and understood them.

"You will die for my family! For my people!" the Ragu roared.

Steph again, dodged the spear with ease. This time he

did not kick the Ragu, just hopped to the side. The creature continued to roar the same words and try to attack Steph with the spear over and over and Steph just dodged it skillfully over and over. The words weighed on his mind and his conscious.

Then Ansai yelled. "Good you understand it. Now, don't be fooled by this slime's lies and trickery! It wants only to eat your flesh and bones. Slay the beast Steph!"

When Ansai yelled, the creature stopped and looked in his direction, it roared at Ansai screaming "Lies and trickery! You Na'gee are monsters as bad as the dark ones! We will kill you all!"

The creature rushed towards Ansai, who pulled his knife and stepped towards the approaching beast. When the beast was almost upon him, Ansai turned back towards the wall and jumped up at the wall. The result was amazing to Steph, as he watched Ansai, leap off the wall, flip in the air and land behind the lunging creature. He took its head clean off as he landed.

The roaring ceased and the area around the lake was filled with silence.

Ansai, stalked angrily towards Steph, stopping face to face with him.

"Why would you hesitate? Why would you not dispatch this disgusting beast?" Ansai asked without any attempt to hide his frustration. Even as he was asking, he realized his task to train a top sider would be harder than he thought. Top siders didn't remember all the stories that Na'gee were told as little ones about the dangerous creatures they would one day kill or grow up custom to the creatures that the Na'gee preyed on for food. It was all new to them.

Steph looked into Ansai's eyes. "Why would the creature lie to me? What would it gain?" Steph asked.

Ansai thought about the question. He knew the creatures had been hunted and slaughtered for years by the Na'gee. Their resources stolen and their people were eaten like top siders ate cattle. He also realized he could not expect this weak soft hearted top sider to understand that, so he tried a different approach.

"To distract you Steph, to get you to let your guard down so it could kill you. Don't you have stories or legends about creatures like this in your world? Monsters that eat people and hunt them and lie to them? Look at the creature Steph." Ansai said.

Ansai counted on the top side legends he'd heard so much about scaring the boy into compliance or at least to eliminate any empathy that he felt towards the Ragu. He counted on the fact that many top siders had stories of creatures that had slipped through to their world and believed them to all be fictional. He did not know if his plan would work but figured that Ragu would think every human was a Na'gee and attack on site.

Steph looked closely at the beast and said, "Maybe. I don't know. Kind of like some old monsters in story books with dragons and dwarves or something I guess, maybe, but its different. It doesn't make any sense Ansai." Steph said.

"We have many vicious creatures here Steph. Many things that don't seem real in your world come from this world. It is the same for us here. Things from your world come through and we are shocked because many believed them not to be real. Not long ago, people here did not believe these were real." Ansai said and he pulled out the large pistol he wore in the holster on his belt.

"Or these." Ansai continued and he pulled a strange old Nextel looking device from the back of his belt. "Your world's creatures are not like ours, but your machines and technology are things that children here dream of Steph. It is the same." Ansai paused, letting Steph soak it all up and felt proud of his ability to explain it all so convincingly. Then he continued. "If you are so easily fooled, you will be no match for the demon that took your sister and parents from you."

As soon as Ansai said it, he saw Steph's entire face change. He saw tears build up in the young man's eyes and more importantly he saw fury and rage building up behind the tears.

"I am ready to learn. I will not hesitate again. What's next?" Steph said coldly.

Ansai did not respond, he just began walking further around the lake and Steph followed.

He stopped on the far side of the lake, opposite the crevice that they had entered from and once again two warriors appeared on a ledge. This ledge was higher, about twenty feet in the air. One of the warriors threw down a black leather belt, with a large pistol in the holster that hung on it and several clips fastened securely around the belt.

Ansai, caught the belt in the air and then turned and tossed it to Steph. Steph noticed the large sheath for the knife he still held and quickly sheathed the knife and strapped the belt on. He pulled out to the pistol and looked at it familiarly. Memories of his father and mother flooded his mind. His parents had taught him to shoot from as far back as his he could remember.

As he thought of them, he thought of his sister and the things that Olo had told him. His sadness was replaced by anger. Steph smoothly checked the clip in the gun and the chamber, then cocked the pistol.

Ansai had retreated to the wall once again and the two warriors on the ledge above went into motion. Steph saw the wall beginning to move and faced it with confidence. He felt he had figured this training game out already.

"Something comes out and I kill it. Simple enough. No talking this time." Steph thought.

Sure enough, an opening began to appear in the stone wall before him. This time the creature that ran out, looked very much like the beast that Olo had killed when they first arrived. To Steph it appeared to be a small sort of dinosaur.

It had very small arms in front of it with long curved talons, big strong legs that also had long curved talons and huge head and gaping jaw full of huge teeth. The thing stood just over eight feet tall and had a large tail that did not touch the ground.

It ran straight at Steph, jaws gaping open.

This time Steph didn't think about what he had learned in the aging process at all, he just willed his new body to do exactly what he had seen Olo do earlier. He charged the beast, fired the pistol into its body three times and then flipped over its head, pulling the knife while in midair and sinking it in where the head met the neck on the creature's back.

The beast collapsed and slid to a stop several feet away.

Steph did not look at the men on the edge or at Ansai. He simply walked over to the dead beast and pulled his knife free, wiped it clean on the dead beast's body and sheathed it.

Ansai walked to his side looking at the dead creature and then at Steph. "You did not learn that from the aging Steph. That is not how the young warriors fight these creatures, it could leave you exposed if executed poorly." Ansai said.

"Then I will not execute poorly Ansai." Steph said, then he added "And it still looks like a dinosaur to me."

Ansai did not respond, he simply began walking further around the lake and Steph followed.

He made it about halfway back to where they entered the strange opening in the center of the mountain and stopped. They were three quarters around the pinkish red lake and again two warriors appeared on a ledge.

This time, the warriors threw down a giant massive club. Ansai, let it hit the ground and instead of walking to the wall he turned and faced Steph.

"You will face a potent Na'gee foe, the T'kche. There are different tribes of T'kche and the Na'gee war with most of them. One in every three Na'gee warriors that go through training, don't make it past a T'kche alive. We need you to live Steph and to kill the 'Brite', so I will give you a piece of advice that is never given… if he gets to the club, you will die." With the grim words spoken, Ansai, retreated to the side wall and the warriors up on the ledge began moving. As Steph watched them move, he noticed that unlike the other ones, they carried large rifles on their backs.

Steph steeled himself and although he hated his father for sacrificing his sister, he found himself thinking of what his father would do right now, more than of what he had learned from the aging.

The stone face of the mountain side opened up and large man like creature covered with thick brown hair emerged. It stood nine feet tall and had massive arms, legs, and feet. It stepped out and surveyed the lake and the area around it. It glanced at Ansai, standing far off to the side with his back against the wall and then at the two warriors on the ledge who now had their rifles aimed at it.

The T'kche looked at Steph standing before him and then at the club on the ground. The large beast did not move, it simply looked back at Steph and spoke, in growls and gurgles that Steph clearly understood.

"You are not like them young one. They have stolen your youth. Do not let them steal your life as well. Step aside and I will escape this place and these evil Na'gee, refuse and I will kill you before they shoot me." The beast stopped growling its broken words and simply stared at Steph.

"Why do you call them evil when they hunt demons and saved me T'kche?" Steph replied with growls and gurgles that came to him more easily than he thought they would.

"They worship the demons and work with the dark ones foolish boy! They are evil! Now step aside. I will not say it again." The beast growled.

Ansai had seen many young warriors fail at this part of the training, but he had never heard the T'kche talk to one. They usually just attacked.

"It must notice he is not Na'gee. Damn pale skin of that boy." Ansai thought.

"Do not fall for the hairy demon's lies Steph or you will never avenge your sister!" Ansai yelled.

The T'kche turned to look at Ansai and growled. It looked back and Steph and spoke again. "You are a fool to believe them young one."

Once the words were spoken the beast took off for the club. Steph ran to cut it off and pulled his large pistol while running. He fired and hit the T'kche in the side twice. The beast roared, but it did not slow down.

Within feet of the club, the creature dove and slid across the stone, grabbing the club and jumping to its feets in a rolling motion. It turned to face Steph who was running at it.

The T'kche growled and planted its feet, drawing the massive club back. Steph kept running at it and then within feet of the creature, he threw his large pistol in the air far above the T'khce's head, yelling "here!"

The T'kche looked up and Steph leaped into the beast's chest with both feet, knocking the creature to the ground on its back, with Steph standing on top of the creature. Before the beast could move, Steph drove the massive knife into the T'kche's neck with both of his hands. The beast died instantly and Ansai let out the breath he had been holding while he watched.

Ansai walked over to Steph and clapped him on the shoulder. "You have done very well Steph. Many true Na'gee have failed to perform with such courage. Now let us go inside, darkness approaches and you must never be out in the dark in this world." Ansai said with genuine praise.

Steph didn't know how he knew, but he knew why. "The dark ones?" he asked.

"Yes, young Steph. The dark ones." Ansai replied.

As the two walked towards an opening that had appeared near the entrance to the clearing, Steph noticed warriors from the very top of the high mountain sides with ropes pulling up the bodies of the three creatures he had slain.

"What are they doing?" Steph asked.

"They offer sacrifices to the dark ones." Ansai replied.

"If we offer sacrifices to them, why isn't it safe for us to be out after dark?" Steph asked.

"The sacrifices just keep them from hunting us in our caves. They own the night, if we trespass, we are considered sacrifice. If we offer them flesh and blood, they do not hunt us in our homes." Ansai said grimly.

Steph noticed two other ropes on either side of the entrance to the clearing each had a young Na'gee woman tied to it by her arms and being raised similar to the bodies.

"And what of them Ansai?" Steph asked.

"Some sacrifices must be alive Steph." Ansai said, frustrated that the wise ones had kept so much knowledge from the top sider, but also making a note to himself to be very careful with what he said to Steph.

"The top sider is not like the Na'gee. The wise ones may have had very good reasons for keeping things from him." Ansai thought.

As the two entered the cave, it closed shut behind them and they walked towards a small fire where some kind of meat roasted on a spit over it. There did not appear to be anyone else in the small cave but them. There was a pot of water on the ground between two large stones by the fire and in each corner was a stack of what appeared to be fur blankets.

Ansai sat on one of the large stones and gestured for Steph to sit on the other. Steph did as he was expected to and was offered the water once he was sitting.

He didn't realize how thirsty he was until he began drinking but forced himself to stop and save half of the pot of water for Ansai. Ansai took the pot of water, drank himself from it and then set it back down between them. He then reached on the other side of the stone and picked up a circular stone talisman that was attached to a long leather string.

"Lean your head forward Steph so that I may place the talisman of the Na'gee around your neck." Ansai said.

Steph dipped his head forwards and Ansai placed the talisman around his neck.

"It does many things for the Na'gee, but most importantly

for you, it opens doorways to your world Steph." Ansai said.

Steph gasped and asked "How?"

"It is like a lock young one. Trace your fingers on it in the same motions that I do." Ansai said and then began slowly tracing his fingers on the talisman in a series of motions. A blur appeared in the air and Steph gasped again. Ansai moved his fingers quickly in a reverse motion and it disappeared.

"Do not go to your world, until we meet with Olo, and he feels you are ready to hunt the demon. Once it is time, you now know how." Ansai said.

Then Ansai, stood and pulled out his large knife. He approached the roasting meat and cut off a large chunk that he handed to Steph. He then cut a large chunk for himself and sat back down.

Steph ate the meat like he was starving and finished it in seconds.

"That was great! What was it?" Steph asked.

Ansai stared at Steph, debating on how he would answer. Finally, Ansai chose to tell the top sider the truth.

"Enough with the lies. If he is to be a Na'gee for any amount of time, he must understand and embrace our ways." Ansai thought.

"It is a Ragu young Steph." Ansai said.

"What?! You mean the creature that yelled at me?" Steph asked, horrified at what he'd just eaten.

"Not that Ragu, but yes, a Ragu nonetheless." Ansai

replied calmly.

Steph felt sick. He was disgusted. "How could you eat one of them? No wonder it hated you and wanted you dead! You probably did kill its family!" Steph cried out.

Ansai remained calm and slowly responded. "Do you not eat creatures in your world for strength and sustenance?" he asked.

"Yes, but not ones that can talk and have families Ansai!" Steph yelled.

"So, the living things that you kill for food, do not make babies?" Ansai asked.

"Well, yeah, but it's different. They don't talk and wear clothing. They're just animals." Steph said. His voice had slightly calmed, even though he still felt sick.

Ansai continued to press the matter. "So, the difference is that our 'animals' as you call it can be understood by us and that makes it different Steph? Do your 'animals' not make sounds and communicate with one another? The only difference seems to be that top siders are too stupid to figure out how to understand their prey." Ansai said somewhat proudly.

Steph was at a loss for words. It didn't seem right, but he couldn't seem to think of a decent argument. On one hand he could not fathom how anyone could kill and eat a creature that could reason and raise families, but on the hand, he wondered was there any real difference.

He was confused. So much had happened in such a short amount of time. He felt he had lived a lifetime in the last twenty-four hours. He knew that he didn't entirely trust the Na'gee.

Steph decided then and there that he would learn as much as he could, but he would find his parents and confront them about this demon before he just blindly killed them because Olo and the Na'gee said too. Something just didn't feel right.

"Still… that wasn't Mila." Steph thought. He stood up choosing to eat no more Ragu, no matter how compelling Ansai's argument was and stomped off to one of the piles of fur blankets in the corner. Steph laid down and thought about his mother, father, and sister. He thought of how much they all got along and the love he felt for them all. He thought of how lost he felt without them.

He knew he was a man now. He felt different. He knew a lifetime of things, but deep down in his heart, he was still a six-year-old boy that passionately missed his family more than anything else. Tears began to stream down his face and Steph cried himself to sleep.

CHAPTER 39:
"ANYONE KNOW HOW TO COOK SNAKE?"

Vic stepped onto a cold forest floor. There were shadows everywhere, but orange rays of sunshine shined through brightly here and there between the trees. He was holding Mila's little hand tightly with his right hand and held his pistol just as tightly with his left hand.

Mila's other hand clasped her mother's hand tightly. The three of them slowly walked out of the blur, Eva still limping and in obvious pain. The air was cool, the trees were huge and the forest around them was dense. Vic's head was on a swivel, looking everywhere. He expected Na'gee to be surrounding them, but nothing seemed to be there.

All around him was beautiful forest and in the distance through the trees, he thought he saw the glimmer of water.

"This way. Stay close." Vic said softly to his wife and daughter. While he thought to himself "They shouldn't be here with me. It's not safe."

Vic led them cautiously through the thick woods towards

the glimmer of water he saw on the other side of the trees. They all kept holding hands as they silently made their way in the shadows of the trees.

They seemed about twenty feet from the edge of the woods, when Vic heard the faint sound of leaves crunching or moving. The noise came from the bushes to his left. He slowly let go of Mila's hand, and pushed her further from him toward her mother, as he turned in the direction of the noise. Eva instantly caught on and pulled Mila close, backing a few feet away from her husband. She knew she had to give him room to move.

Peering through the bushes, Vic caught the glimmer of sun reflecting off scales. He stepped back away from the bushes and heard the noise to his right. When he looked up, he saw a giant snake raising its head and flickering its tongue at him. Its body slowly came into sight and formed a wide half circle around Vic.

"Holy shit! That things got to be at least sixty feet long!" Vic said softly to himself.

In his peripheral he saw Eva and Mila further away, ducking behind a nearby tree.

At this Vic felt a slight sense of relief, knowing that he wouldn't have to worry about them. Then the size of the giant snake staring at him, like he was a rabbit, started to sink in.

The snake was solid black, and its head was bigger than Vic's entire body. It was at least ten feet in diameter at its widest section from what Vic could tell. He didn't think snakes like this existed. He thought they were only seen in fake news articles on the internet, and yet here he was staring at one.

The large snake hissed, and Vic slowly raised his .45 caliber pistol. He didn't know how much time he had, before the thing decided to strike, but he figured it wouldn't be long, so… Vic decided to strike first.

"Bet your big ass didn't think grim reapers existed either did you fella?" Vic said as he squeezed the trigger.

Vic shot the giant snake three times in the head, before it swerved its massive body out of the way. The snake was bleeding, but it was far from slain. With incredible speed, it showed its fangs and struck at Vic.

The tall man was waiting for it. As soon as the snake was near, he dove backwards to the side shooting the snake in the head as he dove. The shots hit at much closer range than the first three and the snake reared back in pain. One of its eyes looked like it had exploded from point blank gunfire.

The snake's body flailed and thrashed, and it tossed it's massive head from side to side.

"That's right you son of bitch, I ain't a damn rabbit!" Vic roared as he ran at the snake's body that held its thrashing head in the air. He touched the body with his pistol and began firing in a tight row across the snake's side. It created a large tear in the snake's body that almost tore it in half.

In what seemed a final attempt to save itself, the beast blindly struck where Vic stood with its enormous jaws. Vic jumped to the side and as the snake's bite hit the ground where he had just stood, he spun back, touched the creature's good eye with his pistol and fired three times.

The beast's eye exploded and Vic kept firing. Almost instantly, the creature's body slumped to the floor of the forest, and it stopped moving. Vic stared at the giant, apparently dead snake. He still couldn't shake his surprise that a snake could get this big. Then the tall man turned around smiling at his wife and daughter who were peeking from behind the large nearby tree.

"Hey babe, you know how to cook snake?" Vic said with a grin.

Eva and Mila shared a 'he's crazy' look with one another and then walked over towards Vic smiling.

"We're not eating that thing Vic." Eva said defiantly.

"Ok babe, I'll just have to kill something bigger when you get hungry." Vic said with a chuckle and the three of them continued walking towards the clearing.

As they walked, Vic heard Eva mutter "Wow, that thing was huge. What is this place?" He pretended not to hear her, even though he was wondering the same thing. Mila was silent and stoic, she seemed unphased by the incident.

As the three of them emerged from the forest in the clearing, they immediately saw the vast lake before them. Its bright blue waters reached out farther than they could see with their eyes. The shores seemed flat and rocky, while the landscape around the lake was open and rocky, with scattered trees and bushes. Far ahead of them was a rocky mountain and small hills that led up to it. They could see shadows here and there on the hills that looked like small caves. As they looked around, Vic noticed that the sun was starting to set.

"Let's head to one of those caves and camp for the night. If snakes like that are running around in the daytime, we probably don't want to be out in the open at night." Vic said as he started leading them towards the caves at the base of the hills not far ahead.

Out of nowhere Mila spoke. The voice that came from her, was not like the voice they had known as hers though, it was colder and shallower. "We must hurry father." She said as she quickly, almost aggressively grabbed their hands and started pulling them along.

"Ok Mila, your mother's hurt though. She can't move that fast." Vic said, trying to slow his daughter down and hide his concern at her eerie change in demeanor.

"I'll be ok. Listen to her Vic. She, well, she knows things." Eva said and began rushing as fast as she could, grimacing and limping the entire way.

Just as they got to the entrance of the cave the sun set. As it got darker, Mila started to slightly glow that same white light that she had shined before.

They were still holding hands as they walked into the cave. He was staring at his daughter, when Vic heard the noises behind him.

He turned quickly and saw two shapes dart up towards the cave. They stopped just feet outside of the entrance and stared. The two creatures wore tattered black cloaks of some sort and had pale; almost translucent skin that seemed hairless. They were tall and lean, and Vic immediately noticed their black eyes and long claw-like fingers and toes.

He tried to pull his hand free from Mila and step between his family and the strange creatures, but Mila's grip was too tight. When he glanced down at her, to yank his hand free, he saw that the white light coming from her body was shining brighter and brighter.

Mila's grip was like steel on his hand, and he felt himself being forced behind her. He tried to resist, tried to stay between his precious daughter and these predatory creatures, but he couldn't. She just kind of pushed him behind her.

The light from Mila continued to glow brighter and brighter, until it was almost blinding to look at. The creatures backed away a few feet from the entrance to the cave, holding their tattered cloaks in front of their faces and making loud hissing noises.

As Vic squinted past the brightness of his daughter, he saw two other similar creatures had joined the first two. They crowded the entrance, carefully staying just out of the bright circle of light emitting from Mila.

After what seemed like forever, one of the creatures stepped closer to the light and raised its head. It hissed loudly showing a large mouth full of sharp teeth and two enormous fangs, then it spoke.

"These lands our ours Brite!" The creature hissed in a hollow raspy voice. "You should not have come. We rule here. We will drink the blood of you and your loved ones." As the creature said it all, Vic noticed the parts of its skin that the light touched sizzling.

As Vic began to contemplate the implications of this, he heard his daughter speak back to the creature in that same voice that was not hers, only this time it was louder and more ominous, almost like a crackling loudspeaker.

"You will hurt no one, disease!" Mila roared and then the bright white light coming from her flashed ten times brighter.

Vic and Eva shielded their eyes from the brightness and heard raspy screams and wails, then silence. The flash faded away, but Mila still glowed, just not as brightly as she had moments before. Vic looked past her and saw four piles of ashes with tattered black cloaks lying near them.

Mila looked shaken and Eva grabbed her to hold her steady.

"Come, sit inside the cave with us Mila. It is safe now baby." Eva said compassionately.

Mila looked up at her with bright glowing eyes and said "It will not be safe until daylight. I will sit here."

With that, Mila pulled away from her mother's arms and sat down cross legged in the entrance to the cave, facing outward.

Vic looked at Eva, who seemed heartbroken by what was happening to her daughter and then at Mila, who sat stoically, unmoving, cross legged on the floor of the cave entrance. Then the tall man looked outside the cave and silently gasped at what he saw. About twenty yards away, six more of what appeared to be the same creatures stood. They just stared at Mila, unmoving.

Vic didn't know what to do. He felt helpless. He felt heartbroken. His son had been taken from him, his daughter was going through some strange transformation, and he couldn't do anything. He felt like a failure.

Then Vic looked at his wife. Eva seemed similarly crushed. She stood staring at Mila, tears streaming down her eyes. Vic immediately quit worrying about how he felt, and decided he could do something. He decided he could comfort his wife, the love of his life, right now in this moment.

He stepped towards Eva and wrapped her in his arms. They both sat down against the wall of the cave slightly behind Mila, who still glowed brightly and stared at their daughter while they held each other.

"I can do something. I can always do something." Vic thought. "Tonight, I will comfort my poor wife and watch over my daughter. Tomorrow I will find my son, kill the bastards that took him and then figure out how to help my daughter." Vic felt comforted by his thoughts and determined to do exactly what he planned. He thought the same thoughts over and over, as he held his wife and stared past his glowing daughter at the strange creatures who stared at them all.

Chapter 40:
Dishonored

Camacho stepped out of the small wooden shack, built on the far side of the Na'gee camp. The healer's hut was crude and small, but it was enough for them to get the job done. As Camacho looked around the large Na'gee settlement, he was flooded with the same condescending thoughts that had so often ran through his mind during his time with the Na'gee.

"With all the resources of the top side available to them, why would they choose to live like primitives?" He thought. Camacho couldn't understand it. "They could have anything. They could have everything. Yet they choose huts in caves and fire pits and ancient tribal rituals." The thoughts disgusted him. He didn't understand the purpose of power if it wasn't used to put yourself in a better position.

His disgust with the Na'gee only increased as he looked around.

It had been a long time since Camacho had been back to the Na'gee settlement where he was trained and groomed, to be their top side leader. The large settlement was inside the mountain they called F'rouke. It was on the eastern shore of the great lakes and had been hollowed out over centuries to make the settlement before him.

It was the size of a small town on the top side and was home to about one thousand Na'gee. It was filled with wooden huts that served as homes and small caverns littered the inner walls of the mountain, all serving different various purposes. In the center of the settlement or the makeshift mountain town, was a huge wooden fort. It served as the main hall and the dwelling place of the elders and chieftains. In front of the fort, was a clearing with a large fire in the center that was always kept burning. There was a platform at the head of the clearing that had a walkway, leading to the balcony of the fort.

Camacho knew this place well. Memories of tribal rituals and sacrifices on that plank flooded him. The Na'gee were a superstitious and violent people. They worshipped death and were bent on conquering the other races or species of their world.

Camacho remembered his initial disgust when he witnessed them sacrifice and eat their own, saying it passed along the strength of the Na'gee from one to another.

"Fucking cannibals is what they are." He thought to himself.

He shook himself from his memories and looked around at the settlement again. This was where they trained him, and half raised him. Outside of the strategically placed outposts, this was the only Na'gee home he knew of. Camacho had heard stories of other tribes of Na'gee in other parts of this world, but this was the only settlement and tribe that he knew of.

He glanced back past the healer's hut, at the main cavern leading in. He knew there were only two ways in and out of the mountain settlement. The main cavern was the primary one and about halfway up the one-hundred-foot wall towards the tall ceiling of the cave, there was a small cavern that led to the other.

The main cavern entrance led outside to the base of the mountain and was always guarded with four warriors. They used a large boulder to lower it into place blocking it off as the sun set, so that there was no access in or out after dark. The alternate access point, far up the opposite wall of mountain, had steps leading up to it that were cut out of the side of the mountain's inner wall. The steps ran about fifty feet up the side of the mountain wall to the cavern opening. It was a long, small tunnel that led to the backside of the mountain, facing the forest, not the great lakes that the main entrance faced. Two warriors always stood at this entrance and used a similar boulder technique to shut off access after dark.

As far as Camacho knew, the only other access in or out of the mountain, wasn't really access at all. It lay at the far end of tunnel directly to the left of the great fort that housed the chieftains and elders. Camacho had only seen it once, during his training and was forbidden to return. The tunnel led to a dead end with a large horizontal gap about three feet long and one foot top to bottom.

No one could fit through the gap, no matter how small they were. It was used for the chieftans and elders to speak with the dark ones. They made deals with them and offered sacrifices in exchange for information. The sacrifices were usually left chained up outside the main entrance, when it was sealed off at dark.

Young warriors were taken down the tunnel once, like Camacho was, so that they could lay their eyes on the dark ones they learned so much about. After that, they were forbidden to ever return.

Despite Camacho's arrogance and bravado, he shivered at the thought of the dark ones. They were monstrous beasts. He had seen many left as sacrifices to them, during his time here. He knew that the Na'gee said they had to make sacrifices to them, so that the dark ones wouldn't work to find a way into the settlement. He had learned that in the past the Na'gee had to constantly be on the move, never staying in the same place twice for fear that the dark ones would find their home and break in at night.

He understood their beliefs and the history he was taught, but he just thought that constant sacrifices were only increasing the dark ones numbers. How long before they decided it wasn't enough.

Camacho had voiced his concerns during his time with the Na'gee and they had assured him that's why they only chose the women and the weak men for their live sacrifices. To Camacho it didn't matter. To him any creature that can feed on its victim's blood and then use its vile tongue to plant eggs of an ancient conscious into the victim's body like a parasite, that takes over the body and the mind of the same person it just consumed, would only turn on everyone sooner or later.

To Camacho it made more sense to work on a strategy to wipe them out, not grovel to them and increase their ranks. Ultimately, his arguments didn't matter. To the Na'gee he was a hardheaded top sider with more brawns than brains. He was a warrior who was perfect to dominate their top side interests and provide them with weapons, food, and other resources, but nothing more than that.

"I should be leading these foolish people and instead I'm just a damn tool to them." Camacho thought.

"Oh well, better damn get on with it." He said to himself, and he began to make his way towards the massive fort. He knew that getting lost in his memories was nostalgia, it was procrastination. He didn't know exactly how they would react or what they would do, but Camacho knew the migration had failed. He knew many Na'gee were slaughtered, and he knew that somehow, they already knew that top siders had followed him back to this world. He didn't know exactly how the elders would react or what they would do, but he knew it wouldn't be good.

He decided that if they sentenced him to death, he'd take as many of them with him as he could. Camacho knew he would not just bow and wait for the death blow.

"You can leave that submissive shit to the pure bred Na'gee! They want my life; they better damn take it and they better hope that lucks on their side." Camacho thought as he approached the massive fort entrance.

The four warriors that stood at the entrance to the fort, were tattooed, bald and wore black leather pants that shined in the fire light like other Na'gee warriors. The fort guards, however, were not armed like the other Na'gee warriors. They had sub machine guns strapped to their bare chests and held large pole axes. These warriors also did not wear the stone circular talisman around their necks that the 'traveling warriors' wore.

As Camacho approached them, they stepped forward, blocking his way.

Camacho knew what they wanted but stared at each of them defiantly for a long moment before choosing to comply. Once he felt he had made his silent point and show of strength, he reached under his shirt and handed them his pistol with one hand and his long dagger with the other hand.

The guards took his weapons and then stepped to the sides, allowing him to walk between them and enter the fort.

Camacho walked down the large wooden hallway that led to the main chamber. The walls were littered with torches and skulls of various creatures. On the large double doors to the main hall, there were two oddly shaped skulls with their mouths mounted open to show the huge fangs. They were dark one skulls. This decoration or trophy or whatever it was always bothered Camacho.

"You show off their skulls, yet still sacrifice your own to them. Fools." Camacho thought.

He pushed the double doors open and entered the great hall.

There were small tables and chairs sitting off to either side of the hall and long large table in the center that sat fifty.

At the far end of the huge hall, past the large banquet table, there was a wide empty space and past it were the chieftains and the elders.

They sat facing the double doors that Camacho had just entered through in a row of chairs. There were six of them sitting in their crude thrones, that sat on a platform, raising them about three feet above the rest of the floor. To Camacho the scene had always reminded him of a kind of stage overlooking a dance floor. He remembered Primo saying it was like a viking hall from the top side. Either way it didn't matter, Camacho didn't want to be here and dreaded facing them. Not many things were harder for Camacho than swallowing his pride and he knew that in this moment he would have to.

The two chieftains sat in the two center chairs and two elders sat to the side of each of them. There were three fort guards standing on the floor level on either side of the platform and to Camacho's surprise, in front of the guards on the left stood Olo.

He noticed Olo still had his weapons belt. He disregarded this and made his way towards the platform.

Camacho stopped when he stood directly in front of the center of the platform, facing the two chieftains. He nodded his head forward, in a halfway kind of makeshift bow and then stared at them. The chieftains stared back. Silence filled the hall for several long minutes.

Finally, one of the two chiefs spoke. "You have failed to pave our way to the top side Camacho. You had time to prepare and yet the migration was a failure. What say you to this disgrace?"

Camacho clenched his teeth. "The arrogance of these old fools." He thought. "I'm the reason your damn guards even have their fancy guns." Camacho pushed away his angry thoughts and forced himself to remain calm.

"It is as you say Chieftain. There were unforeseen adversaries that sabotaged my well laid plans. It is unfortunate." Camacho said. Despite his best efforts to hide his anger, the tone of his voice gave him away.

The Chieftain on the left, who had remained silent roared loudly in response. "Unfortunate?! The top siders are weak fools, how weak and foolish are you to let them sabotage the migration?!"

Camacho didn't respond. He just stared at the older chief who had yelled at him with fury in his eyes.

The chief on the right, who had spoken first, continued. "Is it also true that the same top siders that made a fool of you, followed you back to our world, injured you and sent you running to the shelter of the Na'gee in shame?"

Camacho was furious. He stopped trying to hide his anger and decided he would speak freely to the old fools. "I ran from the dark as you trained me to! I did not run from any top sider!" He yelled.

As soon as he yelled it, Camacho saw the movement to his left from the corner of his eye and instinctively used his unnatural speed and strength to catch Olo's fist that was speeding at his face.

Camacho held Olo's arm in place and slowly turned his

head to stare into the warrior's eyes. Both men were furious.

"Enough!" roared the chieftain on the left. "Release him you fool! Olo, we will let you know when it is time to dispatch of this insolent top sider."

Camacho stared at Olo a moment longer and then let go of his arm. Olo stared back and then slowly backed away to his previous position, staring at Camacho the entire time.

"You will fix what you have broken fool, or you will die a tortured death!" The same chieftain yelled at Camacho.

The calmer chief on the right chimed in. "Take a hunting party at first light and find the top siders that followed you and defeated you Camacho. Bring us back proof of their deaths."

"They are already dead or dying as we speak. They do not know of the dark ones. I left them out at night. They will not survive." Camacho said in response.

"Then find their corpses and bring us proof as you have been told to do." The chief replied.

"What if they have been infected? What if the dark ones have laid eggs in their bodies after feeding on them? I will have no way of getting to them then." Camacho said, less angry now and more concerned. He knew that if the top siders had been consumed while alive and had eggs laid in them, then there wouldn't be bodies laying around for him to find.

The angry chief on the left yelled again. "Then you will find the newly born dark ones and bring us their heads or we will take your head! You are responsible for your failures

Camacho, you now are responsible for trying to redeem your honor!"

Once again silence filled the great hall, only broken by the sounds of angry huffing and puffing from the chieftain in the left seat.

Camacho finally nodded his head and said "It shall be done. Top sider or dark one, it doesn't matter. I'll bring you their damn heads."

Once Camacho had said the words, Olo stepped towards him again. Camacho prepared himself for another attack from the warrior, but instead of attacking, the warrior stood almost next to Camacho and turned to face the Chieftains.

"There is more." Olo said. "There is a Brite. I believe it to be on the top side, with its mother. The wife of the man that betrayed Camacho. He is dead though." Olo paused to let his words sink in, as he watched the expressions of concern appear on the faces of the chieftains and the elders before him.

After a moment he continued. "I faced the Brite and took its sibling. Ansai has aged him and is training him now. I will use this top sider to kill the Brite, since they can only be killed by their own blood."

After Olo spoke, one of the elders on the far end, an older woman with white braids in her hair and the same dark skin and tattoos that the Na'gee warriors had, got up and walked behind the row of chairs to where the chieftains sat. She leaned down her head between the two chiefs and whispered to them both. After some time of whispering, she stood straight and went back to her seat.

Camacho didn't know what was happening, but he was glad the attention was off him for a minute. Truth be told, he didn't really care what was happening, he had his own problems to deal with and knew if the top siders didn't survive the dark ones tonight, his problems would be much bigger.

The calmer Chief finally spoke, directing his attention to Olo. "You are mistaken great warrior. The Brite has entered our world and it travels with two top siders. One man and one woman."

Olo hid his shock. "How did it get here?" He thought. Then his thoughts latched on to the last part of what they said. "What does the man look like wise one?" Olo asked.

The elder woman on the end spoke up in response. "He is very tall and has pale skin Olo. Is this the Brites father that you believed to be dead?"

"Yes. It is him." Olo said. He raged inside. "How could the man survive?" Olo thought.

"He is more resilient than I thought. I will need to dispatch him and the woman, before we send the boy for the Brite. We cannot risk them convincing the boy to show mercy." Olo said.

The Chieftains both nodded. The one on the right that had remained calm throughout the entire event then spoke to both Camacho and Olo. "You both know what must be done. Go. Gather your hunting parties and leave at first light." Once the instructions were given, the men both turned and started to leave.

The words of the Chief on the left, who was obviously

still angry stopped them in their tracks. "Camacho! You have one day and one night to complete your task. If you are not back with heads by then, we will send for your head!"

Camacho didn't turn around or respond. He just stalked off towards the door. There was nothing left to say.

CHAPTER 41:
A DIFFERENT WARRIOR

Steph awoke in the small cave and saw light streaming in from the entrance. He silently rose to his feet, momentarily shocked at how tall he stood, then it all came back to him. He remembered everything in an instant and the confusion and questions that plagued him the night before returned.

Driven by a strong feeling of distrust, he silently made his way towards the light coming from the cave's entrance. He heard Ansai's voice talking quietly into the Nextel device, just outside the cave, so he paused in the entry way, just out of sight and listened.

"How long do I need to keep him busy?" Ansai said in a hushed tone.

Another voice blared from the Nextel, not nearly as quiet. "Until I tell you it's clear. It shouldn't be more than a day or two. The risk is too high if the boy runs into them and has a change of heart. They are here in our world, so I must deal with them first. You have your instructions, now tell me how he did Ansai." The voice said from the device.

Steph knew that he was the one they were talking about 'keeping busy', but he didn't know who they were so worried about him running into. He stayed out of sight and continued to listen closely, trying to piece it all together.

"He was different Olo. The Ragu and the T'kche both spoke to him, instead of attacking, he listened, though I do not think he believed them. When he fought, he didn't use the standard moves that newly aged warriors have ingrained in them. Well, he used some, but he did it differently. He killed the second beast exactly like he saw you do it." Ansai said it all in a rushed whisper.

Steph listened closely, but it stayed silent for a moment. Then he heard the loud voice from the Nextel, that he now knew to be Olo, respond. "His bloodline is not like other top siders Ansai. His sibling is a Brite, his father should have died but lives and fought stronger than most Na'gee warriors. Watch him closely Ansai and teach him well." After Olo's words stopped blaring from the Nextel, Steph heard the sound of movements that clearly signified Ansai returning to the cave.

Steph silently crept back to the fire pit and stood staring at the remains of the Ragu. His thoughts dwelled on the conversation he had just heard. Despite the aging process, despite having so much knowledge seemingly implanted in his brain in an instant, he was still a child when it came to people's plots and motives. Regardless of his confusion, Steph clearly took a couple things out of the conversation he overheard. One; he heard Olo refer to his sibling as a 'Brite', which was what they called the demon. So, Steph figured that the demon story had to be true. His sister was dead, and some vile entity had taken her body. Two; his father and someone else were both here in this strange world with his sister and Olo didn't want him to run into them. Olo intended to kill them before sending Steph to kill the demon that took over his sister.

Based on these two conclusions, Steph firmly made up his mind. He would kill this demon, but he would also confront his father first. He wouldn't let it dissuade him from killing the demon, but he needed to learn more about what had happened to his family. He needed to understand how the wonderful people who he cherished more than life itself had turned to this and he knew the Na'gee would not help him understand. Whether they were lying about some or a lot, they were not being honest about everything.

He snapped out of his thoughts and realized he was staring at the roasted remains of the Ragu.

"These Na'gee are not good people. Every creature that can communicate here, screams of their evilness. I must be careful.

Ansai approached Steph quietly and stopped about three feet from him, watching in silence. Steph heard his approach, he heard his silent breathing and was amazed at what this new body was capable of.

He turned to face Ansai and saw the warrior grin.

"Hungry today young Steph? Ragu doesn't sound too bad now, does it?" Ansai asked.

Steph looked at him with steel in his eyes and determination in his voice and responded. "I will kill this demon 'Brite' Ansai and I will kill my treacherous father that let this happen. I will not be dissuaded. Teach me what you must and let us be off. I will not wait for Olo to kill the man I need to face. He is my responsibility. Let me do this or I will refuse to face the demon." Steph said with confidence.

He didn't know how Ansai would respond. He braced himself for an attack.

Ansai simply nodded, seemingly unphased at what the boy knew. "Let us train first then young Steph, lest you die by your evil fathers' hands before you have a chance to kill the demon. I am told he is a much greater warrior than most top siders." Ansai said.

"Very well. Where do we begin?" Steph said.

In response Ansai turned and headed out of the cave, Steph followed and on the way, he said "Actually, you heard he was a much greater warrior than most Na'gee warriors Ansai."

Ansai did not respond.

Once they had left the cave and entered the clearing around the eerie aging lake, Ansai turned to face Steph. He held a wide stance and twisted his feet into the ground, almost seeming to ensure his footing was secure.

Staring into Steph's eyes, Ansai spoke. "When you best me young Steph, we will leave this place and I will teach you to hunt. Once you are able to defeat a true Na'gee warrior and face the creatures of this land, you will be ready. Then we will hunt your evil father and this demon. It is up to you if we leave today or if we remain here for weeks. Now, attack me when you are ready. We will start without weapons." Ansai held his wide legged stance and placed both hands behind his back. He did not speak again, and he did not move. He just stared at Steph.

Steph stared back. He thought about protesting, about arguing with the man that the idea of him defeating one of these warriors was insane. In his mind he knew it would be useless.

"He's counting on me failing. He's counting on me failing over and over until Olo tells him to bring me and then he'll say, I did good enough. That's why he didn't argue with my demands earlier." Steph thought to himself.

With these thoughts in his mind, Steph realized he needed to win. He needed to beat this Ansai and he needed to do it quickly. His mind was full of fighting techniques that he just knew. Steph understood this had to be from the aging process. He also understood that everything he knew they taught him or planted in his brain or whatever.

"The only chance I have to beat him, is to fight him in ways he doesn't expect. I will not win using what he taught me." Steph thought.

He remembered seeing his father train in martial arts. He remembered the wrestling shows and action movies he saw not long ago, when he was living out a normal childhood. Visions of moves and fights and mostly of him watching his father's exercises flooded his mind.

Steph took off towards Ansai, full of drive and motivation. His body told him to leap with a flying punch towards the man, but his mind knew Ansai expected it. As his body's muscle memory and momentum started to propel him in the air towards his opponent, he switched gears and used the same momentum to dive.

Instead of a flying punch, he dove into Ansai's left leg. As Steph crashed into the leg, he latched on with a deathlike grip and twisted, while he rolled himself up out of the dive. The move instantly had Ansai on the ground face down, with Steph standing behind him holding the man's left leg up over Ansai's back and twisting it at the same time.

Steph felt Ansai, starting to twist out of it and he used all of strength to lunge forward, shoving the mans twisted leg much further over his back, while still twisting it. Steph's feet were now straddling Ansai's body as he kept leaning in, bending, and twisting the man's leg over his body.

He had been trying to do a figure four move that he had loved watching some of his favorite wrestlers do, but somehow ended up in this position. Steph felt like it was good enough. He felt like with a little more force, Ansai would either submit or Steph would break his leg. In the moment he didn't care which one came first.

Then Steph felt something else. He felt the boot of Ansai's free leg, kick his right ankle out from under him. As Steph fell to the right from the hard ankle kick, he landed on Ansai's free right leg with his body and while holding onto the twisted left leg, still in his grasp. As soon as Steph's body had hit the ground, he made one strong jerking twist on the leg he held and heard a loud "pop".

Ansai, roared! He squirmed and wiggled, trying to get his good leg free from under Steph's body and Steph jerked the twisted leg again. This time it went further than before, but it did not make the same 'popping' sound. Ansai did roar much louder than before though.

The Na'gee warrior was lying sideways on the ground, with Steph on top of right leg and twisting his left leg in an impossible angle. Ansai did the only thing he could, he bent forward in a sideways kind of sit up, holding himself off the ground with his right arm. This positioned him in range of Steph, and he took full advantage of it, swinging his left fist hard at the top siders head, over and over.

Before Steph knew what had happened, he had been hit in the head hard several times. He saw stars, was dizzy and let go of the leg, scrambling backwards to escape the devastating blows.

He managed to crawl backwards out of Ansai's reach and jumped to his feet. As soon as his feet were under him, he began staggering sideways and had to force himself to stop and get his bearings. He had never taken a hit like that to the head and was disoriented and shocked.

He looked up and saw Ansai had risen to his feet but was leaning heavily on his right leg. When the Na'gee warrior tried to lunge at Steph, it looked like his left foot was stuck in place behind him. Ansai staggered himself at this, trying to keep his balance with only one leg appearing to be functional.

Still dizzy, Steph didn't think, he just let his instinct take over and leaped in with a flying right hook. It caught the staggering warrior on the side of the head and sent him crashing to the ground several feet away. It was like Steph's brain was turned off, he didn't think, he just let his body take over. He ran at the Na'gee warrior on the ground and kicked him in the face hard. Ansai rolled over several times from the impact of the kick. Steph was on him, before he stopped rolling, stomping his head in.

He didn't realize he was crying and screaming, he just stomped his opponent's head with all the force he could muster. Then he was flying through the air and smashing into the ground about ten feet away.

The two elders were standing by Ansai. Their tattoos glowed blue, as did their staffs. Ansai wasn't moving. Steph was still disoriented and filled with rage. He jumped to his feet and began charging, with tears still streaming down his face and one of the warriors raised his glowing staff and jerked it at him. He felt his body go flying backwards through the air again and crashed into the ground several feet further away.

This time, when Steph slowly got to his feet, he did not move. He just stared at the elders and Ansai on the ground by their feet. He slowly wiped his tears away and fought to regain his senses and take control of his emotions. He watched as one of the elders leaned down, checking Ansai's neck and chest. The man looked up and nodded at the other elder. With that the other elder began walking towards Steph.

Steph didn't move, but he readied himself. He didn't understand how this man had thrown him through the air, but just pointing his staff at him, but Steph decided in that moment that if the man attacked, he would shoot him with the gun on his belt. Unconsciously, he moved his hand to rest on the handle of the large pistol that rested in its holster.

By now the elder was less than three feet from Steph, he

stepped a foot closer, and Steph wrapped his hand around the pistols handle tightly.

"There is no need for that top sider. Your fight is over. Only one warrior has ever won their first training battle after the aging before. Now two have, as you have won top sider." The elder looked at him sternly, but also with a sense of wonder and surprise deep in his eyes.

Steph didn't know what to say, but he moved his hand away from the pistol.

"There is fruit and water under the tree where we sat in the shade. Go eat and rest, while we attend to Ansai. He is severely injured. You did well young warrior." With the words spoken, the elder turned his back on Steph and walked back over to Ansai, who still laid motionless on the ground with the other elder wiping some bluish salve on his head.

Steph was shocked at what he had done, but slowly the shock turned to pride.

"With this new body, I can do anything" He thought. "I defeated a seasoned warrior on my first try. No one can stop me. I may be the greatest warrior to have ever lived." Stephs thoughts flooded him with confidence. He didn't worry about Ansai, he knew the man was trying to stall him and figured he got what he deserved.

Steph walked over to the tree and sat in the shade. As he ate fruit and drank water, he watched the elders attend to the bloody warrior on the ground and casually wondered if he'd killed the man.

CHAPTER 42:
HIGH GROUND

Just before the sun started to rise, Vic saw the strange creatures disappear. They all just darted off through the woods in the same direction, at incredible speeds.

It had been a long night. None of them had slept a wink. Mila didn't speak or move, she just sat cross-legged the entire night staring out the cave door.

Vic had held Eva and watched the creatures watching them for a while, but eventually he and Eva got up and moved around. They couldn't sleep, that was for sure, but they also couldn't just sit there.

Vic got a fire going several feet behind the entrance and Mila, for them, with twigs and sticks that he found littered about the small cave. He had found a large branch in the cave, that was extremely hardened, and he started whittling on it with his knife. They spent the better part of the night sitting by fire, warming up as they watched Mila with concern and Vic carved away at the long branch.

As the sun rose, Mila collapsed over on her side and Vic

quickly rushed to her to check her breathing. Her pulse and breathing seemed ok, but it seemed like she had passed out from exhaustion. Vic didn't know how she had done the bright light thing but figured that doing it all night had taken everything that the little girl had in her.

He gently laid her down, further into the cave and looked at Eva.

Before Vic could say a word, Eva spoke. "I'll stay with her. I have my gun and plenty of ammo. Go look around. See if you can find tracks or any signs of these damn Na'gee or whatever they call themselves. The sooner we can get Steph and get out of here the better. Just be careful and be back before nightfall."

Vic had trouble responding and he always had a quick response ready. His voice was just caught in his throat.

"To think how much she's been through in these last days and she's still so strong willed and levelheaded. Damn, I'd be lost without her." The tall man thought.

Instead of sharing his thoughts that filled him with emotions, he simply walked over to his wife and hugged her. "I'll be back. Be safe and stay out of sight babe. I love you." Vic said.

Then he quickly let go of his wife, picked up the branch that over the course of the night had been carved into a solid thick spear or maybe it was a staff with a pointed tip. Vic hadn't been sure which one he really intended it to be, he had just needed something to keep him busy throughout the night and figured if he was better equipped to hike and had something with a little reach for the next giant snake, it would be a win win. With his staff-spear in hand, he headed out of the cave.

Vic took in the landscape as he shook off the emotions that had washed over him with his wife and daughter in the cave. They were at the base of a large hill, the hill seemed to bump up against an even larger mountain. He saw the forest that they had hiked through and large body of water opposite it across the valley from the hill. He figured the higher terrain would give him a better lay of the land and maybe even give him a glimpse of where the strange warriors were holed up, so he started up the hill. Vic's long legs carried him quickly up the hill. He was stiff and sore from the recent events that had taken place, but the more he moved, the more it all went away. It had always been that way with Vic.

"The only way I'll ever die is if I sit around and do nothing." Vic thought and he approached the top of the hill.

He looked around and only saw more of the forest and the great lake that he had seen from the bottom of the hill. He saw movement in the woods and large boat sized ripples here and there in the water and chose not to speculate on what all was creeping around in this strange place. The mountain that the hill butted up against obscured the rest of his view. It was large and stone, with grey and purplish tones in the rock face. The side of the mountain went straight up, but Vic saw some small paths and enough outcroppings along the way that he figured he could easily hike and climb his way up to the top by mid-day, so he took off.

About halfway up, the makeshift path disappeared, and the face of the mountain turned into a flat wall of rock. Vic had seen this coming as he hiked his way up and was prepared. He took the spear-staff and tucked it into his belt behind his back, grabbed the closest outcropping of rock and began to scale the side of the mountain. Straight up he went, moving quickly from one spot to the next, evening having to leap upwards or sideways to get to the next handhold. He did it all with grace and seeming expertise and by midafternoon he had reached the top of the mountain.

Vic pulled himself up over the edge onto the top of the mountain and maintained a crouching position as he looked around. Most of his view was blocked by a giant thicket of branches and sticks. It was like someone had stacked a giant pile of debris, right in his way. He stood and started to work his way around the pile of branches that lay very close to the edge of the mountain, when he heard faint noises coming from the other side of the pile. Curious and cautious, he grabbed the branches sticking out of the large pile and pulled himself up on top of them. It wasn't until he got to the top of the pile that he realized it wasn't a pile at all. It was a giant circle of huge branches and sticks, that seemed to be about the size of a large truck. The center was almost hollowed out, making almost a bowl shape and several large grey rocks were thrown about in the middle of the bowl shape.

One of the boulders on the far side of the pile looked like it had crumbled and then Vic saw the movement that had made the noise he had heard. A small, weird looking grey colored reptile was moving around awkwardly, in the pile of crumbled rock. It was about the size of a large dog and had a pointed head that seemed to get wide in the middle and point out far behind it. The front of the point came down in a sort of beak that opened and closed repeatedly. The creature had dark blue, beady eyes that were about the size of softballs. As it stumbled about the rock debris, Vic saw that it had stubby little legs that ended with clawed feet. Its body was also about the size of a large dog, but it stood upright and had arms almost like a human, with strange bat like wings that seemed to attach to its wrists and run to it waist.

As Vic stared at it all in awe and wonderment, realization flooded over him.

"Oh shit, this isn't a pile of damn branches. This is a giant nest." He thought.

"Wait, if this is a nest, then those aren't damn rocks… those are huge ass eggs and they're hatching weird dinosaur bat birds or some shit." Vic said to himself. He quickly eased himself back over the outside edge of the nest and started to make his way around the large mess.

As soon as he cleared the nest and was on the open top of the mountain he started to look around. He immediately noticed another mountain not far from this one. It was in the opposite direction from where he had hiked from, but it seemed promising, as smoke poured up through what appeared to be several small cracks in its top.

"Well, its either some type of camp or a damn volcano and the top of that thing sure doesn't look like a volcano. That's where I start." Vic said.

For a moment Vic contemplated whether he could get to the other mountain and get back by nightfall or not, but he quickly discarded those thoughts.

"I'd be pushing it to make it there by night." Vic thought

to himself.

He approached the far edge and looked over. He saw what appeared to be almost a path leading around the mountain he stood on over towards the one he saw with smoke rising from it in the distance. He followed the trail of sorts, back towards his point of origination and saw that there appeared to be a way to hike around the hill he had come from, to the path and straight towards the other mountain.

"If we start early, we can make that in a day, no problem." Vic thought.

Feeling like he had a solid plan, he surveyed the rest of the landscape. As he began to take in the strange features of the landscape, he noticed a huge shadow moving towards him in the sky.

"What the hell is that?" Vic thought as he squinted, trying to get a good look at it, past the glare of the sunlight.

The thing grew closer at an alarming rate and by the time Vic realized what it was, he didn't think he'd have time to get off the mountain top before it was on him.

"Fucking momma dinosaur bat bird. Great. Just great." Vic muttered. He backed up, until his back touched the huge nest and the creature skidded to landing in front of him, screeching loudly upon landing. Vic debated for a brief moment and then pulled the staff-spear from his belt, instead of pulling his pistol.

"Better save as much ammo as I can for the damn Na'gee." Vic thought as he squared off against the enormous flying reptile that was slowly moving its head from side to side, as it cautiously walked towards him.

Vic followed the head movements with the pointed end of his staff-spear that he held out before him.

"Just like spear fishing, you follow the movements and strike. Come on bat bird, come get you some." Vic said out loud.

The giant reptile bird did just that. With blinding speed, it dipped it's head down low and speared it in towards Vic's midsection. It kept its jaws tightly closed, attempting to stab him with the point of its makeshift beak. Vic stepped to the side and stabbed down hard with his spear-staff. The creature was in and out too fast and Vic hit its beak instead of its head, causing the spear-staff to rattle in his hands and appearing to do no damage to the large creature.

The reptile bird pulled its head back and screeched incredibly loud. Seeming to yell out in frustration.

"Yeah, yeah, I'm pissed that I missed too. Betcha it doesn't happen twice dino mom." Vic said to the creature, while aiming his spear-staff out in front of him.

The reptile bird stopped moving and eyed Vic strangely. It seemed that the creature had caught on to what Vic had attempted to do and was reconsidering before spearing its head towards him again.

Vic, who had never been described as patient seized the moment and hurled his spear and the reptile's large neck. The spear struck and sunk deep into the neck of the creature. The reptile bird stumbled backwards and its head kind of rolled back behind its body.

Vic raced in towards it and shoved the spear, further into the creature, then he twisted and pulled the spear free. Black blood squirted out all over him and onto the ground. He stabbed the bird again, this time in its midsection and the creature fell over to its side and slid off the side of the mountain.

Vic peered over the edge and saw that it had crashed to the ground, making a huge splatter, not far from where he had started to make his way up. As he looked at the body of the creature, he noticed movement towards the forest. It was hard to tell from this far up, but it looked like three Na'gee warriors emerging from the woods, studying the ground closely, following the same path that he had taken his family on the day before.

"They're tracking us and I'm way up here! Shit!" Vic thought as panic and helpless feelings washed over him. He heard movement from behind him and flipped around expecting another reptile bird, but instead saw another giant snake coming over the far side of the mountain. It was at least as big as the one he faced the day before, if not bigger. The giant reptile did not move slowly, as it headed in Vic's direction. He braced himself, thinking that he didn't have time for this, thinking he had to get down to his family.

He debated on if using the pistol would lead the warriors to him instead of his family or if they would know he was away, and it would encourage them to strike while he wasn't around to defend his family. He was torn and undecisive, when the snake slowly changed direction within feet of Vic and slid over the side of the nest. Heard squealing noises and knew that the snake had chosen a different lunch option today.

Vic tucked the spear-staff through the back of his belt and took off over the mountain edge, scaling his way back down as quickly as he could.

425

CHAPTER 43:
A PROMISE

Olo and the two warriors with him had went to the place where the elder had sensed the breach into their world. From there it was easy to find and follow the tracks of a child, a man and a woman. The fraction of respect Olo had developed for this resilient top sider dissipated quickly as they followed the tracks. It was clear that these top siders had no clue about how to leave no trail. It appeared that they had just trotted through the forest, purposely leaving a guide to their location.

"Foolish top siders. They deserve to die for their stupidity." Olo thought.

As he and his men emerged from the woods of the forest, he saw a large beast fall from the top of the mountain in the distance. He was concerned by this, as most of the creatures of the land hunted for food, they would not carelessly toss good meat off a mountaintop.

He thought of the T'kche, who refrained from eating meat, well most of their tribes anyway, but they would only kill if attacked.

"The T'kche are weak and peace-loving creatures, why would they slaughter a beast and throw it off a mountain." He became irritated that no reasonable answer for what he had witnessed came to him and then even more irritable at the fact that the two warriors with him didn't even notice the creature falling off the mountain.

"I am surrounded by fools." Olo thought.

In truth, Olo had thought this much of his life. Since his aging, he had thought condescendingly of most of the warriors and elders around him. He was the only warrior ever to have killed his teacher in the trainings after the aging and rather than taking pride in that accomplishment, it left him despising the weakness of those that came before him.

As talks of the migration had increased, his feelings towards his tribe only increased. He was sickened by the fact that they would even consider running from their homes to the weak shade of the top side. It bothered him as much as the pacts that the chieftains had made with the dark ones. Olo believed they should be hunting and killing the dark ones, like their ancestors did, not bargaining with the beasts and offering them sacrifices.

Angered by his thoughts and still frustrated that he could not understand what would throw the large beast off the mountaintop, Olo decided that they needed to do this quickly. He knew that dispatching the parents while the 'Brite' was with them, could be tricky, but it had to be done and had to be done fast.

"Hurry. We must do this with speed." Olo said firmly and the two warriors with him began to hurry their steps, still studying the ground as they went.

As they approached the hill, Olo grabbed each of the warrior's shoulders. "Stop. The tracking is over. Look up, is it not clear?" Olo said in a quiet voice.

The two warriors looked up towards the hill and immediately saw what Olo was referring to. There was a small cave near the base of the hill and in front of it they could make out several small piles of tattered black robes. They laid in heaps before the doorway to the cave.

One of the warriors turned back to Olo and said, "They have killed several dark ones and left their remains as a warning to others." He said it all with a hint of fear in his voice.

Olo grabbed the warrior by the throat and pulled him close. "I have told you we hunt the companions of a 'Brite'! Have you not heard what 'Brites' do? You shame yourself with fear. Redeem your honor and proceed with courage fool." Olo said harshly in barely more than a whisper.

Having been reprimanded, the warrior steeled himself and began moving towards the cave at the base of the hill, with a renewed sense of purpose.

Olo, waved for the other warrior to circle around the right and he took off to the left at a run. Olo and the other warrior made wide circles and in no time were jogging towards either side of the cave entrance, while the reprimanded warrior headed straight up to the mouth of the cave.

Mila had finally woken up and come to sit by the fire that Eva had kept going. She would not say much about the events of the previous night, only that the dark ones were evil, and she wouldn't let them hurt her family. When asked for more details, she had just told Eva that she didn't know how she knew these things, she just did.

Finally, Eva stopped hounding her with questions and let her rest in silence by the fire. They remained away from the doorway, hoping to draw no unwanted attention. Eva found herself constantly staring out the entrance to cave, without getting close to it. She waited for Vic to come back, she watched for more strange beasts of this weird place, and she worried.

As she stared out, late in the afternoon, she noticed movement not far from the cave. Cautiously staying near the side wall of the cave, she eased towards the entrance with her gun in hand and peered out.

Sure enough, she saw a Na'gee warrior not ten feet away from the cave entrance and coming straight for it. She did not see any others with the lone warrior, so she steeled herself, stepped away from the wall and started for the cave entrance. As she moved, Eva said "Stay back Mila. There is danger."

She faintly heard Eva say something, but couldn't make out what it was, she too focused on the man approaching.

Eva raised her pistol and stepped out of the cave firing. The warrior took three shots to the mid-section and one to the head, falling backwards. Eva saw a flash of movement to her left and turned to fire, before she could get a shot off, she was kicked in her back.

The kick sent her hurtling towards the warrior she had intended to shoot, Olo. He caught her and flung her through the air several feet away from the cave, in the direction of the woods. She hit the ground and rolled another few feet, and Olo came running and kicked her mid-section as she started to rise. It sent her rolling across the ground several more feet.

Olo pulled his knife and looked back, to see his warrior entering the cave, followed immediately by an explosion of bright white light that sent the warriors body flying twenty feet through the air. When it landed on the ground it was burnt and sizzling. The Na'gee warrior was obviously dead.

Eva started to rise to her feet, coughing and gagging from the powerful kick she had taken to her stomach. Olo, turned back towards her with his knife, figuring he would kill her and then figure out how to kill the man on his own.

As he turned, he glanced in the distance towards the mountain to see if whatever had killed the beast and thrown it off the mountain had been alerted to the 'Brite's' explosion. What he saw was a man, scaling down the side of the mountain. He instantly knew who the man was. It didn't matter how far away he was, the tall man dressed in black was unmistakable. Suddenly, it all made sense to Olo.

The man had taken to the high ground to understand the terrain, that was why the woman came out firing. Olo, turned back to the woman and hesitated before swinging his large knife.

Finally, Olo decided against it. He decided that if Steph had second thoughts, the life of his mother would be a strong motivator for a child of his age, despite the aging. Instead of taking Eva's head with the knife, Olo slammed his booted foot into her face and the woman fell unconscious to the ground.

He picked her up and threw her over his shoulder. Before leaving Olo looked back and saw the shape of a young girl standing in front of the cave. A brilliant bright white light came from the girl's body, and she stared at Olo, with eyes that shined like headlights.

Olo stared back at the child for several minutes, the two gazing at each other, then he turned and ran off into the forest with Eva slung over his shoulder.

Vic scaled down the side of the mountain face as quickly as he could. The third time he had moved to fast and lost his grip, almost falling to a major injury or death, he decided he had to slow down.

"I won't be helping anyone if I end up splattered on the ground like damn dino bat-bird over there." Vic thought. "Still, have to hurry." He thought.

Despite him coming down at least twice as fast as he had climbed up, it seemed like it took ten times as long. The worry and fear for his wife and daughter weighed him down and tormented him the entire way down.

He had a little ways to go, before he could drop safely onto the path and begin to run, when he heard the gunshots ring out. He could tell from the sound that it was Eva's pistol and not the huge .50 caliber pistol that the Na'gee wore… it didn't make him feel any better.

Vic moved faster, careful not to let panic send him falling to his doom. Moments after the gunshots, he heard a loud explosion. Hanging on the side of the mountain face, he forced himself to lean back to try to see what was going on. He couldn't make out the cave from his vantage point, but what he did see caused his gut to wrench and gave him a stinging feeling in his heart. He saw a tall Na'gee warrior almost at the tree line, looking in his direction. Vic couldn't be sure from this distance, but it looked a lot like the warrior that had kicked him off the parking garage wall and left him for dead. The same man that had taken his son and threatened his family.

Vic paused staring for a moment longer and saw the man throw Eva over his shoulder and trot off into the forest.

"No! First Steph and now Eva! I'll kill everyone of those bastards!" Vic thought as he moved faster than before. Trying to get off the side of the mountain as quickly as possible.

It seemed like forever, when he was close enough to drop off the side of the mountain and land on the rocky path. As soon as his feet touched the ground, Vic took off running.

He ran as fast as he had ever run before.

"Mila has to be alright! She just has to be!" Vic said to himself as he ran for the cave. He had decided during the final stages of his descent that the warrior had too much of a head start to catch him in the forest and it was evening now. He'd never catch him before dark when those 'things' came out. So, he ran for Mila as fast as he could. Praying that his daughter would be ok.

He also felt fairly confident that he knew where this man that called himself 'Olo' would be taking Eva.

"It has to be the mountain with the smoke. Someone's

making that fire and there the only someone's I've seen in this godforsaken place." Vic thought.

As Vic rounded the corner, he saw his little girl. She stood in the remnants of the exploded doorway to the cave. Still shining a brilliant bright white light and still staring at the forest, where the man had taken off with her mother.

Vic slowed down as he got close, noticing that she had not even glanced at him and not wanting to surprise her or frighten her.

"Mila baby. It's going to be ok. I know where they're taking her. We're going to get her back. I promise." Vic said softly and compassionately to his little girl.

Mila turned to face him, and when she did the light disappeared from her body and from her eyes. When it did, he saw tears begin to stream down her face. Mila wrapped her arms around him and squeezed him, crying.

He hugged his daughter and felt a fire ignite inside of him. Tears did not stream down Vic's eyes, but an overwhelming anger flooded through him.

"These damn animals have taken my son, taken my wife and crushed my poor little girl! I'll kill everyone of them if it's the last thing I do. Nothing else matters now." Vic's thoughts fueled the rage growing inside him. He was so caught up in his furious thoughts that for a moment he didn't realize that Mila had released him and had spoken to him.

"What baby?" Vic asked.

"I said, do you promise Dad? Do you promise you'll get Mom and Steph back?" Mila said softly.

"Yeah, Mila. I promise… and I'm going to kill all of those men." Vic said in response.

Mila stared at him and then wiped up her tears. "Let's get inside then Dad. The dark ones will be here soon. We can leave when its light again." She had that ominous tone when she said it, like she had earlier. Vic didn't know what to think, but he did what she said.

The two moved enough debris to climb back in the cave. Vic started another fire and as the sun started to set. Mila sat back in front of the opening to the cave cross legged and glowing once again. Neither Father nor Daughter spoke a word as they prepared or while they watched the dark ones stare at them from twenty feet outside the cave, all night.

CHAPTER 44:
THE T'KCHE

The long tunnel was dark and dank, lit up only by the bluish glowing symbols or hieroglyphics or whatever they were. The tunnel was about six feet wide and about twelve feet tall, but the further they went the taller and wider it seemed to grow. Samuel continued to carry Flutter, who had slightly moved and made a groaning noise here and there. He thought that was promising but couldn't be sure. Halbred marched on in front of him, staying a few feet back from the huge hairy man-ape creature or whatever it was.

As they walked, Samuel tried to get a better look at the creature, but it was hard because of the darkness and being behind Halbred. The 'T'kche' as it had called itself, had thick black hair covering all of its body, except its feet, hands and some of its face. These seemed more ape like, with tough black skin. The creature's feet were huge, as were its hands, and it stood at least eight feet tall. Samuel thought it might actually be taller, but the way it slightly leaned forward when it moved, made it difficult to tell.

The tunnel ended into a huge underground cavern. There

was a small stream at the far end and shelves that seemed to be growing various types of mushrooms in neat rows. The walls and ground were mostly dark brownish black dirt and rock, with huge bluish glowing designs and pictures covering almost every inch of the walls. It gave the cavern a light blue glow, that made it relatively easy to see.

Outside of the strange landscape, Samuel saw five more of these so called T'kche. There were two small ones by the water that appeared to be about five feet tall, but still massive in girth. They were both covered in a lighter shade of brown hair. They appeared to be children. A large dark brown T'kche sat by the water near them.

The other two were standing together directly in front of the large black-haired one that had led them down the tunnel. They did not appear to be greeting him kindly, rather they seemed less than pleased that their counterpart had arrived with unexpected guests.

One of the two was about the size of their guide. It wielded a similar club and was covered in dark brown hair. The other was much bigger than both of them. It stood about ten feet tall with a massive chest and shoulders. It was covered with black and brown hair that almost seemed to make swirls and it held a massive club that had spikes carved into it.

Samuel watched what he assumed was a standoff and listened to the beasts make strange growls at each other, then he realized he could understand them and he listened closer.

"They not Na'gee D'knr! All man not Na'gee!" He heard their guide saying to the largest one. Samuel figured the big one must be in charge.

Their black-haired guide continued. "They kill many dark ones. They good warrior. Female hurt. Need help."

Then Samuel heard the large beast respond. His deep voice seemed to make the cavern rumble. "No man good G'noch. All evil. You should no bring here. You young and stupid G'noch." The beast scowled at their guide when he said the words.

Samuel did not like the way things seemed to be going. The fact that the dark brown beast that had confronted them with the large one, slowly eased himself around them, cutting off their retreat back into the tunnel, did nothing to ease his concerns.

Right when Samuel decided that he'd need to set Flutter down and try to smooth things over, he heard Halbred speak up.

"We're no Na'gee D'knr! We're hunting the damn Na'gee!" Halbred said in his usual angry tone. "G'noch here helped us out while we were fighting those damn blood sucking things up top and the fact is, if my friend here wasn't hurt so bad, we'd have just stayed up there and killed all the damn things for you." Halbred finished his angry update by gesturing to Flutter, who Samuel still held.

Samuel was impressed at how quickly Halbred had picked up on their names and used them, but he wasn't sure that yelling at the giant beasts that were already wary of them was the most tactful approach that he could have taken.

There was a long moment of silence and then their guide, G'noch spoke up loudly as he roughly patted the largest beast on the arm. "See D'knr! Told you they no Na'gee. Not all man bad." As G'noch spoke and patted D'knr on the arm, he walked right past him and over to the large brown haired T'kche with the children. He apparently considering the conversation over.

This left Halbred staring up at the giant D'knr and Samuel uneasily watching them, while holding Flutter and keeping an eye on the other T'kche with the club, that now stood directly behind him.

"What you mean you hunt Na'gee?" D'knr asked Halbred, staring at him, like he could look through him.

Halbred seemed unphased. "I mean we're hunting them. Those damn Na'gee killed my men. Good men and a shitload of innocent people. Now I'm gonna kill all the damn Na'gee. Every one of them." Halbred said it matter of factly and stared right back at the giant beast.

As the two faced off, Samuel saw G'noch take the place of the dark brown T'kche that sat by the children, and that one stood up and approached. It walked right past D'knr gently touching his arm as it went by and saying "If they kill dark ones and Na'gee, they ok with me D'knr. Now stop. Let them rest. I help hurt one." The T'kche said it, sounding strangely more feminine than the others had, and walked right up to Samuel.

"I T'jin. I help hurt friend." Said the T'kche who had approached Samuel, as she reached her large arms out and gently took Flutter from Samuel's arms. She, as it was obviously a she, walked a few feet away and gently laid Flutter down on what appeared to be a bed of moss, directly under one of the rock shelves growing what appeared to be some strangely shaped and colored kind of mushrooms.

Halbred turned from his staring contest with the large T'kche and followed the one that leaned over Flutter.

She immediately began rubbing some sort of salve over Flutters forehead and neck, being very delicate the entire time.

"I am Halbred. Thank you T'jin." Halbred said, in what Samuel figured was the nicest voice he was capable of, that still sounded somewhat angry.

"Her head hurt bad Halbred. We fix her." T'jin said.

The large T'kche, D'knr set his club down and stood over them both watching.

Samuel turned to the T'kche that still stood behind him and stared at him for a moment. Finally, he decided he had better break the ice with his hosts for the night and said, "I am Samuel."

The T'kche in front of him growled and stomped off over to the stream by G'noch. Samuel heard G'noch make the same weird growling gurgling sound from the tunnel and then say "He no like your face Samuel. No worry. T'sko no like anyone."

Samuel stood unamused and decided that the weird noise was definitely laughter and this time it was at his expense.

For what was definitely several hours T'jin continued to massage different salves onto Flutters head and neck, while Halbred crowded close. The man didn't seem to be much help, but Samuel understood.

"She's the only one he's got left to lose." Samuel thought. The thought made him think of Dante and Vic. He felt bad that he had let those men die. It seemed strange to Samuel that he felt anything for them, after all, they were just a means to an end, but still he felt responsible for their deaths.

It angered him to think about and it made his thoughts wander to that of the family that he had lost. So much death and loss. He was still enraged about what had happened to his family and while he blamed Camacho, he now also saw that the blame was to be shared by all the Na'gee. Samuel silently vowed to himself that he would kill them all. He would avenge his family and he would avenge Dante and Vic too.

Samuel was pulled away from his thoughts of loss and vengeance, when a wall with a large design on it opened up, forming one of the strange doorways and a large brown T'kche came stumbling through.

At a glance it appeared to be a female like T'jin, with slightly darker hair. It was holding it's side and stumbling, before it crashed onto the floor. T'sko roared from across the cavern and came rushing to the female T'kche's aid. He rolled her over and they all saw the blood gushing out of her side.

As her arms fell to her sides, her hands opened up and large brown mushrooms fell out. They did not look like the mushrooms growing in the caves, but like the ones Samuel had eaten on many occasions. As he peered past the concerned T'sko to see the wound, he realized it was a gun shot wound.

"She's been shot." Samuel said.

Halbred jumped to his feet and rushed over. T'sko tried to push him back, but Halbred held his ground and said "I can help T'sko. I can take out the bullet and fix her. I cannot help my friend, but I can probably help her. Let me try."

D'knr still stood over T'jin, who did not stop her efforts to help Flutter and the children stayed at the far end of the cavern by the stream, but G'noch now stood by Samuel and they watched the exchange between Halbred and T'sko.

T'sko seemed to wait for only a moment and then he stepped back and allowed Halbred to approach the female T'kche.

"I am Halbred. What is your name?" Halbred said as he crouched down and looked her in the eyes of the large T'kche laying on the floor of the cavern.

"I am S'tku." The female T'kche softly said as she lay there bleeding.

"Ok, S'tku. I am going to take the bullet out and try to sew you up to stop the bleeding. It's going to hurt, but it will help. Tell me what happened." Halbred said. Despite the natural gruffness to his voice, compassion was evident. It seemed that the man had seen so much death, that he relished at this chance to save a life.

"I harvest food on other world. Man see me. He shoot with long club." S'tku said. It was clearly an effort for her to get the words out.

Samuel glanced down at the mushrooms that had fallen out of her hands and contemplated her words. Unless he misunderstood, it seemed that this T'kche was in his world harvesting mushrooms and got shot in the woods by somebody with a rifle.

"So, they can come and go from our world like the Na'gee." Samuel thought. He looked closely to see if any of them wore any Talisman or could have one on their persons, but they did not wear any clothes.

"They must have a different way of traveling from world to world." Samuel thought.

Halbred pulled a few tools from one of his many pouches and began to work on extracting the bullet. S'tku writhed in pain, but did not cry out, while T'sko crouched on the other side of her watching it all with pain in his eyes.

Minutes later, from across the room, a fist sized rock fell from a hole in the ceiling of the cavern and landed on a large hollow log that looked like it had been placed under the hole purposely. It made a loud echoing thump throughout the cavern and everyone stopped what they were doing and stared.

A second later, another fist sized rock came through the same hole, hitting the log and filling the cavern with loud echoing thump again. Moments passed and no other rocks came.

"Two stones mean Na'gee. Maybe find door." G'noch said.

Everyone heard him clearly.

Halbred looked up at Samuel and said, "If I stop now, she'll die."

Samuel nodded and then turned to face G'noch. "Show me where. I'll deal with the Na'gee."

G'noch gave Samuel a weird tooth filled grin and turned to D'knr "Told you they good warrior." Then G'noch looked back at Samuel and said "I take you. We kill Na'gee together Samuel."

Samuel nodded and G'noch grabbed his large club from where it had rested against the wall. With club in hand, G'noch began rushing back down the same tunnel that they had arrived from the previous night. Samuel followed closely.

As the two quickly moved through the long tunnel Samuel asked, "How many more T'kche are up there?"

"No more. Lot of T'kche tribes, but not many in each tribe." G'noch replied. As he kept moving quickly up the dark tunnel path.

Samuel had to half jog to keep up with the large T'kche's long strides. As he hurried along, he kept thinking about G'noch's answer. Finally, Samuel asked, "If there are no more T'kche, who dropped the stones alerting you to the Na'gee?"

"The S'kte. They like T'kche, only tiny." Without slowing down, G'noch looked back and gestured with his hands indicating the creatures were roughly one foot tall. Then he turned back around while kept talking and walking. "We protect S'kte. S'kte lookout for T'kche. Warn us when evil close. Two stones, mean Na'gee." G'noch explained.

Samuel was intrigued by the strange relationship between the two species. Before he could ask any more questions though, G'noch abruptly stopped and turned to his right, staring at the wall. It seemed to Samuel that they were only a little more than halfway to the door that he had followed G'noch through the night before. He watched closely as G'noch seemed to examine the wall.

Like all the walls to the tunnel, it was covered with designs and pictures that glowed a blueish color. G'noch stared at the design for but a moment and then placed his hand directly against it, on a specific symbol on the wall. Immediately, a doorway or opening appeared in the cavern wall.

Turning to face Samuel, G'noch said "You go back to end. Use that." He pointed at the stone circular talisman of the Na'gee, that Samuel now wore around his neck, then he continued with his instuctions. "Open same door we come through. Kill Na'gee. G'noch go this way. Meet you other side. G'noch kill Na'gee too." As he said it, G'noch made a circular motion with his hands. It appeared to Samuel that G'noch intended for him to hit the Na'gee from one side, while G'noch attacked from the other side.

Samuel didn't reply, he simply nodded and walked off towards the end of the tunnel, where they had entered the dark tunnel from initially.

G'noch watched Samuel for a moment, nodded in satisfaction and then took off through the new doorway that had formed in the side of the tunnel wall.

As Samuel approached the end of the tunnel, he forced himself to push away the enraging thoughts of avenging his family and Vic and Dante. He forced himself to focus on the task at hand. The long sleepless night, coupled with being alone with his thoughts, made it difficult.

"These warriors demand my full attention, not to mention the damn creatures of this world." Samuel thought as he inspected the end of the tunnel wall before him and raised the talisman he wore around his neck. When he placed it against the stone wall, the symbol that matched the one on the talisman glowed brighter. He matched the talismans placement to the that of the symbol and then the wall opened up, creating a doorway, the same doorway they passed through the night before.

As soon as it opened, sunlight streamed into the cavern tunnel and Samuel found himself standing face to face with two Na'gee warriors who looked as shocked at his sudden appearance as he was at theres.

"Shit." Samuel thought.

Chapter 45: Re-Match

Earlier that day in the wee hours of the morning, as the sun was about to rise, Camacho approached the blocked entrance to the Na'gee's mountain settlement with the six warriors he had gathered. He waited for the settlement's entrance guards to move the boulder at first light as was the custom.

As he waited Camacho noticed, Olo approaching with two warriors and staring at him. Camacho turned to face the Na'gee warrior and stared back, feeling challenged by the seasoned warrior's stare. His pride and ego had been tested much in the last several hours and his patience was thin. He felt anger bubbling up as he watched Olo approach him staring.

Olo walked directly up to Camacho and stopped within inches of him, still staring. After several tense moments of the two men standing close and staring at one another, Olo spoke. "How many warriors must you take Camacho? You dishonor yourself to bring so many to hunt weak topsiders. Na'gee hunting parties are in threes."

"I have two hunting parties then Olo." Camacho snapped back.

"What of you then Camacho? You make seven. Are you no longer counted amongst the hunters?" Olo responded coldly.

Camacho stared. He hated being challenged. He wanted to tear Olo's head off with his bare hands. He knew if he attacked the senior warrior he would be hunted by all the Na'gee. He knew how tradition worked, he knew the rules were different when facing a tribe leader then a they were with a warrior who considered a peer.

"I could challenge him, but I would have to request the right to challenge from the elders. They will not grant that until I have redeemed myself." Camacho thought. He got angrier at the thought and was tempted to try to kill the man anyway and deal with the consequences.

He stared in Olo's eyes and knew that Olo knew exactly what he was thinking and was tempting him on purpose.

"He really thinks he can stand up to my enhanced speed and strength. Foolish Na'gee!" Camacho thought.

Finally, Camacho replied, forcing himself to say the words instead of scream them at Olo. "I hunt soldiers and warriors that are enhanced from the gene, as I am Olo. You hunt the mother and father of damn child that glows and you still need help. Don't talk to me about honor." As Camacho finished spitting out the words, the boulder was removed from the entrance and the first signs of daylight streamed in.

"I face the greater threat you top sider fool. Do not

underestimate the significance of a 'Brite'. I will find this Brite, and her mother and father will die by my hands." As he finished his rebutle, Olo walked past Camacho and out of the mountain, his two warriors following closely.

Camacho, fumed silently for a moment and then exited the mountain as well, his hunting party of six warriors followed him closley.

As he went outside Camacho saw Olo and his two warriors running off towards the smaller mountain that was near the lake and hills on the other side of the forest.

Camacho looked out at the vast landscape before him. The view was incredible from the mountain settlement entrance. He was able to see for many miles in three directions. The view only being broken up by forestry, hills and smaller mountains. He remembered clearly where he had crossed over from the top side during the failed migration battle.

"We'll track them from where they crossed over. Keep up." Camacho said to the hunting parties that stood by him, awaiting his instructions.

He began to run in that direction, straight through the nearby woods.

Camacho did not run as fast as he could, or his hunting party would never be able to keep up. His enhanced speed would take him there in minutes and leave them following nothing but the blur of colors he left behind. Camacho did, however, run just fast enough to make the warriors push themselves hard to keep up. He knew it was harder than he should have pushed them, but he wanted to remind them of how weak and slow they were compared to him. After the challenging interaction with Olo in front of these warriors, Camacho wanted to make sure they remembered why he was in charge of them. So, he made them run, struggling to keep up with the pace he set.

It was about midday when Camacho and his party arrived at the same spot he hand crossed over to the previous evening. He immediately noticed the two black cloaks by piles of ashes. Two dark ones had died here last night, that was for certain.

Camacho knew that the warriors with him noticed this as well and figured it would keep them sharp. Not many could kill a dark one. The thought that a handful of top siders could kill two, unnerved the hardened Na'gee warriors greatly.

Camacho started inspecting the tracks that to a trained eye mapped out a story of the fight that had taken place here the night before. He followed them and found a large spot on the ground, where a massive man must've laid. Based on the size of the indention on the ground, Camacho figured it was the massive solider he had hit on the roof. He remembered hitting the solider with everything he had and not long later had seen the huge man killing other Na'gee on the roof. Camacho knew that the blow he had delivered would have easily killed a normal man.

"His strength must be incredibly enhanced by the gene. It's the only way he could've survived, let alone shook the devastating punch off with no seeming effects, so quickly." Camacho thought to himself.

As he continued to inspect the tracks, he noticed that despite the fact that the man had clearly laid on the ground, there was no body, no blood, and Camacho saw that the large soldier's tracks showed that he had walked away through the clearing and over the edge of the hill.

The age of the tracks made it appear that he had walked away long after the rest of the battle had ended.

"It could mean nothing, or it could be very bad." Camacho thought. "If those parasites laid eggs in the large one, with that unnatural strength we could have a very different kind of dark one. That could change things drastically." He thought. Camacho decided that was a concern for another day, figuring he had enough to think about right now without that distraction. Although, it continued to haunt him in the back of his mind.

He didn't know of anyone being effected by the 'gene' in this world. Sure, some of the tribe's elders and wise ones had special gifts, but they had always seemed more magical or spiritual than genetic. No, as far as Camacho knew, the 'gene' was only prevalent in the top side world. His true home world. He did not know what would happen if dark ones had the chance to lay their eggs or implant their ancient entities as the Na'gee believed they did, into a topsider with the 'gene', but he knew it could mean trouble for them all.

As he looked around more, he noticed that two other sets of tracks went off in the opposite direction into the woods. Camacho did not expect them to split up, and that it had happened only added to his concerns. Pushing the troubling thoughts away, he decided that they would follow the other two sets of tracks. Based on the way the tracks changed, one of the pair appeared to still be carrying the woman he had knocked out.

"That punch should've killed her too. Still, it wasn't nearly as hard as I hit the big one." Camacho thought.

"Forget the large tracks that go off by themselves. We'll follow the pair of tracks into the woods. Come on." Camacho shouted to his warriors, and they all began slowly following the tracks deeper into the woods.

Before long Camacho and the large hunting party arrived at an area where two large boulders were positioned against a giant tree on either side, making a kind of half circle enclosure. The massive tree's branches hung low and almost created a roof.

The tracks went directly inside of the nature made shelter.

Camacho made several hand gestures to the hunting party, that told them to be silent and instructed two of the six to remain outside the encloser on either side. Camacho and the other four warriors entered the clearing cautiously. They saw signs that their prey had been there, but no one was there now.

"Search the walls for old T'kche paths. If they stumbled on one and used it to escape the night, we'll find them." Camacho barked out in a hushed voice. As he looked around, he pretended not to notice the dark tattered cloaks and piles of ashes on the ground. The warriors with him tried to follow his lead, but their eyes kept going back to the black cloaks on the ground and they were clearly rattled.

"Four more dark ones dead. These fools are definitely more than I expected." Camacho thought.

The four warriors began holding the stone circular

talisman that they wore around their necks at the walls, slowly making their way around the inside of the clearing.

When one warrior got to the spot, where G'noch had led Samuel and Halbred into the tunnel, the boulder glowed blue, showing a design that matched the one on the talisman.

The warrior made a quiet whistling noise, and the three other warriors were on him. One stood directly next to him and the other two stood behind them both. Camacho watched eagerly from the doorway to the enclosure.

The warrior that had whistled, held his talisman up, but right before he touched the boulder with it, a door opened up seemingly on its own. The Na'gee warriors froze in shock as they stood face to face with a muscular, dark skinned top sider. He had a shaved head and was wearing black jeans, a black t-shirt and black sports coat.

Samuel had just opened the doorway and saw the warriors in his face. He saw them all momentarily freeze in shock at the site of him. He was equally surprised, but he didn't freeze up. He never froze up. A moment of them hesitating in surprise was all he needed, whether he was surprised or not.

Samuel quickly pulled both of his pistols, raised them simultaneously and shot the two Na'gee staring at him in the head at the same time. The shots echoed loudly in the enclosed space, deafening everyone. As their bodies started to fall, Samuel reached past them and shot the two warriors behind them in the head. All four shots were executed in a fluid motion that happened in a blur of speed.

It was mere seconds, and Samuel had killed four Na'gee warriors. Camacho saw it happen. In an instant he went from hunting the top sider with a large group of warriors to facing him by himself.

"What the fuck just happened?!" Camacho thought. Feelings of shock and rage ran through him. He decided in that moment he would kill this man if he did nothing else.

Camacho took off, starting to rush his opponent from the doorway and Samuel just started firing as he turned the pistols in that direction before he even had them fully aimed at his target.

"Just got to keep shooting and hope I hit the fast bastard again. If I can slow him down, he's mine." Samuel thought.

Camacho was too fast for Samuel to land a direct hit, but he managed to hit him in the leg, before diving to the side and barely dodging Camacho's charge.

Samuel spun around and kept firing both pistols, forcing Camacho to use his incredible speed to run in circles around the inside of the clearing to avoid being shot.

The two warriors from the outside of the natural clearing heard the gunshots and started to make their way in, when a large black haired T'kche came roaring out of a doorway that appeared on the base of a giant tree, just outside of the clearing.

G'noch swung his massive club high into the air and brought it crashing down with incredible force on the closest warrior to him. A large splatter was all that was left of the warrior, who was instantly crushed from the T'kche's mighty blow.

The second warrior started to pull his large pistol and

G'noch switched his grip on the club and swung it sideways into the man's midsection. The blow sent the man flying into the enclosure, past Samuel, who was still firing both pistols and almost into Camacho who was running around the inside of the enclosure.

The near collision with the flying Na'gee warrior, made Camacho slip and one of Samuel's bullets caught him in the waist.

The impact of the bullet, combined with the trip up while running at an incredible speed sent Camacho crashing to the ground, his momentum sending him skidding right past Samuel and out of the enclosure.

G'noch saw Camacho's body come sliding past him before stopping just feet away and he ran at it, club raised high. The large T'kche was within range in a split second and brought his club down hard attempting to smash Camacho, but Camacho rolled over on his side several times.

He rolled as fast as he had run, and it took him several feet away from G'noch, dodging the club's swing. Camacho jumped to his feet but struggled to stay up. He had been shot twice and one of the wounds was bad. He knew he was losing a lot of blood fast.

He looked up and saw the black haired T'kche approaching and then he saw Samuel rounding the side of the boulder with pistols in hand.

As much as he hated it, Camacho knew he didn't have much of a chance. So, once again, he turned and ran off through the forest, leaving a trail of blood flying behind him.

Samuel and G'noch saw the man take off in a flash. Before they could consider another attack, he was just gone. G'noch let out a furious roar that echoed through the dense forest around them.

"I will not let him get away again." Samuel thought, as he calmly turned around and surveyed the enclosure behind him. He saw the bodies of the four Na'gee he had shot lying on the ground. He also saw the one G'noch had knocked into the enclosure rolling around on the ground, holding his ribs in agony.

Samuel walked up to the injured warrior and kicked him hard in the midsection, where the man held himself. The warrior let out a cry of pain and looked up and Samuel.

"Tell me where he's going. Where is Camacho heading?" Samuel said coldly.

He was aware that G'noch had stepped inside the enclosure and now stood behind him watching the exchange, but he didn't care.

The Na'gee warrior stopped rolling from side to side in pain and stared up and Samuel but did not say a word. He tried to hide his pain behind a stoic expressionless mask, but it was evident that he was severely injured.

Samuel kicked him again, hard. The man's expressionless face was replaced with a look of pain as he cried out. Blood began pouring out of the man's mouth and his eyes rolled back as his head the floor.

"He no answer now Samuel." G'noch said, through the same sound of growling and gurgling that Samuel now recognized as the T'kche laughing.

"I'll have to follow the blood trail and track him, to find out where he's run off too. Then I'll kill them all." Samuel said darkly, coldly and seemingly to himself as he turned away from the now dead Na'gee warrior.

He walked over to the four dead Na'gee by the doorway to the cavern tunnel, that still remained open and snatched the talisman off each of their necks.

"These things seem to come in handy. I'll hang on to them for now." He thought. Then Samuel turned to G'noch and said, "I need to tell Halbred that I'm going after him. He has a right to come if he wants. He's lost a lot to these damn Na'gee too. Take me to him G'noch, then I'll follow the blood trail and find Camacho."

"No need follow trail. G'noch know where Na'gee live." G'noch said to Samuel in return. "Na'gee in mountain. Too late today. Dark soon. Early tomorrow, G'noch take you Samuel. We kill all Na'gee together." The large black haired T'kche gave Samuel another tooth filled grin, then walked past him into the cavern doorway and began walking down the tunnel. Samuel slowly followed, frustrated at the thought of waiting until the next morning, but noticing how late in the day it was already, he chose not to argue. He knew the large T'kche was right.

"No sense in having to fight those night creature the entire way there." Samuel thought as he entered the tunnel and doorway closed behind him.

When the two arrived back at the large cavern, they saw the scene had changed. Both Flutter and the large female

T'kche that had been shot, S'tku, were now sitting up side by side with their backs resting against the cavern wall. T'jin and Halbred hovered over them, while the two other large T'kche stood close by staring at them with obvious concern and relief.

All eyes shifted to Samuel and G'noch as they entered the cavern.

"We kill most. One run away. They find door. We must kill tomorrow." G'noch said loudly.

D'knr the large apparent leader of the tribe looked incredibly angry in an instant. "You let one run away?!" he roared. "Now we must find new home G'noch. Na'gee come back and hunt tribe."

Samuel had, had enough of all of it. He shared the large T'kche's frustration at Camacho's escape, but he also knew exactly what he was going to do at first light. He interrupted the exchange in his loud deep voice.

"G'noch will show me the Na'gee settlement at first light." Samuel glanced at Halbred and then looked back at the rest of the gathered T'kche. "We'll kill them all. You do not need to move your home. The Na'gee will not survive us, no matter how many there are." Samuel had gestured at Halbred when he had said 'we'll' and upon finishing his bold statement he just stared silently at everyone in the cavern. In his mind, he wondered just how many Na'gee they might truly end up facing.

Halbred stood and moved slightly to stand by Samuel. "That settles it then. Those bastards die in the morning." He said gruffly.

"G'noch go too. We kill Na'gee together." G'noch said.

D'knr looked from the two men to G'noch. Then he spoke in his growling, cavern rumbling voice. "This a man fight, not a T'kche fight, G'noch. Show them Na'gee home and come back. You no fight."

G'noch looked at the two men and then back at D'knr and simply said "No."

The two large beasts stared at each other for long moments and then G'noch spoke again, apparently losing the silent staring contest with the much larger T'kche.

"G'noch hide no more. G'noch kill Na'gee with good warriors. Nothing here for G'noch. D'knr and T'jin. T'sko and S'tku. Little ones. Nothing for G'noch. G'noch warrior. I leave and kill Na'gee." The other T'kche in the cavern shared concerned looks with one another for several moments and then finally D'knr turned back to G'noch.

"G'noch true warrior. You go. Be safe." D'knr said sternly.

Surprisingly to all of them, including D'knr, T'sko spoke up. "T'sko go fight too. Man save S'tku life. T'sko go save man life." T'sko said it viciously, but with an ominous sort of honor.

In a faint pained voice Flutter spoke from her seated position by the wall. "What the hell are they all growling about boss and why did you growl at them too?"

All eyes turned to Flutter. Halbred seemed momentarily perplexed by her statement, but instantly caught on, when he saw Samuel walked over to her and gently put one of the talisman that he'd confiscated from the dead Na'gee around her neck.

"You will understand them now. We're going to hunt the Na'gee at first light and those two have decided to help us." Samuel said coldly.

"Good enough for me. I'll be good by the morning. Let's kill those bastards." Flutter said and then she adjusted her position so she could lay down against the wall and she closed her eyes.

With the decisions seemingly made, everyone got comfortable and tried to get some rest while they waited for morning to come.

Chapter 46:
To the Settlement

Steph had spent most of the day just sitting under the shade of the tree, munching on some types of dried fruit, and drinking cool water, while he watched the two older Na'gee with the white braids and beards, leaning over Ansai.

As the hours had drifted by it occurred to Steph that he had hurt Ansai much worse than he'd initially thought. More than anything, the man's leg appeared to have sustained some serious damage. As time went on Steph mentally sorted through what seemed like an endless amount of knowledge that he just had now about this world and the Na'gee. There were gaps that left questions, but he understood so much. The time alone, in silence gave him the opportunity to think through it all, to kind of process it all and try to make better sense of the world around him.

Throughout the afternoon his thoughts took him to the recent events. They took him to what the Na'gee had said about his family. He somehow knew there was more to it all that they were keeping from him. He did not trust them at all. He had heard enough and learned enough during the aging and testing that he believed they were at least a violent and primitive people. He wasn't sure if they were evil or not, but he didn't feel that they were the 'good guys' that Olo had made them out to be.

Still, he knew something was wrong with Mila. He had witnessed her weird predictions, strange voices and the glaring bright light that came from her. He had seen the explosion at the hideout that see had caused.

On the other hand, Steph also knew that for whatever reason, the events all seemed to be in defense to the Na'gee attacking his family. His family that was supposedly here in this world now, based on what he'd overheard. His family that Olo planned to dispatch before he could confront them. Defeating Ansai, was supposed to have given him that opportunity, but instead it had just left him sitting under a damn tree.

Steph decided he would confront his parents. He decided with this new body, and this knew knowledge, he would force his Father to tell him the truth about Mila and what had happened. He would do whatever it took. He knew his parents; he would be able to tell if they were lying to him.

In that moment Steph resolved that if what the Na'gee claimed was true, he would kill both his parents and the demon they had allowed to kill his sister and take her body. On the other hand, if there was something else to it, he would kill Olo. After what he had done in his testing and what he had done to Ansai, in his first fights with his new body, Steph felt confident that nothing and no one could defeat him.

In his mind he had become like the heroes he had watched in movies as a child, in what seemed like only yesterday.

With his mind made up, Steph stood up and walked over to the two older Na'gee with Ansai. He stopped less than a foot from them and confidently addressed them both.

"Ansai and I had a deal, that if I defeated him, he would take me to find my family. I have clearly defeated him. If he cannot take me, I expect one of you too." Steph said with confidence.

The older Na'gee looked from Steph to one another and without saying a word, one of them grabbed Ansai's arms and began dragging him off towards the cave where Steph had spent the night. The other turned to face Steph.

"I care not for your deals with Ansai top sider. The young warrior does not speak for the wise ones. However, because Ansai can no longer train you or take you anywhere. I will take you to Olo at the Na'gee settlement. He can decide what you do and where you go from there." The wise one paused and stared at Steph, almost challenging him to protest, when Steph said nothing, he continued.

"We will leave shortly. It will be dark before we reach the settlement, so you must be sure to follow my instructions without question or you will die at the hands of the dark ones." The wise one said it firmly and stared at Steph obviously to make sure the statement was weighed heavily. The wise one then turned and walked off towards a different cave, not far from the one Steph had slept in.

About thirty minutes later, the wise one returned. He had several large packs tied securely to the belt around his waist and now carried a large knife similar to the Na'gee warriors. He did not carry one of the large .50 caliber pistols though. He walked right past Steph and gestured for him to follow as he headed for the path that led out of the mountain's center and away from the aging lake. Steph followed as it was indicated for him to and the two of them began their journey to the Na'gee settlement.

Based on the sky, Steph figured it was late afternoon/early evening when they exited the strange mountain path and headed into the forest. He wasn't sure how he could tell the time so definitively from the look of the sky, he just could now.

After hearing Ansai's descriptions and warnings of the dark ones the night before, he wondered how the old wise one planned to handle this danger. Although he wondered, Steph wasn't concerned, he felt with this new body that he could do anything.

"Let a dark one, or anything else for that matter try me and it will be the last thing they do." Steph thought.

The wise one, who had been leading in silence seemed to know his thoughts and spoke up without looking back at Steph. "The dangers of this world are real young warrior. You have come out of the aging strong and done well in the testing, but you are still a child. Do not underestimate the risks around you, just because you are stronger now than you were yesterday boy." The wise one, did not try to hide his dislike for Steph.

All Steph really took out of the statement was that the old Na'gee didn't like him, but still was forced to admit that he did well.

"Yeah, I did well enough to kill your beasts, even when the big one had the club and then kick Ansai's butt." Steph thought arrogantly.

As the two journeyed through the dense forest, Steph heard noises around him here and there. He didn't see any creatures though as the wise one, seemed to silently and swiftly take him through bushes and small creeks, always leading away from the noise before Steph even heard it. It was almost as if the wise one could sense the creatures of the forest and avoid them, before Steph even heard their sounds.

As he followed, Steph tried to concentrate on doing the same thing. A couple of times, he thought he sensed something before he heard the noise, but there were far more instances where he failed to do so. He kept at hit, trying to kind of tune in his senses as he walked. In the back of his mind, young Steph thought that he could end up confronting the Na'gee and have to travel this world on his own. He figured if that happened, he needed to be ready.

As they walked along it got darker and darker, before Steph knew it the sun was setting. As it started to set, the wise one stopped and waved Steph to him. He reached into one of the large pouches he wore on his belt and pulled out a leather bag that seemed to be full of some sort of liquid.

The wise one, rubbed the thick blue liquid substance all over his arms, face, neck chest and back. He continued to run down his exposed legs, until all the man's skin was covered in the dark blue goo. It made him difficult to see in the failing light and seemed to eliminate the odor of the old Na'gee.

The wise one stepped closer to Steph and began to rub him down with the same substance. Steph did not move, he just stood still and let the man cover his skin, as he watched him do to himself.

By the time full darkness had arrived, they both were completely covered in the blue goo or gel or whatever it was. The wise one, put his finger to his lips gesturing for Steph to be quiet and then silently climbed straight up the closest tree, high into its branches.

Steph felt icky from the blue goo and yet was still amused that the old Na'gee had used what seemed to be the universal sign for 'be quiet'. He stealthily followed the wise one up the tree and continued to follow as the wise one leaped from branch to branch, seemingly continuing their journey high in the air moving from one tree to another.

Steph followed. The movements came to him naturally, like he'd done them his entire life. He didn't know how he knew how to do them, he just did. Not long into their tree bound leg of the journey, Steph also knew to stop and be silent and still without the Na'gee instructing him to do so. He didn't know how he knew this either, but his instincts forced him to. His skin tingled as he crouched on the branch of a huge tree.

He looked down and saw two creatures wearing tattered black cloaks creeping along the forest floor, far below. Steph knew instantly that these were dark ones. They appeared to be sniffing the air and leading with their noses, slightly leaned over as they crept along through the forest.

Steph stopped staring at the strange creatures, to look up

at the old wise one and noticed he was also stopped and similarly crouching on a branch. Not moving an inch.

After a few minutes, the creatures took off in a blur of speed. As soon as they did, the wise one stood up on the branch, gave Steph a reassuring nod and then took of again. Steph followed closely.

This same sequence of events happened so many times through the rest of their journey through the trees in the dark of night, that Steph stopped counting. The dark ones always seemed to appear in twos. Steph couldn't tell if all of the incidents were the same two creatures or different pairs, but deep down he knew he couldn't let them see him. No matter how confident and powerful he felt with his new body and skills, it didn't wash away the feeling that these creatures were very dangerous.

Hours into the night, the wise one scaled about halfway down a tree and jumped to the forest floor. Steph followed closely and the two of them stepped out of the woods at the base of mountain. Steph looked up and saw smoke rising from the top of the massive mountain.

He followed the wise one to the what appeared to be a hole in the mountain face, that was blocked from a large boulder seemingly on the inside of the opening. The wise one raised his wicked looking staff with the curved blade on the top and it glowed a bright blue. He pointed it at the boulder and the boulder glowed blue as well and started to move aside.

Concerned by the brightness, Steph looked around and as he did, he saw two of the creatures with the tattered black cloaks appear at the tree line of the forest. The creatures smelled the air and looked around. When their eyes landed on Steph and the wise one, long black tongues flickered out of their gaping mouths and the creatures kind of hissed, showing off sharp teeth and massive fangs.

They took off, moving at an incredible speed towards Steph. All he could do was watch in awe as the terrifying creatures came for him. Then suddenly Steph was jerked off of his feet and into the mountain. He landed on his rear facing the doorway and watched the boulder slide back into place just before the dark ones made it inside.

Chapter 47:
Rebirth

arkness surrounded Roid, but somehow, he could still see clearly. There were other shapes and figures huddled near him. They all started moving slowly, milling about like a group waking up from a deep sleep all at the same time.

Roid recognized the beings around him as the same creatures he had battled upon arriving in this strange world. He remembered it all very clearly. He remembered everything, including things that made no sense to him. He remembered dying or something close to dying, he didn't really know what it was. What he did know was that he stood up, changed, before the sun had risen and was drawn to the place where he now stood. It was a large pyramid constructed of giant grey stones, that were each bigger than a large truck. The place looked ancient. He was in a large room, that had several hallways of somesort leading from it in every direction. The large room's walls were covered with murals and strange pictures roughly carved into and drawn on the walls. He found that he clearly understood them, they told of the history of these creatures that he felt an attachment too now. They were somehow his people now or something of the sort.

Roid struggled to make sense of it all in his head, it was like he another voice or conscious residing in brain. It almost whispered to him, like a split personality, yet was one with him. He could not explain or even clearly figure it out in his head. What was clear, was that he craved 'the hunt'. He was overwhelmed with an insatiable urge to hunt, to kill, to feast on his prey and to convert others to this way of life. It was almost like a primal survival instinct that felt deeply rooted in his core now.

As he tried to figure it all out, memories of the recent events that led up to this moment flooded his mind and seemed to mix with his new feelings and ancient memories that seemed to be from someone else, yet they were still somehow his memories now.

He thought of his unit being slaughtered, he thought of Halbred and Samuel and Flutter. He thought of how they had left him for dead. Left him to this unnatural new state of being. The thoughts fueled him with anger. Throughout it all, he still was consumed with an overwhelming urge to hunt. He channeled his angry thoughts and embraced these new urges. He didn't try to fight or even understand the voice in his head, he embraced it or welcomed it as part of him now. He had nothing else. The only people he had cared for were either dead or had left him to this fate without a second thought.

In that moment Roid decided that if he must hunt, and he knew that he must, then he would hunt the Na'gee that had killed his friends and he would also hunt Halbred,

Flutter and that Samuel character that had betrayed him and left him to this fate. He would kill them all and everyone they cared for.

"No, I will consume them all." Roid thought to himself. The thought came with a strong sense of power and violent urges that he seemed to relish. It was a foreign sensation to him, to feel so pleased and warmed by thoughts of violently tearing all of them to shreds. Thoughts of feasting on their blood warmed his spirit and the voice in his head encouraged it.

Roid snapped out of his thoughts or trance of some sort when all the other creatures that were somewhat like him started pouring out of the room down a large tunnel. He somehow knew that it meant darkness had arrived. He somehow knew that it was time to hunt, so he joined the flow of creatures and headed down the tunnel.

The long tunnel went upward and led to a giant stone wall that stood at least twenty feet tall and was ten feet wide. It sat on a track of sorts. All the beings gathered in front of the stone wall, staring at it eagerly. Then two of the creatures approached the wall and pushed on it, sliding it sideways along the tracks, and opening up to the darkness of night outside the pyramid.

The creatures took off in pairs, darting off this way and that way in a blur of incredible speed. While Roid felt akin to them, he realized he was not like them. They were of this world, whether transformed into their current state or not, they were close to being like him, but still different.

They were all much smaller than Roid, who had lost

none of his size or strength during his transformation or whatever it was. In fact, he felt stronger than he'd ever been and that was saying a lot. He also felt this new speed that he now possessed and quickly noticed that his fingers were significantly longer than before, ending in sharp pointed claw like tips. He embraced the feelings of sheer power that flooded through him and looked at the creatures running around him with condescending thoughts.

"They are my people now, but they are fools. They embrace primal tendencies without thinking past the night ahead." He thought. Although he couldn't tell if it was his thoughts or the new voice in his head or some strange combination of them both. What he could tell was that he thought differently than the creatures around him and he knew he was far more powerful than any of them.

"At least any of them that you've seen so far." The sinister voice in his head seemed to tell him.

Roid focused his thoughts, embraced the urge to hunt and took off for the last spot he remembered being with Halbred.

"I will start with him. I will track, I will watch, I will wait, and I will kill them. The traitors I thought to be my friends first and then the Na'gee." Roid thought. "They will all die, slow tortured deaths, one by one, feeling the agony of loss before they suffer similar fates."

As he ran towards the last spot he remembered, he was invigorated by the sinister thoughts, the plan and the purpose he now had. For Roid, the hunt had begun.

In what seemed like only minutes, Roid had covered several miles and skidded to a stop at the clearing towards the base of the hill, right next to the tree line. The same place he had been left for dead, by the people he had considered friends.

He immediately began examining the tracks in the area. It took him a while to make sense of them all, as it seemed that a second large group had come through here earlier that day. After some time though, he realized that the second group's tracks followed Halbred's and Samuel's tracks.

"Na'gee must be hunting them too." Roid thought.

He began to follow both sets of tracks through the woods. Very slowly and methodically, he crept through the forest. Careful to make no noise. He still wore his dark military fatigue pants, belt full of all his usual tactical gear and combat boots. His shirt had been torn off him during the last battle he remembered, so remained shirtless. Despite this he felt no cold, or even heat for that matter. He did not understand how he didn't register temperatures as his skin seemed the same, only paler in color, but he didn't nonetheless.

Almost half the night seemed to have gone by, by the time he arrived at the natural enclosure made of the two large boulders and the giant tree. He saw a smashed Na'gee body lying outside of the enclosure. The body seemed several hours old. Roid leaned down and sniffed it, then he licked the blood.

As it touched his tongue it seemed to intoxicate him. He felt a momentary sense of euphoria, followed by an overwhelming sense of power and strength. He licked more, then stood and turned towards the clearing. As he took the steps to enter, he noticed a thick trail of blood going off through the forest.

Roid froze, momentarily unsure if he should follow the blood trail or continue to look around the site. The voice inside him urged him to chase the blood trail. To find whoever was bleeding and devour them, but he also felt that he needed to look around and search the area.

He controlled his primal urges for the moment, telling himself and the voice in his head, that he would follow the trail once he finished looking around the site. He smelled the bodies before he saw them. Five more Na'gee lay dead in the enclosure. The tracks were difficult to understand, however he noticed something with huge bare feet had tracks mixed in with the rest of them. He followed the strange large bare foot tracks and they seemed to go directly into the side of the boulder.

Confused he searched the site more, examining tracks and stopping to taste the blood of each of the slain men. The euphoria washed over him again. The feeling of absolute power consumed him. He raised up, feeling the rush of power flowing through him and doubled his efforts to make sense of the tracks his prey had left. He searched the inside of the clearing thoroughly and nothing added up. He searched outside again and slowly it began to all come together for him.

He deduced that the large barefoot thing had rushed the smashed Na'gee from a large nearby tree. There were no tracks around it, so he figured the creature must have come down from the tree. Then it had attacked.

Inside, several Na'gee had been killed by a man wearing

boots. They didn't leave tracks like Halbred's boots, so he figured it must be the dark-skinned man, Samuel. He could tell that one Na'gee had run away through the forest wounded, but where had Samuel and the large barefooted creature gone.

Hours went by and Roid's frustration built up more and more, as the euphoric sensation from the blood slowly faded.

"They couldn't just walk into a damn boulder! Where have they gone?!" He roared, in a deep raspy voice that he didn't recognize as his own.

Furious, he went back into the enclosure and stared at the boulder where the tracks ended. In a fury of rage, Roid delivered a mighty punch to the spot on the boulder where the tracks ended. Cracks splintered and spider webbed out from where his fist had damaged the boulder. He punched it again and again, hissing and growling while he let his built up frustrations out on the boulder. The enclosure echoed and boomed from the loud sounds of unnaturally powerful fists hitting stone. Then the section of the boulder seemed to explode inward, opening the way to what appeared to be a dark tunnel beyond.

Roid curiously looked past the debris from the explosion of rock, he looked at the ground closely and sure enough, he spotted the same pair of tracks. His senses told him that the sun would be coming up in a few hours. The voice inside his head told him that it was almost time to head back to the pyramid, it urged him to go.

He discarded the urges and the voice's warnings. He knew deep down, that facing the sunlight meant death. He didn't know how he knew it, he just did. Despite that, Roid figured there were many places he could hide from the sun. He fought the feelings of being pulled or drawn to the pyramid and instead focused on his hunt. He was too close to turn back.

"Besides, if the tunnel stretches far enough downward, there'll be no sunlight anyway." Roid thought as he began to creep down the tunnel path. He smelled faint whispers of Halbred, of Flutter and of the strange man Samuel, mixed in with strange animal scents.

"Yes, I'm close now." Roid hissed out loud to himself as he crept down the dark dank tunnel that glowed an eerie blue from the strange designs on the walls.

Roid heard the quiet movements and smelled the strong scents of some type of large hairy animal, before he got to the end of the tunnel. He could see from the shadows that the tunnel opened into some larger below ground room ahead of him. He could see that it glowed a much brighter blue than the tunnel he was in.

Without hesitation he walked into the entryway from where the cavern met the tunnel and stopped to survey the scene before him.

What Roid saw was a giant, beast staring at him about six feet away. Roid guessed that the creature was around ten feet tall and noticed the black and brown swirl patterns it is fur or hair or whatever it was. The creature was holding a massive club, with what appeared to be some crude sort of spikes carved into its sides. It had obviously sensed his approach.

"Or it heard me punch through the boulder, as if that was

discrete." Roid thought.

Despite the massive beast's attempt to cut off his access to cavern and make a defensive stand, Roid could see past it. He saw two other large brown hairy beasts, that were big, but nowhere near as big as the one that stood before him. He also saw two smaller beasts in the far corner.

Somehow his sense of smell told him that the small ones were children, and the two large brown ones were female. He seemed to be able to smell the blood coursing through their veins and it helped him to identify these things. He also could smell faint remnants of his true prey.

"Yes, Halbred has been here." Roid thought.

Out of nowhere, the giant beast rushed him swinging the massive club. It seemed to Roid that the thing was determined to crush him in a single blow.

Roid didn't attempt to dodge the blow, in truth, the thing moved so fast, he wasn't sure that he could, even with his enhanced speed. Instead, Roid lunged upwards with both hands, caught hold of the club that was crashing down towards him and jerked it right past his right side.

The quick movement was a disarming move he had learned in some of his unique special unit training and the result was that he managed to yank the club right out of the hands of the huge beast. Without hesitation, he lunged forward with the club's handle pointed at the beast that had just wielded it. He put his entire body into it and rammed the club straight through the chest of the massive creature.

The beast roared and with a club stabbed through its entire

chest, still managed to rear up both arms into huge fists and attempt to bring them down in a smashing motion on the Roid who was still holding onto the club. Before the beast could bring its arms down though, Roid let go of the club and rammed each arms pointed claw like hands straight into the monster's armpits and into its body from the there. He grabbed whatever internal organs his hands felt and ripped them out.

The creature fell to the ground with blood and organs coming out from under its arms and huge club still sticking completely through its chest.

The two large female beasts roared in unison at the gruesome site. Roid licked the blood off his fingers while he watched their roaring approach, feeling the powerful feelings from the blood. They got about halfway to him, and he acted, not giving them a chance to make the first move.

He rushed the closest one and punched it so hard in the face that it went flying into the wall at the end of the chamber, headfirst. The other beast rushed his back, and he grinned and evil fang filled grin, before spinning around with his mighty claw outstretched and ripped its neck wide open.

In that moment of blood gushing out of the neck of the creature, instinct took over. He lost all thought and control and leapt on the beast, sinking his fangs into its exposed neck wound and drinking the blood. He cherished it, consumed by the euphoric feelings and the animalistic instincts that seem to overtake him. Time seemed to stop, as he lost himself in the moment.

Roid didn't know how long it had been when he finally

pulled his head away from the beast's body, but he did know the blood was all gone. There was nothing left in the corpse before him. As his senses and wits came back to him, he looked around the cavern.

The other large beast was slowing pulling itself up, using one hand on the wall to help and holding its head with the other hand. Blood was pouring out of its mouth and shattered eye. Upon seeing the blood, Roid felt the urge to attack it, to consume this blood as well, but this time, he fought the primal instincts and ignored the raging voice in his head. This time, he thought clearly.

Instead of going for the beast, he ran for one of the young ones, grabbing it quickly off the ground by its neck. The smaller beast tried to hit him, and he ripped its arm off with his free hand.

The female roared again and rushed towards him, but he kicked it in the chest without letting go of the young one, sending it flying back to the wall.

"Tell me where they went and I'll let you and your young live." Roid hissed at the beast. He was battling the voice in his head and fighting every urge in his body not to drink the blood pouring from the creatures missing arm, but he held strong.

The creature roared at him, in the passionate type of rage that only a mother could muster up when her child was in danger.

Roid stared at the creature and then slashed the young creature's throat and threw in on the ground. His anger helped him fight back the urges to feast.

In a flash, he had the other young creature by the neck as well.

"Where did they go?" He hissed. This time he pointed at the boot tracks on the ground when he asked it.

The large beast hesitated, and then quickly turned and walked to the wall it had been punched into. The creature took a moment feeling on the wall and then came to spot and placed its hand in the center of a glowing blue spiral type design. The wall opened into a doorway that seemed to lead to another tunnel.

Roid grinned, showing the massive fangs that were his now. He tossed the young creature aside and started for the tunnel. At the last moment before entering the tunnel, he turned and leapt onto the large creature. Holding its arms down and tearing into its chest with his teeth. He treated himself and drank the blood, all of the blood, drowning in the power and euphoria that came with it.

This time when he finished, he didn't argue with the voice, he let the voice have its way and he rushed the young one he had tossed aside and tore into its throat with his teeth and fangs.

CHAPTER 48:
PREPARATIONS

Several hours before dawn, G'noch and T'sko got up from their seated resting positions in the cavern. Samuel, who had not really slept, eyed them and rose to his feet. He noticed Halbred doing the same thing. The gruff military man, gently nudged Flutter with his boot and she rolled over and rose to her feet as well.

The two T'kche watched silently, obviously waiting for them all to rise and ready themselves. Samuel was ready in an instant. Halbred and Flutter took a few moments to arrange the belt full of tactical pouches that they each wore. Flutter adjusted the vest that she had and checked the clip on the sub machine gun that was tightly secured to the front of it.

"I guess she's back." Samuel thought.

Upon completing her inspection, she nodded at Halbred and together they approached the T'kche and Samuel who had moved to the opposite end of the cavern from where they had entered. G'noch approached the far wall and slowly examined it. After a moment, he placed his hand in the center of a spiral like glowing blue symbol and the wall opened up forming a doorway to another tunnel.

The large, black-haired T'kche motioned for them to follow and took off down the corridor. Samuel followed him closely, with Halbred and Flutter not far behind. T'sko came last and the doorway closed shut behind him.

This tunnel did not have many of the glowing symbols for light. There was one here and there, but mostly it was dark, very dark. Samuel's eyes adjusted as best they could, but he found himself following blindly more than anything. He assumed Halbred and Flutter had some sort of flashlights in the many pouches they wore, but that they probably felt darkness was a safer bet in this strange world.

The group marched through the twisting and turning tunnels for hours, before finally coming to a sharp curve and an opening. As they rounded the curve, they saw the horizon and the faint signs of the sun starting to rise. They also saw a large mountain directly in front of them.

Samuel stepped forward and noticed that they were on some sort of ledge. It was about twenty feet from level ground, on the side of what appeared to be a rocky hill about one hundred yards from the much larger mountain they were facing. The larger mountain seemed steep and had weird trails of smoke coming from the top. The smoke trails were less like a volcano and more like several vents letting out smoke from whatever lie inside the huge mountain.

Samuel could see a rocky path of sorts leading from the ledge they stood on to the bottom of the mountain. G'noch stepped forward and stood next to Samuel, looking at the mountain before them.

"Na'gee home." G'noch said, pointing at the large mountain before them. "Big door there, on ground." At that he pointed towards the right side of the mountain. "Little door there, up side mountain." He said pointing to the left side of the mountain.

Samuel couldn't see any entrances and figured there were either more hidden doors, which were starting to seem fairly common in this weird place, or that G'noch was referencing around the left and right sides of the mountain.

Halbred, who had approached silently behind them and apparently been listening in, spoke up. "Let's do a little reconnaissance and see exactly where these doors are Samuel. Flutter can take us through the air. This may be our best shot, as the sun is just starting to rise. We should be able to dodge the creepy black cloaks and check things out before anything else decides it's safe to come out." Like always the man said it gruffly and seemed to expect no debate.

Samuel nodded and looked at G'noch. The large T'kche seemed to be catching on to how they said things, as he just nodded and said "T'kche stay here. We know doors. Be safe. Many many Na'gee."

Halbred gestured for Flutter, and she touched him and Samuel on the arms, and the group instantly began floating. She leapt in the air and pulled them along behind her like weightless balloons.

"Little door first boss?" Flutter asked without looking back, while she flew effortlessly through the air with both men in tow.

"You know it solider." Halbred responded, with a hint of

relief in his voice to have his companion back to seemingly full health.

Flutter pulled them behind her and quickened her speed. In minutes they were rounding the left side of the mountain, almost over top of it. As they curved around it, they all immediately saw the 'little door entrance' that G'noh had been referring to. It was about halfway up the large mountain and seemed very similar to the ledge they had just stood on. The ledge here was more of an outcropping or over hanging flat rock that jutted out the side of the mountain. It appeared that the 'little door' was blocked by a massive boulder. There was a steep path, but a path nonetheless that ran from the ledge down the side of the mountain to the ground.

As Samuel looked at the path, movement brought his attention back to the boulder, it was slowly being raised. He figured Flutter must have seen it too, because without a word, she took them much higher in the air. She stopped with them floating about fifty feet directly overtop of the boulder that was definitely being raised. When it stopped, it kind of locked into position with a loud 'clanging' noise and two Na'gee warriors walked out onto the ledge. They each sat on a large rock on opposite sides of the entrance and stared off into the distance.

Halbred made a hand gesture and Flutter took them up and over the top of the mountain. They passed directly over the cracks in the top of the rocky mountain that let out streams of smoke, which smelled like a campfire.

As they went, Halbred spoke up. "Speed it up Flutter, the natives are starting to wake up."

With the command given, their speed rapidly intensified. She took them straight across the large mountain in no time and then quickly slowed them down to a cautious crawling speed as they cleared the far side. The three all seemed to strain their necks to look down. Far at the bottom of the mountain, they saw a boulder at least four times the size as the other one, latched into a similar mechanism. They didn't need to go further, they knew this was the big door.

"Want me to ease us in to try to see how many guards they have posted on the front door boss?" Flutter asked.

"Nah, we're pushing it now. It'll be two, four or six, not gonna matter either way. Let's get back to our damn bigfoot guides and figure out how we want to kill all these bastards." Halbred half shouted in response.

Once again, the instructions were given and like that, they were off.

Moments later, they found themselves sitting on the ledge of the small rocky hill, soaking up the morning sunshine.

It didn't take long for Halbred to break the peaceful silence. "The way I figure it, we got two options. One we hit them in the daytime and try to take them all out by ourselves or two, we hit them in the evening, keep the doors open and let the black cloaks help us wipe them out. Either way is risky." The gruff military man stopped and seemed to wait for responses.

Samuel had been thinking similar thoughts. He figured that using the natural threats around them to bolster their numbers was the way to go, he just didn't like the thought of having to fight his way through who knew how many of those creatures.

"Let's hit them in the evening. Give us a couple hours, to get in, take out damn Camacho and as many of their commanders as possible to make sure they don't skip back to our world." Samuel paused for just a moment to give others a chance to object, when they didn't seize the moment, he continued.

"If you're comfortable hitting them hard from the front Halbred, I'll take the back door by myself and sneak in. That way, even if things go sideways, we know there's an open door for the black cloaks. If plans go great, we'll wipe them out and one of them will open a doorway home for us to take. If they don't, well then, we fight our way out past the creepy black cloaks and rendezvous here." Samuel finished laying out his plan and looked around at the group.

"That's it then. You big fellas ok following my lead in the front door?" Halbred said looking at the T'kche.

T'sko simply nodded. While G'noch showed his tooth filled grin and said "G'noch hunt Na'gee with you Halbred."

With the plans, or general direction of attack at least, decided on, the companions sat in silence staring out at the mountain that housed their enemies. As the group stared Halbred noticed an opening at the bottom of the mountain on the side that faced them.

It was a rectangular opening about eye level for a normal man, that looked to be about a one foot from top to bottom and maybe three feet from left to right. At this distance, he wouldn't have noticed it, except for all of the scratches in the rocks on either side of it. From where he sat it looked like it had been getting clawed at for years.

As he strained his eyes to look closer, he noticed that the ground around it was covered in layers of tracks that went off in every direction from the opening. It was impossible to tell what types of tracks they were from here, but they were tracks of some sort, that was for sure.

"What is that?" Halbred asked roughly, while pointing towards the opening. He didn't specify his question to anyone in particular, just asked the group.

Oddly enough, it was T'sko who spoke up in response. "Na'gee deal with dark ones there. Speak together, no risk dark ones killing them. Na'gee evil like dark ones." He said it all quietly and calmly.

Halbred listened intently but did not fail to notice that G'noch seemed as surprised as everyone else to hear this. "So, the quiet ones been around the block. Probably did all the spying and hunting that our young bigfoot friend did before the female and child. He may be more valuable in this fight than I thought." Halbred thought to himself, mentally rolling around tactical approaches to the upcoming assault.

Halbred, reached into one of his many pouches and pulled out two small square devices that fit in the palm of his hand. He held his hand open before the group, showing them the devices.

"These are explosives. Don't let their size fool you, they'll take out as much or more as a brick of C4. They work off a timer. I'm going to place them on that wall." Halbred said to everyone, while he still stared at the mountain target before him. His expertise in assaults and combat missions in enemy territory was evident and it shined bright when he got going.

"The way I figure it, that's about halfway through the mountain. We don't know the layout inside, so we're going in blind. This will do three things for us… one, it will provide a distraction. Two, it will provide another exit, one that heads straight for our getaway route and three, it will provide another way for the black cloaks to join the fight." Halbred seemed to be talking himself through his plan more than talking to anyone else, but they all still listened intently.

In truth, everyone there, including Samuel, found it difficult not to get caught up listening intently to everything the old soldier had to say, when he started talking strategy.

"The only question is, how long do I set it for? I'm thinking one hour into our attack. That's an hour before we can expect the black cloaks and may prove to be a vital distraction if they're putting up a fight. Then again, if we cut through them like butter, it gives us a nice quick getaway." Halbred finished talking and jumped up from where he had been sitting on the ledge like everyone else.

"I'll be back" he said.

"Wait, let me fly us down there." Flutter protested.

"Too risky soldier. They may notice flying in the sky, they won't notice me. This isn't our first mission Flutter and it's no different than dozens we've been on. Just another target." Halbred finished and took off down the path, moving quickly and quietly, yet still somehow blending in with the rocky path he ran down. Everyone sat and watched. They had all heard his planning session with himself, and the logic was sound, there was nothing left to do but wait.

As Samuel processed all that Halbred had just talked through, he turned to Flutter and asked "You don't happen to have any of those do you? If I'm sneaking in the back door, while you all hit the front, a couple of those strategically placed could double down on his strategy."

Flutter looked at him with no emotion. It was clear she wasn't fond of Samuel whatsoever.

"She may blame me for the deaths of her friends. Probably right, I'm responsible for the death of… well, I guess they were about as close to a friend as I would call anyone." Samuel thought and his mind wandered to the guilt he strangely felt for the deaths of Dante and Vic.

He snapped out of his thoughts when Flutter bumped his arm with her closed fist. He realized instantly that she was trying to hand him something.

When he opened his hand, she dropped three of the little squares in it.

"You know how to use these Agent 17?" Flutter asked.

"Yeah, I know how. Thanks, and… it's just Samuel now." Samuel said.

Flutter ignored him and turned her attention back to watching Halbred creep down the rocky path towards the opening.

Roid listened intently from the deep shadows of the tunnel. He dared not even attempt to peek around the curve that led to the cave and the ledge that the group sat on, due to the bright morning sunlight. From back in the safety of the tunnel's shadows though, the curve created a wall that kept the sun from him. He stayed in the deep darkness and listened to their plans while he starved for vengeance on these people that had left him for dead.

"Just let one of them wander into the shadows." He thought sinisterly. "Other than that, I'm stuck waiting for dark. Sounds like they'll have a couple hours head start into the mountain, but they're also giving me a quick way in. Soon, very soon, I'll have my revenge." Roids thoughts helped to quench his thirst for their blood and warmed him in a way.

CHAPTER 49:
ARRIVAL

Steph waited by the great fire in the center of the Na'gee mountain settlement for Olo, as he was told to do. He kept thinking of the strange creatures they called dark ones that had tried to attack him only hours before. Despite his new size, skills and confidence, it had scared him. He had frozen. He had no desire to face one of those things again.

The wise one who had traveled with him, had pulled him inside just in time. Then walked him to the fire. Steph had heard him whispering to what appeared to be other Na'gee wise ones. Steph wasn't able to make out everything they said, but he did hear them say 'he is securing her now. She will serve as leverage or sacrifice if no leverage is needed.'

"They're always trying to hide things from me. They're treating me like parents treat children, only telling them what they think they need to know." Steph thought with frustration. The thoughts made his mind wander back to his parents.

"My parents didn't do that though. They shared everything with Mila and I. I know my dad hurt bad people. I know that was his job. They never lied to us or kept secrets from us, they treated us differently that most parents." Stephs thoughts made him second guess what the Na'gee had told him about his parent's evilness and sacrifice of his sister. He continued to question the truth to their claims more and more, but when he did, he kept reminding himself of how strange his sister had become… of the strange incredible feats she had managed to pull off.

"Still, she did it to save my mom and me. Why would a demon fight to save us?" Steph thought.

He was shaken from his thoughts by Olo placing a hand on his shoulder.

As he turned to face the intimidating Na'gee warrior, Olo spoke. "They tell me you have tested well and severely injured Ansai on your first face off young Steph." Olo said it sternly and stared into Steph's eyes.

"I didn't mean to hurt him, I mean, well he said that if I could beat him then…" Steph started, attempting to excuse his actions to the scary Na'gee warrior before him.

Olo interrupted him harshly. "Do not whimper and make excuses! You are a warrior now. You have done well. If he was weak enough to be defeated by a newly aged warrior than you should of killed him Steph. Next time you battle, you deal death. Understood young one?!"

Steph nodded and the confidence he felt before, after defeating Ansai, flooded back to him. Something about Olo inspired him. Olo's words and tone and look filled him with the feeling that he could do anything and eliminated doubts. He pushed away his questioning thoughts and steeled himself once again to avenge his sister and murder this demon and his traitorous parents that had led him to this fate. He still did not trust the Na'gee or Olo, but he believed them in this one matter.

"After all that has happened to me, this must be my destiny." Steph thought.

He turned back and stared at the fire, while Olo continued to stand slightly behind him, stoically staring at the fire as well.

As the inspirational feelings slowed died down, Stephs thoughts wandered again. The confidence of a child who thinks that can take on the world and come out unscathed was back full force.

He turned, still sitting and looked up and Olo, unafraid to stare the man in his eyes and asked, "Who is this woman that you intend to use as leverage Olo?"

The seasoned warrior stared back into Sephs challenging eyes. Olo's instincts told him to strike down the young warrior and forever put him in his place for daring to question him. However, Olo felt that the top siders egos and pride was too fragile and delicate, to handle that… yet.

Olo knew he needed the young man, fully bought in for the task that lay ahead, so he controlled himself and responded more tactfully. "She is of no concern to you or your mission. There are many matters that I must oversee to protect our people young Steph. You must focus on steeling yourself for our mission. Tomorrow, I will verify that you are ready. I will personally teach you the best ways to kill a 'Brite' and the next day we will hunt this demon down." Olo stared at Steph and could tell that he had successfully shifted his thoughts to the task at hand and away from the suspicions that previously plagued him, so he continued. "The demon travels with your father. They will both try to deceive you and convince you to stray from your mission Steph. The demon and your father who serves the demon, know that only one of their own blood can kill the 'Brite'. You must prepare yourself mentally so that you are not fooled into becoming their next victim."

Steph thought for a moment "Dad's with her or it, huh. He'll pay for destroying our family. He'll answer for what he's done, explain himself and then die by hands." He thought.

Then Steph looked back up and said, "If the demon travels with my father, what has become of my mother Olo?"

"We cannot be sure young Steph, but we believe that they have sacrificed her, having decided that they had no further use for her. That is how the demon works. It uses its servants until it has no more use for them and then it kills them." Olo said, watching closely to gauge Stephs reaction.

Steph didn't know what to think. He was devastated to hear that his mother was likely dead, yet he felt conflicted as he had intended to kill her. He didn't understand why the demon would kill its followers, he didn't understand why the demon and his father would even be in this strange world, none of it made sense. He questions, suspicions and feelings that he was only getting half-truths from the Na'gee returned, but he said nothing.

After a few moments of silence Olo said, "Time to get some rest Steph. I will lead you to a small cave where you can rest. We will train for the final hunt tomorrow." With those words spoked, Steph rose to his feet and silently followed Olo to where he would sleep. He laid his head down and thought through everything that had happened and all that he had been told. He did not sleep, instead he laid there trying to make sense of it all in his head.

After Olo finished getting the top sider settled he made his way to the healer's crude hut on the far side of the settlement. Once there, he went inside and immediately saw the healer leaning over the injured man on the table.

The healer was working vigorously to heal the bullet wound in Camacho's side. Olo watched for a moment and the stopped the healer, with a firm touch to the arm and an intense look. No words were needed… the healer clearly understood and stepped away.

Olo eased closer to the injured Camacho who lay face down on the operating table of sorts and then jammed two fingers into the wound in Camacho's side.

Camacho roared in pain! He tried to rise, but before he could move, he felt the cold steel of a blades point touching the back of his neck. He froze, knowing that any sudden movements meant death. He knew that his strength and speed would not help in this precarious situation.

"Yet again, the top sider returns injured while all the warriors with him are left dead. You did not learn this cowardice from our training. What type of warrior leads his troops to their deaths and scurries away time and time again?"

Camacho gritted his teeth in anger but did not respond.

He did not trust his words, to hide his disdain for the arrogant Na'gee.

Olo let the silence add to the sting of his words while the tip of his knife dug into the back of Camacho's neck. After several long tense moments, he continued. "Should I not kill you now and save the lives of all the other warriors that you will inevitably lead to their deaths, while you run and hide top sider?"

Camacho continued to hold his tongue. He knew that the moment he opened his mouth, the anger inside him would erupt into a verbal assault on the Na'gee warrior. Ultimately, Camacho knew that it was either silence or death.

While still holding his knife tip against Camacho's exposed neck, Olo leaned in close and spoke softly into Camacho's ear. "This will be the last time you survive failure. The Na'gee will not be dishonored by you again top sider."

The last words from Olo were too much. Camacho decided death would be a welcome reprieve from the arrogant babbling of Olo, so he responded, loudly and harshly. "Do you forget how quickly word travels in this tribe Olo?! You speak of failure hypocrite, but everyone with you died as well and for what?! For you to return with one woman prisoner?! I thought your mission was to kill, yet no one died except the warriors you led! Do not lecture me! We have both been thwarted by this ragtag band of fools! We are the same in this!" Camacho had yelled the response. He was steaming with rage and didn't care that the knife was digging deeper into his flesh. He felt the trickle of blood running down his neck and didn't care.

Finally, the knife was removed. Olo made a grunting acknowledgment and turned away. Camacho quickly sat up, to face the man and as he did he felt the stinging agony from the wound in his side.

Olo did not turn back, but he paused in the doorway of the hut. "Once you are healed, meet me at the great fire Camacho. We will discuss how we are to finally kill these troublesome fools and their cursed Brite." Olo said the words and walked out.

With Olo gone, the healer approached Camacho and gently pushed him back down on the table and resumed the work of healing the injured man.

Chapter 50: The "Back Door"

Shortly before the morning sun began to peak out over the horizon, Vic watched the black cloaked creatures take off. Disappearing through the woods, off to wherever they came from.

He rose from the small fire that he'd been able to keep burning all night, grabbed his spear-staff and approached Mila. The brilliant bright white light coming from her began to fade and she shakily rose to her feet from the cross-legged position she had maintained all night.

Vic had expected this, after their first night in the strange new world, so he had spent the sleepless hours of the night carving her a walking cane. He grabbed it, from where it had leaned against the wall and handed it to his daughter. No words were exchanged, just a compassionate look between father and daughter as she took the cane and leaned heavily on it.

Vic wrapped his long arms around her and squeezed her tightly. "I love you, Mila. I don't know what it is that you're going through, but I'm here to help you through it. First though, lets go get your mother and brother. Are you ready?" He said it softly to his daughter and patiently waited on her to respond, still squeezing her tightly.

"I am ready." Mila said, in the voice that didn't seem like hers. She still slightly glowed, but it was nowhere near as bright as it had been throughout the night. Her eyes had no pupils. They just shined like headlights.

Vic chose not to stare or even think about it. He needed to focus on something he could control. Something he could do, which was get back his wife and son.

"And kill all these damn Na'gee, especially the one called Olo." Vic thought.

Mila and Vic left the small cave and began heading for the tall mountain he had spotted with the smoke rising from its top. He had spent the night thinking over the landscape and their destination while he had carved the walking cane for Mila and had come up with what he thought would be the fastest and least demanding route to their destination.

Vic figured they could make it there a couple hours before nightfall if they maintained a modest pace. His plan was simple, by now he knew that Mila could keep these strange creatures that stalked the night back. He figured if they could get to the mountain and scope it out, he could make his way in and find a way to let the creatures in as well.

His hope was that the Na'gee would end up being so caught up fighting the creatures that Mila and him could find Eva and hopefully little Steph and get out of there safely. Vic had made up his mind that, once he found the family, he'd have Mila take them back to their world. Vic planned to stay behind. He didn't want to leave his family again, but he knew he needed to end this. He needed to kill Olo and Camacho. Once the family was gone and safe, he'd be able to focus on that.

As he had formed the plan throughout the night, he had decided that he wouldn't tell them until the last minute. They would protest, but he would insist.

"These monstrous Na'gee have tortured my family, not to mention they killed Dante and Samuel. I won't leave with them still breathing." He had vowed to himself in the wee hours of the night.

The journey was long, and Vic had worried about Mila constantly as they went, but she seemed to be holding up just fine, despite the lack of sleep. They encountered no beasts or otherworldly terrors along the way, which Vic liked to think was just plain lucky, but deep down he suspected it had more to do with the glowing light from Mila than luck.

They arrived at the large mountain base a couple hours before night, just as Vic had planned it. As they emerged from the forest trail that had taken them most of the way, Vic immediately noticed that a little more than halfway up the large mountain was a large ledge.

He saw the two Na'gee warriors sitting on the ledge and instantly he knew his suspicions were right.

"This is where they're holing up. I've got the bastards now." Vic thought. A surge of fresh energy and adrenaline seemed to flow through him.

He gently grabbed Mila's arm and stopped her, before they left the cover of the last trees. He pointed at the ledge, and she nodded.

"If we can get to that path without them seeing us, we should be able to hike our way up right under their noses. We'll have to be quiet though. We don't want a shootout with these guys, we need to take them out silently and see what we're up against inside before we let everyone know we're here." He said it softly, looking at Mila's shining eyes.

He had been tempted to tell her to wait for him here but had decided along the way that splitting up from her in this strange place would be far riskier than letting her follow him into combat. He didn't like either option, but it didn't matter, it was still the best of the bad decisions available.

"I understand." Mila said in the ominous tone she had used all day, although she'd barely spoken. Vic figured that whatever change she was going through, this was a sign that she was prepared for what was to come… well, as much as she could be.

"Ok, stay close behind me." Vic said. Then he looked around at the ground and picked up two small pebbles. "Here, if you need me to stop, throw one of these at me, don't say any words. If I feel it, I'll come back to you. Got it?" Vic said as he placed the two small pebbles in her little hand.

"Yes" she said.

"She's so cold and well, distant." Vic thought with concern. "Enough of that. I've got work to do. Time for the grim reaper to make a house call. These poor bastards are going to regret fucking with my family." With that final thought, Vic took off running for the path. He crouched while he ran and moved quick.

The path that led to the ledge was about twenty yards from the tree line and he covered the distance in a couple short minutes. To his surprise, Mila kept up with him the entire way, staying right on his heels.

Once they had made it to the trail, they knew they were out of sight of the Na'gee warriors.

"Unless they look over the edge, we should be good. So, keep it quiet and don't give them a reason to look." Vic whispered to Mila and the two began the hike up the long path.

The time had come. The sky made it clear that nightfall was only a few short hours away. Halbred looked around at the gathered group standing on the ledge.

"You all ready? Once we start hitting them, we don't stop until they're finished. If the black cloaks start tearing through them, we'll ease out and let them do their thing. Samuel, you find that little Camacho shit and take his head. We'll keep them distracted. See you in the middle." Halbred laid it all out and then extended his hand out to Samuel.

The two stared at one another and firmly shook hands. The mutual respect that had developed between the two hardened men was evident. Samuel nodded and said, "Be careful. I'll find you." Then he turned to Flutter and asked "Care to drop me off on the top? I can hike down from there."

Flutter did not respond, she simply looked questioningly at Halbred.

"She definitely blames me for all of this." Samuel thought.

Halbred half grinned, obviously thinking the same thing and said, "Get him up there Solider, and then come down the front side of old smokey mountain. Me and the sasquatch duo over here, will hike down and meet you there."

"No Sasquatch, we T'kche little man." G'noch said as Halbred and the two T'kche headed down the trail towards the main entrance of the mountain settlement.

Flutter turned to Samuel and without saying a word, she grabbed his arm and took off into the air. Once again, Samuel felt himself being weightlessly pulled behind the flying soldier, only this time he felt a little more concerned than the previous experiences.

"She obviously doesn't like me. Nothing would stop her from dropping me to my death right now and no would ever know. They'd just think I didn't make it past the Na'gee." Samuel thought as he stared at the ground far below them.

Flutter, seemingly reading his mind spoke up out of nowhere. "I should do it, but I won't agent 17. This shit we're in is all your fault. The death of my team is your fault. I will deal with you, but I won't disobey Halbred. You won't die now." she said coldly.

Samuel stayed silent, feeling no more confident about her not dropping him than he did before she spoke.

In no time at all, they were over the top of the mountain. Flutter took him right to the backside of the mountaintop that overlooked the large ledge with the two Na'gee warriors and let go of his arm, letting him drop about ten feet to the top of the mountain. Without a word or even a glance back, she took off heading over the top for the opposite side of the mountain, where Halbred and T'kche approached the front entrance.

Samuel landed skillfully and watched her fly away. Then he turned his attention to the edge of the mountain. He leaned over and looked at the various ways down. From his vantage point he could see the top of the Na'gee warriors shaved, tattooed heads. He thought of shooting them both from here but knew that it would be unwise to let his presence be known.

So, instead he carefully and silently began to climb down the mountain face just to the left of them. He hoped he didn't knock any rock or debris loose on his climb down but decided that at least in this position, if he did it might fall past them unnoticed instead of falling directly on top of them.

After several long minutes of strenuous climbing, he found himself close enough that he could jump down onto the ledge. So far, they had not seemed to notice his presence. He was close enough that he could smell their sweat and hear them trading seemingly embellished stories of their hunting feats.

Samuel decided he'd jump in front of the closest one and freeze him quickly, then try to either freeze the other one or kick him off the side of the mountain before he could make any noise.

With his plan of attack decided, he jumped down onto the ledge. Both warriors immediately leapt to their feet in surprise, at the site of large the dark-skinned man in black landing in between them, seemingly out of nowhere.

As soon as Samuel's feet hit the ground, he lunged for the man on his left. The warrior was fast and the shock at Samuel falling from the heavens to interrupt their bragging session did nothing to slow him down. He sidestepped Samuel's lunge, positioning himself slightly behind Samuel's left side and quickly pulled his large knife out of its sheath.

As Samuel turned to face the warrior, he swung his knife downward in a slicing motion which was obviously meant to open Samuel up from his right shoulder to his groin.

Samuel stepped under the swing, bringing him face to face with the Na'gee and touched his arm, freezing the warrior in place.

With one adversary down, he pivoted to face the other Na'gee who stood across the ledge from him. This warrior, however, seemed to have no intention of knife fighting Samuel. He stood with an evil grin on his face that seemed very uncharacteristic of the Na'gee, pointing his large .50 caliber pistol at Samuel.

Samuel knew the distance on the ledge between them was too far for him to cover it before he was shot. He thought of jumping off the side of the ledge and trying to catch himself but knew that even if he managed to do so, the warrior would have no problem gunning him down from the ledge.

He steeled himself and prepared to attack, knowing that he'd probably be taking at least one bullet in the attempt.

Just before he made his move, he saw a large spear come

shooting out from the warrior's chest. The warrior's eyes rolled back in his head, blood instantly began streaming out of his mouth and the pistol fell clattering to the rocky ground of the mountain ledge.

The spear seemed to retract from the now dead Na'gee's chest, and the body fell to the ground. Standing in the warrior's place, the source of the brutal stabbing stood tall.

Samuel was shocked to see Vic there, with his sinister grin. "Good to see ya Samuel. Looked like you needed a hand." Vic said.

The two men looked at each other, neither man attempting to hide the looks of relief and a sort of joy that they felt at seeing one another.

"I thought you were dead Vic." Samuel said.

"Yeah, so did the damn Na'gee. Takes a lot to kill the grim reaper brother." Vic replied in his signature cocky tone. Then Vic's face took on a serious look. "They've got my son and wife in there Samuel. We're here to get them back."

It was the word 'we're' that brought Samuel's attention to Vic's daughter that stood half behind him. He noticed that she was glowing. It was like a faint white light was being emitted from her and her eyes shined like the high beams on a car's headlights.

"Is she ok Vic?" Samuel asked as he looked at Mila.

"She's ok for now. Not sure if you've ran into those damn creepy things in the black cloaks or not, but they won't come near her light. We're going in, freeing Eva and Steph and plan to leave the door open for those bastards to finish off anyone I don't kill. It should be fun Samuel, care to join?" Vic said.

Samuel realized in that moment how much he'd missed Vic. Not only was the man a valuable asset to have in a fight, but his carefree nature in even the worst of situations was somewhat motivating.

"It's good to have him back." Samuel thought.

"Sounds like we're planning about the same thing Vic. Halbred and Flutter are with me. They're hitting the front any minute now, with a couple of the T'kche. There's a bomb about to go off on the far side of the mountain over there. The chaos should allow us to slip in the back door here and find your family, along with Camacho who I plan to end once and for all." Samuel said flatly.

Vic listened intently, seeming to soak it all up. Then said, "This is the back door huh? Wait, what the hell is a T'kche?"

Before Samuel could answer an explosion rocked the mountain.

Chapter 51: Family

That's our cue Vic. You'll know the T'kche when you see them. They're big, hairy and swing huge clubs. They're on our side. You ready?" Samuel said calmly as he eased towards the opening into the mountain.

"So, you recruited a couple cave men, while I was stuck fighting giant anacondas and dino birds?" Vic asked as he started to follow Samuel inside with Mila on his heels.

"Think more bigfoot than cave man and you're about there." Samuel said and then he fell silent as he made his way into the mountain with Vic and Mila following closely behind him.

The three came emerged on a high ledge inside the mountain overlooking the large Na'gee settlement in its entirety. There were rough stone steps carved into the rock wall, leading down from the ledge to the ground level. Before them they saw Na'gee running here and there in what appeared to be utter chaos.

They heard gunshots from the large entrance that they

could see on the opposite side of the cave from them. To their left was a large structure that seemed to be the center of the mountain city and past it there was smoke and dust coming from a large tunnel, that seemed to be the source of the explosion.

Past the large fort-looking structure in the center, far off behind it, were rows of cages with what appeared to be all sorts of different creatures and some people in them.

"They're probably holding them in the cages. Let's head there first, then we'll clear their main building once the family is safe Samuel." Vic said eagerly. The tall man was obviously readier than ever to free his wife and son, now that they seemed to be so close.

Samuel nodded and began to hurry down the stone steps, taking two at a time. He pulled both of his pistols while he ran.

Vic stayed on his heels, his knife was tucked in the back of his belt and his pistol was still tucked in the front of his pants. He held his spear staff tightly and took off behind Samuel, glancing back every few steps to make sure that Mila was still behind them. Somehow, she kept up, step for step.

By the time they hit the ground level, all the Na'gee they could see were either headed for the battle at the main entrance or running for the exploded tunnel. It actually seemed they were more worried about the tunnel than the attack.

Samuel could see fading sunlight streaming in from the area of the explosion and figured that they understood the greater threat was letting the black cloaks into their settlement.

With no one seeming to notice them at all the three ran off to the left, towards the cages that they had seen from high on the ledge.

It didn't take long for them to get back there, moving quickly and staying close to the wall the entire way. They focused on keeping as much distance between them and the large structure as possible, to avoid being noticed on the way to the cages. The wall of the mountain turned sharply, creating a type of corner and as they cleared the corner, they saw the long rows of cages.

There were three rows that went back quite ways, creating two walkways or paths to walk down between them, providing access to the prisoners. While some cages were empty, many had strange creatures, weird looking people or even Na'gee warriors locked up in them.

As they approached the cage rows Samuel said. "I'll take the first row, you two take the second one. If they're here, we'll find them. Vic nodded and took off with Mila close behind.

Samuel ran down the first row, looking from left to right while he ran, his head on swivel. He tried to keep himself from getting caught up staring at some of the strange beasts that were locked away, forcing himself to keep running. He was flooded with concern when he made it to the dead end at the end of the row without a sign of Vic's son or daughter. He turned and began to run back, hoping that Vic had better luck on his row. Hoping that his wife and son were still alive.

Vic and Mila ran down the second row of cages looking

this way and that way, growing more and more worried the further they went without a sign of Eva or Steph. About halfway down Vic heard Mila say "She's there." She said it in that same cold distant voice that she had been using and pointed three cages down to her right.

Vic couldn't see into the cage she had pointed at from where they were and wondered how Mila could, or if she could even see it, regardless he didn't slow down. He ran up to the cage she had pointed at, and sure enough Eva was there.

Without a moment's hesitation, Vic pulled his pistol and shot the large lock holding the cage door shut. The lock exploded and he kicked open the door.

Eva looked bad, she was bruised and bloodied, but she was on her feet. She rushed into Vic's arms and hugged him tightly, then she pulled away and hugged Mila. "I'm so happy to see you two!" Eva said.

"We're just glad you're ok babe. Can you move?" Vic said.

"Yes, let's get out of here." Eva replied quickly.

"Great. Let's see if little Steph is in one of these cages too." Vic said, as the three began to jog further down the row of cages, looking from left to right.

It didn't take long for them to hit the dead end, with no sign of Steph. They all turned around and began to jog back the way they had come. Although their hearts weighed heavier on the return trip.

"Please let my little boy be alive." Vic thought to himself.

When they finally emerged from the row of cages, they saw Samuel waiting for them. He smiled at Eva and said, "Good to see you in one piece Eva."

"You too Samuel. Now let's find my son." Eva responded curtly.

They all turned their attention away from the cages and ahead of them, facing the back of the large structure in the center of the settlement.

As they looked at it, they were all shaken from another mighty explosion. This one seemed to come from the main entrance at the front. As one and without words, they took off jogging towards the back of the large structure, Eva holding Mila's hand tightly as they ran.

The group had just arrived at the base of the planked walkway that led up to the tall platform on the back of the structure, when Olo and six Na'gee walked out onto the platform facing them. There was a seventh warrior with him that didn't look like the rest. This one was pale and very, very tall with only a fraction of the tattoos that the others had. Whatever he was, he was definitely not Na'gee.

Olo, the six warriors and the strange tall one all leapt from the platform, landing directly in front of the companions. Before they had hit the ground, Samuel had shot two warriors.

Mila's voice rang out loudly, ominously, before any other shots were fired and everyone froze. "It is Steph father" she said.

Everyone there, Na'gee and companions alike froze at the overwhelmingly loud voice that Mila produced, and Vic turned his attention to the tall warrior that was unlike the rest. The one that Mila pointed at. He could see it now. He didn't understand it but somehow, he knew this grown man was his son. He could feel it and see it in the eyes.

Eva must've seen it too because the next noise anyone heard was her screaming "Steph my son! What have they done to you?!"

"Enough!!! Kill them!" Olo yelled at the top of his lungs as he ran forward and jump kicked Vic in the face, sending the tall man flying backwards and crashing to the ground.

One of the other Na'gee followed Olo and swung a hard fist hitting Eva in the head. She managed to dodge the brunt of the blow at the last second but still took enough of the impact to go staggering backwards, letting go of Mila's hand.

Samuel aimed his pistols at the two Na'gee before him but was hit from behind before he could fire. Another two warriors had approached from behind and one of them had kicked Samuel in the back, sending him staggering forward towards the two he had intended to shoot.

One of the two warriors stopped his forward momentum with a hard round house kick to the face and Samuel fell onto his back.

His head spun, but his eyes remained open, and he saw the booted foot come stomping down towards his head. He moved his arms quickly and caught the foot with both hands and twisted it hard. A loud 'snapping' noise filled the air.

Samuel didn't wait for the next boots that he knew were coming. He rolled to his side, jumped to his feet, and ducked under the left hook that was swinging at his head. He came back up smoothly, like it was a dance he had danced a hundred times and punched the attacking Na'gee in the side of the head, freezing him on contact.

He saw the warrior next to him on the ground, holding his ankle and Samuel kicked him hard in the face, knocking the man out and relieving him of several teeth as he did. Then Samuel swung his elbow backwards at the other warrior who was coming in fast, swinging a large knife at him.

He hadn't really saw the attack coming from behind, as much as he felt it. Kind of knew where each of them were and what would come next. He felt the man's nose crunch under the impact of his elbow, and then he caught the arm coming down over his shoulder and flipped the warrior into the last attacker running towards him. As they crashed to the ground, he leapt forward touching them both and freezing them in the place where they fell.

While Samuel had been fighting his attackers, Vic and Olo traded blows. The tall man, fought with a fury that he didn't remember feeling before. He blocked and countered every punch and kick that Olo threw at him, despite the Na'gee warrior's incredible speed and strength. After flurries of blows back and forth the two backed a few steps away from one another and slowly circled each other, both winded and bleeding.

Vic was winded but he felt no pain, only a burning desire to kill the man before him. The man that had attacked his family, abducted his wife and son and done who knew what to his son. Nothing else mattered to Vic, no one else existed, it was just him and the man before him.

"This 'Olo' dies now, no more hunting, no more running. It ends right here." Vic thought as he readied himself for his next strike.

Eva wasn't faring half as well. The attacker that had punched her, had now also kicked and hit her several times. She had dodged and blocked as much as she could, but the Na'gee warrior was just too fast. Suddenly, a stream of bright white light coming from Mila seemed to engulf the warrior attacking Eva and instantly melted him into a puddle of blood and ashes.

Mila had not yelled this time. There was no mighty explosion. She had just stared hatefully at the man attacking her mother and the blinding stream of white light had seemed to come from her entire body and consume him.

Steph watched the battle before him without moving. He watched Samuel, seeming to have no problem fighting four trained Na'gee warriors at once and could not help but feel admiration for the strange man's skills. He wanted to hate the man, as he remembered this man coming into their home after his father had left for work just days ago and then all this had begun, but still he had seen his father and this man bond and fight to protect him and his family. He could not hate him, even though he felt he should.

He watched his father go toe to toe with Olo, who he had believed up until this point was the mightiest warrior there was. His father made him think twice about this. No matter what move it was, how fast it came or how much strength seemed to be behind it, his father was able to block and counter Olo almost every time. He felt the love a son feels for their father wash over him and found himself looking up to his father in that moment, like he'd always looked up to him. He knew that he was supposed to hate him, supposed to kill him, but none of that mattered. He was proud of his father and proud to be his son, he could not hate him.

Then he saw the man hitting his mother. He was about to intervene, protective instincts kicking in and before he could, he saw the stream of light from Mila melt the warrior to nothing more than a puddle. The bright light and raw power that came from his little sister shocked him. Instantly, it all came back to him. He remembered why he was here. Steph remembered that this was not his sister, this was a demon. He knew something had to be done, but for some reason he could not make himself attack his sister or his mother. He didn't know why, but he just couldn't.

This frustrated him even more and he turned his eyes to his father. This man that he loved, respected, and idolized had ruined his life and killed his sister. He had turned her into or over to a demon, nothing else could explain what this little girl who used to be his sister had done. This man, he could be hit. It didn't matter what he felt for him, someone had to avenge his sister and that someone was him.

Steph rushed past Olo and punched Vic in the side of the head with everything he had. Vic went staggering back several steps but maintained his footing. He turned his eyes to his six-year-old son, who was now somehow grown and said "No Steph. I won't fight you, Son. Step aside, this man must die for what he's done."

Steph roared and swung at Vic again. This time, Vic managed to sidestep the swing. Then he dodged the one that followed. Refusing to swing back.

"You killed Mila! You gave her to a demon! You've ruined everything!" Steph roared as he lunged into the air aiming a jump kick for Vic's chest.

Unable to move out of the way in time, Vic caught the kick and flung Steph through the air away from him. As soon as he threw him, he saw Olo leaping towards him, attempting to catch him in the midsection and tackle him.

Vic jumped up with a flying knee and caught the strong Na'gee warrior in the chin. Olo, having thought Vic's attention was on Steph, never saw the counter move coming. The Na'gee warrior felt his jaw break from the impact of Vic's knee as his body went crashing backwards. Steph came running back, behind Vic now and grabbed Vic under the arms, locking him in a full nelson hold. Vic fought the urge to ram his head backwards and break the face of the man holding him, like he usually would. He couldn't do that to Steph. Instead, he pulled and jerked his arms trying to break free, but Steph was too strong, his grip too tight.

As Steph held him, he yelled "Why?! Why would you and Mom kill Mila?! Why?!"

"She's different, but she's not dead son. I'm here to save your mother and you. These bastards keep trying to kill us… how could you believe anything they tell you son? You've seen them try to kill us over and over. This man kidnapped you son and then he kidnapped your mother and stuck her in a damn cage like an animal!" Vic roared in desperate frustration. He couldn't believe that these monsters had convinced his son that his own family was the cause of all this.

Steph was filled with hate and rage and confusion. Still

holding his father, he glanced and saw Mila helping Eva up. Immediately he remembered Olo telling him they had sacrificed his mother. Then he looked up and saw Olo on his feet running towards Vic with his large knife in hand.

In an instant his mind was made up. He released his father, shoved him to the side and pulled his own knife in one quick motion.

Olo saw Vic helpless in Stephs strong hold and rushed in with his knife. No need for finesse when your prey couldn't move. His next steps were clearly laid out in his mind, he would gut this man, make the boy kill the 'brite' and then slit the boy's throat. So confident in what he was going to do, that Olo didn't even realize the boy had released his father and shoved him aside, until the boy's knife was deep in his gut.

Olo gagged as Steph twisted the knife's handle and opened the large gut wound wider. Olo dropped his knife and stared at Steph in his last moments of life, unable to utter a word.

Steph looked into Olo's eyes and watched the life slowly drain out of the man. Softly he said "You lied to me Na'gee. You are the evil one." And then he let Olo's lifeless body fall to the ground. He sheathed his bloody knife, not bothering to wipe it off and turned to face his father.

Vic was standing there, watching. He wrapped his arms around his son and hugged him. The embrace only lasted a moment before Steph said, "Is mom, ok?"

The two released one another and with tears in their eyes, they rushed over to Eva, who was half being held up by Mila. They all embraced, together again.

Samuel stood from his reckless dive that had frozen both warriors before and quickly picked up the pistols he'd dropped in the skirmish. He shot each frozen warrior in the head, as well as the one he'd kicked into unconsciousness.

When Samuel turned to survey how the others were doing, he saw Vic and what was supposedly his son, which made no sense at all to Samuel, embracing and then watched both of them run over to Eva and the glowing Mila and all embrace one another as a family.

The scene warmed his cold heart and reminded him of the family he'd lost. He let himself get washed away in the emotions for but a moment, before it evolved into a renewed lust for vengeance. However, it was now different. He still intended to kill all the Na'gee and especially Camacho, but it wasn't just about his family anymore, it was about what they'd done to the family before him and what they'd done to Dante's family. It now seemed more about protecting other families from similar fates then about avenging his. These were new feelings for Samuel, but he embraced them and felt invigorated and full of purpose.

Samuel snapped out of his deep thoughts by the sight of Vic walking over to the body of Olo. The tall man pulled the large .45 caliber gun from his waist band and unloaded it into the body of the dead Na'gee warrior. When the gun was empty, he finally stopped pulling the trigger, spit on the corpse and dropped his gun on the ground. Then he casually confiscated the dead man's belt which held the .50 caliber pistol and the spare clips. When Vic looked up, he saw everyone staring at him and said "What?"

"He was already dead Dad." Steph said. While everyone

else remained silent.

"This son of bitch kidnapped my son and my wife, now the bastards dead twice." Vic said, then he added "plus he kicked me off a damn parking deck."

Everyone looked somewhat confused by his last comment, but before they could ask, Vic spoke again. "Samuel, Mila can open a portal home. Let's get out of here. We can deal with the rest of them later."

Samuel looked at Vic and his family for a moment, soaking up the sight of the re united family before him. Finally, he responded. "You go Vic. Get your family to safety. I'm not finished here and I'm not leaving Halbred behind. I'll find another way back."

Samuel's words seemed to bring Vic back to reality. He stepped back from his family and looked at them. "You all go. Hurry. I'll catch up with you. I'm going to finish this with Samuel. He's right, if we don't kill them now, we'll never be safe." Vic said it passionately, not wanting to leave his family again, but knowing that it all needed to end here.

Steph spoke back first. "I know how to use these now," he said as he patted the stone talisman he wore around his neck. "I'll help you kill them Dad, then I'll get us out of here. Mom, Mila, you go. Hurry." As Steph said it, he eased over to stand next to his father.

Despite the emotions and urgency of the situation, he was blown away that he now stood just as tall as his seven-foot-tall father.

Eva walked away from them all and leaned over one of

the dead Na'gee warriors. She unbuckled the warrior's belt and removed it from him, before standing and strapping it onto her. It held a large knife on one side and the .50 caliber pistol on the other side. The pouches were full of spare clips. It was the same as the armaments that Steph and Vic now wore.

Having secured the belt into place, Eva pulled out the large pistol and said, "We're not splitting up again. Let's do what needs to be done and get the hell out of this damn place. Come on Mila."

No one said a word, they all just turned to the structure before them. Samuel pulled out the two remaining explosive timer squares that Flutter had given him. One, he had previously placed on the back ledge entrance when they had come through. He had that one set to go off about an hour after they entered, right about the time he guessed it would be getting dark. Part of his reasoning was a later distraction, and the other part was to alert the black cloaks to the opening in the mountain. He figured it was almost that time.

He placed the other two side by side on the back of the structure. Then he looked up at Steph. "You know what or who is in there?" Samuel asked.

"It's the wise ones and the elders. From what I can tell, either they run the place or Olo does… I guess did." Steph said, glancing at the body of Olo lying on the ground.

"You know where Camacho is?" Samuel asked.

"The short guy with the mohawk who dresses differently? Yeah, Olo sent him to defend the attack at the front while we came to defend the back" Steph said.

"Then we go to the front. Halbred could probably use a hand anyway." Samuel said as he reloaded his pistols from one of the many clips secured to the inside of his black sports coat.

Just then the back of the mountain ledge where they had entered from earlier erupted in a giant explosion.

CHAPTER 52:
SHOWDOWN

Halbred crept around the side of the mountain, staying silent and out of sight. The two huge T'kche followed closely, creeping as stealthily as any soldier he'd ever served with.

He saw four guards in front of the massive entrance, two on each side, and decided there probably wasn't a much a chance of doing it quietly. He motioned for the T'kche to lean in close to him as he peered around the corner at the guards.

"I can take the two closest to us. Do you think either of you can get from one side to the other before they alert everyone to our presence?" He asked. The two T'kche looked at one another, trading what appeared to be amused looks. Finally, T'sko nodded at G'noch and scrambled straight up the side of the sheer face of the mountain. Halbred watched the large hairy beast move like a spider, somehow able to hold itself against the flat surface of the rock.

"What the hell is your bigfoot buddy doing?" Halbred asked G'noch.

"You say kill quiet. T'kche kill quiet, little foot buddy." G'noch said in response as he crept past Halbred towards the two guards closest to him.

"Oh hell." Halbred said to himself, while watching with pistol in hand.

As he watched, he saw T'sko climb the mountain face over the entrance and out of view. The next thing he knew G'noch moved quickly behind the two closest Na'gee and grabbed each by the neck, one with each hand. A loud crunching noise followed and both guards fell dead with broken necks.

When Halbred stepped forward behind G'noch, he could see that T'sko had done the same thing on the other side of the entrance.

As they started to ease inside the opening of the mountain, Flutter came flying down from above and landed softly behind Halbred, sub machine gun in hand.

Halbred took the lead, with Flutter close behind, and marched straight into the mountain. The T'kche each kept their backs to either side of the wall and followed closely with clubs in hand.

Several Na'gee warriors were gathered directly ahead, just inside the entrance and Halbred opened fire with his pistol, dropping several before they seemed to realize they were under attack.

Flutter followed Halbred's lead, firing her sub machine gun just over his shoulder and spraying several more Na'gee with showers of lead.

The first group was wiped out and the T'kche took off in

opposite directions running quickly and silently, seeming to disappear into the rocky background of the cave as they ran off.

"Guess they fight their own way, might just be us. You ready Flutter?" Halbred shouted as he jogged straight ahead towards what appeared to be a massive gathering of Na'gee by a giant fire.

In response Flutter leapt about six feet into the air, still moving forward at the pace that Halbred had set and opened fire on the gathering by the large fire.

Halbred joined in the shooting as he ran towards their opposition. The two of them dropping several Na'gee warriors who stood by the large fire in front of them.

Out of nowhere, they saw the T'kche come running in from the far side of the fire, opposite from where they were, swinging their clubs wildly and sending dozens of Na'gee bodies flying through the air.

Then the tunnel exploded in a deafening thunderous noise and the mountain air filled with dust.

In minutes, the Na'gee had organized themselves and were firing back, while dozens of other Na'gee seemed to be scrambling to barricade the demolished tunnel with large rocks and debris. Halbred still stood front and center, barely flinching as the high caliber bullets bounced off his impenetrable skin, while Flutter flew from here to there through the air at incredible speeds laying down flurries of bullets on the Na'gee from every direction. The two fought as one and decimated ranks of skilled warriors, making it evident that this is what they were trained to do.

Halbred was shocked at how well the T'kche were able to run into the fire fight and decimate large numbers of Na'gee with their mighty clubs and then seem to run off and disappear without getting hit by the gunfire all around them. They just seemed too big to be able to do something like that, but they did it right before him over and over, like giant hairy ghosts that vanished at will.

The only thing that was more surprising to the seasoned soldier than how the T'kche fought, was the fact that the Na'gee seemed less interested in them and the attack than they did at trying to rebuild the destroyed tunnel. They were getting shot down and smashed in large numbers, and yet very few were fighting back, while dozens scrambled to block up the exploded tunnel that was letting fading beams of sunshine in from outside.

Then all of the sudden, Halbred went from surveying the scene and dropping Na'gee with precision shots to flying through the air and crashing into the interior mountain wall. He turned to see what had hit him and saw nothing more than a blur of color, just before a large stone club shattered across his face.

Although his skin couldn't be penetrated, he felt the impact, just like he felt the impact from every bullet that hit him. This was harder to shake off, as he now had chunks of stone and grit in his eyes.

Halbred, half blinded, pushed himself off the wall and felt a flurry of rushing air surge past him, then he felt it again and the next thing he knew he was taking gun fire to his face at point blank range. He was shot at least four times, before he was able to reach out and grab the arm of the person shooting him. Still unable to see, he yanked them forward and delivered a mighty headbutt.

He felt a nose crush beneath his forehead and then he felt the grip reverse. The arm that he had held now held him and flung him with incredible force off his feet and into the wall again.

Before he could move, he felt himself jerked back by the same arm and slung into the wall again.

"I'm getting slung around like a dog's chew toy! What the hell am I fighting?!" Halbred thought while trying helplessly to catch a hold of something, anything that would allow him to stop being slung into the wall over and over.

Then gunfire exploded all around him, some of it hitting him and he felt the grip on his arm release and rush of air as something seemed to run away from him.

Flutter landed next to him and was wiping his eyes out, quickly.

"It's the one from the roof boss. Heads up, he's coming back!" Flutter yelled as she leapt back into the air flying high and laying down gunfire behind her.

Most of the debris having been cleared from his eyes, Halbred looked up and saw a blurry shape coming his way at an insane speed. He didn't have time to think, so he just kicked up debris and stone from the wall that had been smashed by his body.

The debris he kicked into the air hit the approaching thing head on and Halbred stepped to the side, watching Camacho crash into the wall where he had just stood. Before the man could recover, Halbred swung hard and hit the smaller man in the side of the head with the butt of his pistol.

Camacho felt the pain of crashing into the wall. He had expected the man to try to dodge him but was caught off guard when instead he kicked dirt and rocks into his face. Then he was suddenly hit and seeing stars. The pistol struck him in the temple and sent his head spinning. Fearing another blow would follow or worse a gunshot from what was obviously a gun hitting him in the head, Camacho used his unnatural speed and strength to turn towards the direction of the attack and without looking unleashed a flurry of punches.

They were jabs, but jabs at the speed he could deliver them and with the force he could exert were more powerful than any normal man's hook or uppercut. To Camacho's surprise it felt like he was punching steel. Then he took a punch to the throat and gasped.

Both men were face to face against the wall, Camacho gasping while Halbred delivered another massive blow to his throat. Then the back of the mountain exploded.

Halbred knew that meant it was about dark and he knew what the darkness would bring.

Camacho couldn't breathe. He didn't know how this had happened. He'd hit the grizzled red haired solider a dozen times over with incredible force and the man seemed to take the blows, like they were child's play and respond with two hard hits directly to his windpipe.

He didn't know what to do next, nothing that should have killed this man had seemed to work. Then the mountain shook with the deafening sounds of a mighty explosion, that seemed to come from the opposite side of the Na'gee settlement.

Halbred was startled by the explosion and Camacho took advantage of the momentary reprieve of getting his windpipe crushed by the soldier's fists. In an instant Camacho realized that one thing had seemed to work, was when he went for the soldier's eyes.

In a blur of incredible speed, the short man pulled the dagger from under his shirt and jammed it directly into Halbred's left eye.

By the time Halbred saw the knife, it was already stabbing into his eye. He felt immense pain, roared loudly, and shoved the man away from him. The dagger stayed tightly held in Camacho's grip though and was stuck deeply into Halbreds eye. Resulting in Halbred's eyeball being yanked from its socket as Camacho was shoved backwards away from him.

Halbred could still see out of his good eye and what he saw was the smaller, mohawked man grinning a sinister grin at him.

"I'll take both your eyes and torture you until I find a way to kill you fool!" Camacho roared. Then slightly more softly he added "Don't worry we'll leave you your ears so you can hear what we do to your flying little lady soldier."

Halbred reached into his pouch and wrapped his hand around one of the small square explosives he had. He knew there was no way he'd be fast enough to stop the man from taking his remaining eye, but figured he could blow them both up. It wouldn't be pleasant, but he'd survive, and his attacker wouldn't, that was all that mattered now.

Before any of it happened though, a large club came swinging in and smashed Camacho's head against the wall. It crushed his head into a splatter of blood and brains on the stone interior wall of the mountain. Halbred released his grip on the explosive and let out the breath that he had been holding.

With his one good eye remaining he looked over and saw G'noch standing there with club in hand.

The large black haired T'kche looked at Halbred and said, "Little man take Halbred's eye. G'noch take little man's head." Then a concerned look washed over the grinning T'kche's face, and he suddenly looked up towards the main entrance. "Dark ones here. Need to leave." G'noch said.

Flutter landed next to them and T'sko appeared by them as well, coming from who knew where. T'sko had the same concerned look on his face that G'noch had.

Halbred looked up and saw the black cloaked creatures beginning to slowly creep in from the front entrance, then he looked the other way and saw them coming from the back entrance as well.

"We'll fight through the Na'gee and head down the tunnel and back to the T'kche lair. You all start heading that way, hurry." He rushed them to go and they all hesitated.

"What about you Boss?" Flutter asked, reluctant to leave her commander, not to mention the only person she had left.

"I've got to find Samuel. I'm not leaving any other soldiers behind Flutter." Halbred said firmly.

Flutter saw it was obvious that there was no arguing with

him, so she took to the air and surveyed what was left of the battle field that was previously the Na'gee settlement. She saw more and more black cloaks creeping in from the front and the back. They were leaping on Na'gee here and there and seemed to be eating them alive or something like that. Then Flutter saw Samuel, heading their way from the large structure.

The tall man from the hotel battle was somehow now with him, as well as another tall man that looked eerily similar except for the Na'gee attire he wore and the tattoos that adorned him. There was a woman with a large pistol and a child that appeared to be glowing with them as well.

"At this point there's nothing that could surprise me." Flutter thought, just before something knocked her out of the air and sent her crashing to the ground in front of the tunnel exit.

Samuel led the way in a hurry, leading Vic and his family towards the tunnel they were planning to use for their exit. He hoped he'd run into Halbred somewhere along the way, since this was the route they had all planned to take once darkness came.

He saw the black cloaks starting to pour in from the front and rear entrances. Here and there, he saw them beginning to pounce on Na'gee warriors. He looked up and saw Flutter in the air. Samuel saw her surveying the area and then saw her eyes land on him.

As he ran and looked up at Flutter, he also noticed movement on the ceiling. He slowed to see what it was and noticed black cloaks crawling on the ceiling. Then he saw one leap onto Flutter in midair and bite into her as they came crashing down to the cavern floor.

They landed across the cavern, directly in front of the exit to the tunnel that he was headed for. Flutter hit the ground hard and the creature bit into her. Samuel doubled his pace, heading to help her as fast as he could, but knowing deep down that it would be too late.

Halbred saw the thing leap onto Flutter and bite into her. He ran for where they had crashed and was hit as one of the creatures landed on him, trying to bite into his neck. He reached up with his pistol and shot the thing in the face several times, until it fell off of him. He didn't bother to decapitate the creature, there was no time. He could see the thing that had had its teeth sunk into Flutter, rear its head up and then extend the strangely long black tongue into the open wound.

He was almost there, but T'sko beat him to her.

With a devastating blow of the club, T'sko took the creature's head clean off. The massive brown haired T'kche leaned down, appearing to examine Flutter and then stood back up, his eyes looking everywhere for the next attack.

G'noch was not far away. Black cloaks cautiously circled him, not shying away even when he smashed one after one with his huge club.

Halbred finally got to Flutter and T'sko and the large T'kche stepped in front of him. "It too late man friend. Dark one take her" he said.

Halbred shoved past him and saw what was left of Flutter.

Her neck had been completely torn open and her body was blue. There was no blood. Halbred leaned down and felt for a pulse. There was nothing.

"Not you too! Not you too Flutter!" Halbred yelled as he crouched over her.

A mighty roar snapped his attention to T'sko who stood over him. When he looked up, he saw a huge, clawed hand sticking out the front of T'skos chest. Then he saw the hand disappear back where it came from leaving a gaping hole in the center of the T'kche.

Halbred jumped to his feet, only to see the large T'kche's head get ripped clean off its body and tossed to the side.

Before him stood Roid. Hissing and showing long fangs and rows of sharp teeth. There was no doubt it was Roid, but he looked much different than the Roid Halbred remembered. This version of Roid had pale almost translucent skin and extremely long fingers that ended in sharp pointed claws. There were also the eyes that were larger and black. Outside of those obvious changes, it still was the same abnormally large and muscular Roid that had been given great strength and size from the effects of the gene.

Roid stood shirtless, still wearing his tactical pants and boots, with arms covered in blood up to his elbows. He looked at Halbred with solid black eyes and hissed. "You have let another die Halbred. Did you plan to leave her like you left me and all the rest to die? Doesn't matter, it's your turn now!" As Roid spoke the last hissing word, he leaped forward and smashed his large fist into Halbred's face, sending the seasoned soldier flying backwards into several black cloaked creatures who had been approaching to pounce.

Roid roared "He is mine!!!" and the creatures backed away. Halbred shakily got to his feet and stared at Roid.

"I didn't leave you Roid. You were dead man. What the hell has happened to you?" Halbred yelled back.

"Doesn't matter now Halbred. I'm back and better than ever, and as for you…well, now it's your turn to die." Roid hissed back. He rushed towards Halbred and swung both hands clasped together in one powerful blow that sent Halbred flying backwards ten feet in the air.

Halbred came crashing to the ground directly in front of Samuel, who skidded to a stop to help the old solider up.

As Roid was about to rush Halbred again, he noticed something coming quickly towards him in his peripheral vision and turned just in time to dodge the massive club swinging at his head.

He lunged in towards the attacking G'noch in an upward uppercut motion, with his large claws extended and G'noch stepped back just in time to avoid having his neck skewered.

As quickly as G'noch stepped back and dodged the claws coming for his throat, he stepped back forward ramming the end of his club into Roids massive chest, sending Roid stumbling backward several feet.

Many dark ones still darted here and there devouring the Na'gee, but now several began crowding around the battle between a giant one of their own and the massive T'kche.

Roid made a loud furious hissing noise and lunged for

G'noch. The T'kche danced out of the way, moving much faster than it appeared was possible for a creature of his size and swung the club downwards attempting to crush Roid as he'd done to so many other dark ones.

Roid rolled out of the way and squared off against the large beast.

Then the blinding light erupted and seemed to fill the cavern.

Samuel helped Halbred to his feet and asked, "You alright?"

"It's Roid, but it's not. He killed Flutter and T'sko. We've got to stop him, Samuel." Halbreds voice strained with anger and sounded of desperation. The two men turned their attention to Roid, who was going toe to toe with G'noch, and quickly saw that the large T'kche seemed to be getting the better of him. They also saw the dozens of black cloaked creatures gathering around, forming a circle around the battle.

Before they could join in the attack, they each felt a small hand grab their arms and pull them back with strength that didn't seem to match the size of the hands.

They looked down to see Mila, shining brilliantly.

She did not look at them when she spoke in the crackling ominous voice that echoed like a loudspeaker. "Step back and be safe. I will deal with the darkness before us" she said eerily.

The two men let themselves be pulled back, entranced in some sort of awe and the little girl's words and the light that shined from her.

Mila stepped forward and an explosion of light erupted from her towards the large gathering of dark ones before her. Some of the creatures melted into ashes while others further away from the center of the light erupted into flames. In mere seconds the dark ones between her and the battle between Roid and G'noch were no more.

Momentarily blinded by the light, G'noch and Roid stopped fighting. They both looked over seeing the brightly shining child slowly approach.

The remaining dark ones begin to scatter at her approach. Roid looked from her to the beast before him and then towards Halbred.

"I'll find you and kill you yet Halbred!" He yelled then he turned and looked towards the demolished tunnel that he had emerged from.

"You will not escape the light!" Mila shouted in an eerie voice and a large beam of light streaked toward Roid.

He saw it coming and grabbed two nearby dark ones, one in each hand and threw them at the light, as he dove behind G'noch, attempting to use the large T'kche as cover.

The two creatures that were hurled at Mila, disintegrated in the air.

Then the large Na'gee structure in the center of the settlement, that Samuel had placed the two explosives on erupted in a massive explosion. The entire mountain seemed to shake, and chunks of rock started falling from the ceiling.

One large chunk was coming straight for Mila and Halbred quickly stepped over her taking the blow and protecting the child.

Roid took advantage of the distraction, darting off towards the tunnel. He grabbed Flutter's ankle as he passed, dragging her body roughly down the tunnel behind him.

Steph rubbed the talisman, in the way that Ansai had taught him and the blur or path to their world appeared in the air.

"Come on! Let's get out of here!" Steph yelled. He ushered Eva through the doorway and gave his father an urging look. Vic rushed past Halbred and Samuel and grabbed Mila's arm.

"Let's go baby girl." Vic said gently and he began walking Mila towards the blur.

Rocks continued to come crashing down from the ceiling all around them.

Samuel yelled "G'noch come on! With us!" and the big T'kche immediately began running towards them.

Vic and Mila stepped through the blur, followed by Samuel and G'noch. Halbred hesitated before entering, staring back at the tunnel that Roid had run through.

"Come on man! Let's get out of here while we can!" Steph yelled to the seasoned soldier. The comment seemed to snap Halbred away from his thoughts and he stepped through the blur. Steph followed and the pathway closed behind him.

CHAPTER 53:
THE JOBS NOT DONE

The group appeared in a wooded forest a good way outside of the city. There was nothing around them but woodlands. No one said a word, as they all looked around seeming to expect an attack from one of the dark cloaked creatures.

After several tense moments of nothing but the sounds of crickets and frogs in the night, they relaxed a little. Halbred pulled out a square electronic device of some sort from one of his pouches and typed away on it. After a few minutes, he said "I've got someone I can trust coming with a chopper about five miles west of here. There's a clearing. They should be here within the hour." He looked around at the faces that the gathered group gave him and realized that he'd need to explain more.

"We're not in that strange world anymore. Here they think of me as the government." Halbred thought.

"Look, I know what you're all thinking. I lost everyone I cared about in the last few days. The way I see it the jobs not done. It seems these Na'gee have an infrastructure that reaches much further than this city and the settlement we wiped out. I plan to kill every last one of them. Once I know this world is safe from the Na'gee, I intend to find a way to go back and kill every last one of those dark cloaks. Any of you with me?" Halbred said it all gruffly, as he usually did, but there was something different to his voice now. This wasn't just the soldier's mission anymore. No, now this was something much deeper. This was his life. His purpose now.

Samuel was the first to speak up. "I'm with you. Where's the chopper taking us?"

"I've got a spot up north. It's high in the mountains, it's fully stocked and it's off the grid. I figure after everything we've all been through; we can regroup there. The pilot owes me, and he can be trusted. He'll drop us off and leave. From there you can go if you want, or you can join me in keeping our world safe. It's up to all of you." Halbred explained.

The man spoke with an intense sense of duty and seemed not to even notice the blood leaking out of the gaping hole where his left eye used to be.

Vic nodded, and with his arms wrapped tightly around his wife and daughter he said "I told Samuel when we started this thing, I was in it until we wiped them all out. We ain't done yet soldier. I'm in."

Steph said "I'm in too. The Na'gee are evil. They're not just a danger to our world, but to everything in the world they are from too. They must be stopped."

"G'noch hunt Na'gee and dark ones with you, little foot Halbred." The large T'kche said as he gave his now seemingly signature tooth filled grin and laid a heavy hand on Halbred's shoulder.

Halbred nodded, clearly a signal for the group to begin their trek through the woods towards the clearing where their ride would be waiting.

Before they all started walking, Vic spoke up with a perplexed look on his face. "Why does that big thing keep growling at you guys?" As he asked the question, he shifted his gaze from Samuel, to Halbred and finally stopped, staring straight at G'noch.

In response, Samuel reached into his jacket pocket and removed the three remaining talisman, that he had confiscated from the dead Na'gee warriors. He handed one to Vic, one to Eva and offered one to Mila. While Vic and Eva accepted theirs, Mila simply shook her head and said, "I understand the T'kche."

Before Samuel could respond, Vic spoke up. "What the hell is this for?"

"Put it on, it's like a translator." Samuel said.

With that, the group all turned and began to make their way through the wooded landscape.

As they were walking, everyone heard Vic mumbling loudly "Open's doorways to alien worlds, translates bigfoot… this thing is definitely gonna give me cancer."

THE END

EPILOGUE 1

Flutter woke in a dark cavern of some sort, with strange eerie blue lights. She felt confused and somehow different as she slowly sat up.

Across the room from her was a huge beast of a man, standing shirtless before the body of a Na'gee warrior that had been staked to the wall and was missing most of its limbs. Scattered about the cavern there appeared to be bodies of large hairy creatures she remembered to be T'kceh.

She shifted her attention to the large shirtless man that had his back to her and after a moment of staring at she realized it was Roid.

"What is this place? What's happened to me?" Flutter asked, in a voice that sounded deeper and raspier than hers had ever sounded.

At the sound of her voice, Roid turned around and looked at her. To Flutter he looked nothing like he had before. His eyes were black, and his skin was so pale that it almost glowed in the dark. Despite the sinister look of her old comrade, it didn't disturb her. She seemed rather comfortable with it, although she didn't know why.

"It's ok Flutter. You're with me now." Roid said in a

hissing kind of voice. "Halbred and that damn agent 17 we hunted left you for dead, just like they left me, but I saved you. You're healed now and we'll hunt them down together. Our kind hunts better in pairs."

It took a moment to process what he had said, and then a strange voice in her head that she did not know, yet seemed to now know very well encouraged her to hunt them, to kill them, to consume them. She embraced the voice and the angry feelings of vengeance and bloodlust that flooded her.

"Yes. They must die. Let us feed on them." She said without even meaning too, in the voice she didn't recognize as her own.

Roid grinned a sinister grin, showing off his massive fangs and said, "I thought you'd say that. I found a friend on the way here and look what he taught me." As Roid said it, he lifted a stone circular talisman in his hand and rubbed it this way and that way in circular motions. To Flutter it looked like he was working a combination lock. Then all of the sudden a blur appeared in the center of the room.

Flutter stood, staring at it peculiarly.

"It takes us to our world. That's where they went. That's where they're hiding. You ready to hunt Flutter?" Roid said.

She nodded, the thoughts of killing running through her mind and the two of them stepped through the blur.

Epilogue 2

Primo watched the battle at the hotel unfold through video links he had tapped into, using the hotel's camera systems. He saw skirmishes on the different levels and had been in communication with Lieutenant Riker.

Primo knew Riker wanted to be in command of the elite mercenary unit. The man despised his commander and despised Camacho for letting them turn into a glorified security service. Riker believed that they were one the most capable mercenary squadrons on the planet and felt that what they had become was insulting and embarrassing.

Primo agreed with him. The two often worked together unbeknownst to anyone else to further each other's ambitions. As Primo watched the migration being thwarted, he decided that this was the moment. He saw the teleporting knife fighter get knocked out by Camacho and contacted Riker, giving his orders.

The Lieutenant was more than eager to finally put their plans into motion. He knew this meant that Primo and him would take over everything and he was ready.

Riker got the call from Primo just as he and his men arrived on the rooftop. He saw the fighting on the other side of the roof, but that didn't interest him.

What did interest him was his commander, Captain Venco walking towards the smaller unconscious man with knives strapped across his chest.

Riker unholstered his pistol walked up to Venco who was approaching the unconscious man, obviously intent on killing the knife fighter. Without a word he shot his commander in the head and kicked his body off the rooftop before it fell.

Riker turned, picked up the unconscious knife fighter and threw him over his shoulder, while his men threw ropes over the side of the building. They all took off, repelling down with ease, even Riker who still held the unconscious man. They hit the ground in no time, where multiple hummers sat idling waiting on them, poured into the vehicles and took off. Seconds after they were speeding away, they saw the entire hotel explode in their review mirrors.

Dante woke up on a cot in some sort of war room office. There were monitors everywhere. He saw a thin man with a ponytail sitting behind a desk and a tall man in black military gear standing behind him. It only took him a second to recognize the thin man in the suit as the man that was with Camacho after the club exploded, killing his family.

He slowly rose to his feet and pulled a dagger with each hand.

"These idiots should have taken my knives when they had the chance." Dante thought. His head pounded, but thoughts of vengeance seemed to dull the pain.

Primo saw the young knife fighter rise and slowly pull his knives. He knew he had to talk fast. He'd seen the young man at work.

"Dante, before you take our lives, look at the screens before you." Primo said calmly.

Dante looked at the screen and saw that it was paused with a clear picture of Samuel standing outside of his black sedan, holding a rocket launcher. The rocket launcher he held was pointed at the club where his family had been murdered.

He stared at it. The image triggered the thoughts he'd had in his last interactions with Samuel. As he looked at it, he believed what he saw to be true.

Primo watched the emotions in Dante's face and then hit 'play' on the video. It clearly showed the rocket being fired and the club exploding.

"I did not kill your parents, nor did Camacho, Dante." It was this man in the black coat that did this to you.

"Samuel. His name is Samuel." Dante said as he watched the video.

Then the video changed and it showed the hotel exploding.

"Camacho and the Na'gee are evil and they would killed us all if we had not stopped them." Primo said, pretending that he had something to do with the explosion caused by Fuse.

"I intend to hunt down and kill this Samuel. Then I will wipe out the Na'gee and take over their infrastructure. No families should have to work for their freedom. No young men should be forced to fight to save their families as you did Dante. I am Primo and I intend to make things right." Primo paused for effect and then resumed his speech.

"These people attempted to kill you on the rooftop, but I instructed Riker here to save you. I feel responsible for what has happened to you Dante and I intend to make it right. Will you help me?" Primo left the question hanging in the air and said no more.

After several long minutes of silence, Dante sheathed his daggers and looked at the thin man in the suit who called himself Primo.

"Ok Primo, but Samuel is mine. He dies by my hands, understood?" Dante said coldly.

Reflections of Worlds:
Volume 2

"Dark Crossing"

Coming soon!

www.ingramcontent.com/pod-product-compliance
Lightning Source LLC
Chambersburg PA
CBHW022250310726
48973CB00001B/26